FOREIGN AND DOMESTIC

A JACK WIDOW THRILLER

SCOTT BLADE

Black Lion Media

ALSO BY SCOTT BLADE

1

ONE THING LEADS TO ANOTHER.

Cause and effect.

A bullet leads to a target, and a democratically-elected president dies. A fragile country is thrown into upheaval, and the world changes, and somebody benefits.

Simple. Cause and effect.

A son shoots his father in front of an entire nation, and the entire world sees it, and politics shift. Power struggles happen, and a country's destiny changes forever.

On this occasion, the equation equaled three bullets fired—two center mass and one miss, with one trigger pulled, three times, and one father killed by one son, his eldest. The son had no choice.

Three bullets. That's all it took.

One thing leads to another: cause and effect.

Moments before he was assassinated, in the small African country of West Ganbola, President-elect George Biyena stood offstage in a freshly pressed suit with a black and gold tie—his country's colors.

Not just on his tie, but the same colors were ahead of him on the stage, sewn into a large West Ganbola flag that waved proudly in the wind, standing next to and at equal footing with the flag of the African Union.

The African Union's flag also waved.

A big part of Biyena's platform had been to move West Ganbola more in line with the rest of the union's humanitarian and democratic policies.

He was a champion of his country's poor and impoverished.

His wife stood on a provisional platform, built the day before in preparation for his first speech as West Ganbola's president-elect. She faced out toward his constituents. He gazed over them through a black and white curtain, surveying the crowd of hundreds of supporters, non-supporters, and the media, both foreign and domestic.

Biyena had just emerged from a vicious election cycle, fraught with back-and-forth political character assassination ads and propaganda. Some true, most lies. He had almost lost the election, but not because the other guy was more popular—or even popular at all— and not because the other guy was the sitting president. It was only because the people of his country were terrified of the other guy. He had been an extreme dictator, a warlord, categorically.

The other guy wasn't a legitimately elected official, not in the sense of what an elected official was supposed to be. The other guy was a dictator, a military leader who overthrew a democratically-elected government fifteen years ago and then installed a fake democratic one over it. He installed what a lot of strongman-types did. They would hold elections, make it all look real, make it all look legitimate, but under the surface, the votes weren't counted. The whole thing was staged to make it look like the other guy was mandated by his population.

It was all a scam.

The other guy was nothing more than a criminal.

Not this time. Part of Biyena's campaign was to get the votes counted by a new third-party institution. This time, Biyena had made enough friends in government, and the other guy had made enough enemies, that the vote was counted, and Biyena had won.

He was proud of his political victory, a road fraught with more than just potential political defeat. It had been dangerous for him and his family. His path to leadership had led him through treacherous waters and political acrimony. Where so many others had failed, forced out of the previous presidential races against the incumbent socialist dictator, or were simply the other guy's patsies, Biyena had succeeded.

Any of his close, personal friends would attest to his patriotism. He believed his country deserved a fresh start, a new beginning. It was truly a great day for democracy and a great day for West Ganbola.

He had not appeared publicly in the three days leading up to the election because of concerns from his head of security. Death threats against him had risen the week before, and it looked as though he would legitimately win the election. This meant he had to be under close guard. He waited in secret, in a secret location, until the ballots were counted—and he won. Now he was about to give the speech that would move his country into a new era of peace.

He had rehearsed the process many times in his head. Walk up the steps. Cross the raised platform. Go over to the podium and hug his wife. Stand and recite his speech, eyes locked on his people.

Don't show fear.

Biyena had stayed up the entire night before, practicing his speech in front of his two most trusted advisors. When they had run out of energy, he had practiced it in front of a mirror at the Royal Hotel on Webiga Street, the street with the hospital that he was born in fifty-three years ago. It was not on purpose, just one of life's coincidences, like dying on the same street.

English was the official language of West Ganbola, but over eighty languages were used in the region. Languages other than English were especially common in the more rural areas, which were almost everywhere.

Near the craggy mountain ranges and olive jungles to the east, you could walk into a village, hear a regional language that had originated there, and then travel a few miles inland only to hear a completely different vernacular and see completely different jungles and mountains.

He loved his country.

Biyena waited for his wife to announce him to the crowd. He heard her voice. He heard her rehearsed annunciation paying off.

She said, "I'm so proud to announce my husband as President George Biyena."

Biyena took a deep breath and held it, and another, and held it. He felt the air go in through his mouth and expand his chest, and then he released it. He repeated the whole thing and then stepped through the curtain, releasing his breath as he did.

The crowd was already standing and chanting his name.

"BI-YE-NA! BI-YE-NA!"

It grew louder and louder as he stepped onto the stage.

"BI-YE-NA! BI-YE-NA!"

He was overwhelmed by the chants and the distant sounds of beating drums and blasting trumpets to mark his arrival, by the sea of faces, and the rows of children brought out to see him. They waved little black and gold flags to show their support. He watched as the flags swayed in the air, not knowing it would be his last time seeing them.

The children in the crowd were dressed like the adults, most of whom were dirt poor. They couldn't afford the kinds of clothes that the richer citizens could, the ones who stood closer to the front of the crowd and on the balconies of the two- and three-story buildings lining downtown.

Even though most the onlookers couldn't afford suits or ties or decent shoes, they were dressed in the finest clothes that they owned. Many of the children wore threadbare, button-down shirts that didn't fit them, with long ties that belonged to their fathers. Many of them were barefoot, toes digging into the gritty dirt. They weren't barefoot because they couldn't afford dress shoes for the occasion, but because they couldn't afford shoes at all. Many of them didn't own a single pair—not all of them, but many.

Biyena noticed. There were far too many children who lived wretched lives because of how poor they were. This was one of the reasons that he'd joined the presidential race in the first place—no matter the risk, no matter the chance of losing his life. In a country filled with the oppressed and the poor, ethics mattered. Honesty mattered. That was why winning was Biyena's only option. He had to change things.

It called to him like God called to him.

Biyena walked out onto the stage and held his arms out and open in a gesture of embrace as if to say: *I'm here, my friends. I'm your new president.*

The crowd never stopped chanting his name. Instead, they upped the ante and roared on.

"BI-YE-NA! BI-YE-NA!"

They repeated it over and over.

They grew louder and louder. They too had felt the rush of hope. Hope for a new future for their war-torn country—freedom from the political corruption and the fallacy of a government that had enslaved them into poverty instead of freeing them to enjoy a better economy and a better life. Parents hoped for a better life for their children. Grandparents hoped for a better future for their grandchildren. Wives hoped their husbands could go to work and return home with a decent wage. Husbands hoped they could pay for clothing for their children and food for the entire family.

To them, George Biyena was a beacon of hope. They wanted a nation without terrorism. Without war. Without fear. Without overwhelming crime. Without brutal poverty. Without instability.

Biyena was what they had longed for. He would change their lives and alleviate their struggles.

Biyena sauntered to the center of the stage like he was taking a stroll. He wanted to savor the moment. He earned it. He had worked hard for this victory.

The months of moving secretly from one location to the next had taken its toll on his wife and four grown boys—especially his first-born son, Nikita.

Nikita was his pride and joy. He had grown into a successful man in his own right. He was the father of three children. He was a good husband to a good wife.

Biyena couldn't be prouder of Nikita.

President Biyena looked across the stage and saw that, near the bottom of the steps, his son Nikita was passing through the capital police. He was waving frantically at his father.

He wasn't supposed to come up on stage, but the policemen recognized him and let him pass. What were they supposed to do? He was the new president's firstborn son.

Nikita wore an intense look of concern on his face. He was normally the only one of his sons who always kept his cool—nothing ever fazed him.

Whatever was worrying him must've been something urgent, something that couldn't wait. Or maybe Nikita was so proud of his father's victory that he just wanted to share the stage with him in a show of support. Perhaps he wanted to hug him tight and was worried he wouldn't make it. Perhaps.

After all, Biyena had been so busy for months that the two had barely had any time to speak.

Biyena reached the podium and leaned in toward an old, worn-out microphone, the kind with the steel vented face that an old-timey radio station might have. It was a vintage Shure microphone, but Biyena didn't know that, and it didn't matter. He knew that his country had modern equipment. Just because they were a third-world nation didn't mean they were lost in the nineteen fifties.

He wondered whose idea it had been to set up the old-style microphone. Maybe it came from his campaign manager. Maybe it was supposed to represent a more traditional appearance to his constituents and countrymen. Maybe the microphone would make him look like a mid-nineteenth-century revolutionary who had just won a similar election battle, or maybe it made him resemble an American leader like Martin Luther King Jr., giving a speech that would change a nation. Perhaps his people were waiting for him to give a groundbreaking, game-changing speech that would inform his enemies that the people of West Ganbola were no longer afraid. Or perhaps it was because there was an international news crew there covering his speech. Whatever the reason, Biyena liked to be included in all decisions, no matter how small. He believed that every little detail about his televised appearance was crucial. He believed people remembered the details.

He dismissed his concern and stared at the microphone.

A black wire ran down the front of the wooden podium and offstage like a long, thin snake, disappearing below gray cedar boards that made up the platform.

Biyena leaned forward to the microphone and spoke.

"Good morning!"

His voice *boomed* across the crowds and city streets.

The crowd went crazy—chanting and hooraying, waving their flags, and stomping their feet as if they were at a sporting event.

The smallest sons were picked up by their fathers and held high on their shoulders. Mothers hugged their daughters. Brash cheers filled the square, echoing past the low buildings, carrying over the corrugated iron roofs, and dipping down the other side to fill the ears of people standing farther away.

Biyena asked, "How are you doing today?"

The crowd roared, repeating all the same chants and waves and stomps as before.

The capital police stood in front of the stage in a tight perimeter, preventing overzealous citizens from rushing the stage.

The cops directly in front of the stage wore body armor and antiriot gear: helmets and vests, but no guns. They had only batons and stun guns, as they weren't allowed to carry guns—Biyena's orders.

He had clarified that this was an unwavering policy. He strongly believed in it. It was his opinion that guns created a temptation for violence, and the last thing that Biyena wanted was for his police force to be tempted to fire their guns.

The days of cops haphazardly shooting off their guns were over, as far as he was concerned.

Shooting guns into a crowd of civilians was the kind of measure his predecessor would've taken, and had taken many times before. It was not the kind of image Biyena wanted to project for the new direction of his country. He had forbidden guns for most of the police. The only guys with guns were the snipers, Biyena's personal bodyguards who stood in the wings offstage, and the soldiers who stood guard on the outskirts of the capital in case of an external threat.

Unfortunately, the armed soldiers were necessary.

Biyena's predecessor was nowhere to be found. It seemed he was hiding out in one of the many presidential houses—some of which were secret from the public.

No one knew how he would respond to being beaten by Biyena. In fact, no one had seen him in almost seventeen hours, ever since it looked as if Biyena would win.

The soldiers were a precaution, but Biyena had no fear of the old leader returning because he had been told by his advisors that the old dictator had already fled across the border and would probably never be seen again.

So far, transferring power seemed to go off without a hitch, which made sense. Biyena's predecessor was old. He had no children of his own. There were no sons to follow in his footsteps.

He had ruled over West Ganbola so viciously that he never allowed one person to rise to second in command. No one would follow him.

Biyena concluded that the old guy saw the writing on the wall and just ran. He was too old to fight a civil war. And he didn't want to go to prison.

Likely, the new president would have him executed. Why not just run?

The old guy could retire somewhere warm, like the coast of Brazil or Venezuela, countries he had strong relations with, allies.

Biyena and his advisors figured the old guy would most likely spend the rest of his life on a beach rather than in a jail cell, where he belonged, but that was fine with Biyena. He could live with it if the old dictator never again showed his face in West Ganbola.

Biyena looked out across the crowd and then over his shoulder at his son.

Nikita was fighting with two of his father's personal guards, who had stepped in after the police allowed him up the stairs to the stage.

Biyena could see the guards trying to frisk his son, which annoyed Nikita.

Biyena turned back to the crowd and held his hands up high and spoke into the microphone.

"This...this is because of you. All of you. We deserve a better country. We are on our way."

Cheers roared.

He repeated slowly, "This is because of you. All of you."

The crowd cheered again, and people continued to wave the little flags with West Ganbola's colors, more and more, harder and harder. A sea of black and gold flowed across his sightline.

The spectacle kindled a sense of patriotism deep down in Biyena's bones, igniting that sense of nationalism a man feels at his core. He felt like he was dreaming.

Suddenly, he heard his son call out to him over the roars, from behind him.

"Father!"

Biyena turned and looked at Nikita. He looked into his eyes. They were laden with emotion and a look that seemed to be regret and panic all at once.

Perhaps his son was overwhelmed with pride, and that was the look he was seeing. He wasn't sure.

Biyena waved at the guards to allow his son on stage. Then he turned back to the microphone.

"This is because of my family. This is because of my wife. My sons."

He glanced back at the spectators and then at his wife and his son, again.

Nikita walked toward him, and Biyena saw in his eyes that something was off.

Suddenly, fear shot through Biyena. He didn't know why. It was deep down in his bones.

Nikita said, "Father."

There was a tear in his eye.

Biyena didn't step back from the podium or the microphone, but simply turned halfway.

The crowd quieted to a murmur.

Biyena said, "What's wrong, son?"

His voice was low and deep. It fired into the microphone and echoed over the crowd in a low boom from the speakers near the foot of the stage. The crowd fell silent in a cohesive hush, as if they were listening to a sermon. A hiss from the speakers resonated over them in the dead silence. Whispers could be heard wafting through the air.

Nikita walked past his mother without looking at her. Not a glance. Not a nod. Not a flicker of his fingers in a partial wave. Not a single acknowledgment.

As he closed in on his father, the tears multiplied. They filled his eyes.

Biyena knew it was bad news. No—it was the worst kind of news. He had seen nothing rattle his eldest son, and he would never again because right there, Nikita pulled a Colt 1911 handgun from under his jacket. It had been stuffed in the inside left pocket of his suit jacket.

Now it was out and visible, and gripped tightly in Nikita's right hand.

Biyena stared into the end of the barrel. It looked like a single, eyeless, black eye socket staring back at him.

The gun was matte black, but it appeared black and polished in the bright morning sunlight.

Nikita wielded the gun, pointed it at his father's center mass, and, in three quick strides, he closed the gap between them.

Biyena froze in utter terror.

His son was pointing a gun at him.

Confusion filled his mind at first, but then he had a split second of absolute clarity. He was going to die, and his oldest son would be the one to deliver his death to him.

The worst thing a parent can witness is the death of his own child, but the reverse is also true.

With tear-filled eyes, Nikita pulled the trigger, as he had been instructed.

Once. Twice. Three times.

Boom! Boom! Boom!

The sounds were deafening in the silence. The flashes were all bright, fiery orange sprays, small explosions thrust out of the muzzle.

With each shot, the muzzle climbed like Nikita was pulling the trigger recklessly and not squeezing it, which he was.

He had never fired a gun before, not once, but the bullets hit where Nikita aimed. That was what usually happened at close range.

The first bullet ripped through Biyena's upper chest. Red mist burst out and colored the short distance between them.

By the time the second bullet fired, Mrs. Biyena had gone off into a howl of frantic screaming, the shrieks of a banshee.

The second bullet blasted upward and to the left, sending it on a trajectory that ripped through Biyena's right upper side, where the shoulder joins the neck.

The third followed but deviated on a slightly higher path and barely missed Biyena's head. It fired off into the air over the crowd of spectators and rocketed another sixty-four yards before crashing through an office window and embedding itself into the back of a thick wooden bookshelf.

Nikita never got the chance to fire a fourth bullet because Biyena's personal guards had drawn their own weapons and shot him dead.

Two guards fired a pair of classic M9 Berettas and killed the son of the president. They fired nine-millimeter parabellums straight through Nikita's back, rupturing his pancreas and collapsing his lungs and severing his spinal cord.

The guards were well trained and overzealous. They knew how to shoot their weapons, and they didn't miss. They fired into Nikita until he fell, face forward—dead. It was overkill, but the job was done.

Biyena died before his son, but both were lying on the same stage, dying, bleeding out.

Biyena's wife dropped to her knees. Between them, almost perfectly centered, perfectly framed, like a morbid painting of a scene right out of a Shakespearean play.

She watched, her head moving back and forth between them.

First, she saw her husband gasp his final breath. Then she watched the light from her son's eyes die away to nothing.

She wailed and screamed, never uttering a single word.

Only once did she glance up at the crowd. That was when she saw the news cameras. Her eyes fell on them, and she stared as if she was staring at a train barreling down.

All the major stations from West Ganbola and the neighboring nations were there.

Al Jazeera was there, and one crew from an American-owned network was there. It was *CNN International*.

She never spoke.

2

ON LAND, Jack Widow was used to being the apex predator. More than ten miles off the coast of Miami, it was the tiger shark swimming beneath him.

Widow walked aft and stopped at the stern of an eighty-foot rust bucket with a fresh paint job and twin John Deere 6125AFM 400hp main engines. The boat was called the *El Pez Grande*, which meant *The Big Fish* in Spanish.

The John Deere maritime propulsion engines used to be in top working condition, but that was on another vessel—two boats ago—before the last boat ran them virtually into the ground.

They were third-generation bought engines.

Widow could tell they hadn't been well-maintained because one of them had shuddered and smoked at least four times since he started working for Jorge Calderón. And he wasn't even sure that it had been the same motor all four times. Looking back, it seemed probable that both had problems.

Widow dressed comfortably for the weather, which was end-of-August hot, but windy on the open water. There was nothing to see in all four compass directions but the open blue-green Atlantic Ocean. Miami was behind him to the west, and the Bahamas were to the east.

The waves swayed the boat gently. Two narrow metal cages, painted white, were sunk into the water at the back of the boat. The rooftop doors were padlocked closed for safety reasons.

Behind Widow were three young college guys, the clients. They looked like frat boys. All three were students at the University of Miami.

One had hair covering his forehead. One was brawny like a jock. And one, the youngest and meekest, was freshly shaved bald, like a grunt about to ship out to boot camp.

The grunt was all geared up in a wetsuit with a single oxygen tank strapped to his back, with a diving mask strapped to his head, not yet pulled down over his eyes.

In the wetsuit, the boy shivered like he was terrified. Which he was. And he should've been.

The jock stood behind the grunt and said, "You're going in the water, Teddy. There's no turning back now."

The grunt named Teddy muttered, "I don't want to go. Don't make me go. Please. There's got to be another thing I can do?"

The one with the hair in his face moved like a pawn taking directions from the leader. He circled around both guys, stood on the other side of Teddy, and placed his hands on Teddy's shoulder. Implementing a hard, quick massage, like a coach with a player he's trying to encourage before shoving him into the big game.

The pawn said, "Ted, you gotta go in. It's what you signed up for."

Teddy said, "No. I can't. Let's go back to shore."

"There's nothing to be scared of. They're just overgrown fish."

Widow stood near the cages at the stern of the boat. He knelt over the stern and peered down to the empty cages.

Widow had only worked for Calderón for about a week, but he already knew the man's situation was less than fruitful. The third-hand, burned-out engines, the paint covering the rust on the boat, and the spotty-looking workmanship on the shark cages all pointed to a dying business. Not to mention the fact that Widow was the only crewmember.

What did that say about him?

Either he was dumb enough to get on the barely-held-together boat, or he was Calderón's cheapest option. Widow thought the answer was probably both things.

He was cheap labor, and he was dumb enough to get on board the boat.

Widow didn't need the money. The only reason he'd taken this job was a total twist of fate.

A week ago, Widow walked the concrete pedestrian walkways along Biscayne Bay in Miami, sipping the last of an espresso he'd bought from a street vendor. Walking along, he saw Calderón fire two crew members, right there on the pier, headed out to a small boat dock.

Widow watched the two disgruntled guys come in and saw Calderón's look turn to despair afterward.

As hard as Widow was, he had a soft spot, right in the middle of him somewhere. He approached Calderón and inquired about what was what.

Calderón gave him the story about a failing business and tons of debt, and how he needed a big score to make his overdue installments.

This is where the dumb part came into play. Widow blurted out that he had been in the Navy and missed being at sea. Casual conversation.

And right there, on the spot, Calderón offered him a job—first mate, which was actually the *only* mate. The first offer of money was low, and Widow refused, but the second offer was double while still low. Calderón added the promise of adventure and open waters. The man was a damn fine salesman.

At sea the first day, Widow learned Calderón was a fine salesman but a bad skipper.

Widow ended up doing most of the work and improved most of the launch procedures, which bled over into the at-sea procedures.

By the end of their first voyage, Calderón joked that Widow should be the skipper, and he should be the first mate. It was true.

In the last seven days, they had only a handful of clients wanting to go out to dive in cages with sharks.

Calderón's shark-diving business was living on fumes. Widow said nothing about it. He didn't have to. The writing was on the wall, and Calderón knew it.

It wasn't a real job for Widow. His livelihood wasn't based on it. He had plenty of money in a bank account that his mother had left him. Plus, there was some inheritance from stocks and IRAs. And he had money from his old job in the NCIS. He wasn't hurting for income. And whenever the day would come that he might be, he was no stranger to physical labor.

Widow showed up every morning to work on Calderón's boat, partially because he felt bad for the guy and partially because he was enjoying the open air, the end-of-summer breeze, and just being out on the water once again.

The jock continued to pressure Teddy, psyching him out, while the pawn talked in the other ear, trying to psych him up.

Widow reached down and checked the shark cage's durability with two hard tugs on the top of the wires.

Right off, one of his tugs pulled the metal away from the corner, where it was supposed to have been welded together.

Oops, he thought. Better not put the kid in that one. He let go of the cage and shimmied sideways to the other one.

The sunglasses on his face slipped forward on his nose as he looked down. He pushed them back into place with one finger. Then he reached down and tugged at the second cage's top corners, checking its durability. It held together.

Satisfied, Widow reached a hand around behind himself and into his back pocket. He came out with a set of two keys on a ring that dangled from a large orange floating bobber, a precaution in case they fell into the water. They were copies of the keys to the padlocks on the cages. Calderón had the original set in his pocket, or on deck somewhere, or in the cabin. Or possibly, back in his office onshore.

None of those locations would've surprised Widow, which was why he held on to the copies himself. The last thing he wanted to happen was to lock a client into a cage and lose the keys.

Widow reached down and gripped the cage's padlock and unlocked it. He re-pocketed the keys and pulled the cage door open. He left it leaning on its hinge, and stood up.

Widow looked out over the water. He saw nothing on the surface in all directions, until, suddenly, he saw a dorsal fin come up out of the water. He watched it. It swam down under the boat. He looked down and saw a huge tiger shark circling the boat slowly, like a dog waiting for dinner.

That tiger shark was joined by another. Both were roughly the same size—large. They both had the same empty blackness in their eyes.

They swam almost in figure eights around the boat like a choreographed dance.

Calderón was at the starboard side, chumming shark bait at the end of a long pole. He dragged the pole's tip and the bloody shark bait along the surface of the water.

Blood pooled on the ocean's surface from the large chunk of meat at the end of the pole. Calderón swept the pole and the meat back and forth across the water as if he was stirring a pot. The bait and the blood lured the sharks close to the stern of the boat.

After a moment, the two large tiger sharks were joined by another, even bigger than the first two.

Widow saw another shark in the distance, swimming up to join the game, to find out if the blood was meant for him or not.

The new shark wasn't a tiger. It was a solitary hammerhead.

Only Widow was mistaken because two others popped up behind the first. It wasn't one hammerhead. It was three—three large tiger sharks and three large hammerheads. The kid was going to get his money's worth. That was for damn sure.

The jock and the pawn continued to bait Teddy, gearing him up for the cage. They saw Widow staring at them and lowered their voices, but continued to pressure him.

Widow recognized the hazing process. Any military man worth his salt knew the signs, knew the procedures. The pressuring, the daring, the crazy stunt the newbie was expected to go through. There was a pecking order in the military, both spoken in the ranks and unspoken among the enlisted.

The same was true in college frats.

Teddy was at the bottom of the pecking order. He was a pledge.

Calderón looked over his shoulder at the boys and spoke.

"Okay, guys. It's now or never. The sharks aren't gonna hang out all day."

He jerked the pole up and took the bait out of the water just as one of the tiger sharks dove and circled back and came at the bait fast.

The boys, Calderón, and Widow all watched in awe and horror as the huge tiger shark breached the ocean surface and came all the way up and out to his dorsal fin. Gravity kicked in, and the shark fell back to the ocean, splashing water high. Some sprayed on the deck of the boat.

Calderón barely got the meat out of the water in time to avoid having it ripped off with the pole.

Teddy flipped out.

"No. No. I'm not doing this."

The jock said, "You have to. There's no turning back now."

The pawn said, "Dude, you have to. It's not that bad. They can't get you in the cage."

Widow looked back at them again.

Teddy saw him.

Widow motioned for him to come over.

Teddy pulled loose from the others and waddled over to Widow.

Teddy's eyes stared up at Widow and then he peered down slowly to the water. He stared at the bloodthirsty sharks circling.

Teddy shut his eyes tight and stopped within arm's reach of Widow and shivered.

Widow intercepted the kid and put a hand on his shoulder.

He said, "Open your eyes, kid."

Teddy opened his eyes and stared back down to the cages and then the water and the sharks.

"Oh, God!" he uttered.

Widow said, "Look at me."

Teddy looked at him.

"It's no big deal. They can't get you. You have nothing to be afraid of."

Teddy said, "But. They're sharks. Look at them."

Widow released the kid's shoulder and reached his hands down to the bottom of his T-shirt. He grabbed the cloth and pulled the shirt up over his head and took it off. He held it down by his side, one-handed.

Teddy, the jock, the pawn, and Calderón all stared at Widow's naked torso.

Unlike most of Widow's SEAL brothers, he hated working out. Widow liked regimen, but only when it was a part of a bigger functionality. Run uphill? Sounds good, but only if it was to cross over to the other side. Climb a tower? Absolutely, if it was to watch the sunset from the top. Do push-ups? Of course, if it was to impress a girl, but just going to the gym day in and day out? That wasn't his style. Every exercise should have a functional purpose.

Widow moved a lot. He walked a lot. He carried himself with good posture. He had a combination of great genes and lots of get-up-and-go, which amounted to an abdomen like the side of a brick wall, shoulders as rock hard as boulders, and biceps like bowling balls with huge hands on the ends of long forearms.

Widow's bicep size was naturally offset by his long arms and long forearms. He didn't walk around looking like he constantly had a bodybuilder's pump. Guys with long arms have to squeeze their biceps harder to make them pop out. When the bones are longer than normal, the muscles lie flatter.

This was all good for Widow. He didn't like being stared at any more than he already was.

Calderón, the jock, the pawn, and Teddy continued to stare at Widow's torso.

The jock was the first to speak.

"Bro, you should try out for the NFL."

Widow said, "I played ball once."

The jock asked, "Pro?"

"No. High school."

"Why didn't you go pro?"

"I only played one game."

"Why? What happened?"

"I killed a kid," Widow lied. He hadn't really killed a kid, but he had put a kid in the hospital. It was all an accident. They were both decked out in football pads and helmets. But Widow's raw force destroyed the kid's pads and his helmet.

Widow broke the kid's jaw. He heard the kid had to eat from a straw for six months after that.

Widow never picked up a football again after that except on the decks of countless supercarriers and other naval ships. And that was only to throw the ball back to other sailors who asked him to. Throwing around the ball was fine. But he refused every game, even touch football.

Calderón stared at Widow as if he were having second thoughts about hiring him.

Widow saw it on his face. The guy was asking himself: *What kind of animal did I take out to sea with me?*

Suddenly, the sharks weren't the only things to fear.

Widow ignored the looks of fear and smiled and turned around. He faced away, showing his back to them. Then he heard the audible gasps from all four of them as they saw what his back looked like. They weren't gasping at his tattoos, which covered much of his body. They weren't gasping at his defined, chiseled back muscles. They were gasping at the three bullet wounds at the center of his back.

Three round scars. Three bullet hole scars. They formed the three points on a triangle.

The scars left behind were white and rigid, with the appearance of dead flesh. They were hardened from the passing of time. They were reminders of a life he'd lived long ago and a betrayal that he'd rather not think about.

Calderón asked, "Widow, are those bullet holes?"

"Yes," he said.

And no, he thought.

Suddenly, they all had questions.

"Who shot you?"

"Was that in the military?"

"How're you alive?"

Widow turned back around and faced them.

He said, "It was a long time ago, a different life."

All four of them had to close their gaping mouths. They looked as stunned as if they'd just seen an alien spaceship fall from the sky.

Widow said, "Teddy, come here."

Teddy shuffled the rest of the way, reluctantly, and stopped in front of Widow. No one stopped him. His friends no longer hounded him. Everyone was quiet.

Widow pulled his shirt back on.

He spoke directly to Teddy the way he would to a kid who was a sailor under his command.

"There are worse things than sharks in this world. Sharks don't pretend to be your friends. They don't betray you and shoot you in the back. People do that. You've got nothing to fear from them. You know why?"

"They're not people?"

"You got nothing to fear from them because you know without a doubt what their nature is. They eat and swim. They don't want. They don't lie. They don't betray."

"Isn't that why I should be afraid of them? Cause they want to eat me?"

"Ted, I was in the Navy SEALs. I've been on lots of ships and boats. I've been in shark-infested waters more times than I can count. They don't want to eat *you*. You know why?"

"Why?"

"People taste like shit."

Teddy slowly smiled and then laughed.

Widow put a hand on his shoulder again and said, "Know why you're going in the cage and not your friends?"

"I'm the pledge?"

"It's because they're pussies."

"I'm not?"

"No way. Look at you. You're all geared up to go down there with sharks. You don't see your buddies wearing wetsuits, do you?"

Teddy looked back at his friends.

He muttered, "I'm the only one going in."

"You're the only one brave enough to go in. You came all the way out here. You got in the wetsuit. The hard part is over. Sharks hate the taste of humans. We're stringy and bony—not much nutrients for them. Plus, no blubber for flavor. They prefer seals to humans. Hell, they prefer starvation to humans. Trust me."

Teddy cracked a smile and nodded to himself.

"Okay. Let's do this!" he called out to his friends.

Teddy pulled the diving mask down over his eyes. He turned to his friends and nodded and waved at them, expecting to go in the water a terrified boy and come out a man.

Widow led him to the cage that seemed sturdier and grabbed Teddy's forearm. Widow lowered him through the cage's door and reminded him to put the breathing mouthpiece into his mouth.

"Test it now," Widow said.

Teddy tried it and nodded and gave a thumbs-up. He sank down into the blue water.

Widow closed the cage door and locked it. He stepped back off the cage and hit the lever to lower the cage until it was fully submerged.

Calderón whipped the pole and the bait at the sharks.

The tiger sharks and the hammerheads circled and swam under the boat. They followed the bait and the blood around Teddy's cage.

Widow knew Teddy was scared. But after a while, he saw visible cues from the kid that he had relaxed.

There was nothing to fear.

3

A PHONE CALL skipped and bounced through several international phone carriers and towers across the planet until it was rerouted back to the United States. To remain untraceable, the cell phones being used were burners.

Traceable or not, none of that bothered the man known to only one other man in the world by the codename Jekyll. He wasn't concerned about anyone listening to his conversation. No government scared him. Even if some flunky from the National Security Agency had stumbled upon their phone conversation, none of it mattered now.

The first mission was already complete.

The only thing that scared Jekyll was the man known to a handful of people in the world as Hyde.

Hyde answered the phone, his voice dark, calm, and eerie. There was no sense of urgency in it, but there should've been, considering the stakes of their business.

His voice sent chills down Jekyll's spine—and Jekyll was not a chills-down-the-spine type of guy. He had plenty of training and was a formidable adversary, but Hyde was the scariest guy he had ever known, which forced Jekyll to maintain a certain level of caution when speaking to Hyde.

Hyde said, "Mission complete."

"I know. I saw it on CNN. They're playing it everywhere, as prominent as if it had happened on American soil. It's all anyone's talking about."

"They may play it where you are, but it's not getting much attention in Middle America where we want it to get attention."

"What did you expect? Americans don't care about some country in Africa they never heard of. They barely care about the parts of Africa that they *have* heard of. No one's going to care until it happens here. Happens to them."

Hyde said, "That'll be soon."

"How did you get the son to go through with it?"

"Same way we'll do it there."

"How's that?"

Silence fell between them.

Hyde asked, "Does it matter?"

"No. I guess not. Just curious is all."

Jekyll thought, *How far do you expect me to go?*

"We used leverage."

"Leverage?"

"The children. We took his children. Told him if he didn't kill his father in front of the cameras on that stage, then we would kill them, and not quickly."

Jekyll swallowed, and Hyde heard it.

Jekyll said, "Obviously, he believed you. How'd he not know it was a bluff?"

Silence fell over the line for a brief second.

Hyde said, "He believed us because there was no bluff. We were serious. We made him understand that."

"How?"

"He had three children."

"Yeah?"

"Now, there're only two."

Jekyll swallowed hard again.

He had no confusion about the kind of man Hyde was. He was no good guy. He wasn't on the side of any government, not anymore.

After the mission he was about to embark on, no one would see him as anything other than a traitor. He would have to leave the US. There was no way around that.

He'd already accepted that he would have to disappear forever.

He'd already bought plane tickets on the dark web through a reliable source. And he'd made his travel arrangements after he got a fake passport and a whole new identity to go with it.

He was ready to run. He was already a man on the run as soon as he linked up with Hyde. It's just that no one else knew it yet.

The plane tickets were freshly printed and stowed away in a bugout bag he had stashed someplace safe, where no one would find them.

He took every precaution because he knew what they would look for. He knew intimately what Homeland Security, the FBI, the Secret Service, all of them, would look for after the upcoming mission was complete.

Of course, he wasn't flying out of the United States. That was far too risky—and would be almost impossible for him afterward.

In the movies, things usually worked out whenever someone was trying to get away after a bank heist or some other illegal act. The bad guy wore a disguise and showed up at the airport, boarding pass in hand—no problem.

Movies never explained how he got the ticket. They don't explain it because they can't. There was no such thing as getting plane tickets with fake identification, not in the United States. Those days were long gone. Doing that now was next to impossible. Wherever it could be done, it was almost certainly because of government corruption, like in a third-world country like West Ganbola.

Getting out of there after what Hyde and his team had done wasn't impossible. It was a cakewalk compared to getting out of the United States after the operation they were about to embark on.

West Ganbola was only a trial run.

Jekyll had procured his tickets in Mexico—much safer.

After the mission was over, he'd ride in the back of a hollowed-out gas truck all the way to Georgia, where he would get out and spend the night in a predetermined safe house.

Next, he'd hop on a bus, ride it down to Texas, where he would meet a contact who would drive him across the border in a transport van for an American oil company. He would be disguised as part of the work crew, a bunch of guys who were paid to keep their mouths shut.

They were already well versed at smuggling people across the border, both ways. Not that any of it would matter because the Mexican government wouldn't stop them, and even if they did—that sort of thing could be handled as well, with cash money.

All of this was okay with Jekyll—the mission, the risk, and certainly the money, which was his only motivation. He didn't care that much about country or patriotism or the president or the United States Secret Service or anyone who might be collateral damage.

Hyde was paying top dollar. And top dollar was a lot of dollars, enough to last him the rest of his life. In a month, he would be nothing more than a cliché, lying on a South American beach, sipping piña coladas. No guns. No guards. No sentry duties. No flags. No one giving him status updates in his earpiece. He would be free. He would live his life on his own terms.

All that said, he wasn't crazy about killing children. Even a traitor has his limits.

That was the major difference between Hyde and himself.

Jekyll was in it solely for the money—no question about it. But Hyde was in it for other reasons, which even he didn't completely understand.

Hyde was psychotic. His whole crew was unhinged.

Hyde asked, "Having second thoughts?"

"Of course not."

Jekyll answered without hesitation. Hesitation would get him killed.

"Good. Then, you're ready to do this? On American soil?"

Jekyll ignored the question.

He said, "So far, the media still thinks the son was acting alone. They're buying the motive we put in place. The jealous son thing."

"Of course, they're buying it. They'll swallow it whole. I knew they would. The media are a bunch of stupid, headline-hungry dogs. They'll believe whatever scraps I feed them."

"What now?"

"Now, we move forward with our real target—no more third-world bullshit. We're ready. How's your end coming? Did you find him?"

Jekyll gulped.

"Find him?"

"You know who! The one I want to use as the patsy!"

Hyde's voice blasted over the phone. Jekyll pulled the phone from his ear and could still hear Hyde. He waited for Hyde to stop and put the phone back to his ear.

Jekyll said, "I'm trying. I've been trying. It's been months of this. He's off the grid. Untraceable."

"No one's untraceable. Not in America. Not unless he's already dead. In which case, you should've produced a death certificate by now."

Jekyll said nothing.

"What about his family?"

"His family?"

"Yes. Everyone has a family. Find them and put the squeeze on them. They'll give him up."

Jekyll said, "Jack Widow. Born in Mississippi. No brothers. No sisters. Mother deceased. Her parents are deceased. His father was unknown. The story goes he was a drifter. He probably knocked up the mother and vanished. He probably doesn't even know he has a son, if he's still alive. Otherwise, there's nothing else."

"Nothing?"

"No. Nothing. No family left. No wife. No kids. Nothing. He's a ghost."

Hyde said, "You agreed you could find him. Using your resources. Using the resources of the damn United States Secret Service, you promised you would locate him."

"I'm sorry. We can use another patsy. Doesn't have to be him."

Hyde breathed in and breathed out, loud. He repeated until he was calm and collected.

He said, "You've had five months. You promised you could get the job done. Widow is who I want!"

"I know, but the guy's a ghost."

Hyde slammed a heavy fist down on a countertop. The noise resonated through the phone.

Hyde shouted, "He's out there somewhere! Go get him!"

"I'll keep trying. But..."

"But what?"

"We need to have a backup plan just in case I can't find him. Or he turns up dead."

Hyde said, "I got a backup plan in case you don't find him. And trust me, you won't like it."

Jekyll didn't respond to that, but he swallowed hard.

He said, "I'll call you tomorrow. At midnight. I'll know more then."

Jekyll clicked the burner cell phone off and slipped it back into his pocket. He stood on the perimeter of a big Victorian house in a rich and quiet gated Virginia neighborhood. A place where only the most elite senators, congressmen, and their families lived, a place that was guarded better than the ancient palaces of Rome.

It was watched over by the most elite guards in the world—the United States Secret Service.

Each house on the block appeared normal from the street, all except for the patrolling Secret Service agents.

Jekyll had pretended to step away from his post to take a smoke break. He looked around the street and saw that most of the other houses were pitch black except for the occasional flicker of late-night TV through the curtains of upstairs windows.

The United States Secret Service was as ubiquitous to them as the neighborhood garbage man. They were present, armed, and ready to die for them. Ready to take a bullet if necessary. But the people locked safely in their houses were used to that. They were complacent. It was business as usual. Nothing special. The people in the houses worried about nothing. That was something that Jekyll was going to change, but for now, there was nothing for them to worry about and nothing for him to worry about.

He looked back at the large house behind him, his post.

No one watched him. No one had listened in on his conversation. No one had even noticed that he'd left his post.

Nestled under his left arm and holstered in a shoulder rig was a SIG Sauer P229. It was chambered with a .357 SIG round, eleven more in the magazine. He kept the gun chambered and ready for use. It was concealed nicely. He had a shoulder holster that didn't bulge or lean out. It had as small a profile as any holster on the market.

Jekyll scanned the yard, the street, and the other houses one last time before tossing his cigarette onto the driveway and letting it burn down to a dull, smokeless nub. Then he turned and walked back toward the quiet house. Back toward the sleeping family, back to the people who thought they knew him, back to the people who trusted him with their lives.

4

THE NEXT MORNING, Widow was up at the crack of dawn. After they'd returned to shore the night before, and the three frat boys left, and Widow sprayed and hosed the boat down, Calderón asked him to come in super early the next day. He said they had a special job to do. He said nothing more about it.

Widow was up early as ordered, picking up two black coffees, to go, from the counter of a posh Starbucks-wannabe coffee shop that he'd never heard of before. The coffee shop was posh because it had chrome trim, chrome railings, and glass dividers between the guests and the staff. The seats were tall swiveling apparatuses that belonged in a stylized nightclub with a space theme and not in a coffee shop near the docks.

It wasn't his preferred scene, but it was on his route and close to where the *El Pez Grande* was docked.

Widow didn't complain—all he cared about was that a coffee shop did its one job right, which was to serve coffee, and preferably good coffee.

The attendant took his money and nodded for him to step aside and wait for the coffee down by a curved section of the counter where several other early morning people were waiting for their orders to be filled.

Widow moved down and stood as far back against the wall behind the other customers as he could. He didn't want to stand in front of anyone. It made him feel impolite to block the views of shorter people. And most people were shorter people.

He got comfortable against a wall and glanced up behind the counter at a flat-screen TV. It was mounted on the back wall above the pickup station. It looked newly bought and newly installed.

CNN International played a muted report about a Confederate statue being removed from its official display in front of a government building in a distant southern town in a distant southeastern state, which was all to the north of him.

Widow turned away from the TV and stared out over the coffee shop. There were empty tables because the time was far too early for the typical early riser. But the line for coffee was building. He saw two uniformed cops walk in and order and wait by the pickup counter.

Widow let his eyes scan the room and gloss over the people who were there. He paid no attention to the news. If he had, he would've seen a news crawl scrolling on the bottom of the screen, showing headlines from across the world.

One headline, creeping by, read: *African son kills president-father.*

5

RAGGIE ROWLEY WASN'T Jekyll and Hyde's target, but she was a part of their plan. She was an important part of it, only she didn't know it. Not yet.

Raggie was known to her friends and family as Raggie and not by Nicole Marie Rowley, which was the name her parents had given her at birth.

But the name *Raggie* had come along a year ago, and with it came the event that would scar her life forever.

Right then, she was fourteen years old, thinking back about when she was thirteen.

One person she thought about was her best friend, Claire.

Claire and Raggie had been best friends since they were seven. They met in an after-school dance class that both their mothers forced them to attend. The two young girls entered, hating the idea of joining a dance class. It wasn't their thing. Neither of them wanted to learn dance, ballet, or the like. And they especially loathed the idea of learning to dance with boys.

Claire and Raggie were best friends until Raggie left with her family to live in South Africa, where she got the nickname Raggie.

Raggie's father had an important job. He was a secret agent. At least, that's what he used to tell her when she was little. He worked for the

United States Secret Service. He was the team leader for an advance protection unit, meaning he was sent out to secure locations before the president arrived.

Back when Raggie was still called Nicole, she was forced to say goodbye to her friend Claire and their little clique because her parents wanted the family to be together. They were moving away together.

Her father, Gibson Rowley, was assigned to an unpopular vacancy. He was to head the advance protection team for the southern region of Africa. This meant he would devise a protection plan within forty-eight hours for any location in his region.

It wasn't the most desirable post, but it meant that the family could be together all in one place for a while.

Rowley's job was divided into two parts. First, he had to evaluate any location within his region and with little to no notice. This meant that he and his team had to travel to the location where the president would visit and scout it out.

Rowley was a hands-on kind of leader with his team. They evaluated all the risks. They looked at every escape route. They addressed every security concern.

His team reconned the locales and then coordinated with local law enforcement officials to have escape plans ready as well as to arrange transportation details.

South Africa and much of the region was known for government corruption. Rowley made it a habit to make secret backup escape plans of their own, without the knowledge of local law enforcement agents.

Breaking laws or pissing off the local officials wasn't their concern— protecting the president was, and at any cost.

Their second mission was to guard the locations and routes after they were swept and cleared. This was to ensure that the locations remained secure until after the president had come and gone.

Being on the advance protection team meant Rowley needed to remain onsite. He had to live in South Africa as long as the mission was ongoing. He and his team had to remain in place at all times.

Not long before Nicole earned the nickname Raggie, she and her mother had to go and live in South Africa with her father. Not that this made much difference because even though the president didn't visit the region that much, her father was always gone.

He was too busy for her. All that effort to be together as a family didn't amount to much.

While Raggie lived in South Africa, she made friends with the local girls. They soon grew into a small, tight-knit group, and Nicole felt a part of something special. Immediately, she picked up on something about these girls that set them worlds apart from the girls back home. These girls weren't girlish, not like the ones she knew. They were different. They weren't the gossiping, baking cookies, and wearing dresses kind of prissy girls she was used to.

They didn't sit around talking about boys, hanging out at a mall, or watching the Kardashians on TV. Most of them didn't even own TVs.

These girls lived life. They were all about fun. They were outdoorsy.

Whatever instilled conventions of American girls that Nicole held before, these girls tore them down and set those ideas on fire.

The girls became Nicole's best friends.

Six weeks after winter that year, the girls introduced her to something that would change her life forever.

Nicole's new best friends were surfers.

Not knowing what to make of it at first, Nicole took lessons from them to fit in. But over that first summer, she spent every afternoon —with or without her new friends—on the beach, learning to surf.

She learned everything that they could teach her, and then she sought local surfers to pick up more tips and tricks.

Surfing had been missing from her life. By the end of that summer, she was full-blown addicted to surfing.

The first time she caught a wave without tipping over or crashing into the unforgiving breaks was one of the best moments of her life.

Sometimes she wished Claire could've been there to know that feeling, to feel the rush of the wind and the unpredictability of the surf, but Claire was thousands of miles away and light years behind her now.

Nicole's first surfing injury was a sprained left knee after she had tried to ride a wave the wrong way. She had to stay out of the water for the rest of the summer, which killed her on the inside. All she thought about the rest of the summer was the crashing waves.

It took the rest of that year to convince her mother to let her return to the water.

Nicole spent her time away from the ocean thinking about nothing but the ocean. While her parents thought she was studying for school, she was researching the sport of surfing.

She watched videos on the internet on how to surf, where she ended up finding a *YouTube* channel for a guy who wanted to be a pro surfer.

The guy produced a series of instructional videos teaching surfing, including techniques and tricks for getting the most out of a surfboard.

The guy had few followers, but he had an account with patreon.com so that he could accept donations from people to finance his video lessons.

By watching all his videos over and over, Nicole trusted him and, eventually, she used her mom's credit card to donate money to him monthly as a subscription.

She had never met the guy, but she learned a lot from his lessons. Why not give back?

They became friends.

When the first rays of warm weather hit the beach the following summer, Nicole was ready to get back on the board.

She rejoined her friends and surfed with them every day.

Over time, she got good enough to look like a surfer and not just a wannabe.

Her new friends celebrated Nicole's newfound ability with encouragement and partying, which they kept a secret from her parents.

One of her friends asked, "Nicole, how you get so good? After that injury, we all thought we'd never see ya again."

Nicole replied, "How does anyone get good at anything these days?"

She paused and smiled like she was making a joke.

She said, "*YouTube*!"

6

NICOLE WATCHED the surf from the shore, ready to spring into action.

Her break was coming up. She knew it. She felt it in her bones.

She wore a form-fitting wetsuit, even though she still looked like a boy in it. That might've bothered her back home in the States, but not here. Here, she felt fine with how she was built.

Nicole had a teenaged boy's frame—athletic arms, stringy legs, and a flat chest. But that was all good. It made her smile.

She thought about the girls back home in Virginia.

She thought about Claire, who was most likely praying that she would grow breasts. Claire was back home, probably hoping for curves. She probably imagined herself filling out the latest trendy clothes at the local mall.

Claire was probably trying to convince her mom to take her to *Bebe* or *GAP* or whatever department store to buy clothes that would be out of style in a season.

Nicole didn't care about that, not anymore. She wasn't concerned with boys, or styles, or status, or her first kiss, or how to fit in with the other cliques.

Right then, all she cared about was the surf. The crashing waves, the ocean, and the surfboard were the most important things in her life.

All she concentrated on was trying out the new trick that she had been working on. She had watched the advanced videos from her guy on *YouTube*, and she had practiced the jump every day at sunup. She practiced while the other girls were still asleep.

She wanted to surprise them with it.

Nicole wasn't the only surfer around at sunup. In fact, most dedicated surfers were at the beach by dawn. What they referred to as the "tourists" were the rest of the surfer wannabes who showed up later in the day.

If midnight was the witching hour, then sunrise was the surfing hour.

Today was a weekday.

Nicole came out at dawn, practiced the jump over and over on the sand, feet planted on her board. When she was ready, she took the board out into the waves. Soon, as she was landing the jump, the so-called real surfers took notice of her. She was getting smiles from them like she was now accepted into the club. She was one of them. She'd broken through.

Her new jump had gone off without a hitch, but she still had to do it in front of her friends. That would be the real showstopper. Just then, she saw them arriving.

This was the moment she was waiting for. She wanted to impress them.

Three of her new best friends stood behind her on the beach. Their surfboards were laid out on the sand like seals lying in the sun.

The tallest girl, Saffron, was Nicole's closest friend of the bunch.

Saffron was fifteen and already had a sleeve tattoo—all tribal. She was the opposite of Claire.

Saffron was her new best friend, and she was also the best surfer out of the group, which was why Nicole had kept her new trick a secret from them. She wanted to impress Saffron the most. She wanted Saffron to see her perform a jump that not even Saffron could do.

She wanted Saffron's approval.

The trick Nicole wanted to do was a high jump with the surfboard over a wave. It wasn't anything special in the eyes of true-blooded surfers, but for a thirteen-year-old girl who had a knee injury several months before, it was quite impressive.

Nicole watched for the perfect break.

The beach was getting crowded, but few people were out in the surf because a warning flag had been thrown up. A small crew of lifeguards had arrived for duty, and one of them had spotted a dark shadow in the water about a hundred yards from the beach. The shadow was probably from a school of fish or sea turtles—it could've been anything really—but the beach wasn't far from a popular place known for the likelihood of spotting Carcharodon carcharias, the scientific name for the great white shark.

Whenever there was the tiniest possibility that a shark had been spotted, the lifeguards threw up a red flag, which meant danger. Which usually meant shark. And today, for the last hour, the red flag had been up.

Nicole watched out over the sea and saw her waves coming and crashing down. The perfect chance. No one else was on the water, nothing between her and her chance to show off her new jump.

This was her chance. She felt it in her bones. Nicole scooped up her surfboard, ignored the flag, and waded out into the surf.

7

NICOLE PADDLED out past the first crashing waves and the shallowest parts of the beach. She felt the waves underneath the board. She cleared her mind and paddled forward. First, she passed the three-foot depth and then five and then seven, and she kept going. She felt no fear. She had practiced and practiced the jump and was ready to do it in front of her friends. Nothing would stop her.

She passed the ten-foot depth and then the twelve and the fifteen.

The ocean wasn't too brutal, but the surf was much higher than normal. Of course, she was getting farther out so that she could ride in longer and then take a deep breath and find the right wave to jump from. She paddled, feeling her arms strain. Her elbows bent, fighting the current. The salty water splashed her face. Her eyes blinked involuntarily every time, and she forced them back open and stared ahead.

She got to a comfortable place and stopped paddling. The waves splashed in over her, and she held her breath and held onto her board with each pass. She came out on the other side and was ready for her wave. It barreled toward her. She grabbed the board, turned back to shore, and paddled. Her hands pounded into the water, and her feet kicked and kicked. Her left knee throbbed from the healed knee injury. She powered through the pain and paddled and kicked.

A huge wave swept up underneath her, and she leaped to her feet. Both feet landed on the board like they were supposed to. She balanced and rode the wave. Everything went off without a hitch. Her form was right on the money.

She looked to the shore and saw her friends leaping and waving their hands. At first, she thought they were cheering her on. A split second later, she noticed the bystanders were joining in on their cheers.

She looked for the opportunity to make the jump, her instincts controlling her every move. She was ready.

But suddenly, she saw the lifeguards speeding out to her on wave runners. There were two of them—on red machines with white stripes on the bottom. They were still close to the shore and far from her. The closest one must've been going full speed, bouncing and crashing back down into the water. The idiots were headed right for her. The worry that they would crash into her swept over her like a sudden swell of high water.

They were going to ruin her jump. Suddenly, she feared they were headed toward her for breaking the rules and going out while there was a red flag. They might arrest her. She wasn't sure if it was breaking the law in South Africa to ignore a red warning flag.

She had to make the jump now. There was no time. She was ready. It was now or never. Her friends were watching. Saffron was watching.

Nicole bent her knees, dipped down, and locked her feet. She geared up to make the jump. The wave was almost perfect.

Suddenly, the second before she jumped, something big and dark and rough slammed into her board. The force of the blow knocked her clear off the board. Instantly, she plummeted into the wave. Her body crashed and sank, and rolled violently. She felt the safety string from her surfboard jerk at her leg. The waves crashed over her. She was dragged down into the ocean like a rag doll.

Under the surface of the water, she must've flipped and twisted several times. She couldn't feel anything but the violent pounding of the waves. The fear of drowning overcame her. She had had little time to take a breath before she had been pulled into the water.

Her lungs pounded worse than her knee. Her mouth flew open. She couldn't help it. She swallowed saltwater for a second before she closed it. Her eyes stung from the sudden impact of the water. She shut them tight and tried to stay calm. She knew that the most important thing was to remain calm. In the ocean, panic caused death faster than anything else.

The water pummeled her like a million clubs. Suddenly, she felt an undertow drag her down farther into the wave.

Abruptly, a shooting pain came from her wrist. She thought it must've been the pull of one of the lifeguards as he dragged her back to the surface. She strained and opened her eyes. Under the ocean and the booming of the waves, there wasn't much to see but shadow and darkness.

Finally, she saw some light. It was rays from the sun. It contrasted with the darkness of the depths below her. She knew that something was pulling her down toward the darkness, where she didn't want to go. She twisted her head and stared back at the reddish hues of distorted sunlight that reflected in her sightline.

The thing that immediately confused her was that the lifeguard was supposed to pull her to the surface. He should've been pulling her up and not down. But he wasn't. He was pulling her down.

At first, she blamed her disorientation. Maybe she was confused because she had been rolled several times, perhaps up was down. Maybe her sense of direction was completely wrong.

Suddenly, she was snaking and flipping out of control.

Nicole reached up or down—she wasn't sure—toward whatever was clenching her arm, pulling her down.

She reached out toward it with her other hand. She expected to find the hand of one of the lifeguards, but it wasn't a hand. She found something rough and rubbery and dry, even underwater. It was like wet, rubbery sandpaper.

She felt around the thing and felt for her hand. She couldn't find it. Whatever the thing was, it was wrapped around her hand and wrist. She jerked and wrenched and couldn't break free from it.

Seconds turned into minutes, which felt like an eternity. She knew she was going to die if she didn't break free.

Nicole's personal record for holding her breath was under a minute, but she was certain she had been underwater for much longer. Probably it had been at least two minutes.

This was it. This was where she would die. No question.

Suddenly, whatever the sandpapery thing was that held onto her hand and wrist dragged her farther down. And she felt the unmistakable brush of a huge dorsal fin whipping past her head like a rotor.

8

NICOLE THOUGHT, *SHARK!* It was a shark. She was going to die, and she knew it. She stopped struggling against it. She stopped trying to break free. She was out of time. She accepted it.

After a minute and seventeen seconds more of the shark thrashing and pulling her under, it bit her hand off at the wrist, let go of her, and swam away.

The first lifeguard to reach her leaped off his wave runner into the water, dove into the crashing waves, and swam as hard as he could. He caught up to her and grabbed her by the leg. Underwater, he snicked open a three-inch knife and cut the rope to her surfboard and let it go.

Nicole reached out with her good hand to feel the remains of her other hand. Nothing was left but bone and skin.

She clenched onto her bleeding appendage and felt the lifeguard drag her through the surf back to the wave runner. She sucked up saltwater through her nose. He pushed her body over the hump in the back, and then he climbed up onto the machine and sat in the front.

She huffed and coughed and wheezed and spat out saltwater. He turned to face her and examined her wound—quickly. Blood was everywhere. It pooled on the water's surface.

The lifeguard turned back to the front and searched through a saddlebag for emergency bandages. He found the equipment and wrapped her arm up as tightly as possible so that she wouldn't lose any more blood, and then he cranked the throttle and took off back to shore.

Nicole's eyes were open. She felt as though she were on the back of a horse as the wave runner hurtled through the waves. She gazed back to the sea and watched her surfboard as it drifted away, and she saw the dorsal fin of the shark one last time as it swam off and was gone from sight.

Later, the doctors patched her back together—without her hand. Her friends visited her and brought her gifts and get-well cards. She drifted in and out of sleep and awakened each time to a room filled with flowers and different family members and advance protection team members.

Sometimes she saw her mom and sometimes her dad. Sometimes they were together. Other times, it was members of her father's team. They were all close to her and the family, like uncles.

After she recovered, her mother insisted that she never surf again, which wasn't a possibility because the call of the ocean was far stronger to her than one lost hand.

Once she was discharged from the hospital, she rebelled against her mother by attending surfing competitions as a spectator.

Her friends who had witnessed the whole thing told her she was most likely attacked by a shark breed known to locals as the ragged-tooth shark, which was the ugliest thing in the ocean and nocturnal, but still known to attack at any hour of the day. It was a big shark with a mouth full of crooked and ragged teeth. There were so many crooked teeth that far more bone was visible in its mouth than gums. This breed was common in the waters surrounding the local beaches.

After some time had passed, the horror of the incident wore off, and Nicole recovered. She began by leaving her room and venturing slowly into the rest of their rented house. She spent only a couple more weeks inside with her mother, and that was enough to push her back out in public. She called her friends and met them away from home. Gradually, she stayed out longer and longer, and before too much time passed, she was involved again in their social gatherings.

Her friends renamed her Raggie, slang for the type of shark that had attacked her.

Her father relocated back to DC the following year, taking on a more high-profile role in the Secret Service. Therefore, she had to move as well.

Raggie had to leave surfing and her friends in South Africa behind, but she took with her a love of the sport and her new name.

9

IN THE PRESENT DAY, Widow climbed aboard the *El Pez Grande* and found Calderón on the deck.

"I brought coffee."

"Thanks. That'll help. We got a long day today."

Widow handed Calderón the coffee and looked around. He glanced back at the parking lot leading up to the pier.

"Where's the client?"

"No client today."

"No client?"

Calderón took a sip of the coffee to test the heat.

He said, "There is a client, but no passengers."

"What the hell are we doing here so early?"

"We're doing a pickup today."

"A pickup?"

"Yeah."

"Aren't we a shark cage diving company? What are we picking up, sharks?"

Calderón stopped in the middle of the deck and stared at Widow.

He said, "Look around. We ain't got many customers wanting to go out there."

"Yeah. I noticed."

"Sometimes, I gotta do pickups to make the month."

"What're we picking up?"

"Don't worry about it. It's no big deal."

Calderón paused a short breath and repeated.

"No big deal."

Widow stayed quiet.

"Yeah. No big deal. Don't worry. It's actually pretty easy. And we get to go out on open water. With no customers to coddle. You're going to love it."

Widow shrugged and didn't argue.

They undocked and fired up the engines and were off.

Widow watched the dock shrink behind him for a long moment, then turned to the ocean ahead and drank his coffee.

Calderón piloted the boat. They rode off toward the rising sun.

10

CALDERÓN AND WIDOW passed sixty nautical miles by midmorning with no planned stops, except that one of the engines went out every forty-five minutes. It happened so often that they were used to it and knew what to do. The engine needed to stop and stay offline for several minutes until it cooled down.

At sixty-one nautical miles, Widow looked south and saw Bimini Bay about five miles away.

Calderón slowed and swung the wheel, steering the boat northeast. He pushed the throttle up, and they went on for another twenty minutes until Widow could barely make out Bimini anymore.

Widow looked around in all directions and saw nothing but blue-green Caribbean ocean.

The water was so blue and crystal clear that Widow saw the bottom. Not too deep where they were.

Calderón slowed the throttle to a complete stop and cut the engines. They floated. Borderline choppy waves rocked the boat enough to give a landlubber seasickness. Luckily, neither Calderón nor Widow was a landlubber.

Brash winds gusted over the surface of the Atlantic and over the deck.

"Throw the anchor," Calderón ordered.

Widow nodded and walked from the helm out to the bow. The wind was hard, but not hard enough to blow a man overboard. It was enough to whip his hair all to one side and plaster his T-shirt and shorts to his body, silhouetting his muscles.

Calderón wore boat chinos, flip-flops, and a thin coat, not a windbreaker, which Widow would've understood. But a coat? Widow didn't know why he wore the coat. He figured maybe Calderón didn't own a windbreaker.

The sunglasses on Widow's face protected his eyes from being battered by the wind.

Widow walked over to the anchor and knelt and picked it up with one hand and scooped up the chain with the other. He ran it out to make sure it wasn't tangled anywhere.

Widow heaved the anchor over the side of the boat. He watched it sink to the depths below until it was gone from sight.

The first time he'd tossed the anchor overboard for Calderón, he'd wondered why Calderón had an anchor that wasn't automated by a winch, instead of this cheap, manual thing. He'd almost asked about it, but being on board the bucket of bolts with the few customers that they had all summer told him all he needed to know.

Calderón joined him on deck. He held a GPS tracking device in his hand. It looked expensive, more so than any of their other equipment.

Widow stared at it until he figured out that it was a satellite tracker.

Widow said, "Expensive. When did you get that?"

"They gave it to me."

"Who are 'they'?"

Calderón looked at Widow.

He said, "Better not ask questions."

"Calderón, what the hell are we doing out here?"

"Told you. We're picking up."

"What are we picking up?"

"Just a package."

"A package? In the middle of the ocean?"

"Yeah."

"What have you gotten me into?"

Just then, Calderón looked at the GPS tracker. It beeped, slowly at first, and then picked up a steady rhythm.

Calderón said, "Quiet."

He looked at the GPS screen and pointed it around like he was trying to find a signal and then stopped, pointing the device south. He looked up into the air and saw a dot in the sky.

"There!" Calderón shouted, and pointed up.

Widow turned and looked. He squinted his eyes, even with the sunglasses on. The skies were clear, which meant that it didn't matter where the sun was; everything was bright.

He focused and saw what Calderón pointed at. It was a seaplane, small, and bright white.

Suddenly, Widow heard a crackle from a radio, and he spun around and saw that Calderón had another expensive device that he hadn't had before.

It was a small handheld radio.

Calderón clicked the button and spoke in Spanish. He released the button and listened. A voice came on and spoke back in Spanish. Calderón waited, listened to the voice, and responded. All of it was in Spanish.

Calderón lowered the radio and slipped it into his pocket.

They both stood on the deck, watching the plane.

Suddenly, Widow wished he had just stayed to his formulaic life of passing through. He thought maybe he shouldn't be taking on odd jobs. He didn't need the income. He'd done this because he felt bad for Calderón, and he wanted to spend some paid time on the ocean. But this wasn't what he'd signed up for.

He wracked his brain, processing all the scenarios for what they were picking up. None of the answers were good. The cloak and dagger of it all, and heading out sixty-plus miles on open water, and now a seaplane, all meant that whatever the package was, it wasn't legal. No way.

The very best-case scenario that Widow could think of was Calderón was picking up a package of Cuban cigars. But who would fund a trip this far out to sea and provide an expensive satellite GPS tracker and an airdrop by a seaplane for some cigars?

Plus, Cuba was a couple hundred miles in the other direction, which meant the answer was nobody would do that.

Widow repeated, "Calderón, what did you get me involved in?"

Calderón turned back to him.

"I'm sorry, Widow. I need the money. We need the money."

"You should've counted me out."

"No. I need you. You're experienced."

Widow didn't like being called experienced. Not in drug smuggling or weapons smuggling or whatever this was.

Calderón said, "It's only a onetime thing."

"Onetime thing? That's how it always starts."

"Actually, it's a once-a-month thing."

"Once a month? Is this how you afford any of the shit on this boat?"

"This is how I can afford even to run this business."

Widow shook his head.

He said, "When we get back to shore, I'm done."

Calderón stared at him, disappointment on his face.

He said, "No. Please. You're the best first mate I've ever had."

"Sorry. I don't want to be involved in whatever you're involved in."

Calderón's shoulders slumped for a second, and then he spoke.

"Okay. I understand."

The seaplane descended towards them.

Widow looked at it. He recognized the type of plane. It was a Super Petrel LS, an expensive, Brazilian-made seaplane. It was easily distinguishable by its unique design, one of the more unusual-looking private planes on the market.

Widow didn't know the price tag on it, but he bet it wasn't cheap.

The plane had no tail number.

It swooped down. Widow saw something bundled and attached by ropes to the plane's hull. The plane passed over the boat, and the bundle dropped and fell to the water. It splashed about sixty yards past the boat.

Calderón got on the radio and spoke in English this time.

"Got it."

He said nothing else.

The voice on the other end of the radio replied an affirmative in Spanish.

Widow watched the seaplane as it tilted and flew upward and off to the north.

Calderón said, "Get the anchor."

He returned to the helm and fired up the engines.

This was the part Widow hated about the cheap manual anchors. He had to pull the anchor up fast by the chain. It took him a minute, but, finally, he had the whole thing up.

Calderón did not wait for the okay from Widow. As soon as he saw Widow stop pulling, he pushed the throttle and piloted the boat away. They went over to where the package had splashed down.

Widow looked out and saw the package wasn't subtle at all. It was bundled up in a bright yellow floating device. And there was a beacon light flashing on it like a survivor's life preserver.

"Tell me when we get up on it!" Calderón shouted from the bridge.

Widow shot him a thumbs-up and watched out over the front of the bow.

He watched as they got close and shouted out.

"Okay!"

Calderón stopped the boat, and they floated several more feet toward the package.

Suddenly, an uneasy feeling grated in Widow's stomach. He felt guilty for participating this much, but what else was he going to do? He couldn't just storm off. He was on a boat out at sea. There was nowhere to go.

Widow stepped back. He moved to the starboard side and leaned against the rail.

Calderón climbed down from the bridge and onto the deck. He went to the bow and picked up the long pole. The hook was cleaned of the bloody bait that had been on it the day before.

Calderón looked over at Widow.

"Help me out?"

Widow said, "Nah. I'm good."

"Come on. It's probably heavy."

"No. Sorry. This is your show. I'm not getting any more involved than I already am."

Calderón nodded, shame covering his face.

Widow walked to a row of seats bolted on the deck, and plopped himself down.

It took Calderón about ten minutes to lean all the way out, hook the package and haul it up to the deck.

Widow felt no sympathy for him.

After Calderón got the package up on the deck, he dropped the pole and fell to his knees, huffing and puffing like he had run a four-minute mile.

He leaned over the package and pried it open from the top.

Widow said, "I wouldn't do that if I were you."

"Why? Don't you want to see?"

"No. I don't. Right now, I have plausible deniability. I've seen nothing illegal, just suspicious as hell. And maybe that goes for you too. Let's keep it that way."

"But I already know what's inside."

"Don't tell me! And don't open it!"

Calderón froze his fingers over the package. He stayed still a long second and then nodded, returning his hands to his sides.

"Yeah. You're right. I'll just push it to the side."

Calderón backed up and shoved the package all the way across the deck until it was underneath the ladder that led to the bridge.

Widow stood up and asked, "Now what?"

"Let's go back."

Calderón smiled and climbed the ladder, and returned to the bridge. He manned the helm and fired up the engines. Within seconds, they were off, back to Miami.

* * *

AT THE DOCKS, Calderón pulled in, and Widow tied off the boat.

Calderón said, "Don't worry about hosing us off or the other stuff. Just help me get this thing into the office. Will ya?"

Widow looked at the package. It was basically a plastic crate wrapped in a bright yellow floatation device.

Widow said, "No. I'm not touching that."

"Widow, please. It's heavy."

Widow turned to walk away. He stopped at the edge of the boat before stepping up onto the pier. He turned back to Calderón.

Widow said, "You disappoint me. You know? I would've done my best to help you get your business back. But not this. I can't be a part of this."

Calderón said, "Jack! Wait! I can't do this on my own. I can't meet these guys alone. I need you."

"You've never met them before?"

"This is the first time. I'm afraid to meet them alone."

Widow pointed at the crate.

"If I were you, I'd get out now. You don't want to be in bed with people like this."

Calderón looked past Widow at the docks. He moved his head around like he was scanning for any witnesses. Then he reached into his jacket pocket and pulled out a silver object that Widow knew too well.

Calderón reached out his hand and palmed a snub-nosed .38 revolver. A fine, time-tested weapon. Revolvers don't jam, and they're easy to conceal, and they're powerful.

Widow stared at it and spoke, calling Calderón by his first name.

"Jorge, if you think you need a gun to meet with these guys, then you shouldn't meet them. Do yourself a favor. Go to your office now and call the police. Tell them about the package. They'll forgive you. Trust me. If you turn these other guys in, they won't care about you."

Calderón jerked the gun back and returned it to his inner coat pocket.

"I can't do that! They'll kill me! These guys are connected!"

"Even more reason for you to get out now!"

Calderón said nothing.

Widow said, "I'm out of here. I want no part of it. Do me a favor; if you get caught, leave my name out of it."

Widow left.

Calderón called out one last time.

"They're coming by tonight at ten. Please be here! Back me up!"

Widow stepped off the boat, walked away, and didn't look back.

11

WIDOW COULD'VE SKIPPED TOWN. He didn't have to go back to his motel. Everything he owned was in his pockets. He could've gotten on a bus and headed north. He could've left right then. He should've left—maybe—but he didn't.

After he left Calderón on the boat, Widow returned to the room he rented by the week at a shitty motel by Miami Beach standards, but he didn't mind it. It wasn't a roach motel. It was just basic—as basic as they came.

There was a single bed, a single bedside table with a rotary phone on it, a desk chair, a barely cleaned bathroom, and a wall unit a/c that he didn't need because it was windy and cool outside, which was good because the a/c didn't work.

The room had no TV, no clock, no desk to go with the desk chair. The lights worked, but they were as dim as candlelight.

Widow lay on top of the covers in his clothes. His head lay on the open palms of his hands over the pillow. He stared at the popcorn ceiling, letting his mind wander.

Where next? he thought.

Widow didn't need a job, but he had taken one because he needed a change of pace. He couldn't take a vacation, not by definition. By definition, Widow was always on vacation. A vacation from his life was to get a job. He figured, why not? It wasn't a forever thing. He would probably stick around for a few weeks until he got his fill of the ocean, and then move on.

That was nearly two weeks ago, and he was still here.

Widow looked over at the bedside table for the clock. It was instinct. He'd forgotten there was no clock.

He turned back to the ceiling and then glanced to his right at the single window. It was dark outside.

He thought about the package. If he were a betting man, he would bet it was drugs. Probably cocaine. What else would it be?

Whatever outfit Calderón was involved with was not small time. Small timers don't own expensive seaplanes, nor have advanced open-water drug trafficking networks. Who knew how far that package had traveled to get this far north? He knew it wasn't from Mexico. The cartels had their own pipelines established. This was from somewhere else. Hell, it might even have been from the Bahamas. All likelihood was that it came up from South America somewhere, and the drug lords had found a better, cheaper route than paying the Mexican cartels to get their product into the States.

Whoever Calderón was meeting with might've been lower level, but they worked for someone powerful. The head of the snake was always someone who went through hell to get there. Making it that far meant that there was plenty of blood on their hands.

But none of it was Widow's problem. Not technically. Why couldn't he stop thinking about it?

Widow knew why.

He was letting Calderón go into a dangerous situation alone, and feeling guilty about it.

He thought about leaving again. He should've gotten a bus ticket. He should've moved on. Moving on was Widow's preferred style of transportation. Forward momentum was all he knew. He breathed it. He lived it. The only thing that could stop him was that little voice deep down in his bones.

Do the right thing.

It couldn't be ignored.

An unstoppable force meets an immovable object. Forward momentum was his immovable object, but doing the right thing was the unstoppable force.

Damn it! he thought. He couldn't let Calderón meet with some dangerous drug dealers on his own. They would kill him the moment they saw the revolver.

Widow sat up on the bed. He heard his stomach rumble and realized he hadn't eaten all day.

He got out of bed and slipped on the only article of clothing he hadn't been wearing, his shoes. Then he stepped out the door and glanced around the motel parking lot.

The motel was right on the water, but not the oceanfront. It was on Biscayne Bay.

A buoy's bell dinged in the distance. Waves rolled and sounded against a concrete seawall.

It was night out, but Widow had no idea of the exact time. He left his door unlocked. The keys were in his pocket, along with a heavily worn, heavily used, and heavily creased passport, a bank card, and fifty-five dollars and twenty-five cents in cash money.

Widow walked down toward the motel parking lot entrance, past a pair of soda machines, an icemaker, and several occupied rooms. He stopped at the motel office and opened the door, poked his head in.

A girl was working behind a counter with bulletproof glass separating her from the lobby. The setup looked like a bank teller's counter more than it did a motel.

She was playing around on her cell phone. She glanced up at him and set the phone down on the countertop in front of her. She recognized him from seeing him around.

She asked, "Something wrong with your room, sir?"

"No. Just wondering what time it is?"

The girl looked down at her phone and back up at him.

"Nine forty-five."

Widow nodded a thank-you and backed out the door. He turned and walked to the street so he could hail the first cab he saw to take him to the *El Pez Grande*.

On the street, Widow saw no cabs, which didn't surprise him. Uber and other ride service companies had come along over the last decade and put the taxi industry on the ropes. But they were still out there. Especially in major metro areas, and Miami was a major metro area.

Widow wasn't opposed to using Uber, but to use it, you needed an app, and apps needed smartphones with operating systems.

Widow had no phone.

He was about three miles from the docks and the boat. At first, he walked in that direction. After five minutes of no cabs in sight, he stuck his thumb out and continued walking.

After another five minutes passed, no one stopped for him. He ran, which wasn't easy since he was wearing boat shoes. They weren't made for all-out sprinting. But what choice did he have?

12

CALDERÓN SHIVERED as two big guys hovered over him along with their boss, a Russian mobster named Ivan Solonik, the local boss over Miami Beach. He represented the Solonik family. They were small scale on the world stage, but big enough to have a major operation running through Miami.

They had enough palms greased not to have made the news and to have avoided police suspicion—so far.

Solonik was a short guy, barely five feet tall, and that was with inserts in his shoes and two-inch rubber heels underneath that.

He wore a black fedora and a Miami shirt, brightly colored, with white chinos and a white blazer. He dressed like he was some kind of low-level gangster on *Miami Vice*.

The two Russians with him were Igar and Sasha. Both steroided up hard as a brick outhouse, both well-paid, and both ready to break bones even if they weren't well-paid.

Both Russian enforcers wore dark chinos and pastel-colored, short-sleeved button shirts. The collars were wide open at the top, showing off barrel-sized chests and silver chains. None of it was by choice. Not their choice, anyway.

Solonik insisted they dress the part.

The four men stood on Calderón's boat, docked at the pier. He'd met them on his boat, thinking that the familiar territory would give him an edge over the Russians, but it didn't.

Igar and Sasha leered at Calderón. Their heads pointed downward, but they were used to looking down because they were both built like mountains. They towered over most men. Plus, they were always staring down at Solonik, taking his orders.

Calderón shouted, "You promised to pay me now! Tonight! I can't wait!"

Solonik spoke. His voice was all in his throat, like he was doing an impression of a smoky radio voice.

"We'll pay you when we feel like paying you. Now, you tell us where the shit is, and we'll grab it and be on our way."

"But I need money! We had a deal!"

"Look, we can take it off you. I'm being friendly here. I'm being professional because I want us to go forward with a good working relationship."

"But how's it good if you don't pay me like we agreed!"

Calderón was getting a little upset, a little emotional. One hand waved around in front of the gangsters, which was part of the way he spoke to people when he was emotional. He couldn't help it. It was like a nervous tic. The other hand gripped the collar of his jacket, ready to dip in and snatch out his revolver if he needed to.

Solonik grew impatient. It was obvious in his demeanor and in his stance, as he shuffled and his fake, smoky radio voice faltered. The raspy quality of it broke into a squeakier voice—his real voice.

His guys picked up on this. They knew his telltale signs well. They knew when he was losing patience, which meant that they had to step in and do what they did well.

Igar and Sasha were well-trained bodyguards, enforcers, and all-around henchmen.

Both Russians reached into their pants pockets and pulled out black leather search gloves.

Calderón watched them slip the gloves on and pull them tight. Then both Igar and Sasha cracked their knuckles. Calderón shivered, which turned more into shakes as he suspected where this was heading.

Solonik said, "You know, Calderón. There are a lot of boats in Miami. You know why?"

Calderón said nothing.

Solonik said, "Because we're surrounded by freaking water! Do you know what that means?"

"No."

"It means that I can find a thousand new patsies to go out there with their boats and bring back my shit!"

Solonik banged on his chest as he shouted. His smoky radio voice was all but gone. He screamed in Calderón's face. Too close for Calderón to pull the gun.

Solonik finally backed off and circled back to his guys.

He spoke. His natural-born Russian accent bled through.

"Calderón, last chance, amigo. What's it gonna be? You gonna work with us and accept your payment when we say you accept it? Or are my guys going to beat you to death right here on your piece-of-shit boat?"

Calderón shouted, "No one's leaving here until I get paid!"

He jerked the revolver out of his inner coat pocket. It was not a pretty gun pull. It was clumsy as all hell. The revolver got stuck on the lining of his coat. He fumbled with it for a second before revealing it.

Solonik or Igar or Sasha could've pulled their guns faster and shot him dead. They all witnessed the fumbling around of the weapon. They could've drawn on him, but they didn't because the revolver didn't scare them.

All three men had been around guns long enough that guns didn't scare them. It was the man holding the gun that scared them. In the hands of an amateur like Calderón, there was nothing to fear.

Solonik stayed where he was. First, a smirk cracked on his face, followed by a half-smile and then a full-blown smile and finally a chuckle, until he was straight out laughing at Calderón.

Igar and Sasha stayed behind him. They didn't smirk or smile or laugh. They stared at Calderón. Igar cracked his knuckles again. Sasha's veins pulsed on his forearms and biceps.

Calderón gulped.

He half mumbled, half whispered.

"Just give me my money," he begged.

No one spoke.

Calderón muttered, "Please?"

He pointed the revolver at them. He held it all wrong. He held it out one-handed, elbow bent. If he squeezed the trigger, it would've been a hip shot. And a clumsy one at that.

Solonik said, "Hand the gun over to my guy. Now!"

Sasha stepped up and around Solonik, toward Calderón. He reached out a huge hand, palm up, and waited.

"Stay back!" Calderón shouted. He shuffled back, closing in on the port side of the deck.

He pointed the gun at Sasha.

Solonik said, "Amigo, Sasha doesn't like to have guns pointed at him."

Calderón shouted, "Stay back!"

"Amigo, better hand over the gun."

Sasha stepped up close to Calderón and held out his hand.

Calderón shivered and tried to think. His finger was in the trigger housing. He should've shot the gun, but he didn't.

In a fast, violent outburst, Sasha stepped forward, closing the distance between himself and the revolver. He clamped down one hand the size of a baseball glove on Calderón's fist and gun and violently jerked all of it to the right. Faster than Calderón could aim, squeeze the trigger, and hit Sasha with a bullet.

The violent jerk of the gun and his hand forced Calderón to pull the trigger. The gun fired and *BOOMED* over the night air.

It echoed across the water and between the other docked boats.

The bullet burst from the muzzle, zipped past Sasha, and crashed through the surface of the water beyond. Killing no one but maybe a fish somewhere below the boats.

Sasha ripped the revolver from Calderón's hand, wrenched back, his feet planted on the deck. He whirled around like a Major League pitcher and belted Calderón across the face with the revolver.

Calderón's nose *CRACKED!*

He whimpered and clutched the bleeding appendage.

Solonik turned around, rotating all the way, checking out the docks for witnesses. Surely, someone had heard the gunshot, but no one came out to see what the commotion was.

Solonik said, "I love Miami."

Then he looked at Igar and barked an order at him.

"Pick him up!"

Igar nodded and walked, which seemed hard for him because of his thick legs. His calves were as dense as boulders, and just as hard to walk with.

Calderón was slumped over on his knees, holding onto his broken nose.

Igar reached down and jerked him to his feet by the collar of his coat. He moved behind Calderón and wrapped a bicep and forearm around his neck, both thick as his calves and as hard as oak. He got Calderón in a one-armed chokehold and squeezed enough to get Calderón to grasp at the man's tree-trunk forearm, but not enough to put him to sleep.

Solonik walked over to him and pushed back Calderón's forehead with two fingers. Solonik inspected Calderón's face.

"Looks like your nose broke," he said, and then he jabbed a right at Calderón's face, hitting the broken nose. There was no crack like before. Solonik wasn't as strong as Igar or Sasha, but the nose was already broken, and it still hurt like hell.

Calderón screamed in pain.

"Quiet him!" Solonik barked.

Sasha nodded and stepped up and belted Calderón in the gut, knocking the wind out of him and cracking a rib.

Igar wrenched his arm tighter, choking Calderón to the point of almost passing out, and then he released.

Solonik poked at Calderón's broken nose with a short, stubby finger.

"Stay with us!" he said.

Once again, Solonik stepped in. He punched Calderón in the gut, following the same path as Sasha.

Calderón hunched over in Igar's grip. He tried to speak, but only spat blood.

Solonik looked at his guys and said, "What do you guys think? Did Calderón shoot himself with his own gun? Committing suicide on his boat? You know, because business is so bad? His life is worth ending. Don't you think? I think the cops will buy it. Either that or they won't care."

Calderón's heart raced, which sluiced blood out of his broken nose like it was a busted pipe.

He said, "No...please...don't kill me...No one will...buy it."

"I don't know. I think a piece of shit like you, having a failed business, would kill himself. And on his own boat. The captain goes down with the ship and all. What do you boys think?"

Igar and Sasha didn't respond. They knew the question was rhetorical.

Solonik stood there in silence, as if he was looking for the next thing to say.

Suddenly, he froze as if he had seen a ghost.

Silence fell over them. Igar and Sasha stared at their boss, waiting for him to speak. But he just stared past them, past the boat's bridge and up to the docks, past an empty boat slip.

He had seen something. It was brief, and then it was gone like an illusion.

He was speaking, and then he glanced up and saw a dark figure standing tall at the edge of the dock. The figure was like something out of a Halloween movie when someone looks off to the forest and sees the undead killer staring at them. One moment he's standing there, and the next he's gone.

Solonik pointed up to the docks.

"There was someone there. Someone big."

Igar turned and pulled Calderón with him to see. Sasha turned his head, raised the revolver in case he needed to fire it.

They stared at where Solonik had been looking and saw nothing.

They waited.

Soft, ambient noises of a quiet dock at night were all they heard at first. But then there was a loud splash at the top of the docks—something going into the water.

Solonik pointed at Sasha.

"Go check it out!"

Sasha said nothing. He just stared dumbfounded at the place where Solonik said a dark figure had been standing.

"Sasha!" Solonik barked.

Sasha turned around to face him.

"Go check it out!"

"Me, boss?"

"You have the gun! Go check it out!"

Sasha said, "But we all have guns."

"You have the only gun that's not traceable to us, moron!"

Sasha nodded and asked, "If I find him, want me to kill him with it?"

"Yes!"

With orders to kill, Sasha nodded and stepped off the boat onto the pier and headed toward the splash.

13

BACK IN THE DAY, Widow could run a mile and a half in ten minutes flat, which sounds impressive to a novice runner, even better to someone who never runs at all. But for a Navy SEAL, it was just a hair better than what was expected.

In BUD/S, which stands for *Basic Underwater Demolition/SEAL* training school, Widow ran thirty miles a week. Even after BUD/S, Widow kept up with his running regimen at least once a week, doing about ten miles in each outing.

But those days were long behind him. He hadn't run a straight mile in years. But he did tonight. He ran for nearly three miles. Without a watch, he couldn't be sure of the time. He guessed it was around twenty-five minutes, which was pathetic for a SEAL. His brothers would've been embarrassed. At which, he would've pointed out the boat shoes to them. And they would've laughed. Someone would've certainly thrown the second-ever SEAL motto he learned in the Navy in his face, which was: *Get comfortable being uncomfortable.*

Still, Widow had gotten to where he needed to be, even though it was uncomfortable. He ran and ran until he reached Calderón's office.

Out in front of it, he stopped and bent over, planted his hands on his knees, and just breathed—catching his breath. It took him nearly a minute to stop panting. He waited for his breathing to slow to normal and for his heartbeat to settle. He wanted to wait until his calves stopped throbbing, but there was no time for that. His feet ached in the boat shoes, but he wasn't going to kick them off. Better to have shoes on your feet than not.

Once Widow got closer to being comfortable, he checked the door-knob on the door to Calderón's office. It was cold and locked. He glanced between the blinds in the window. The lights were out inside. He turned to the docks. He hoped they were meeting on the boat and he hadn't missed it.

Calderón didn't know what he was doing and was likely to get himself killed. And it would be on Widow. He should've stayed or talked Calderón out of it, or forced him out of it.

Widow walked to the docks, past parked cars, until he stopped at a car that looked out of place. Coming to work at the docks every morning and leaving every evening, he had seen the same basic vehicles over and over. This one didn't belong.

It was a black Escalade with gaudy chrome rims. The paint had been waxed to a shine recently. The hood reflected the stars and moon and the city lights overhead.

Widow slapped a hand down on the hood and felt the temperature. It was warm. The engine had been shut off recently.

He moved to the rear of the vehicle and checked the plates. A bit of advice that he learned in Quantico and not from the SEALs was to always check plates. Witnesses hardly ever did this. License plates were one of the fastest ways to track and identify people.

Widow memorized the Escalade's plate and then looked in the windows. The SUV was empty. He tried the door handles. They were surely locked, but you never knew. The first handle he tried was the rear passenger door, and it was unlocked. It popped right open. His jaw almost fell to the ground. He didn't expect it to be so easy.

Widow looked around and saw no one.

He pulled the door all the way open. The dome lights hummed to life.

Widow made a quick search of the SUV. He found a wallet in the center console. Inside, he found a Miami driver's license for a man with a Russian name, Igar Baranovichi.

Widow looked at the photograph. The guy in the picture had an ugly mug. The face looked like that of a boxer who fought professionally but always lost. He guessed that because the guy looked like he had a history of being pounded in the face.

Widow glanced at the guy's weight and size. He was six foot four, Widow's height, and two hundred fifty pounds, which was twenty-five more than Widow.

Widow ditched the ID and the wallet and searched the rest of the vehicle. He found one thing of interest. In the cargo compartment at the back of the Escalade was a metal baseball bat next to a thick roll of duct tape.

Great, he thought. *They came prepared.*

He also found a pair of black leather gloves hanging over the edge of a shoebox without a lid. Under the gloves, in the shoebox, was a bag full of zip ties and another pair of gloves.

Widow reached for the bat. He could use it as a weapon, but he stopped dead over the handle. He looked at the tip. There was something there. He leaned in and saw bloodstains, dried on the head of the bat.

He retracted his hand. He didn't touch it. He would bet money that the blood was real. The bat might've been a murder weapon if this was the vehicle of the drug dealers that Calderón was involved with. It was a believable scenario. The last thing he wanted to do was leave his own fingerprints on it.

Best to leave it.

Widow left the bat and the gloves and everything else and shut the Escalade's cargo door. He walked down to the pier and stopped at the edge of the road and paused.

Suddenly, he heard a noise he knew too well. A gunshot sounded, and blasted and echoed over the docks and boats.

Widow ducked down and slammed his back against a gate that led to the pier.

He waited and listened. He heard loud voices. He looked around the offices and the cars and then back at the buildings. No one came out.

Widow heard the voices again and what sounded like a scuffle. He stood back up and turned and walked down the pier. He stopped at the first boat slip and saw four people on the *El Pez Grande*. One of them was Calderón. Two of them were big enough to be ex-NFL players. One of those two was a guy with the same ugly mug from the driver's license—Igar Baranovichi.

Widow stopped in time to see the other big guy swipe Calderón's revolver right out of his hand and then jab Calderón in the face with it, breaking his nose.

He watched another Russian beat on Calderón. The one doing the beating was a third man. He was short and wore a stupid fedora on his head. After a couple of hits, the short one glanced up at the entrance to the pier and right at Widow. He saw Widow, but for only a moment.

Widow shuffled to his right—fast. He ended up with his back to a chain-link fence that ran the length of the parking lot and the road, separating the docks from the water.

Widow shimmied along so that he was out of sight, but he soon ran out of foot space. He couldn't go back. They were armed with Calderón's revolver, and probably guns of their own.

Widow saw no choice but to get wet. He knew the water was deep enough to dive into from there. He breathed in hard and fast several times and took a deep breath and held it. He stepped forward, hugged his body, and dropped straight into the water, legs locked.

The splash was loud. He knew they heard it.

He let his body sink as far as gravity would drag him, and then he opened his eyes and saw mostly blackness. He also saw faint starlight above him from the night sky.

Widow swam forward and downward. He traversed underneath the boat in the first slip and stopped near the edge. He looked up. He couldn't hear the Russians on Calderón's boat, but he saw one of them stepping out onto the pier and walking up the way he had come.

They were hunting him.

Widow swam on, staying deep, staying steady enough not to ripple the surface of the water. He swam until he was under Calderón's boat. He swam to the rear of the boat, under the twin engines, grabbed one, and slowly hauled himself up. Then he thrust himself up more and grabbed one of the shark cages. He pulled himself up by the bars and hauled himself out of the water.

He stayed silent. After sixteen years undercover as a Navy SEAL, working black ops, doing wet work and black-on-black missions, Widow was good at silence. He may not run a seven-minute mile so well anymore, but he could do stealth.

Widow clung to the side of the shark cage and peered over the top. He saw the short guy, Calderón, and Igar. They were all staring off at the other Russian who neared the first boat slip.

Widow calculated seconds until the other Russian was in place and saw that no one was there. Widow studied where they were and made a quick game plan in his head.

He fired into action like a racehorse at the starting gun.

Widow grabbed the top bar of the cage and jerked himself up on top of it. Then he jumped onto the boat. His clothes were soaked, clinging to his body.

Widow stood tall and walked straight for the short guy first, because he was closer.

The short guy heard him walking on the deck. He heard the sloshing sounds from Widow's wet boat shoes.

Solonik turned and saw Widow. He studied him from down to up, until he stared into his face.

Widow smiled.

Solonik shuddered. His bottom lip quivered like he was going to burst into cries for help. But he didn't. He didn't have time to. The only thing he had time to do was reach into his inner coat pocket for a firearm that matched the Escalade. It was a black metal Colt 1911 with a chrome grip.

There were etchings all over it. Maybe they meant something to the gangster wannabe, and maybe they didn't.

Widow had no idea, and he never would.

Solonik got the gun out all the way, but only because Widow waited for him to. Then he clamped a hand down on the barrel, the hammer, and Solonik's hand. He grabbed it and jerked Solonik forward so fast the guy came half up off his feet.

Widow slammed his other fist into Solonik's left cheek, smashing bones and chipping teeth.

Solonik cried out in pain. His face and head wrenched nearly far enough back to let him see over his shoulder. He spat out blood and not a single tooth, but shards and chips of several. Maybe enough to make a whole tooth, like a puzzle.

Solonik went down and slammed his face on the deck.

Igar turned and saw the whole thing. He dropped his grip on Calderón, which was dumb. He could've used the guy as a human shield or a bargaining chip. That's what Widow expected, because now Widow had Solonik's firearm.

But Igar didn't do any of that. Instead, he went for a Glock in a hip holster.

Widow already had the Colt in hand, pointed at Igar, but he didn't shoot him, not yet. He waited.

The last time Widow checked, Florida had *Stand Your Ground* laws. But he didn't know if that applied to him in this situation or not. He didn't want to chance shooting an unarmed man. Not without protection from police charges. But he knew that good old self-defense counted in every state.

Igar fumbled around before he got out the Glock. He raised it and pointed it in Widow's direction.

Widow breathed out and squeezed the Colt's trigger.

Normally, he advocated dry firing an untested weapon before relying on it to save his life. But there was no time for that. He took the chance and took the shot. The Colt fired as advertised.

He squeezed off two rounds in quick succession.

BOOM! BOOM!

He wasn't trying to kill the guy, even though he could have. Killing a man led to police and charges and paperwork and probably jail time and possibly prison time—self-defense or not. And Widow didn't want any of that.

He only wanted to immobilize him.

He aimed for Igar's gun shoulder. Taking out the gun arm was on his agenda.

Widow fired two rounds before Igar could shoot a single bullet. Aiming for Igar's shoulder worked out better than Widow anticipated because both rounds exploded into Igar's shoulder capsule, causing an explosion of equal parts blood and agony.

Igar dropped the Glock and grabbed at his shoulder with his good hand.

Widow stepped forward, past Calderón, shoving him back out of the way with his left hand. He stepped up to Igar's face and rammed the Colt into it. The muzzle pushed Igar's nose back.

Widow shouted, "Get down!"

Igar nodded. Fear crept across his face because of the man behind the gun.

Widow glanced up and saw Sasha running back to the boat.

Widow stepped back and planted a hand on Calderón, shoving him all the way back to the twin engines and the shark cages.

"Stay there!" he shouted.

Widow returned to Solonik and reached down, with his left hand again, hauling the short Russian up by the collar. He released the collar and slapped the fedora off Solonik's head. It flew off into the wind and landed on the surface of the water and floated away.

Widow grabbed a tuft of Solonik's hair and jerked him around by it. He turned the guy to face Sasha and shoved the Colt's muzzle into the back of Solonik's head.

Widow used Solonik as a human shield, only it was more like part of a shield because he couldn't hide behind Solonik, not completely.

Sasha raised the revolver and pointed at them. He stepped off the pier, back onto Calderón's boat.

"That's enough!" Widow barked.

Sasha spoke English with a thick Russian accent.

He said, "Who are you, friend?"

"Me? I'm the guy who's gonna splatter your boss's brains all over the deck of this boat if you don't drop the weapon!"

"He's not the boss, friend."

"Bullshit! This ridiculous gun. The stupid hat. He's the boss."

"He's not the boss!" Sasha repeated.

Widow pushed hard on the Colt, forcing Solonik to squirm and wrench forward.

Widow said, "If he's not the boss, then he's related to the boss. No way was he appointed control over you two idiots because he's good at his job."

Sasha took his finger out of the trigger housing and raised the revolver slowly, pointing it up to the sky. He showed his hands.

"Let him go, friend. We'll leave."

Widow said, "Toss the gun!"

Sasha didn't move.

Widow said, "I'm not asking twice!"

Sasha looked down at Solonik's eyes, needing orders on how to proceed.

Widow saw this and jerked Solonik's head all the way back, closing the distance between them to inches. Then Widow put the Colt close to the side of Solonik's head, pointed in Sasha's direction, and aimed at the pier. He fired the weapon next to Solonik's head.

It *BOOMED!*

Solonik screamed in agony and grabbed at his ear.

Widow was sure he'd busted Solonik's eardrum.

Sasha reacted to the gunshot before assessing the situation. It was a natural response. He lowered the revolver back down from the sky and aimed toward Widow and Solonik, ready to shoot. But he didn't shoot. He couldn't. He had no shot.

Widow closed himself tight behind Solonik enough so that even a trained marksman, like himself, wouldn't risk taking the shot unless he was willing to kill the hostage.

Widow said, "Careful!"

Sasha stared over the revolver's barrel at Widow. Then he backed off and slowly lowered Calderón's revolver.

Widow said, "Toss it. Overboard."

Sasha paused a beat and tossed the revolver. It splashed in the water. He raised his hands, surrendering.

Widow said, "Toss the other one."

"What other one?"

"The Glock you've got concealed somewhere. Toss it."

Sasha looked at him, defeated. Then he reached for his waistband.

"Slowly!"

Sasha slowed and reached into his waistband, left side, and pulled out a handgun that wasn't a Glock, but looked just like one. It was some sort of cheap knockoff. Widow didn't recognize the model.

Sasha tossed it overboard. It splashed in the water, the same place as the revolver.

Sasha asked, "Now what, American?"

"Back away!"

Sasha backed away.

"Keep going! All the way to the cockpit!"

Sasha kept his eyes locked on Widow and stepped back slowly until his back was to a wall, and he stopped.

Widow said, "Jorge?"

Calderón said, "Yeah."

"Grab the other gun. Right there," Widow said, and pointed at Igar's Glock on the deck.

Calderón said nothing. He stepped forward, passing Widow and Solonik, and scooped up the other Glock. He pointed it at Sasha.

"Now what?"

Widow didn't answer that. He let go of Solonik and stepped back away from the guy.

Solonik whined and grumbled.

"Shut up!" Calderón barked at him.

Widow said, "Stand over with your friends."

Solonik edged over toward Igar and Sasha.

"What do we do with them?" Calderón asked again.

Widow thought, and then he had an idea.

"We call the police."

"The police?"

"Yeah, I'm sure they got rap sheets."

Solonik said, "The cops? They're not gonna do shit! You got nothing on us!"

"Are you serious? There's a baseball bat in the back of your truck with blood on it. I'm sure that'll pique their interest. And if it doesn't, there's the crate. I'm sure whatever is in that will be enough to put you on their radar."

Right then, as if Miami Metro's ears were burning, a police flood-light from a boat on the water behind Widow fired to life. He was engulfed in bright light. It shone past him and sprayed across the faces of Solonik, Igar, and Sasha.

Suddenly, Widow heard voices behind him, and sounds of footsteps scrambling down the pier echoed like dozens of troops storming an upstairs apartment.

Within seconds, there were police in normal uniforms and some in street clothes with badges hanging from neck lanyards. The boat behind him with the floodlight was the US Coast Guard's.

A street cop from the pier, wearing a bulletproof vest over his clothes, pointed a gun in Widow's face.

Several voices shouted.

"Drop the gun!"

"Drop the gun!"

Widow dropped the Colt and raised his hands to his head.

Calderón asked, "What's happening?"

Widow said, "Cops."

The boat was swarmed by officers within seconds, and Widow was put in cuffs along with the others. But unlike the others, he kept his mouth shut. The right to remain silent was always the safe bet when going into the back of a squad car.

Solonik chose the opposite tactic.

He shouted at Widow as the cops put him in the back of another car. It was all the same crap Widow had heard before. Solonik swore revenge, swore that he would get even, and so on.

It looked like Widow was going to spend the night in jail, all for doing a good deed. And that was the best-case scenario. The worst-case scenario would be prison time.

Suddenly, he wished he had minded his own business.

14

A YEAR HAD PASSED since Raggie lost her hand. She kept in touch with her friends from South Africa.

Her family had relocated back to DC, where her dad was busier than ever protecting the president, which she never thought too much about. To her, it was everyday life. It was his job—no big deal.

Raggie sat in a café on the Maryland side of DC She wore stonewashed blue jeans with large slits cut into the knees. A gray skullcap was pulled down over her head, making her slightly resemble a cancer patient, and her hair was stuffed underneath it. A light patina of makeup dusted her face—her mom didn't like her to leave the house without it. She wore black Converse shoes with pink trim that she'd painted herself. They had originally come out of the box in white, but she liked to modify her clothes. She enjoyed making them a little more her own style.

Her handless arm was camouflaged by the long sleeve of a white hoodie. She dressed like a boy. That was something she was proud of. She enjoyed being different from her American friends. Like her friend Claire, whom she rarely saw anymore. Because while Claire had become more like the girls that Raggie avoided, Raggie had become more like her friends back in South Africa—and right then, she was missing them.

Her love of surfing was her reason for being at the café. She sat at a small round table with a MacBook in front of her, the Apple icon glowing white as she watched *YouTube* videos about surfing. She had lied to her mother that morning. She had told her she was going to meet with her friends and hang out with them the whole day. She told her she was going to the mall—as if she would be caught dead walking around a stupid mall.

She was meeting a boy—well, not a boy, but an older man.

She was going to meet one of her idols—Jai Jai Slater. He was the guy who made the *YouTube* videos she liked and followed. She had watched all his videos dozens of times.

A common mistake was people assumed Jai Jai was related to Kelly Slater, a surfing legend and another hero of hers. There was no relation.

Jai Jai was just a guy from DC who loved surfing. He split his time between a part-time lobbying job in the winters and surfing in Mexico in the summers.

A couple of weeks earlier, Jai Jai had communicated with her out of the blue. Probably because she sent him some big donations through the internet to help fund his videos. It wasn't a big deal to her. The donations were put on her mom's credit cards. Her mom didn't even notice. And, for her family, they weren't that big.

Raggie and Jai Jai started talking daily. Now he wanted to meet her in person. He wanted to show his gratitude for her support—or that's what she thought.

She wasn't keen on meeting an older guy like this. But, she could use a new friend in the surfing community since all her old ones were more than eight thousand miles away. She liked Jai Jai. He was cool, and his surfing videos were informative. They had given her the knowledge she needed to surf, to begin with.

Why not? she thought.

She waited with her MacBook and her hot green tea. And then she waited some more. He was late. She drank three green teas and thought about getting a meal, but she settled for two different blueberry muffins, the second an hour after the first.

The café started its daily closing procedures. Most of the customers cleared out. Her waitress brought in the sidewalk sandwich board.

Another waitress started switching off coffee makers and wiping things down with a bar towel.

Raggie looked at her phone. Time moved toward evening. She checked her phone again, but still no word from Jai Jai. She checked her text messages. And then she called him one more time. The phone rang and rang. No answer. All she got was a robotic voice telling her that the voicemail box was full.

Jai Jai never showed, and the sun started going down.

Raggie paid her check, gathered her belongings, and headed out the door.

15

JAI JAI SLATER didn't answer his phone because he was dead.

The guy sitting in a white panel van in the parking lot of a café on the Maryland side of DC had put a bullet in the YouTuber about an hour earlier. Jai Jai had cried and even wet his pants, but he hadn't fought back. How could he? He had been tied up and gagged for nearly two weeks. The only time the guy with the gun and the black suit, tie, and Secret Service earpiece had let him free was so that Jai Jai could go to the bathroom. And even in those instances, he had never let him out of his sight. At least, that's what Jai Jai had thought. But he was wrong. The guy who killed him hardly watched him.

Jai Jai was fooled because there was a security camera pointed at him the whole time he was ziptied to a pipe in a bathroom he had never seen before. He thought someone was always watching him over the camera, but no one was.

The guy who kidnapped Jai Jai and put a bullet in his head was code-named Jekyll.

Jekyll's main job had been law enforcement. Because of his training and his involvement with Secret Service agents, he knew a thing or two about abduction also. He knew how to watch a prisoner and make sure he consumed just enough food and water so he wouldn't die, but not enough to strengthen his body.

Jekyll knew the best way to keep a captive cooperative was to keep him fed, distracted, and feeling protected. It gave a feeling of security and safety. To break the spirits of a captive meant doing the opposite. Take away food. Take away communication. Take away dignity. Take away hope. Both were powerful tactics for gaining full control over them.

Jai Jai had been an easy captive. But Raggie would be even easier because she trusted Jekyll, always had. He would have no problem getting her into the van, and no problem getting her to eat sleeping pills crushed up and sprinkled onto the Beacon Fizz Pop he got for her. It was just like the ones from South Africa she used to love.

Jekyll worried she might refuse it while she was in the van, because maybe she was full from the café. He had watched her drink several green teas.

But that was okay. He was prepared for contingencies.

In case she didn't want the pop, he would use chloroform on her, which was riskier because she would struggle, as everyone does.

Raggie was only a teenager, and she trusted him, but she wasn't stupid. Certainly, she had seen enough movies to know what chloroform does and why a man would shove a rag soaked in it over her mouth and nose.

Jekyll watched as Raggie exited the café and pulled her hoodie over her head.

He waited until she walked out past the line of sight of the security camera above the door. He never went into view of the café or its windows. He didn't want to be caught by that camera, or the traffic camera mounted to the streetlight on the main turn out of the parking lot.

Once she got farther into the parking lot, Jekyll fired up the van's engine. The motor kicked and whirred. He already had the van's nose facing outward. He tapped the gas and turned the wheel.

The van drifted out of a parking spot toward Raggie. She walked away from it and toward the street. The bus stop was her destination.

Jai Jai's body was under a tarp in the back of the van. Jekyll peeked back and took one last look at it to make sure none of it was visible. He pulled the van up alongside Raggie.

He rolled down his window and asked, "You lost?"

Raggie turned and stared at the van. At first, she was ready to run, but then she looked up at Jekyll's familiar face and smiled.

Raggie said, "What're you doing here?"

He said, "Was in the neighborhood."

Raggie said, "Wait! Did my mom send you?"

Jekyll smiled and said, "She's worried about you."

"Great! She knows I lied to her? She knows I'm not with my friends?"

"She's not stupid. Everyone knows you don't have any friends."

Raggie stopped walking and smiled. She looked down at the concrete and her Converse shoes. Then she looked back up and said, "I guess I'm in trouble?"

"She doesn't know you lied to her. She knows nothing. I'm only supposed to look out for you. You know how protective she is. She knows nothing about why you're here. Promise."

Raggie tilted her head as if something bothered her, but she said nothing. She walked around the nose of the van and reached up to the handle. She clicked it open, and the door squeaked. She reached her one hand up and grabbed the lip of the door frame, and hauled herself up into the seat. She reached across herself and jerked the door closed.

Jekyll tapped on the gas, and the van drove off. They turned out of the parking lot and off onto the street. Things seemed to be going according to plan. But then Raggie said something that was smart, but dumb if she only knew who Jekyll really was.

She asked, "How'd you know I was here?"

"Your internet."

"What?"

"Look. I got you one of those pops like from South Africa."

Jekyll reached into a cooler that was where a center console would've been. He opened the lid and pulled out a cold pop inside a deceptive plastic wrapper.

Raggie ignored it and said, "What do you mean? The thing about my internet? Why're you looking at my internet? How?"

"Your mom. She asked me to."

"Why?"

"Come on. Take the pop. It was hard to get."

Raggie said, "I don't want it. Answer me. Why my internet?"

Jekyll smiled and said nothing. Instead, he jerked the wheel, and the tires whipped up off the blacktop, and the van pulled into the empty parking lot of a Dollar Store or a Dollar Tree or a Family Dollar. He wasn't sure. He didn't look at the sign long enough to read the brand. He pulled around the building and braked the van to a stop and flipped the gear into park.

Raggie asked, "What're we doing?"

Jekyll leaned forward, across her lap, and popped open the glove box with one hand. He did this as a distraction. It was a tactic, but Raggie never realized it until it was too late.

While Raggie watched his left hand across her lap at the glove box, Jekyll swept his other hand around her head and locked onto her face with a rag dipped in chloroform.

Quickly, in a violent upward arc, he grabbed her face and pressed the rag tightly over her mouth and nose.

Raggie struggled and whipped her one arm up but couldn't get a grip on his hand because of the angle. Instead, she kicked and squirmed. But he had a powerful grip on her. She fought and fought as hard as she could.

She thought back to the day in the water with the raggie shark. She saw the same blackness. She felt the same powerful jaws. She closed her eyes a few seconds, and for those few seconds, she saw the shark's dorsal fin. The difference this time was that she didn't escape. No one pulled her out of the depths.

She succumbed to the danger—to the chloroform.

Jekyll held her down for a long second more, but not too long. He didn't want to kill her. He looked around the van and scanned his surroundings. He glanced out the front windshield, the passenger window, and then the driver's side window. No one was around except for a guy walking a black lab, but he was far away. Neither he nor the animal made any sign of turning around and seeing what Jekyll was up to.

Another moment passed, and the dog walker and the black lab turned a corner.

Jekyll relaxed and removed the rag from Raggie's face. He got out of the van and went around to the passenger side, and opened the door. He reached in and picked up Raggie's limp body with ease, carrying her like a new bride to the back of the van. He reached out from under her and popped open the van's cargo door.

He laid her down next to Jai Jai's dead body, over the tarp.

Jekyll took one last look at her and closed the doors. He went back to the driver's side and pulled the keys out of the ignition, then returned to the back of the van and locked the doors with the key. Going back to the driver's side, he took one last scan of the area and saw nothing. No cameras. No witnesses. No sign of life of any kind.

He dumped himself back onto the seat and closed the door. He drove off as if everything was normal—a normal guy driving a normal van through a quiet, forgotten area of a normal town.

16

JEKYLL WAS NERVOUS, but he finally had good news for Hyde. The bonus part of their plan had come to fruition. He knew where Widow was—finally.

He smoked another cigarette, standing in front of the white panel van, parked in a nearly abandoned parking garage downtown. Inside the van, Raggie was completely sedated. She wasn't waking up for another two hours. By then, she would be hidden and secure, away from civilian eyes.

The plan had been to take her and drive her straight to the safe house. It was to keep her there, restrained and out of sight. It was all a part of Hyde's plan. There was no reason to deviate. In fact, deviating came with strict consequences—namely, death.

Jekyll knew this. But here he was—breaking protocol. He had to. There was new information. Vital information. Something had happened. Something that was a game-changer.

Jekyll was driving when he got the call. It was from one of his spiders out there in the world, an informant who only thought he was helping his country.

It was funny because Jekyll had thought it would've been a hit from one of his informants in the Navy that would've come through for him, but it wasn't.

The spider that came through was a low-level clerk down in Florida. He was just a guy working for the justice department, a file clerk responsible for processing communications. Nothing special. No one special.

Last year, Jekyll had done the guy a favor, and now the guy owed him. When Hyde started preparing for the American operation, he gave Jekyll one priority for locating the patsy. It had to be one man.

And now, Jekyll had come through for him, and it was just a stroke of good luck.

Jekyll took out his burner phone and the battery. He reinserted the battery back into the phone and clipped the case back into place. He turned the phone on and redialed the last number he'd called.

The phone rang.

Hyde answered. The sound of fury resonated in the back of his voice.

"Jekyll? What the hell are you doing? This is not a scheduled time!"

"I found him."

Silence fell over the line.

"Did you hear me?"

There was a long pause, and Jekyll thought he'd dropped the call, but then he heard Hyde breathing.

Hyde asked, "You found him?"

"I think so."

"Where?"

"That's the thing. The reason we couldn't find him."

"Why?"

"It's because he's a hobo now. A passerby. A nomad. A drifter. He's been living like a vagrant this whole time."

"Are you sure it's him?"

"Pretty sure. I think it's him. I got confirmation from one of my sources. His name is Jack Widow. Born in Mississippi. Mother dead.

Father unknown. No family. Military record is partially sealed. And get this."

Hyde listened carefully.

Jekyll said, "The sealed part is direct from Quantico."

Silence.

Jekyll heard deep breaths on the other end of the line as if Hyde had closed his eyes and was picturing all the horrible things he had planned for this Widow guy—things that made Jekyll wince, things that he would be just as happy not to know about.

Jekyll said, "That means NCIS. And get this. The dude's record showed he was in the Navy, nothing special; then, his timeline goes dark like he was never there. And then he pops up in the SEAL teams. And there're medals."

Hyde asked, "What about NCIS records?"

"Those are hard to get. What I can get shows him working there, but I found no records of what he was doing. But he worked for NCIS the whole time he was also in the SEALs. It's weird. Why would an NCIS agent be stationed with the SEALs? How's that possible?"

"He was an undercover cop. Like a rat."

"In the SEAL teams?"

"Yes. It's him. Gotta be. He was an NCIS agent posing as a Navy SEAL."

Jekyll asked, "Why would they do that?"

"The NCIS investigates the worst crimes imaginable that involve Navy and Marine personnel. They never could crack the SEALs. The SEALs are a tightknit family. There're only two thousand SEAL operators. They all know each other. Impossible to get a man inside."

"Aren't they like the best of the best?"

Hyde said, "Yes. I was one. We were the deadly boy scouts."

"Why would they need investigating?"

"Lots of crimes happen there, just like anywhere else. The SEALs have their own dirty laundry."

Silence.

Jekyll said, "We're going to have him bailed out and put him on a plane and fly him here. The kidnapping will be a perfect cover."

Hyde asked, "Bail him out?"

"That's how I found him. We got lucky. Like fate intervened. Widow just got himself arrested and booked down in Miami."

Hyde said, "That is kismet."

"Kiss what?

"Kismet. It means fate. Like it was meant to be. Soon, Widow will pay for his crimes."

Jekyll said, "Don't worry. He'll be here. You have my word. You can pick him up soon."

"Good work! You may proceed with the plan."

Hyde clicked off the call, and the line went dead.

Jekyll swallowed. The first part of the plan was his part. It made him uneasy.

He turned his burner phone off and took out the battery again and slipped both into his pocket, until the next scheduled call.

Jekyll was already on his way to do the first part of the plan—the hard part.

He got back into a white panel van and started up the engine again and backed out and drove off.

17

AT EIGHT-THIRTY IN the next morning, an agent from the DEA told Widow he was in a heap of trouble. He used the word: *heap*. But by nine in the morning, the same DEA agent was putting Widow in a car on an all-expenses-paid trip to DC. Which was not a dream destination for Widow, but it was better than spending another day in jail.

DEA Agent Morris left his partner, a chubby guy with a salt-and-pepper beard, alone in the interrogation room with Widow.

At first, Widow thought they were doing a good cop, bad cop thing, but they weren't.

What happened was weird.

Morris's phone rang right in the middle of the interrogation. He took the call and stepped out into the hall.

After several seconds, Morris came back into the room. He walked in, cell phone in hand, and stared at Widow.

The guy looked weird. He had a weird expression on his face like he'd just accidentally walked in on the president in a bathroom stall.

Morris held his personal phone out to Widow.

He said, "It's for you."

His partner asked, "What?"

Widow stared at the phone, and at Morris. His hands were hand-cuffed to a metal rail at the center of the interrogation table.

"It's for him!" Morris repeated.

His partner asked, "Seriously?"

Widow shook his cuffed hands.

"Better put the phone to my ear, unless you want to uncuff me?"

Morris looked at his partner. Then he held the phone up to Widow's ear, the receiver to his mouth. He held it steady like he was some sort of mid-century butler.

Widow said, "Hello?"

"Hello," a voice answered.

"This is Widow."

"Widow? Jack Widow? Formerly of Unit Ten in the NCIS?"

Widow paused a beat. Unit Ten was classified. Last he checked. The voice on the other line shouldn't know anything about it. Not its name. Not its existence. Not anything. But he did.

Widow acknowledged.

He said, "Yeah."

"We've been looking for you."

"Okay? About what?"

"Not here. Not on the phone. I want to talk to you in person."

"Who's this? Exactly?"

"I'm sorry. My name's Sean Cord. I'm a federal agent."

Widow asked, "Cord? Do I know you?"

"No. We've never met."

Widow asked, "You're a federal agent?"

"Yeah."

"Federal agent of what?"

"I work for the Department of Treasury. Well, technically I'm in Homeland Security now."

Widow asked, "You work for the Secret Service?"

"That's right."

Widow stayed quiet and heard a busy street on the other end of the phone. A car motor. The heavy sounds of tires on pavement. And another voice that Widow assumed was a second agent.

Widow asked, "You work the protection side or the financial side?"

The United States Secret Service has two main functions. One is the investigation of financial crimes such as counterfeiting, and the other is protection detail. This side everyone knows about, yet it is the most secretive.

The guys on the protection side are the guys who run alongside the president's motorcade, the guys who are willing to take a bullet for the commander-in-chief.

Cord said, "The protection side."

Widow stayed quiet.

Cord said, "I need to see you. Right away."

"About?"

"I can't tell you over the phone."

"Why me?"

"Can't tell you that over the phone either."

"What's so special about me that the Secret Service wants a chat?"

Cord said, "Can't tell you that over the phone. Listen, come out here so we can have a proper discussion."

"Why the hell would I do that?"

"You don't have to. I can't force you. You can stay there in Miami lockup and see how this drug charge thing goes."

Widow thought about it for a second. What choice did he have? This Cord guy was offering him a get out of jail free card—literally.

"How am I supposed to get there? I'm sitting in police custody right now."

"Don't worry about that. I'll take care of it."

"You going to fix my crime?"

"Did you commit a crime?"

"No."

Then he thought about being on the boat when Calderón picked up what must've been a package of drugs. Just being present made him an accessory—technically.

"Good then. I'll sort it out. In exchange, you come to DC? Hear me out? Deal?"

Widow looked at Morris, who stared back at him in utter confusion.

Widow said, "Okay."

"Okay? Great. I'll have Miami Metro take you to the airport."

"You already booked a flight for me?"

"I'll work that out."

"Okay."

"Keep this number. It's my phone. I'll have someone meet you when you land. I'm busy here this weekend because of what's happening. And the president's returning from a trip. It's all hands on deck. Even though he's not my actual assignment."

"Isn't he everyone's assignment?"

"You're right. Of course, POTUS is always our number one priority. See you, Widow."

Agent Cord clicked off the call, and the line went dead.

Morris put the phone to his ear.

"Hello? Hello?"

He brought his phone down and stared at the screen.

His partner asked, "Secret Service? Is this real?"

Morris said, "It's real. The call was connected through the Director's office."

He was referring to the Director of the Drug Enforcement Administration.

And just like that, by nine in the morning, Widow was headed to Miami International Airport with a police escort out front while he sat in the back of an unmarked car.

Widow stared out the window and smiled because he thought he was out of trouble. Saved by the United States Secret Service. But he wasn't. It was more like out of the frying pan and into the fire.

18

THERE WERE no direct flights to DC open for Widow. He ended up with a layover in Atlanta.

He sat for a while on a stool at a coffee bar counter in the Hartsfield-Jackson Atlanta International Airport, then drained the last of his coffee, got up from his seat, walked to his gate, and waited.

Across from the gate was a set of payphones—only two working phones left out of ten. The others had all been removed. There were empty white spaces where they once were. A sign in front read: "To be removed."

The payphone is on its way to being a relic from old times.

Widow stepped past the sign and picked up a phone, deposited a quarter, and dialed Cord's cell phone number from memory. The phone rang and rang. Cord didn't answer, but his voicemail came up.

"It's me. Widow. I'm in Atlanta. I'll be arriving tonight. I'll be on Flight 1029. See you soon."

He hung up the phone and returned to the gate. The boarding of his plane had started, and his row was called. He boarded the plane and sat uncomfortably in an aisle seat.

He closed his eyes and did his best to sleep during the flight, but this was constantly interrupted by flight attendants trying to pass with the food cart and then the drink cart or by passengers who would wake him up to pass by on their way to the restroom near the rear of the plane. Each time someone needed to pass, Widow had to pull his left knee into his row as best he could.

* * *

BY THE TIME his plane touched down in Washington's Reagan National Airport, Widow's joints were cramped—knees, elbows, and neck. As soon as the fasten seatbelt light went off, he stood and stretched the best he could.

As soon the other passengers began moving, Widow followed suit and exited the plane. He walked the long corridor and then made a left-hand turn to descend a flight of stairs.

Coming out of the stairway, he saw another long corridor with a conveyor belt for people, allowing them to get to the other end of the hall faster. He stayed on the main carpet and walked at his normal pace. He was in no hurry.

He wasn't sure if Cord would pick him up or not. He mentally prepared himself to find his own way into the city and get a motel for the night.

Widow walked through the maze of high ceilings, chrome rails, and foot traffic to the baggage claim until he saw the exits.

At the first exit sign, he saw something that he hadn't expected. He had expected Agent Cord to be there to pick him up. But he wasn't.

Instead, Widow saw a sign with his name on it. A simple white five-by-eight card. Big, bold black letters. Impeccable handwriting.

But even more impeccable was the hand holding the sign—and the stimulating woman attached to the hand.

She was the most beautiful Asian woman Widow had seen in recent memory. She was Secret Service, too. No doubt about it. Everything about her screamed Secret Service agent in a way that said she meant business. She was short and probably about twenty-five years old. She was built like a female UFC fighter—tight shoulders and toned arms. Her hair was shoulder length, and she wore a black suit and plain stainless steel earrings—studs, Widow believed they were called

—in her ears. Her skirt was knee-length. Something Widow was certain was regulated by some clause under a section and page heading issued by the Department of Homeland Security on how all agents, male and female, were supposed to dress. It was something similar to the Military Uniform Code.

He walked up to her and said, "I'm Widow."

She smiled in a way that seemed professional, and oddly inhuman, as if she wasn't interested in who he was, even though she was the one holding up a sign with his name printed on it.

She said, "Mr. Widow. My name is Kelly Li. I'm from Homeland Security."

"Cord sent you?"

"Special Agent Cord sent me."

Widow stayed quiet.

Li said, "I'm here to pick you up."

Widow said, "Are you here to babysit me?"

"No, not babysit. Just make sure you're taken care of. Shown around and treated with hospitality. That sort of thing. Agent Cord is busy with protection detail. He'll meet with you tomorrow. He just wanted to make sure that you were picked up and taken to a hotel."

"That makes you my chauffeur?"

Li said, "If that makes you feel better, sure."

"Let's get going then."

"What about your bags?"

"Don't have any."

"You don't have bags? Not even one?"

"Nope."

"Did you leave your luggage in Miami?"

"I don't carry luggage."

Li said, "Where're your clothes?"

She looked Widow up and down like she was inspecting him, but there was nothing much to inspect. He still wore shorts, a red T-shirt, and a pair of worn boat shoes.

Li asked, "This is the only set of clothes you own?"

Widow nodded.

"Okay."

She led Widow out through the glass doors of the taxi exit and over to a black Ford Taurus parked on the side of the drive. Black tires. Good tread. The rims were solid black and rust-colored—not rusted, just rust-colored, almost as if it had been done on purpose. Widow wasn't sure why. The bolts showed through.

The car's paint was matte black and wouldn't make a lasting impression on anyone who looked at it. The one thing about it that made it obvious that it was a federal car was the fact that it was so unremarkable. Purposefully unremarkable. This car didn't have large antennas bolted to the back like a lot of the unmarked police cars that Widow had seen before. There were no lights hidden in the grille. It wasn't meant for protection or high-speed pursuits. It was merely for transport, or perhaps, for quick getaways.

Li said, "Welcome to Washington, DC. Get in, and I'll take you to the hotel."

Widow said, "You already know what hotel I'm staying at?"

"We booked it for you in advance."

Widow paused, turned to her, and said, "How do you know where I want to stay?"

"We took a guess."

Widow shrugged.

Li asked, "Getting in?"

Widow stayed quiet and opened the passenger door. He dumped himself down in the seat. Plenty of room in the footwell, always something he appreciated in a car.

Li walked around to the rear of the car and shut the trunk. She had left it open, probably because she had assumed Widow had luggage. It was a normal assumption, but not in Widow's case.

She walked around, opened the driver's door, and sat down on the seat. She shut the door, put on her seatbelt, and looked at Widow intensely like he had broken some social taboo.

She asked, "Ready?"

"Let's go," Widow said.

"Seatbelt?"

Widow pulled on his safety belt and snapped it into the mechanism. Then he nodded at her.

Her demeanor made her hard to read. Widow wasn't sure if she was mad at him, or just hated her position in life. He had known a woman like that before. He shrugged and just stared out the window.

She put the car in drive and moved away from the curb.

19

THE HOTEL that Li brought Widow to was a place he would never have picked on his own. Not in a hundred years.

It was a modern, youthful hotel that looked more like a Saudi prince's palace than a hotel in the nation's capital. It was called The Fifth. Widow wasn't sure if that alluded to the Fifth Amendment, or if it meant that this location was the fifth one in the franchise, or that it was on Fifth Street or Fifth Avenue. Widow hadn't been paying attention to the street names when they were driving.

Li parked the car in an underground parking garage, a small dark area with dim lights that might as well have been torches in a cave.

They got out and headed toward the elevators. In the booming echo of the underground chamber, Li's shoes clopped and drummed on the pavement. She wore short heels. Something that Widow was again certain was regulated by a field manual somewhere about Secret Service uniforms, just like the Navy.

Li walked him to the elevator on the eastern side of the underground parking complex. She hit the only button—the up button—and stood by him, waiting. He could hear her breathing in the silence, and even her breathing seemed judgmental. It was a vibe from her that even he could pick up on.

The elevator came. It was a steel contraption—chrome everything, but shrouded in a light that was dimmer than that of the underground parking garage. The back of the cabin had a mirror that spanned half of the wall's length. The elevator's style reminded him of the inside of an oven with no working light.

Widow stood a short distance away from Li. She pressed the ground floor button. The doors closed, and Widow took it upon himself to break the ice or at least try to figure out why she was acting so stand-offish toward him.

He said, "You work for Agent Cord?"

She turned a shade of red that could only be described as mad. She turned to him—didn't move her feet, just twisted at the waist—and stared up at him with furious dark eyes.

She said, "I'm not his assistant or anything."

She was upset.

Widow said, "I wasn't saying that. I meant, does he outrank you? Is he your CO? Do you take your orders from him?"

Li snorted slightly. Breath flowed forcefully out of her nose, making her nostrils flare.

Widow said, "Look, I'm sorry for whatever, but I don't know a thing about you. I don't really know anything about Cord, either. And I don't know why the hell I'm here. All I know is you've been rude to me since we met. What's with the cold treatment?"

Li sighed, and the elevator doors opened in unison, almost on cue.

They stepped out into a short hallway, also dimly lit. The carpet had a modern, artsy black design with white trim. The walls were painted white with more chrome trim and mirrors.

Li said nothing during the walk down the hall, and then she stopped at the corner.

She turned to Widow and said, "I'm sorry I acted like a bitch. I'm not usually like that."

Widow shrugged.

"I was ordered to pick you up this morning. I had to wait in the airport the whole day. It ruined my plans."

Widow stayed quiet.

She said, "They were important plans. Life-changing. I was supposed to take my SAEE today."

"SAEE?"

"Yeah, the exam to become a special agent."

"SAEE? Never heard of it. But then, I'm not that familiar with the Secret Service."

Li said, "And you wouldn't have heard of it. It's not a well-known test—only guys who're interested in the Service talk about it. The contents are secret. It's the Secret Service—everything's a secret, you know? It's an official exam. Everyone takes it if they want to be a special agent. If I do well, I get a better chance of being picked for the best assignments. Top-tier sort of thing."

And then he understood why she was upset. He felt horrible.

Widow asked, "And your test was today?"

"Yeah."

"And instead, you were pulled from it and had to be here with me?"

She nodded.

He said, "I'm so sorry. I don't need you to hang out with me. Can you still make it?"

"Widow, it's evening. It's too late. The test has already come and gone. Even if it was still going on, the agents taking it are locked in— no cell phones. No going out for bathroom breaks. And no entering late. You leave, you're out."

Suddenly, he pictured the shiny, brass bell that hangs in the yard at SEAL training school. The first week of SEAL training is aptly called Hell Week. He remembered his instructors repeating over and over that all he had to do to "end the suffering" was to ring the bell.

Widow asked, "Can you retake it?"

She nodded.

"When's the next time you can take it?"

Li looked down at the floor and stared at Widow's boat shoes.

She gazed back up at him with a slight tear in the corner of her eye, which made Widow feel about as awful as he ever had.

She said, "I can't register for the next exam until next year. It's booked till then. It takes forever to get approved to take it."

"Damn. I'm sorry," he repeated.

He said nothing else because he didn't know what else to say. He had inadvertently ruined this girl's life plans without having a choice in the matter. Not his fault. Not entirely. But one thing led to another, and everything was someone's fault somehow. Even down to the molecular level. Everything had a cause, and Widow felt like he had caused her professional downfall.

Li didn't make a sound, but the single tear on her face told Widow how important it had been to her to take the test. He pictured her taking classes and staying up late at night to study for it. Maybe she had studied for months—perhaps years.

Li said, "I'm sorry for being mean to you. It's not your fault. Come on. Let's check you in, and I'll buy you a drink. If you aren't too tired from the flight?"

Widow felt a little tired, but he never turned down a drink with a beautiful woman. He wasn't an idiot.

He said, "A drink sounds great."

They turned, and Li said, "There's got to be a bar here somewhere."

"Actually, can we get out of here?"

"But this is where your room is. Don't you want to check in?"

"This place isn't really my style. I'm more old-school."

"It's already paid for. Sean paid for it. And you probably won't find anything else tonight. Not in town. The city is hosting a small emergency summit of African leaders in two days because of the thing."

"What thing?"

"You know. The thing."

Widow shrugged.

"You don't know what happened in West Ganbola?"

"I don't watch the news. Let's get out of this hotel. You can fill me in about whatever happened over that drink."

"No checking in first?"

"No reason to right this second. I'm more interested in that drink right now."

She nodded.

"Tell you what," Widow said. "I'll do you one better. Let me buy you dinner? I'm starving."

"I'm sorry. I didn't even think that you might be hungry."

"No big deal. Let's grab a bite now."

She hesitated and looked at his clothes again, like a reflex.

He asked, "What? You don't want to be seen with me? Is it the boat shoes?"

"It's not exactly DC chic."

"Ouch. That hurts."

"It's not that I don't want to be seen with you."

"Just my clothes?"

I could lose them, he thought. Also, a reflex. It couldn't be helped. Li was amazing. She was one of those women who turn out to be as smart as they are beautiful—a deadly combination. Plus, she was armed with a government-issued firearm, and Widow bet she knew exactly how to use it.

He pretended to take off his boat shoes.

Li reached up a hand to stop him. She cracked a smile and spoke.

"That's not what I meant, either!"

"I'm kidding. You want me to get new clothes? These don't fit in. I get it. I literally came from a boat. You know?"

"You did?"

"Not directly, but I was on a boat when Miami Metro arrested me."

Li didn't ask. She just said, "Can we please just grab you some new clothes? No place is gonna let you in wearing that. Not here."

"What places? Where're we going? I can't afford a five-star restaurant."

"You couldn't get into a five-star restaurant. Don't worry about it."

"What's that supposed to mean?"

Li smiled widely, her teeth all white. All straight.

She said, "You got any money?"

Widow nodded.

"Good. Clothes first, then we'll grab that drink."

She grabbed his shirt and pinched it. Her fingers brushed his abdomen. It was quick, but he noticed it.

Li walked out to the street, and Widow followed.

20

WIDOW AND LI were back in the unmarked Secret Service's black Ford Taurus. They drove out of the hotel's underground parking and onto the street, which Widow noted was not called Fifth Avenue or Fifth Street.

The hotel wasn't named for one of those two things. The street was called George Street, which got Widow wondering if it was named after a famous George. George Washington? George Washington Carver? George Bush? George W. Bush? George Patton? Or about a hundred other dead guys named George.

He had no idea, and the question slipped away from him as Li turned a couple more streets and then looped past another and took a left on Louisiana Avenue, which reminded Widow of his boyhood home in the South. Then she turned near the Library of Congress, and Widow stared out the window like a tourist, which he was. He watched the buildings and the cars and the people.

Li asked, "You ever been to DC before?"

Widow said, "I have."

"For work or pleasure?"

"Work."

"After this is all over, stick around and see it. There's a lot of history here."

Widow stayed quiet and kept staring out the Taurus's tinted window.

Widow said, "Maybe I will."

They drove on, and Widow noticed that the sunlight had faded away in the west, dying across the beautiful, historical DC landscape.

Li drove the car around another corner and said, "I know the perfect place for you to get some new duds."

"Why does that scare me?"

"Come on! I doubt anything scares you."

She was partially right, Widow thought.

They came to a stop on a side street, and she parallel-parked the car between two compact foreign cars.

"This is it."

"The alley?"

Li smiled and said, "Get out of the car. Let's go."

They got out of the car, and she led him around the corner and back to the street.

The store that Li had picked was what Widow would think of as overpriced, but that was true in all major cities nowadays.

Li led Widow inside. He didn't want to let shopping suck up his entire night with her. He would much rather spend the rest of his time talking with her and getting to know her. He picked something out about as fast as he ever had in his life. He ended up getting a pair of black cargo pants.

Li told him they were stylish. He nodded along with her. He didn't pick them out to be stylish. He picked them out because they were both tactical and functional.

He also purchased a long-sleeved black knit shirt Li called a Henley. It had buttons running from the neckline down about five inches. The top three were left unbuttoned.

Widow wasn't shy. He found a wall mirror and took off his own shirt in front of it. Li stayed behind him, holding the Henley. She stared back at him in the mirror, but she was staring at his chest.

Widow grabbed the Henley and slipped it on and buttoned it up to the top.

Li grabbed his bicep.

"No. Leave them unbuttoned. Looks better that way."

Widow nodded and did as instructed.

Li stepped back from him and looked him up and then down.

She asked, "You really like the color black, don't you?"

"What's wrong with black?"

"Nothing. It's just very...um...Special Forces."

"Nothing wrong with that."

"You were in the Navy, right?"

Widow nodded.

"The SEALs?"

He didn't answer that. He asked, "Where can I put these pants on?"

Li turned and saw a fitting room area.

"Over there."

She handed him the pants and led him to the fitting room. He entered one of the stalls, which had razor-thin curtains that barely reached his knees.

Li waited out in the corridor by another full-length mirror while a young sales associate stood outside Widow's curtain, either afraid Widow would steal something or wanting to wait on him hand and foot for the commission.

Widow put the clothes on and stepped out barefoot for Li's approval.

"Hey, not bad. You'll fit in okay."

Widow stayed quiet.

Li said, "Here. Put these on."

She handed him a pair of black dress loafers with brown trim. The label read *DeBeer*. He looked at the price tag, but she snatched it away.

"Don't look at the price. These'll look good on you. They're worth it. Trust me."

Widow trusted her. He didn't look at the price. Instead, he asked, "How do you know my shoe size?"

"I guessed. Try them on."

He went back into the fitting room stall, left the curtain open, sat down, and tried them on. Perfect fit. He smiled. She had sized him up well.

He walked back out of the fitting room in his new clothes.

"Where're your old clothes?"

"I left them."

"Better get them, or they'll think you don't want them anymore. They'll end up in a landfill."

Widow smiled and said, "Don't want them back."

"What? You're just going to ditch them?"

"You got it. These are my clothes now. Especially if the price is going to be what I think it is. In which case, they'd better last."

They went to the register, and he watched in horror as the numbers rang up on the rectangle-shaped digital screen above a tiny computer.

The whole outfit was over two hundred bucks—well over. His instincts were telling him to run, but he took out his debit card and paid.

Widow paid and turned while Li tore off all the tags and pulled a long sticker off the right pant leg. She handed them to the girl behind the counter, and they walked out of the store together.

Widow smiled. He knew immediately the clothes were well worth the price because as soon as they started toward the exit, Li put her arm through his and leaned the crown of her head below the top of his shoulder, like they were a couple.

She said, "Now people will think we're on a date. Like cover. Got to keep you being here a secret."

Widow didn't ask why. He was satisfied with the whole process.

Li said, "I bet you're a dive-bar kind of guy. Let's walk to the next street over. There're some hole-in-the-wall bars there I've never been to. This side of town is where all the college kids like to come to drink. Or at least it was when I was in college. The bars are all dives, and they have live music. Plus, the food is probably good. Well, it's the kind of food that you like, I'm sure."

"These college kids. Are they the poor kind or the rich-parents kind?"

"Rich-parents kind, of course. This is DC. Just about everyone who goes to school here has rich parents."

Widow stayed quiet.

"Why? You have a problem with that?"

"No problem. Just curious. Dives that cater to rich kids who're pretending to be middle class aren't real dives."

"Do you want to try someplace else?"

Widow said, "I'm game for wherever you want to go."

21

LI PICKED a bar that was exactly the kind of place that Widow liked. Country music played on a jukebox in the corner—not the sad, twangy kind, but the old-school kind with a real blues feel to it, and not overly depressing. Widow liked it, but then he liked a lot of music as long as it was good.

They sat at the bar. The lighting was low. Numerous beer taps lined the wall behind the bar. The place wasn't crowded, but it wasn't empty, either.

A group of five college guys and two college girls played pool in the back, and a couple sat at the other end of the bar. A few older guys were scattered about, mostly watching a baseball game on TV.

Li asked, "Do you like the music?"

She sat on a barstool next to Widow. She drank a gin martini, dirty, with olives. Widow drank a Budweiser out of a bottle.

He thought about her question, thinking about going into his opinions on modern music, and decided not to. He just nodded.

Li said, "Good. I like country. It makes me feel American."

Widow said, "Where're you from originally?"

"North Korea."

"Really? How did you get out of there?"

She stayed quiet and looked at him, sarcasm in her eyes.

Widow asked, "You're not from North Korea?"

Li said, "No, idiot. I'm from New Jersey. I just meant that this type of music makes me feel at home. American like that. Like it's original to America. I traveled a lot with my parents when I was a kid. We're Chinese. I was born in New Jersey, but my mother still holds onto China like it's the mother ship. But even she doesn't want to go back there."

Widow took a swig from his beer. He understood how her mother felt. He would always consider Mississippi to be where he was from, but he didn't have any desire to return.

Li grabbed her own glass by the stem and took a sip. She looked like she wanted to drink more of it but didn't want to drink it faster than Widow drank his. And then he thought about her test—the one he had ruined by being there.

He said, "I knew you were lying about North Korea. By the way."

"Oh, yeah? Sure, you did."

"How do you spell your name?"

"L – I, Li."

"Li? That's Chinese."

"Oh yeah? You positive? I already told you we're Chinese."

"Li originally comes from China. A guy a long time ago named Laozi was actually named Li Er. That a name you might know?"

She shook her head.

"It's the guy who founded Taoism. A long, long time ago. Sixth century B.C."

She took a long pull from her drink and looked at Widow blankly.

He asked, "What?"

"Nothing."

"What? You don't think I could be smart enough to know stuff like that?"

"I guess I'm the one who should feel stupid. I misjudged you. From a brief I read about you, and the way you dressed. When I first saw you, the last thing I woulda thought was that you were a smart guy. Smartass, maybe. But not the intellectual type."

Did she read a brief about me? Widow thought. Then he was curious to find out what was going on. But he stayed the course. They would have to tell him.

He asked, "Why? Because I dress in cheap clothes?"

"First, cheap clothes? Please! Those were a homeless person's clothes."

She smiled at him.

He smiled back.

Li said, "Second, I guess I just didn't expect that you'd have half a brain."

"You don't pull any punches, do you? Is it because of how I look?"

"No. It's not that."

"Wait—it's because you read I was from Mississippi!"

"That might've been a small part of it, yeah. Sean told me to look over some info about you. You know, so I wouldn't pick up the wrong guy. I guess I saw where you're from and just figured you were a stereotypical Southerner."

"Hey! What's that supposed to mean? You think we're all dumb?"

Li said, "What? I said I was sorry?"

"No. You didn't.

"Well, I'm sorry. I didn't mean it like that."

"Typical Southerner? That stereotype is about as factual as the Asian ones. We aren't a bunch of rednecks running around barefoot with no education."

"You're right. I know. I mean, you're from the South, and you're only half-dumb."

Widow said, "Ever met a Southerner before?"

"I've been to Mississippi before."

"Yeah? What part?"

"We went through Jackson last year. The president's family met with the governor's family—some sort of political nonsense. President Asher couldn't go. He sent the first lady, his kids, and Kerry Fife in his place."

Widow asked, "Fife? Who is she?"

Li said, "Not she. Kerry is a he. And he's one of the most important men in our government."

"I never heard of him."

Li said, "Ever heard of the President of the United States?"

Widow didn't answer that. He took another pull from his beer.

She said, "Mister Kerry Fife is Chief of Staff. He does the behind-the-scenes stuff when the president can't. Anyway, last year, we had to go to your state. It was all right."

"Are you supposed to tell me stuff like that?"

Li said, "Oh, relax. It's not top secret."

"Do you have top-secret clearance?"

"I got some clearance, sure. But not for missile codes or anything."

Widow said, "This Cord guy. What's he like?"

Li shrugged and said, "He's nothing special. I mean, he's a good guy, I guess. The by-the-book type. He wouldn't want me telling you the name of the family his unit is assigned to, but screw him. He pulled me out of my exam."

Widow apologized again for it.

"I'm sorry about that."

Li said, "Forget it. I'm young. There's always next year—no big deal. I probably wouldn't have made the cut. I'm not the best example of an agent. I just want to make it so bad."

"I understand," Widow said.

Li finished her drink. "Hey, let's get another one," she said.

Widow finished his Budweiser and nodded.

* * *

ABOUT TWO GIN MARTINIS LATER, Li was still a good distance from drunk, but Widow wasn't about to let her drive or operate heavy machinery or anything. He'd only had three beers, and he was a big guy, so the effects were pretty much null on him. He could tell that she was a little more unwound than she had been.

Li said, "You wanna dance?"

"I'm not much of a dancer."

"Are you scared?"

"I didn't say that. I just don't dance. Not really my thing."

"You were raised by a single mom, right?"

"You know I was."

"Then you should know how to dance. Didn't your mom teach you that stuff?"

"She taught me how to shoot straight. She also taught me how to shave."

Li said, "Wow. She sounds exceptional. My mom taught me girly stuff. She used to make my older brother dance with me. He hated it. You don't have any brothers or sisters, do you?"

"Nope. Only child."

Li took another sip of her martini. She set the glass down on the bar, and then she eased off her stool. She held out her hand and spoke.

"Come on. We're dancing."

Widow didn't need to be asked twice. He took a long pull from his beer and followed her off his stool. He took her hand.

A slow song was ending on the jukebox. It stopped before they got to a space in the middle of the bar that could be a dance floor.

Li paused and said, "Oh, nope. Not this."

She left Widow standing in the center of the bar and stepped away.

He asked, "Where're you going? Thought we were dancing."

"I'll play something on the jukebox. Be right back."

Li walked away from him, and Widow watched her go. He couldn't help it. He allowed himself to look her up and down. Her calves looked strong. Her legs were smooth. He imagined they were soft. He looked away, not wanting to appear ungentlemanly in case she glanced back at him. He looked around the bar. The room was quiet —quieter than when they were sitting at the bar. And it wasn't just because the jukebox had stopped playing. The rumbling of voices had softened.

Widow glanced at the college guys who were shooting pool. They had all stopped to look at Li from behind as well. Several of them held onto beer bottles. Two had pool sticks.

Widow looked at Li as well, but he only did a standard look, a little more than a harmless glance. These boys weren't glancing. They were leering.

Li noticed them.

"See something you like, idiots?" she called out.

None of them spoke. They stared at her a long second more, and then they looked at Widow. They went back to playing pool. They didn't say a word.

Widow looked back at Li as she continued to the jukebox. She walked slowly and seductively like she knew he was watching. And he was.

She stopped at the machine, laid her purse down on a stool next to it, and pulled out a five-dollar bill. She inserted it and searched through the song catalog.

A waitress came over to Widow as he stood alone, watching Li.

She asked, "Bartender wants to know if you guys need another round?"

"Thanks. Tell him a couple of waters. And a menu."

Widow glanced back at Li. He wasn't sure how many songs she could play with five dollars, but he figured it was at least five. One came up. A pop song Widow didn't recognize—something with a female voice and a decent beat.

Li moved her hips from side to side. And Widow watched.

Li continued to sway at the jukebox. She hadn't pressed the button to select a new song in several seconds.

Suddenly, Widow felt the need to hit the bathroom. The beer had gone through him rather quickly. Since Li still had at least four more songs to pick as she plodded through the list, Widow decided it was a good chance for him to go.

He turned and glanced around. He saw the restrooms at the back of the bar. He walked to them and went through the door marked "Dudes."

The men's room was dark with green-painted everything except for the urinals and the toilet. They weren't quite the standard white, but close to it.

Widow hurried and finished up and washed his hands. There were no paper towels. He shook his hands off over a trashcan and came back out of the bathroom.

In life, things can change fast, and in Widow's case, life was always changing fast.

As soon as he stepped out of the men's room, he saw the dynamics of the bar had changed.

Li was still at the jukebox. The music she played was still playing across the bar. The bartender was still behind the bar. The waitress was still holding a tray and standing up near the front. The other patrons still occupied the same places they had been except for five of them.

The five college boys were not where they had been when Widow walked into the men's room.

They surrounded Li at the jukebox. Some of them drunk. One of them very drunk. All of them were buzzed.

One guy was short and stocky. He had tattooed sleeves on his exposed arms. Probably thought they made him look tough. Another guy wore glasses with steel frames and a red T-shirt with some sort of comic book logo on it. Two of the guys were tall, as tall as Widow. They had arms like bridge supports and hands as thick as railroad spikes. They were built like Spartans. They both wore generic sport team hats turned at the front so that the bills looked slightly off—no tattoos on those two.

Then there was one more guy, presumably the ringleader. He sported a sleeve tattoo on one arm. He was a big guy—not as big as the other two guys, but still big. He was all lean and brawny, like a Roman statue. Maybe he was six foot two inches tall. Maybe two hundred pounds. Maybe more.

All five guys were muscle-bound except for the one in glasses. The one in glasses was also the drunkest. That was obvious. He had his hand propped up on a chair to keep himself balanced.

Widow noted them all. His brain made tactical calculations and operational assessment of each of them. That was natural. He couldn't help it. But the only one he was staring at was the ringleader.

The reason he stared was the ringleader was making a colossal mistake. He stood at the jukebox with Li. His hands were down low, thumb out, while he groped Li's ass.

She was pressed up against the jukebox, face against the machine, trying to maneuver out of his grip. But the short, sleeve-tattooed guy had her pinned from the side while the ringleader held her ass with his hands and whispered something in her ear that Widow couldn't hear.

The two big guys stood behind him in no sort of line, but they looked like they were waiting for their turn to grope Li.

Widow felt his blood boil, and his vision became a little fuzzy. No one knew why, but this was something that happened in all animals. Rage set in, and the body reacted in several ways. One being that the eyes fixated, and sight turned into a kind of tunnel vision like a reticle on a sniper scope. And at that moment, for Widow, the ringleader was inside that reticle.

Widow glanced at all of them, one by one, and he stared at the sleeve tattoo on the ringleader. It was a screaming eagle, big and bold, painted in vivid colors with the United States flag garlanded behind it and four black letters stenciled on his skin in bold lettering —USMC.

United States Marine Corps.

Widow guessed there was no way this guy was currently on the Corps roster for active duty. Not a chance in hell. Marines don't go this far. They're trained to be men and to act like it. Not that Marines were always on their best behavior, especially when drinking in a bar, but Marines were full of honor. It was a big deal to them, and Widow knew that. This guy's actions were far from honorable.

But the biggest indicator that the guy was no Marine was that Marines only hung out with other Marines, and his friends were no jarheads. No way. If they were, they wouldn't let their buddy step out of line. Not to a civilian, and not this far.

And of course, there were the two big guys. They were college football players. No question. All four of the stronger guys were probably college football players. Same team. Same school.

Widow looked at the far side of the bar and saw no action from the bartender. No one at the bar was paying attention to what was happening on this side. Widow looked at the two girls who were with the five guys. They stayed near the pool table, holding the pool sticks.

Widow's eyes locked with the guy in glasses.

The guy in glasses raised his hand and pointed at him. The other four guys had their backs to Widow.

Now was the time to act, before the drunk guy with glasses warned his friends and gave away the element of surprise.

Widow crouched down and walked over along the wall, weaving through tabletops and chairs.

The drunk guy in the glasses saw him plain as day. The guy stood up, took his hand off the chair he was using as a crutch to help him balance, and reached over to grab the arm of his friend, the first big guy.

He almost got his fingers on the guy's arm before Widow stood up straight and lifted the table in front of him and charged with it outstretched like a battering ram. Drinks and beer bottles flew, and glass broke, and liquids spilled and merged onto the floor.

Widow released his grip on the table and hurled it at the two guys. The drunk guy flew back onto the ground and started screaming in drunken agony. He held his right hand out over his chest. The fingers were smashed and broken from his fall. His index finger was bent outward and mangled. The other four were even worse.

The one big guy had fallen on his back under the weight of the table, but he flung the table off his chest and bounced back up. His hair and face were covered in beer and liquor.

The other three guys turned, wide-eyed, and stared.

Widow said, "Guys, your friend looks hurt."

"You broke my fingers, man!" the guy screamed from the floor.

The two big guys moved in closer to Widow, not within reaching distance, but close enough to rush him. Widow stood his ground. His hands fell by his sides. Relaxed. Non-threatening.

He said, "Now, guys, I'm guessing you play for a football team."

The big guy who was dry said, "No shit!"

Widow stayed quiet.

The ringleader walked out in front of the two big guys, and the short guy with the sleeve tattoo stood in the foreground. Widow could see that their natural strategy was to circle around him, which was a common group mentality, but Widow had made sure that this wasn't possible for them. The table he had thrown blocked the right side to the wall, and there were tables standing to the left. Unless these guys started heaving tables out of their way, they were stuck coming at him head-on.

Widow stayed focused on his opponents, but he liked to be aware of his surroundings completely. He took one quick glance at the bartender and other customers. They remained where they were—frozen as if they stared at a train wreck. Everyone knew they should dial nine one one, but in this world, most people assumed that someone else was doing it.

They all watched in silence.

The ringleader said, "Hey, bro! What the hell's wrong with you? That's my little brother."

Widow said, "And *that's* my friend you're feeling up—*bro!*"

Li scooted away from the jukebox. She stayed as quiet as she could and moved back to the left rear wall.

The short guy with the sleeve tattoo turned and ran at her. He grabbed her by the arm.

Li said, "Let go of me!"

The guy jerked her arm and pulled her out toward the rear of the group.

Widow stayed quiet.

The ringleader stepped back and grabbed her by the other arm. He said, "This your woman?"

Widow stayed still; feet planted firmly, hands still down by his side.

The two girls from the pool table moved a little closer.

One of them said, "Come on, Brice. Let that slut go. We're trying to have a good time."

The ringleader didn't look back but said, "Shut up, Holly! No one's talking to you!"

Holly backed off, rolling her eyes.

Widow said, "Brice. What's your last name, Brice?"

The closest big guy said, "Cooper." He looked at Widow like the name was supposed to mean something.

Widow shrugged, still maintaining his non-threatening stance, and asked, "Am I supposed to know that name?"

The second big guy said, "He's the quarterback for the Hoyas!"

"As in the Georgetown Hoyas!" the short guy in the back said.

Widow shrugged again. "No wonder I never heard of you."

"What's that supposed to mean, bro?" Brice asked.

Widow said, "I only follow the good teams—not the shit ones!"

Widow had no idea if the Hoyas were good or not. He didn't follow college football. He was more an NFL type of guy, and only casually. He believed in watching the big leagues, not the next rung down.

Brice said, "We're the only team that matters! You better watch your mouth, bro, or you won't like what happens."

Widow paused a beat and then said, "Here's the play, fellas." He moved his eyes to the two big guys and said, "You two can walk away with your legs still working. But leave your two friends behind."

The two big guys looked at each other and back at Widow.

Brice asked, "What? You're going to let them go, and then what? Kick our asses?" He nodded toward the guy with the sleeve tattoo.

Widow said, "The two of you aren't getting out of here on your own. The two of you have laid your hands on my friend there. And for that, you'll have to be carried out on stretchers."

Brice looked at his friend. Normally, he would laugh, but something in Widow's face made it a deadly serious prediction, and he knew it.

Widow said, "And for you, Brice, the paramedics will need an ice chest."

"What's that going to be for, bro?"

Widow didn't answer but asked, "By the way, which hand do you use to throw the football?"

"Why the hell does that matter?"

"Because that's what the ice chest is for—your fingers. After I'm done breaking the bones in your hand, it's likely some of your fingers might come off. In that case, I'd hate for you never to have them back."

The big guy on the left said, "What the hell, bro?" Then he looked at his friend, who stared back.

Widow lunged in—fast.

Jerked his right arm back. His left tucked in. He shot down and sprang up in a sharp, violent arc. Full force. His right arm pulled all the way back and then shot straight out. A huge fist like a hammer jammed straight into one big guy's neck, a brutal blow that almost shattered the guy's voice box. He would've screamed out in pain if he could have. Instead, he fell over like a puppet with its strings cut. Just a fast fall, straight to the ground like gravity had reached up and ripped him off his feet.

The second big guy didn't skip a beat. He came in at Widow with a right jab. Widow danced back and felt the wind from it rush by his chest.

He grabbed a wooden chair that was left from the thrown table and twisted at the waist and slammed it into the guy's exposed lower ribcage. He looked like an Olympic discus thrower except far less graceful. Widow wasn't a graceful fighter, far from it.

If he had taken a moment to look at the expression on Li's face, he would've seen that she was watching him in utter horror.

The chair had shattered and splintered and broken across the guy's ribs. Widow heard the mixture of breaking wood and bone. He had broken more than a few ribs. No question. He knew it, and the guy knew it because he fell over on top of his friend, just landed on the guy. Now there was a heap of maybe three hundred pounds of disabled football players piled on top of each other like they had been tackled in the middle of a game.

Brice said, "What the hell? Bro! Those're my friends!"

Widow moved toward him, slowly.

Fear came across Brice's face—that was obvious—but he didn't back away like Widow had expected him to. The other guy, however, looked at his two friends on the floor and let go of Li.

She jerked away and ran to the bar.

Widow glanced over at her quickly, then saw the rest of the patrons staring at him. The bartender was on the phone, probably calling the police.

Widow looked back at the last two guys.

He said, "Come on, Brice. What're you waiting for?"

Brice said, "Come on, man. We were only messing with her."

"She's not yours to mess with."

"We get it, man. She's yours."

"She's not mine, either, Brice. She's a person. She belongs to herself."

The short guy with the sleeve tattoo crowded in a little too close for Widow's comfort. Widow kept his eye on his position.

Widow said, "Brice, I made you a promise."

Then Widow exploded into action a second time. He charged at the short guy. The guy jabbed with his left, which surprised Widow a bit because he thought the guy was right-handed. It was a mistake on Widow's part, and the jab hit home right in his midsection. It hurt for an instant, but he had been hit before. His mind overrode the pain, and he whipped forward, powered from the ground up. Toes to his knees. Then he snapped forward from the waist and hit the guy square in the face with a monumental head-butt. Not the hardest he had ever delivered—he didn't want to kill the guy—but powerful.

There were two outcomes.

One. The guy's nose broke. Widow heard it. Brice heard it.

Two. The guy flew backward off his feet, straight into the jukebox, which wasn't as sturdy as the manufacturer had intended. The guy's mass broke through the glass center, and he landed in it. He remained stuck there, grabbing his broken nose. He didn't scream like the big guy with the broken ribs. No, this guy wailed. But his cries were drowned out because the one thing the manufacturer did right was to make a jukebox that would still play music even after a broken football player was flung through it.

And right there, right then, Widow saw something he had never seen before.

Brice Cooper, the starting quarterback of a college football team, started crying. Like a baby. Tears rolled out of his eyes and down his face. His cheeks turned red, and his eyes glassed up.

All his life, Widow had gotten into fights defending the helpless, and in that time, he had seen all kinds of people from bullies to international criminals. But none of them had cried like this—not a single one.

Brice started begging. He said, "I'm sorry." Over and over.

Widow approached, and Brice backed away and continued to plead.

Widow said, "Are you sorry?"

Brice said, "Yeah, bro. I'm so sorry."

Widow stayed quiet. Thought about what to do next.

The guy was an idiot, but he wasn't a murderer. A cheat, maybe. Perhaps a liar. But nothing that deserved broken bones. Plus, he had backed down.

Widow grabbed him by his collar. Fast. Brice didn't expect it and started convulsing.

"Ah, man. Come on, bro. Please don't break off my fingers."

"Relax," Widow said, and he half-dragged the guy across the bar, through the pile of his friends, and over to Li.

He said, "Tell her."

"Tell...tell her what, bro?"

"Tell her you're sorry! Not me!"

"I'm...sorry."

"Now tell her you're nothing but a piece of shit."

"I'm a piece of shit!"

Widow pulled him back from Li and spun him around and said, "You're going to pay our tab. As a gesture of how remorseful you feel about what you did."

Brice nodded like he had never agreed with anything else more in his life, and the bartender acknowledged it with a nod.

Widow said, "And one more thing."

"Wh-what? Anything. You name it, and I'll do it."

"Put your throwing hand across the bar."

"What? Why?"

"Do it. Lay it nice and flat."

Brice shook even more than before, but he did as he was told.

Widow clenched his fist like a hammer and pulled it up over Brice's fingers.

Brice squirmed. He shut his eyes tight.

Widow hovered his fist over Brice's like he was going to hammer down and break it.

He did it once. Twice.

Li shook her head and mouthed, "Please don't."

Widow backed away from the bar and kicked the guy square in the groin. Not full force and not bone-breaking hard, but hard enough to make his point.

Brice dropped to the dirty floor, holding his groin with both hands.

Widow looked at the bartender and said, "He'll pay our tab."

He took Li by the hand, and they walked past the other patrons and out into the night.

Sirens wailed behind them.

22

WIDOW AND LI walked back to her car, and Widow put her in the passenger seat and dumped himself down in the driver's seat. He moved it all the way back, looked at her, and asked for the keys, which she gladly handed over.

Li asked, "Where are we going?"

"Where do you live?"

"Hey, I won't be that easy."

"I can bring you home and take a cab back to the hotel. That's what I was thinking."

She paused a beat and thought about it. It was a logical suggestion.

Widow said, "You can't drive. Not tonight. Unless you want to stay in my room, then this is the best way to go."

Li nodded and said, "Hang on."

She dug in her purse and pulled out her cell phone. She messed with the apps on it and then showed him the screen.

"Just go here. Follow the directions."

She had pulled up *Google Maps*, and it now displayed directions to her apartment.

Li said, "Okay. Safety belt."

Widow put on his seatbelt, and she put on hers. He put the keys in the ignition and fired up the car, and they were off. He held the phone one-handed while he drove and glanced at it occasionally. He couldn't remember the last time he used *Google Maps* while driving.

It led Widow and Li back to her apartment, which took about thirty minutes of driving. And that was with light traffic.

Widow turned onto her street, New Mexico Avenue NW, and drove a little way until he found the parking for her building. He parked on the street and got out, walking around the hood to open her door, but Li was already getting out by the time he got to her.

Li said, "Were you going to open my door for me?"

Widow nodded.

Li said, "That's nice. You're a good guy. Now I really feel like shit for being such a jerk earlier."

Widow said, "Don't worry about it. Understandable. It's your career. Sorry I interfered with your plans."

Widow took her arm to help her walk. Not that she needed it, but that was Widow's way. He was from the South and had been raised by a single mother, and that meant he was always a gentleman, unless fighting. Just the way it was. They walked up a narrow stone pathway and past a matching stone sign that read Sutton Towers.

They didn't speak until they reached the lobby, and Widow went in with her. She walked with him to the elevators and pressed the button.

She said, "You can come up. You don't need to leave just yet. It's only —" Li took her cell phone out of her pocket and looked at the screen. She read the time on the screen.

Widow said, "10:35."

"Yeah. How'd you know that?"

"I don't know. It's like a habit. Sometimes, I just know the time."

Li asked, "Do you want to come in?"

Widow said, "Is the Pope Catholic?"

And he immediately felt stupid after saying it. It was not only the worst line he had ever used, but it was the dumbest thing he ever heard come out of his mouth.

Li didn't seem to mind. She smiled and took her keys out of her purse and held them in her hand.

The elevator came, and they got on. Li pressed the fourth-floor button and stood close to Widow as they rode up. At Li's door, she got it open, and they went inside.

Li's apartment was a small studio, maybe six hundred square feet. But it had updated flooring, and the kitchen was nice—granite countertops in a light color. A deep stainless-steel farmer sink was installed in the center of the north counter. The cabinets were painted black. The appliances were all stainless steel and matched like they were bought as a set. A big double-door fridge with a pull-out freezer drawer on the bottom rested neatly in the wall. The only thing that was lacking was the lighting. Li flipped a switch, and the lights blazed on. They hung down from the ceiling on long wires just above a bar that seated three. And those seemed to be the only lights in the room besides some lamps near the sofa—no light fixtures on the ceilings.

The sofa was right in front of the bed, which was made up, something that Widow had stopped doing in the last six months. It made no sense to make the beds in the motels he slept in. What was the point in that?

Widow said, "Nice flat."

And then he wondered why he called it a flat.

Apparently, so did Li, because she said, "Flat?"

Widow said, "Yeah. That's what they're called."

"What is this, London?"

Widow stayed quiet, and Li stared at him.

She said, "Never mind. Stupid joke."

She laid her purse down on the bar top and then kicked her shoes off against the wall. She turned and slipped her coat off, hung it up in a small closet near the front door.

She asked, "Want some wine?"

Widow wasn't big on wine, but he didn't think that the setting allowed for him to turn it down even though he wanted coffee. Coffee versus a beautiful woman. This was a serious dilemma, but in the end, the woman won.

Widow said, "Sure."

"Take your shoes off. Just leave them near mine."

Widow did as she asked.

Li walked to the cabinets near the fridge, opened them, and pulled out two big red wine glasses. She bent down out of Widow's sight-line and came up with a bottle of wine. Widow didn't recognize the brand, but then again, he wouldn't have recognized any brand. It looked expensive.

Li poured two glasses, pretty full, and stood near him. She placed them down on the bar top.

She said, "Can I ask you a question?"

Widow nodded.

"Why do you live like you live?"

"I like the freedom."

"You're a drifter."

Widow nodded.

She said, "Why? Are you searching for something or someone? Do you think if you live off the grid, you'll find what you're looking for?"

"I never thought of it like that. Maybe. Or maybe I'm just enjoying living without the things I'm *not* looking for."

Li took a big drink of wine.

They sat in silence for a bit at her bar, and then she said, "I like you, Widow."

"I like you back."

"It's weird because we only just met, but I feel like I've known you longer."

Widow said, "Common thing, I guess. Good people meet under fleeting circumstances all the time and form a bond. Like on an airplane or a train ride. You take a long trip somewhere, don't know who's sitting next to you, but you talk. Small talk. Before you know it, you've bonded with them. It even happens with kidnappers and their captives. Happens with prison guards and inmates. Happens all over the world every two and a half minutes."

"Two and a half minutes?"

Widow stayed quiet.

Li said, "I guess you're right."

"We've spent the whole evening together, talking. And we made a connection. That's life. And the world spins on."

Li took the last pull from her wine and set the glass down.

She said, "Want to see something?"

Widow nodded, didn't touch his wine.

She took his hand.

She led him to the bed and sat down on it. He stayed standing. Li patted the space on the bed next to her.

"Sit down. It's okay."

Widow sat down carefully. His weight dipped the mattress down, and she slid toward him a little, and then she twisted back and bent over the bed like she was reaching down to get something out from underneath it. Her backside faced Widow, and he wouldn't lie to himself—he looked. It was a view he hoped to see many more times.

She came back up with a small shoebox. She opened it and pulled out a single picture that was placed on top of a pair of tiny old shoes.

"See this? Look," Li said and handed him the picture.

It was a black-and-white picture. It had to be ancient, or else it was made to look that way.

The picture was of a woman at least ten years older than Li, and a little girl. Both looked exactly like Li. Exactly. The older woman was just as amazingly beautiful, and the little girl was just as adorable as Li must've been as a little girl.

Widow asked, "Is this you and your mom?"

"No way! The picture is black and white! Come on!"

"Sorry."

"It's an old picture. I wasn't born for another thirty-some years."

Widow asked, "Who's this?"

"That's my mom and grandmother. That picture was taken before they left China. It was in November, I think. 1949."

"Wow. The end of the Chinese Civil War. Mao Zedong had just established the People's Republic of China."

Li looked at Widow with a look he had seen before. Before she even asked, he said, "I like history, and I just remember things."

Then he decided it best not to go into greater detail. Instead, he listened.

Li said, "My mom was supposed to perform in a ballet in Shanghai at the time of the picture, but those sorts of things were risky. My grandmother pulled her out, but my mom kept the shoes from the picture. All my mom ever wanted was to be a ballerina."

Widow said, "They're both beautiful women. Look exactly like you."

Li smiled and said, "I know. I love this picture. It's like looking at who I was and who I will become. My grandmother was a good woman."

Widow said, "I'm sure that you will be even better."

Li said nothing else. She just took the picture back from Widow and placed it back in the shoebox and clumsily plopped the lid back on. Then she slid the whole thing off the bed and leaned into Widow. She put her tiny hand on his face, felt his stubble.

She smiled and said, "You need to shave tomorrow. Sean's a professional and will expect to see you clean."

"I don't work for Cord."

"I do. Do it for me?"

Widow nodded and noticed that Li hadn't taken her hand off his face. Instead, she moved it down to his chest, ran it across his abdomen and down, then lower.

She moved in to kiss him. He kissed her back. Her lips were cool, and her tongue was warm. Their tongues danced their own private ballet. He gently caressed the back of her head with his hand. Her hair was soft and smooth.

She whispered, "Lie back."

He did as commanded.

She got on top of him and unbuttoned her shirt, but left it on, teasing him with her breasts beneath it. She was wearing a skimpy, lacy; something Widow wasn't expecting under the by-the-book uniform code of the US Secret Service. He found it tantalizing. Behind the lace, her breasts were magnificent.

She said, "I want you, Widow."

Widow stayed quiet because there was nothing to say with words but a lot to say with actions. He took her and pulled her in and kissed her more. Soft at first and then harder. Passionately.

He rolled her over, underneath him.

Li whispered into his ear, "Take my skirt off."

He reached down and slid it off. She reached out with her hands and fumbled with his belt and then the button and the zipper on his pants.

Widow sat back up and stood up off the bed, took his pants off, and threw them on top of her skirt on the floor. Then she jumped up on her knees and grabbed the hem of his shirt. She pulled the shirt up over his head as far as she could reach, and he did the rest.

She kissed his chest, and then his abs.

He pulled her shirt off completely, unhooked the skimpy bra, and stared at her for a long second.

Li said, "What? You don't like what you see?"

Widow stayed quiet and just stared.

"Widow? What?"

He spoke with a slight lump in his throat. He said, "Earlier, I saw your behind and thought it was the best ass I'd ever seen. Gotta be your best feature."

"And? What?"

"Now, I think I was wrong. Your front side is just as good as your backside."

She smiled and clawed at him and said, "Come here."

Widow obeyed.

He never made it back to his own hotel.

23

WIDOW WOKE up early that morning, groggy. He was in an unfamiliar bed. He rolled over and saw the most beautiful woman he'd seen in a long time. It took a while for his brain to register her identity.

Li slept like a baby. She looked comfortable; one leg bent at the knee and a smile on her face. He wondered what the hell she was dreaming about.

Widow slid out of bed as quietly as he could. He went to the bathroom mirror and sink, turned on the water to cold, and doused his face with it. Then he went back into the room to find his cargo pants. They were bunched up on the floor with Li's clothes. After sifting through his pockets to locate a foldable toothbrush he'd picked up in the airport, he took it to the bathroom and used some of Li's toothpaste to brush his teeth. He didn't run the water until he needed it.

Afterward, he went to the kitchen and searched for the one thing he had to have—coffee. He couldn't find any—not even a coffee pot or a coffee machine. He frowned. Now he knew Li's flaw. She wasn't a coffee drinker. She was not the perfect woman he had thought her to be only five minutes earlier.

He got dressed and left the apartment, locking the bottom lock behind him, then walked through the lobby and left the building in search of the drug that fed his addiction. He went to the street and looked around. There were no coffee shops, but he saw a little diner across the street at a diagonal from where he stood. It was next to a bank and an office building shrouded in black glass.

Widow smiled and went in. He figured that by the time he got a coffee to go and returned to her apartment, she would be awake. If not, he could wait in the lobby for her.

He ordered a black coffee, paid for it, and returned to Li's building. It was eight-fifteen, and he figured that if she wasn't awake by now, she would be awake soon enough. Otherwise, missing the test for Secret Service Special Agent was the least of the reasons she wouldn't make the cut.

Widow knew little about the secretive organization other than it protected the president, and it investigated financial crimes.

In the lobby, there was an empty counter that must be used as a post for a receptionist or doorman. Off to the east, a set of matching furniture was set up like a living room, with a TV mounted on the wall, playing a twenty-four-hour news channel, muted. The sofas were gray and modern looking, and they had a matching coffee table with gray legs, gray trim, and a glass top. Flowers were arranged in a vase on top of the table, and old coffee cup rings were visible in two places.

Widow glanced at the television and saw a beautiful blonde pundit who didn't quite fit the traditional anchor description. As she spoke on mute, the headline at the bottom of the screen announced, "Assassination by Son!" Widow wondered what they were talking about, but didn't bother to unmute the TV. Next, he saw a digital map of Africa appear on-screen. It zoomed in on a small country on the north end of the Gulf of Guinea.

Widow's initial observation was that it was a little unusual for African events to make the news. It was simply a reality that African politics and events weren't covered by American media. Not in fair comparison to other parts of the world. Not that he had anything against Africa, but he wondered why this story was being given so much coverage on an American news channel.

And then he realized why. It was because the assassination had been recorded on live TV.

The twenty-four-hour news channel first ran a warning label. All in red. It said, "Images are graphic and disturbing." After, they ran a clip on-air that showed a politician Widow didn't recognize. The man was onstage speaking in front of a crowd that seemed ecstatic he was speaking to them. It was like he was their religious leader or something. And then the man turned to a younger man walking up behind him onstage. They looked similar—maybe family. The second man raised what looked like an M1911 and aimed it at the politician. The M1911 was a serious handgun in Widow's opinion—serious, but everyone knew about it. Therefore, seeing one wasn't anything new. Normal people wouldn't react to an M1911 they saw on TV the same way that they might react to say a Smith and Wesson Model 686 Competitor, which was a gigantic, menacing thing that held six or seven rounds and fired .357 Magnum cartridges.

Next, there were multiple muzzle flashes, and that familiar red mist burst out from the first man's chest. On the screen, some areas around his chest were purposely pixilated by the news channel to blur out the gore.

The whole thing made him think about the Secret Service. Perhaps that was the reason Li had said they were on high alert. He imagined that any assassination on the planet, no matter how far away, was a reason to elevate the Secret Service's alertness. Related or not, it made sense.

Widow looked over to the corner of the room. There was a little nook with a computer available for use. He went over to it and placed his coffee down and hit some keys, figuring he could kill some time by looking at the Secret Service website.

He waited while the computer came out of sleep and then opened the internet browser, searched for the website, and read over it. What Widow had found was a very bland website compared to what he imagined it would be.

He looked over the information about the history of the Service and how it had come into play. He read that it was created in 1865 and assumed it was because of Lincoln's assassination. But the dates didn't match up in his mind. They seemed too far apart. The creation of a protection agency should've been reactionary and immediate. Lincoln had died in April, but the creation of the Secret Service was in July 1865. Three months later. Why wait so long? He Googled Lincoln and read that Lincoln literally had the legislation that would create the Secret Service on his desk as he was watching his final live event.

He read more about how the original conception of the organization was to protect the American currency, which explained the evolution of the financial crimes side of the Secret Service. Originally, the purpose of the agency was to investigate counterfeiting. After the Civil War, counterfeiting became a real concern for the federal government. The Secret Service's responsibilities were expanded to include hunting down people who perpetrated frauds against the federal government. This alteration of the agency led to investigations into everything from the Ku Klux Klan to smugglers to even false claims of land deeds. They were out to get anyone and everyone who defrauded the federal government.

Widow moved through the site, learning about as much information as was available. His drive to learn about the Secret Service was because of Li, and he wouldn't deny that. She was something new to him. It was different in a way that he couldn't quite put his finger on. Perhaps it was a taste of the normal life, and he wasn't used to that.

He clicked on a link that led him to read about the exam that Li had been supposed to take. Nothing very interesting there. Then he clicked on requirements to be a special agent. The age requirement was twenty-one. Must have great vision. Must be able to pass the exams. Applicants had to pass a background check, and they had to obtain and keep a top security clearance. All things that Widow would've expected to find.

Suddenly, he felt a small hand on his right shoulder, and Li's voice said, "What're you doing? Playing video games?"

Widow turned and found her staring at him with a big smile on her face, which made him smile.

"I was checking out your website."

"My website? I don't think they allow those kinds of sites to be visible down here in the lobby. This is a family-friendly complex."

For a moment, the tiniest fraction of a moment, what Widow would call a hair of a moment. His reptilian brain believed her. He didn't feel guilty about it. He wasn't ashamed of it. He had seen her in less than nothing, and she would've made a fortune on the internet.

Involuntarily, he thought, *Lucky me*.

"I was just learning about your agency."

She wrapped her arms around his neck and hugged him like they were longtime lovers. "Learn anything interesting?" she asked.

"Not really. Just that Lincoln had the paperwork for the Secret Service on his desk the night he was killed."

Li said, "Actually, he signed it that very afternoon."

Widow said, "Really?"

"That's the way the story goes. Lincoln had received the papers creating the agency that day, signed them, and then went to his death."

Widow said, "Talk about a day late and a dollar short."

"Yeah," she said and let go of him.

Widow asked, "Something wrong?"

"No. Just heard that one before. It's common. People—civilians, I mean—always make Lincoln jokes. Or Kennedy ones."

"No McKinley jokes?"

"What?"

"William McKinley. He was the twenty-fifth president and was shot in 1901 by an anarchist named Leon Czolgosz."

"Leon who?"

"Czolgosz."

"How the hell did you know that? Are you really that smart?"

Widow stood up from the chair and looked down at her. He said, "Of course."

She paused.

Then he let out a huge smile and said, "I just read it online. Don't even know if I'm saying the guy's name right."

Li said, "Well. You're wrong anyway. Czolguxman—or whatever—didn't kill McKinley."

"That's what I read."

"It wasn't him. McKinley died later from gangrene. It poisoned his blood. That's how he died. Not the gunshots."

Widow said, "Now who's the smart one?"

And he kissed her.

At that perfect moment, her phone rang from her inside jacket pocket. She withdrew from him and reached in and pulled it out.

The phone's screen read Sean Cord.

She answered. Widow couldn't hear the other end of the line, but it was a short conversation. There was a lot of Li agreeing.

She clicked off and said, "We gotta go. Sean has a busy day and said I need to bring you to meet him. He's out on a job."

Widow followed Li out to her car, and they got in.

He said, "Where to?"

"Springfield."

"In Virginia?"

"Yeah. You been there?"

"No."

"It's about an hour away."

Widow sat back in the seat and waited for Li to fire up the car.

She didn't. Instead, she cleared her throat.

He stared at her. She was making a seatbelt gesture.

"Right. Sorry," he said, feeling stupid that he kept forgetting because his mom used to make him do it. Same thing. She wouldn't move the car until he had his belt buckled.

24

LI DROVE Interstate 395 for about forty-five minutes and then took the exit and wound around an interstate cloverleaf until they were driving through downtown Springfield. They drove for another twenty minutes, leaving the small town center and strip malls. They wove through a residential area and then back onto another road lined with more strip malls and a single community college whose campus was as huge as a Navy base.

Li turned into one of the strip malls. The parking lot was relatively empty.

She pulled the car in front of a quaint, small-town café called Mason's Tea & Coffee House.

Widow wasn't sure if it was owned by a person named Mason or if it was owned by the actual masons. Neither would've surprised him because the place had a very masonic feel to it. White building. Marble and stone everywhere. Engravings on the walls, possibly religious. There were thin white pillars out in front of black windows. The place was like a slice of DC outside of the city.

Maybe it was a tourist gimmick—a guy gets off a plane, heads to his motel, which is probably a Comfort Inn or a Holiday Inn or one of those chains, stumbles upon the masonic-looking café and stops in. At least that was how Widow pictured it in his mind.

The weather outside was warm, early September weather. The sky was clear and blue. The sun beat down, but the temperature was probably a balmy seventy degrees.

Off to the back corner of the building, Widow could see the front end of a black Chevy Tahoe. Tinted black windows. Typical Secret Service vehicle. Widow imagined there were red and blue siren lights embedded in the front grille.

He figured it belonged to Sean Cord.

Li said, "Here we go."

The patio had five tables with big green umbrellas. It was relatively dead. A good-looking woman was sitting with a guy who looked fit. Both were young and had a college-kid look about them. No backpacks or anything. But the guy wore a polo shirt with the collar turned up, like in the old vampire movies. This was a stupid fashion that Widow had seen on frat boys before. But he wasn't judging—to each his own. And Widow liked pluralism. It made America great. He enjoyed walking down a street in Los Angeles or San Francisco or Miami or some other American port and hearing different languages. He liked places that had both a Little Italy and a Chinatown.

But these two were an odd couple in the sense that they didn't belong together in terms of fashion. The guy was obviously a frat boy type, but no way was the girl a part of that crowd. No sorority in her life. She had pink hair, one side completely shaved down to stubble just above her ear. She wore all black. Black top, tight and low-cut. Black skirt. Black boots with silver chains linked down the sides like some kind of fashion statement.

Widow would've guessed that they had sat together by mistake and maybe were strangers, but they were holding hands, and then they kissed.

On the opposite side of the couple, at the far corner of the patio, was a man in a black suit. He looked Secret Service all the way. Black shoes. Black coat. Black pants. No tie. The small clear earpiece in his ear had a curly cord disappearing beneath his shirt. And, of course, he wore dark sunglasses. He looked like agents did in the movies, only more real life and with an ordinary height and weight. He was older than fifty, but not by much. He could probably be mid-fifties.

He had black hair that receded a little from his part on the right temple of his head. Widow wondered what the age limit was for entering the Secret Service. Whatever it was to enter, this guy was way past, but maybe he had been in all his adult life.

Widow said, "That must be Cord?"

Li turned the wheel, and the tires jerked the car up over a speed bump near the entrance to the parking lot.

She said, "That's him."

"I don't see any other agents. He's alone."

"Yeah."

Widow said, "I thought you said he was on duty."

"He is," Li said.

"Where're the rest of the agents?"

"He's alone."

"Solo?"

"Yep."

Widow said, "Since when does the Service assign solo agents?"

"Ask him. I'm sure he'll tell you. But I'd better not say anything."

Widow stayed quiet, and they parked the car near the back.

Li shut off the engine, and they got out. She left the doors unlocked.

They walked from the back around the side of the café. Widow let Li walk out in front, not because he was letting her lead him, but because he wanted to be behind her. To Widow, the view was far better from behind. He liked it a lot. If he were in front of her, he wouldn't be able to see her at all.

One of the problems with the nomadic life was that it left him free but alone. In Widow's mind, there was no future Mrs. Widow. There was no white picket fence and no car in the driveway because there would never be a driveway.

They walked on and turned the corner to the front. Li led him past the young couple and around the entrance to the café and between the large white pillars.

Cord stood up when he saw them.

He said, "Widow? I hope your trip up was ok?"

Cord spoke with a warmer voice than what Widow had expected from a Secret Service agent that he had never met before.

Widow said, "It was ok. Better than Miami jail."

Li introduced them.

"Agent Cord, this is Widow. Widow, this is Agent Sean Cord."

Cord held his hand out to Widow to shake. Widow accepted it and shook it.

Cord said, "Please, sit down."

Widow nodded and took a chair across from him at the table, and Li remained standing.

"I'm sorry to drag you all the way out here, but we need your help."

Widow said, "I'm here. Let's get to it."

Cord said, "Ok. No reason to linger. Let's go."

"Ok. Great. Thank you."

Cord got up and pulled out his wallet, a black leather thing that looked as if it had seen better days. He rifled through it and pulled out a ten-dollar bill and left it under an empty coffee mug on the patio table. He said, "You can follow me. Ride with Li."

"Ok," said Li.

And they walked back to their cars and got in them and drove away.

25

CORD DROVE THE SPEED LIMIT. Not that he was worried about the police stopping him, but because he didn't want any attention. Li stayed four car lengths behind and used her turn signals just as Cord did.

Widow stared ahead and stayed quiet.

Li said, "I really have no idea what this is about."

Widow said, "I know."

"I just didn't want you to think I was keeping something from you."

"I know. You were ripped from your test yesterday. I believe you."

Li said, "Good. Because I don't want you to think I was lying to you. I..."

She stopped talking, and Widow turned his head and said, "What?"

"Nothing."

"What is it?"

"I like you. I really wouldn't lie to a guy that I liked right from the beginning."

Widow said, "Beginning of what?"

"You know. The beginning of whatever this is. For us."

Widow stayed quiet because it wasn't the time to talk about it.

"What, you don't think there's an *us*?"

"I haven't had time to process it," Widow lied.

"You're right. It's only been one day. Not even. Not really. It's been what, like twenty hours?"

Widow thought fourteen hours and twenty-seven minutes, but he didn't say it out loud.

They stayed quiet and drove.

Cord led them onto I-495. The early morning sun shot waves of sunbeams across the sky. They drove on for another thirty-five minutes.

26

CORD TOUCHED the navigation screen embedded in his SUV's dashboard and waited for the female computer voice to speak.

It said, "Hey there, Agent Cord."

Cord said, "Redial last call."

The voice said, "Redialing."

Cord's iPhone was synced to his dashboard, and the female voice that operated it paused a beat and redialed the phone.

He looked in his rearview mirror and watched as Li and Widow followed.

A voice answered on the other end of the line and said, "Did you get him?"

The voice was male, older, and had a deep echo of desperation in it.

Cord said, "I got him. He's following me now."

The voice asked, "Good. Does he know why he's here?"

"No. Of course not."

"Did you mention my name?"

"No. You asked me not to."

"That's right. Good. Thank you, Cord."

"Of course, sir."

The voice asked, "Do you think he'll help us?"

"I don't know. Maybe. We'll be there in twenty minutes, and you can ask him yourself."

The desperation almost overwhelming, the voice said, "I hope so."

And then the person on the other end hung up.

27

AFTER ANOTHER TWENTY MINUTES, they followed Cord as he turned off the freeway and down a string of roads and into a rich-looking subdivision.

Big Victorian houses were perfectly threaded along the streets. Widow saw high roofs and red brick and big windows. Some houses had tall walls surrounding the properties.

They followed Cord past a gate that looked more like a military base checkpoint than a gate to a residential community.

Li said, "This is where some of DC's most elite politicians live."

Widow looked around. "Looks expensive. Who else could afford to live here?"

"Staffers live here, too."

"They make enough to live here?"

Li said, "You'd be surprised what they make. Especially senior staff for the upper politicians. And I think the speaker of the house's chief of staff lives here."

Widow nodded and asked, "Where're we goin'?"

Li said, "I don't know."

They trailed close behind Cord as he stopped at intersections and looked both ways and then headed either straight or left or right.

And he did all three, each time following the rules of the road to the letter. Widow couldn't recall the last time he'd witnessed someone so strict about their driving. This guy stopped completely at each stop sign before he continued. And not in how most drivers stopped. Even the safest drivers on the road weren't this by-the-book. He couldn't imagine this guy deviating far from the rules. A side effect of working for the Secret Service, he supposed.

Li said, "Looks like we're going to that house at the end."

"Looks like it has Secret Service detail guarding it."

Li nodded.

"Why? Who lives there?"

"I don't know."

The house at the end of the street was red brick with white shutters and white-trimmed portholes placed throughout. The house was two stories and set far back on the property, with a bricked-in privacy fence around the yard. No pool. There were two cars in the driveway and two Secret Service SUVs on the street in front, just like the one Cord drove.

He pulled alongside one and waved at a guy who stood at the top of the driveway. Then he pulled up and parked across the street, far from the parked SUVs.

Next door, Widow saw two Secret Service agents standing post outside the neighbor's house. They remained still. Good posture. They gave off the impression that they didn't move. No matter what.

Li said, "Someone important lives there too. I guess. Must be a Congressman or something."

Li pulled out past Cord's SUV and parked in front of it.

She killed the engine and said, "That's odd."

Widow said, "What?"

"The agent Cord waved at. I don't recognize him."

Widow looked at him. He was old—older than Cord. Much older. The guy looked like he should be retired, not a working agent. He looked sixty plus, at least. But he was dressed in Secret Service getup.

Black suit. No tie. There was an earpiece in his ear, and a SIG Sauer fitted into a pancake holster on the side of his belt.

Widow said, "He looks old to be an operational agent."

"I don't know if he's too old. But he's a bit out of shape. Maybe he just lived a rough life. Maybe drinks too much. That can age you, you know?"

Widow nodded.

Cord waved at them to follow.

Widow opened his door and pulled himself out. He shut the door behind him and followed Li to the house.

Cord stopped and shook hands with the older guy.

The guy was bald with a gray beard. He was taller than Cord, probably six foot three. He was shorter than Widow, but weighed more. Maybe two-fifty or two-sixty. He had some muscle left in his forearms and biceps. Widow figured that when he was younger, he was probably no stranger to the gym. Maybe he would've been a bodybuilder in his prime.

Cord said, "This is Jack Widow."

The older guy reached out his hand and said, "Jim Lucas. Retired."

"Secret Service?"

"Yes."

Widow took his hand and shook it. The guy still had a powerful grip.

Cord asked, "Are the others inside?"

"They're here."

Cord led Widow and Li through the neatly trimmed yard and shrubs to an entrance with a black door. The paint was glossy and streamed perfectly to where Widow couldn't tell one brush stroke from the next. He thought it had most likely been hand-painted.

Lucas then led them into a small foyer with a high ceiling. Everything was painted white, even the frame around a full-length mirror on the opposite wall. White walls. White ceilings. White beams. White everything.

Widow looked past the front staircase and straight down a long hall that cornered and turned off out of sight. Beyond that, the house opened into an open floor plan with a second staircase. Lucas, Cord, and Li walked in front of him and led him down the hall, around the corner, and into the living room.

Sitting on a gray couch was a woman who was about forty years old. She had a black dress on. Nothing fancy. And not like a funeral dress. It was just work attire and made it seem to Widow like she did something important and wasn't just a housewife. He assumed she was the lady of the house. Maybe her job was being a politician's wife. As Li had said, this neighborhood was the home of politicians and staffers—DC's regulars and America's elite.

Widow walked up to the edge of a sofa and stood at attention like she was the wife of an admiral, not an official commanding officer, but not treated any differently.

The woman was attractive in that kind of political figures or first ladies or royalty way. She clearly had access to fashion consultants, either that or she had impeccable taste. The dress she wore might even have been made exclusively for her because when she stood up, it fit her like an extra layer of skin. To say it was form-fitting would be an understatement. Not that she was an example of a woman who put in serious gym time, but she was a woman who looked after herself. Maybe it was expected. If she was a politician's wife, she would have to be on camera from time to time.

Widow imagined how difficult it must be to always be camera-ready.

She was a beautiful woman. Widow had noticed that fact, but her looks and how she carried herself took a distant second to one glaring fact—she had been crying, and she had been doing it a lot.

The skin underneath her eyes and above her nose was caked in dried eyeliner. It ran down her face like war paint. She looked like she had been captured and tortured by the enemy, and there was no escape. No future.

Widow smiled at her, ignoring the smeared, runny makeup.

"Good morning, ma'am."

A third man stepped into the living room from out of the kitchen. He was close in age to Lucas. He wore black-rimmed glasses. They had thick lenses. The guy must've been close to being legally blind— maybe not right at the door but seriously in the neighborhood. He wore no jacket but sported a blue button-down shirt with a red tie and khakis. He had no gun holstered in his belt like Cord and Lucas had, but something about his pose made Widow believe he was one of them. He carried himself like someone in law enforcement.

Lucas said, "Karen, this is Jack Widow and Kelly Li."

The woman rose from the couch, and a look of relief came across her face like a doctor had just come to tell her that her husband had survived a high-risk surgery.

Widow said, "It's nice to meet you, ma'am."

She nodded, but said nothing. Her eyes stared at him. Desperation was the only thing he saw on her face.

Lucas said, "Widow, this is Detective Douglas Graine. He's one of us. One of the *Navy* us. Not the Secret Service *us*."

Widow stuck a hand out to shake.

"Nice to meet you."

Graine's prescription glasses must've helped him see because he looked in Widow's direction. But he didn't shake Widow's hand. Maybe he didn't notice it.

Widow wondered how blind the guy was without the glasses. The other two agents carried sidearms—even Lucas, who must've been retired. But Graine didn't have one. Widow suspected a big part of the reason for that was his bad eyesight.

Li asked, "So, what's this all about? Why's Widow here?"

Cord looked at Widow.

"Karen's married."

Widow nodded.

"Her husband's a man named Gibson Rowley."

Cord stared at Widow like he was looking for a reaction.

Widow stared back, blankly.

"Do you recognize the name?"

Widow thought for a moment. He knew the name, but it was far back in the memory banks. He couldn't quite pull up the face.

He shook his head slowly.

"No. Can't say I do. Should I? Is he a Senator or something?"

Li cocked her head for a fraction of a second. She recognized the name.

"Director Rowley? This is the Director's house?"

Cord nodded.

He said, "Widow, you don't know the name?"

"No. Can't say I do. Who keeps up with the names of top Secret Service agents other than Secret Service agents?"

Cord didn't respond to that.

Karen swiveled her head and looked at from face to face like she was only just first noticing all of them for the first time. She swiveled her head upward, and her gaze stopped on Widow. She stepped forward, away from the couch, and over to Widow. She stopped right in front of him, close enough to reach up and kiss him.

She stared up into his eyes. Her purplish lips quivered like she wanted to say something, but couldn't speak.

Widow paused and smiled at her. He waited.

The room was silent. No one spoke.

Li was the only one who looked confused.

Karen Rowley said, "Please. Please help us."

Widow reached his hands out, palms up, lovingly like he was greeting a widow at a funeral.

Karen Rowley slipped her hands over his. He embraced them warmly.

He said, "Ma'am, I'll do whatever I can."

"Promise me?"

"I promise."

Graine was the first to interrupt.

He said, "Better show him."

Lucas nodded and said, "Come with me."

Cord said, "I'm going to call Gibson. Be right behind you."

Lucas nodded.

"Follow me, Mr. Widow."

Widow followed Lucas. They climbed a staircase, first one flight, and then the next.

As he walked, he heard the wooden floorboards creak under his weight.

At the top of the stairs, Lucas turned right and headed down a carpeted hall. They walked past an open doorway. Widow glanced in and saw a bathroom. It was immaculate. Spotless. No scuffs on the tile. No trace of lint on the rug. The toilet seat was down and wrapped in one of those fluffy lid covers. It was blue and matched the rug and the shower curtain—not even the slightest shade of difference in any of them. They must've come in a set.

Widow stopped at the doorway, and looked in the bathroom, looked for toothbrushes. There was only one. It was a girlie pink color. This wasn't a shared bathroom, but it was in the hallway. Must've been used by a girl. The Rowleys probably had a daughter.

Lucas led Widow into a teenage girl's bedroom. There were surfing posters on the walls and posters of young guys on the beach with shirts off. But none of it was sexual, not like the rock star and celebrity posters marketed toward teenage girls. These posters were of real surfers. The Rowleys' daughter was into surfing. That was clear not only from the posters but also from a broken surfboard that hung over the perfectly made bed.

The surfboard hung like a keepsake, a reminder.

The board was torn into more than one piece, but the Rowley's daughter had only one large piece on display. It was yellow with twin white stripes down the sides. It looked like it had survived a violent encounter with a shark.

Widow studied the rest of the room and saw a table lamp that shined a dim light over a computer desk. There was a closed laptop on it with stickers that looked like more surfer stuff covering the casing, like surf company logos and such.

There were pictures littering the walls—pictures of teenage girls laughing and hanging out, of them making funny faces, and of girls with surfboards on different beaches—ordinary teenage girl stuff.

They were the Rowleys' daughter's friends, Widow guessed.

Widow stayed quiet and touched nothing in the room.

Lucas said, "You know anything about the Rowleys?"

"Cord already asked me if I knew them. I don't. Don't remember the name. Sorry."

"The Rowleys aren't famous unless you live here in DC."

Widow stayed quiet.

Lucas asked, "Did you tell anyone you were coming?"

"Why does everyone keep asking me that?"

"Did you?"

"No."

"That's good."

"I'm going to ask the same question I've been asking. What the hell's going on? Why am I here?"

Lucas turned to the right like an old turret rusty from a long-ago war. Then he swiveled from the hips and grabbed a picture off the desk. It was a six-by-nine-inch frame with bright blue edges. The picture inside showed two people in the foreground and a small crowd of people far in the background. It was another beach setting. Lucas reached out his arm; a gold watch was turned upside down on his right wrist, not the left. He handed the picture to Widow.

"Look at it."

Widow took it from him and examined it. There was writing in permanent marker on the bottom edge of the picture. It looked like an autograph. The two people in the picture's foreground were a man and a girl. The man had what Widow's SEAL buddies picked on him about—a pretty face. He sported a dark tan, like someone who spends all day on the beach. He was bald, lean, and built like an Olympic swimmer. And he looked familiar.

He wore a white shirt and a red ball cap with a logo on it that Widow was familiar with. It was for a surfing company like the stickers on the laptop's shell.

The girl in the picture was another teenager. She was in all the photos. She was probably fourteenish. She had shoulder-length blond hair and a serious tan. Her sun-bleached hair was damp, as if she had just been swimming. There was a huge smile on her face. She glowed like she was thrilled. Her features were young and familiar.

Widow felt like he had just seen her ten minutes ago. It was because she looked just like Karen. The girl in the photo had the same regal look about her, but the innocence of youth showed in her face and eyes.

Blue eyes, blond hair, and a tan.

Suddenly, Widow thought that Gibson Rowley must've had a lot of problems with boys coming around for his daughter.

Widow closed his eyes for a moment and imagined Rowley's daughter coming home with her first boyfriend and Gibson Rowley waiting for her with his Secret Service agents all scattered around the entrance and the living room, his department-issued SIG Sauer resting on a table in plain sight of the suitor.

He smiled.

Widow opened his eyes again and looked at the picture. Directly behind the pair was the same yellow surfboard above the bed behind him. It was broken in the photo. Widow wondered what happened.

Widow looked at the girl in the picture and noticed something else— something he wasn't expecting. Her right hand was missing.

Widow read the autograph on the bottom of the picture.

"To Raggie. Keep On! Love, Kelly Slater."

That's when he knew how he knew the guy. It was Kelly Slater, a famous world champion surfer. Of course he knew who Slater was.

Lucas interrupted Widow.

"That's Raggie and some famous surfer guy. One of her heroes. World Champion Surfer. Raggie's a surfer, too. She's pretty good."

"It's Kelly Slater. He's won eleven world surfing championships. He's unbelievably good at it."

"You surf?"

"Sometimes."

Lucas choked up for an instant. It was a choked-up feeling that only happened once or twice in the life of a hardened Secret Service agent, and it happened to Lucas at that moment. But he never lost composure. He never lost his cool.

He said, "Raggie is Gibson and Karen's daughter."

Widow heard footsteps down the hall and on the stairs. They weren't Li's. She was too tiny to make loud, audible steps like that. These were too heavy. Probably Cord or Graine, but Widow wasn't sure if Graine could find his way up the stairs with those Coke-bottle glasses. He figured it had to be Cord. And then he heard another set of footfalls on the stairs. They were lighter and probably belonged to Li.

Widow asked, "How good is she at surfing?"

"Damn good. We three used to go watch her. I've seen her surf all over the world. I saw her in Australia, California, and South Africa."

He paused and then said, "We've all seen her."

"So, what, where is she?"

Lucas said nothing.

Widow asked, "What's happened to her?"

Cord reached the room, with Li behind him. He answered for Lucas.

"Someone kidnapped her."

28

WIDOW STARED at Raggie's picture again. She looked like an ordinary teenage girl with a bright future in front of her.

Widow could feel the love in the house, in her room. It was normally a warm, loving home, only, now, Raggie was gone.

Kidnapped was the word Cord had used.

A phone rang somewhere in the house, tightening the silence between them as they waited for someone to answer it. The phone was somewhere out past Raggie's bathroom and down the hall and down the stairs. The sound bounced off the walls and carried throughout the house, coming into existence like a screaming newborn. First, it wasn't there, and then it was.

It rang twice before it was picked it up. Widow doubted it was Karen Rowley who had answered, since the information he had just received let him know exactly why she looked as though she had been crying, and explained why she hadn't cleaned her face. Most likely, every time she washed the eyeliner off and reapplied it, she started crying again, causing more streaking makeup. Why continue to clean it?

Widow asked, "Where's the FBI?"

Cord said, "We haven't told them."

"What? This is their deal! The FBI should've been your first phone call!"

Widow felt himself getting heated.

Cord threw his hands up and nodded. He looked at Lucas, whose hands were clamped together under his extended gut, fingers interlocked. Some kind of bodyguard stance, Widow figured, and from the looks of Lucas, he'd had a lot of assignments standing sentry duty in his career.

Lucas said nothing.

Li asked, "Why haven't we called the FBI yet?"

Widow stared at Cord and pointed a finger at him.

He said, "Because there's more to it. Something they're not telling me. Something involving me?"

Cord nodded.

"What the hell is it?"

Cord said, "You're right. Follow me. Rowley's going to call us. He'll explain."

He stepped back and turned and led Widow and Li back down the hall. They turned a wide corner and stepped onto a landing with a bedroom entrance. The door was open.

The room was large. It was the master suite. Widow looked around. The ceilings in the space were higher than those on the rest of the floor, almost twice the height. Everything in the room was clean and polished and gleaming. The furniture was eclectic, with a heavy emphasis on dark wood. A full-length mirror stood framed on the wall next to another doorway, which Widow thought probably led to the master bath.

Cord waited at the door for the others to enter and then closed it.

He said, "I don't want Karen to hear this. She's really going through it now."

Widow stayed quiet.

Li waited, her eyes locked on her boss. There was disappointment and anger in them. She was upset that he didn't tell her beforehand, that he didn't trust her. But mostly, that a girl was taken, and they were playing detective without calling the FBI.

She tasted the anger in her mouth, but she kept quiet.

Cord took out his smartphone and pushed a little button at the bottom. A small kickstand whipped out, and he set the phone down on the dresser.

He said, "Open Skype."

The phone responded in a generic female voice and opened a blue application called Skype.

Li, Cord, and Lucas faced the phone screen and watched as the application came up.

Cord said, "Call Gibson."

The phone made a notification sound, and Widow waited.

The Skype application rang for a moment, and then the screen showed a face.

That's when Widow's jaw dropped. Only for a moment. He hadn't fully recognized the name, but he knew the face. Now he remembered the name.

It was Gibson Rowley, Director of the United States Secret Service, but Widow knew him long before that as Commanding Master Chief Rowley.

Suddenly, Widow thought back fifteen years when he was a brand-new Navy SEAL. In one of his early missions, Rowley was in charge. He wasn't involved in the ground mission, but he was the one who gave the briefing and commanded the mission from a battle carrier.

Gibson Rowley was the same age as Cord, but looked younger. He had gray hair and a darkening five o'clock shadow. But it was him. The same face that Widow worked for only that one time, fifteen years ago.

Behind Rowley was nothing but light blue metal walls. He sat at a foldable table in a chair. There was a phone on the tabletop. It was a tight space.

On the wall behind Rowley was the US Presidential Seal. And nothing else.

It took Widow a second to realize Rowley was inside a SCIF, a Sensitive Compartmented Information Facility. It's what top government officials used to communicate classified information in order to keep outsiders from eavesdropping. SCIFs are impenetrable to hacking and listening devices.

They look like the inside of a bank vault.

Rowley said, "Sean."

"I'm here with Jack Widow and Kelly Li."

"I know. I recognize him. Hello, Widow. It's been a long time."

Widow said, "Sir."

Rowley was dressed professionally, as guided by the United States Secret Service Uniformed Division. But he changed that right then because he reached up and unclipped his tie and undid the top button on his shirt. He set the tie down off-camera and looked up at Cord and Widow on-screen.

He said, "Cord, I need to ask you to step out of the room. Widow and I need to talk."

Cord was surprised, but he nodded and turned to leave.

Rowley said, "Take Li with you."

Li already knew that would happen, and she stepped first to the door. They both stepped out and shut the door behind them.

Widow said, "They're gone. What's going on, Master Chief?"

"It's been a long time, Widow. Twenty years, maybe?"

"Fifteen, I think."

Rowley nodded and said, "I want to tell you I'm sorry to put you in this position. Sorry to call on you like this."

Widow stayed quiet.

Rowley said, "You know about my daughter?"

"Only that she was taken."

Rowley's face changed. His demeanor changed. A single tear leaked out of the corner of his eye and streamed down his face.

He said, "You have to get her back for me, Widow!"

"I'll help. Of course, I will. But why me, sir?"

Rowley wiped the tear from his face.

He said, "I know about you."

"How's that?"

"I know about Unit Ten."

Widow said nothing.

"I know that fifteen years ago, you worked undercover for NCIS and Unit Ten. I know you were a SEAL, but not really."

Widow said, "It felt real."

"I don't mean disrespect. I'm saying that for you it wasn't the same. Those guys were in all the way. But you could leave whenever you wanted. You weren't really enlisted. Your orders were fake. You walked like a SEAL, but you weren't. You were an undercover cop. Right?"

"You know I can't confirm or deny that."

Rowley smiled and said, "A true agent until the end."

"Why am I here, sir?"

"To get my daughter back."

"But why me?"

"Because we have a common enemy. Someone from the past."

"So, you have an idea who did it?"

"I know exactly who."

Widow stared at the phone screen.

Rowley said, "John Lane."

Widow's mouth dropped.

"John Lane? I thought he was dead by now."

Rowley paused a beat, and then he spoke.

"Let me tell the story like you weren't there. To refresh your memory."

Widow remembered it, but there were gaps. So, he said nothing.

Rowley said, "I needed to read the files to refresh mine. I haven't thought of John Lane in years. Honestly."

Widow nodded along.

"Fifteen years ago, I was in the United States Navy, as you know. Special Ops. I commanded special operations in Africa. And one mission was bad. It went real bad. A top-secret mission that you took part in.

"We were supporting a CIA op. Or rather, they were supporting us because we were doing all the dirty work. We were there to help the rebels eliminate a target named Julian Sowe. He was the president of a little country called West Ganbola. A real son of a bitch. This guy would spend the country's tiny budget on weapons from Iraq and Syria. He tested them on his own people. He gassed hundreds of people once just for the hell of it. Not to mention, he wasn't a friend of the United States.

"We were asked to help get the rebels into a small town called Sane, which is basically just a way station between one slightly bigger town and another. Locals would use the river to travel because the jungles around that region are impenetrable. We had intel that Sowe and a small force of men were traveling by river, so we choppered in at night and met a small band of rebels outside the town—including their leader, a guy named Chang, who wasn't a very nice guy, either, but enemy of my enemy and all."

Widow closed his eyes and pulled up the memory in his mind. He could still hear the jungle noises and helicopter blades from their entrance into the area.

Rowley said, "We were supposed to set up and wait for Sowe and his men. A simple ambush. Chang wanted to kill Sowe himself. It was a symbolic gesture to show his men he meant business, I guess. I don't know. I didn't think of him as some sort of revolutionary. He was just one bad guy trying to overthrow a worse one. I don't go for that sort of thing, but it was our job.

"Anyway, when we got there, we were the ones who were ambushed."

Rowley paused a quick beat and said, "Chang's men turned on him. Not all of them, but most. They shot the others, and a firefight broke out. As you may or may not know, in situations like that—situations where the mission was already over, and we weren't supposed to be there—my priority as the CO was to get my men out alive. But if I thought there was a good chance to save the mission or our allies, I took it.

"We were outgunned and outnumbered bigtime. The local army came out of nowhere—hundreds of them. They were stationed in the town, hiding for hours. We ended up cornered in a structure that was basically a two-story hut."

Widow could still see the hut in his mind.

Rowley took a deep breath. He inhaled and exhaled. He reached up and scratched the stubble on his face.

Widow saw his wedding band, gold with an engraving he couldn't make out in that split second.

Rowley said, "The guys outside had us by the balls, but we had enough bullets to kill a lot of them. Soon the firefight stopped, and we were all still standing. Chang, too. It ended up just being him and us.

"There were six guys in your unit. Four of them I'd known for years, but two of them I'd only known for six months. You and another guy. He was a Petty Officer 3rd Class. When he joined my unit, he seemed okay—at first. But there was something about him. Something unsavory. I couldn't quite put my finger on it, but it was there."

Widow remembered. It was one of his first assignments from both the SEALs and NCIS. He had been sent to watch Lane, to investigate him for past crimes he had gotten away with. But he didn't tell Rowley.

Rowley continued, "The rest of the guys I knew. Just you and this other guy I didn't know. You remember Petty Officer Third Class John Lane?"

Widow said, "I remember him."

"There we were...stuck in this hut. After a few minutes, the guys outside said something on a bullhorn. They repeated the same shit over and over for twenty minutes. None of us spoke the language—except for Chang, and he wouldn't translate anything for us—so we didn't understand a thing except for the word American.

"I never told you, but I remember being a little scared. Which is something I never admitted to my friends. My wife. No one. Not once. Not in fifteen years. But I was. I was a little scared that we were going to die."

Widow heard a noise on the ledge outside the window. He looked over and saw a small bird pecking at the glass. It was white with brown feathers. He wasn't sure about the species. It pecked again and cocked its head, and then it flew away.

Rowley said, "There was no way out. We were dead men. Jones, remember him? He tried to radio overwatch, but our comms were down. I told him to stay on it, but I knew it was hopeless."

Widow remembered Jones. He remembered all of them.

"Finally, the ranting from outside stopped for a bit, and we wondered what was next. Then a voice spoke in English. The voice said that all they wanted was Chang. They told us if we gave him up, then we'd be free to go. We were never going to give him up, but I wanted to get my men out alive. We all wanted to get out alive. I wanted out alive.

"You," he paused and looked at Widow, "you were the only one of us who stood strong. I mean really. It makes me feel shame to this day what I did. What happened next."

Widow stayed quiet.

Rowley said, "The voice continued to repeat the same deal. After about thirty minutes, a different voice came on, speaking more broken English, but it was the same message. Exactly the same. Like they were reading from a script.

"After an hour passed, the original voice was back again, and we waited—not a peep from any of us. We just sat there, quiet."

Widow thought back. He remembered it being longer than an hour. He remembered it being more like three hours.

"After an hour and maybe forty-five minutes, Lane started insisting that we give Chang up. He said he hadn't come to Africa to die. He said other things, too."

Rowley paused and looked around the room at nothing.

"After a while, he made sense. Remember? And then more sense. We were in a standoff for our lives. Sowe was smart. He could've had his men kill us. They could've blown us up with a couple of grenades, or they could have burned us to death. They could've done either of the two and been done with it. They could've killed us and left us charred and dead. We weren't expected to check in for hours. We were dark, and they knew it because they never tried to enter the building. They just figured they'd out-wait us.

"I started to break. We all did. Except you. You stayed steadfast. Strong, like you weren't afraid at all."

"I was afraid, sir. I was terrified like the rest of you, but I could never agree to what you ordered us to do."

Rowley looked at him with shame on his face.

"I know. I know."

He paused and then continued.

"I wasn't the first to agree with Lane. One of the other guys did first. But by morning, I was on board. We all were."

"No. We weren't. I protested."

"I know. I'm sorry."

"You guys pointed weapons in my face, remember?"

Rowley nodded.

"We took him hostage. But it was worse than that. We handed him over to those butchers. I'll never forget it. I nodded to the other guys, and they pointed their guns at him. Lane even shot him in the leg to disarm him. I didn't authorize it, but he did it, and then we were all committed to the act. What was I supposed to do? Arrest Lane right there and then? And we were just as guilty."

Widow said, "You were guilty. You pointed your weapons at me, too. You took my guns."

Widow remembered. He had stood up to them, but they took his guns and shut him down.

He said, "I don't feel shame because I tried to do the right thing. But I regret. I regret not turning you all in when we returned to the ship. I regret that part."

"Why didn't you turn us over to NCIS?"

Widow paused a beat and recalled the situation in his head.

"I tried to turn you in. But they didn't want to hear about it. Even NCIS is a bureaucratic part of the Navy. They protected themselves and swept it under the rug. Reassigned me to a new SEAL team and a new case."

"That's why you were taken from my team so quickly?"

"That's why. You belonged in prison. You all did. Every one of you should've rotted behind bars for betraying Chang."

"I know. And now we are all getting our just desserts."

"Why do you say that?"

"The other guys on our team. They're all dead except you, me, and Lane."

29

WIDOW SAID, "Tell me the rest. What happened with you and the others after we got back? That part, I don't know."

"When we got back, we told our story."

"You mean, you lied?"

"I did. We all did. Except you, I guess. The brass listened. I don't know what Lane told them. I asked none of you to lie."

"That doesn't make it right."

"I know. It turned out all the guys lied for us."

Widow said, "For you. Not us."

"Whatever. The brass wanted to blame someone, but they were facing two problems. The first was that this was a black op that no one wanted to be made public. Americans didn't want to know that we were involved in secret missions in Nowhere, Africa. We were only invested in the region because we were searching for proof of WMDs being sold throughout the region. And this guy Chang had information."

"He'd only help if we helped him?"

"Right. We scratch his back sorta thing."

"Okay. Continue."

"Anyway, the Navy decided there was nothing they could publicly do to Lane. They broke us up for a bit, and I never saw Lane again."

"But that's not the end of the story, is it?"

"No. I had heard that the CIA wasn't happy about what we had done. I also heard that Lane later went on another mission back into West Ganbola. Back into the jungle."

"What happened?"

Rowley said, "He never came out. He went in on an unofficial, and probably illegal, rescue mission to get Chang back. A kind of penance for giving him up in the first place, I guess. My guys were lucky that the Navy didn't make us a part of it because Lane and his guys never came out again. It turned out it was mostly a CIA affair."

"What happened to Lane?"

"I have no idea, not until he took my daughter. Next thing I knew, he was calling me."

"What did he say? Did he ask for a ransom?"

"Not exactly. He told me he got caught in-country and was sentenced to hard labor for ten years. They put him in a vile and gut-wrenching prison, a real hell on earth. The government there used him as a symbol. Gave him a trial and all, but I forget the official charges.

"The rest of us were separated, sent off to different posts, including you, I guess. All I got was a slap on the wrist."

Widow said, "Until now. Now, you're all dead, except you and Lane."

"And you."

Widow ignored that.

He asked, "How did Lane get ahold of your daughter in the first place?"

Rowley said, "The Secret Service doesn't have protection on our families. Not usually, unless we get a credible threat to their safety. Our job, first and foremost, is to safeguard the president and the vice president, as well as their families."

Suddenly, Rowley's hardened face took a turn, and his eyes watered up again. He tried to speak but couldn't. He put his hand over his face for a second.

He said, "Lane took Raggie. I guess she was meeting with friends. At some café. I've already had Graine check it out. No one saw anything."

"When did he grab her?"

"Last night?" He responded, a little confused.

When I was arrested? Widow wondered.

Rowley corrected himself and said, "I mean two nights ago."

Widow asked, "Do you have proof of life?"

"Lane posted a video on *YouTube*. It has no tags, but there's a video of her. Go check it out yourself."

Rowley paused and looked at his wristwatch.

"I gotta go. Can't be inexplicably missing from my duties for too long. Widow, I need your help. Only you understand what we did, what I did. Lane wants me to do something that I just can't do, and I have little time. Watch the video, and you'll see. I gotta go now."

Rowley clicked off the phone, and the screen went back to Cord's phone's wallpaper, which was the logo of the United States Secret Service.

Widow sat down on the bed and thought for a second.

He muttered to himself.

"What the hell have you gotten yourself into?"

He got up off the bed, picked up Cord's smartphone, and went out into the hall. He heard voices and walked toward them. He passed Raggie's room and stopped and looked in. He looked at the made bed and wondered if she'd ever see it again. He wondered where she was and thought about what she must feel and how scared she must be.

He turned and walked out of her room. He passed the bathroom and followed the voices down the stairs and saw that Karen Rowley was seated back down on the sofa next to Graine, who said little. He merely looked at her and nodded, listening to her stories about her daughter. She clutched a bright green frame that held a picture of Raggie. It was a plastic thing that looked cheap from a distance but, judging by everything else in the house, had probably cost over a hundred dollars.

Widow walked down the stairs and stopped and said, "Cord."

Cord turned from his conversation with Li and walked over to him.

Li followed.

He leaned in and said, "What do you think?"

Widow handed him back his phone.

"Show me the video."

"Of course."

"Did he tell you everything?"

"Not everything. I know about Lane, but I don't know why. He must want something."

"He does. But not money."

Cord turned and looked at Lucas, and nodded at him. Lucas nodded back and gestured for Widow to follow him out of the room again, away from Karen Rowley. She must not know the details, just that her daughter wasn't at home where she belonged.

They walked out of the living room and went past a ground floor bathroom. There was no shower or bathtub, just a toilet, a sink, and a mirror.

Widow followed Li. Cord led them through the kitchen. The tile was white and diamond-shaped. He saw four workstations, an island with two ovens, eight burners, a griddle, a major grill, a salamander, and a black farm sink big enough to make a restaurant proud. This was a major kitchen.

Widow wondered if Karen Rowley cooked in there or if the Rowleys had a housekeeper who doubled as a chef.

They walked past the kitchen to a set of French doors that led out onto a covered patio in a backyard with high privacy fencing.

In the back, Cord looked around and waited for Lucas to follow and shut the door behind him.

Outside, the air was crisp and breezy, but not cold, not really. Widow wore a long-sleeved shirt, and he was glad to have it, but Li had on a business suit and skirt. He imagined her legs froze with every gust of wind. He wanted to reach out and fan his hands across them to warm them, but knew he couldn't do that with her boss watching. Besides, he wasn't sure what the rule was for touching her legs in public. He wasn't sure about her rules or about the etiquette for that sort of thing between boyfriends and girlfriends.

Li didn't complain about the wind. Nor did she ask about his conversation with Rowley. She was a good soldier. If she needed information, then Cord would give it to her—and such was every relationship between infantry and commanders since the dawn of warfare.

Cord ignored Li and pulled out his phone again, and went to his *YouTube* app. He pulled up the screen and handed the phone to Widow. He said, "Hit play."

Li moved closer and stood next to Widow. They faced the house. Widow watched Lucas move about and scan the area to make sure no one was around to see the video over their shoulders.

Li reached up and flipped the phone horizontal, and they watched as an image of Raggie came up on the screen. There was a look of sheer terror on her face. There was a gag in her mouth, and she had one black eye. It wasn't a grisly sight, not something to suggest she had undergone a tremendous punch to the face or even repeated blows.

Widow had seen bruises and black eyes before. He knew exactly what wounds from torture and fighting looked like. This was mellow as far as violence went. He figured her abductors wanted to show her face with a bruise because any sign of violence would convey to normal parents that their child was in grave danger. Maybe they had punched her just enough to force her into submission and not enough to damage her.

All Widow could see was her face, neck, and shoulders. And her hair, which was long and blond. It was matted and dirty and flat compared to her pictures. Her face looked just like Karen Rowley's, only years younger. She had green eyes, and her cheeks were slightly sunken. He could see that, just like her mother's, her eyeliner had run down her cheeks.

Widow thought, *she's been locked up all night. She must've cried the whole time.*

He stared into the background. He saw nothing but darkness and shadowy walls. She was somewhere with no windows. There was no artificial light except for some coming from behind the camera. It lit up her face and eyes. Bright halos reflected from her eyes like she had been forced to stare directly into the light and couldn't see past it. She shivered every few seconds as if she were cold, but it was probably from fear.

There was no sound except for Raggie's breathing, which was more like whimpering. It was low and muffled like she was trying to be tough and fight back. And then at the ten-second mark on the little bar at the bottom of the video, words scrolled up in front of her face. The text was short—six words, two exclamation points, and all caps.

KILL THE PRESIDENT! OR SHE DIES!

30

THE TEXT MOVED UP and over her face. It held its position for five long seconds and then vanished. The video played for another five seconds, and there was more of her whimpering. Then a single sound boomed in the silence. It was unmistakable, but just in case a completely deaf person was watching the video, there was a visual image as well. A switchblade appeared in front of the camera, and the blade fired out of the handle with a loud snick sound.

The effect's intent was achieved because both Raggie and Li jumped at the image. Li grabbed Widow's arm, digging her nails through the fabric of his shirt and into his bicep. It was painful, but he didn't resist or make a sound.

He watched as the image faded to black. Then more text rolled across the screen. It read, "24 HOURS." And then, "TELL NO ONE! WE'RE WATCHING!"

And that was all.

Widow looked at Li and then back at Cord. He said, "I wish you would call the FBI."

Cord said, "We can't. Don't you see that? We can't tell anyone. They want Rowley to kill the president. If he's not dead, then they'll kill Raggie. If we tell anyone—she's dead. If Rowley tells the president or anyone on his staff, they'll strip him of his position immediately, and then he won't have access. If anything changes, we're convinced they'll kill her."

Widow said, "I get that. Tell me about Lane. He called?"

"Yes. He called Gibson personally. He wanted us to know. It was a short conversation. He wanted Gibson to know who was doing this."

"When was Raggie taken?"

"Two nights ago. None of us have slept yet."

"When did they post the video? How much time do we have left?"

"Last night. Maybe ten hours left. Lane told Rowley that he wanted him to murder the president when he lands because the president is going to do a Q and A with the press corps."

Widow said, "What's the Q and A about?"

Cord asked, "You don't watch a lot of news, do you?"

"I don't watch anything. TV will rot your brain."

"It's about an African thing."

"What exactly?"

"What difference does it make?"

"I don't know. Maybe something. Maybe nothing."

"Some African president was killed on TV."

Widow asked, "He was killed on TV?"

"Yes. Live. It's been replayed all over the news."

"That sounds related to me. Potentially."

"How so?"

"One president is assassinated on live TV. Another is being threatened. I'd look into it."

Cord nodded and said, "We figured that."

"Why act like you didn't?"

"I just wanted to see if you were any good at investigations."

"Well, this one's pretty obvious. Any half-brain with the IQ of a goldfish could've put that together."

Cord nodded and said, "At least we know you're better than a goldfish."

Li finally spoke.

"We don't have a lot of time. Shouldn't Widow get started?"

Cord said, "Get started?"

"Yeah. Don't you want him to find Raggie? Isn't that why he's here?"

Cord looked at Lucas and then back at Widow.

Cord said, "No, that's not why he's here. Not exactly."

"Why the hell is he here?"

She recoiled a little after realizing how she probably sounded to her boss, but Cord didn't seem to mind. In fact, he seemed to show a glimmer of respect for her sudden backbone.

Widow said, "I'm here because Lane wants me here."

Cord said, "Yes."

Li asked, "Why?"

Widow spoke, ignored Li's question.

"Did Rowley mention a swap? Me for the girl?"

"Not exactly. We haven't heard from Lane except for the one time."

"But you're hoping to use me as a bargaining chip?"

Cord nodded and said, "I'm sorry. But it's crossed our minds. Lane's killed off the others from your old unit."

"All but me. The one he couldn't find."

"Maybe we can appeal to his sense of revenge."

"You think he's doing this whole thing out of revenge?"

Cord shrugged and said, "Maybe he'll trade Raggie for the only man left he couldn't track down.

Widow said, "And you guys figured I would agree to this stupidity? That I'd roll over and turn myself over to a lunatic?"

"Sort of. Yes. We're hoping you'll play along."

Widow said, "That's insane. What makes you think I'd go along with this harebrained scheme? Besides, what good would that do to save the girl? Or the president?"

"We're desperate."

Lucas reached into his coat pocket—right inner—and pulled out a wallet. It was a thick brown leather wallet. The leather was worn and creased with age. It could've been two years old or twenty. Neither would've surprised Widow. Lucas opened it and pulled out a picture from one of those old, milky plastic picture cases for family photos. He held it out and showed it to Widow.

He said, "She's just a little girl."

Widow looked at it. The photo had been preserved perfectly, sealed, and protected like a collector's item. In it, he saw Lucas as a younger man. He was still fat and had the same eyes, but next to him, hugging him close, was Raggie when she was a young girl, maybe ten or eleven. She still had both of her hands. The background looked like a school auditorium of some sort. She wore a clean dress and clean shoes. She might've been in a dance recital or a school play or maybe even some kind of graduation. Did middle schools have graduation ceremonies?

Widow looked back at Lucas. He saw a hard face with unbreakable features. But right there at that moment, he realized Lucas cared a lot more about Raggie than the others did. In fact, her safety was more important to him than his own life.

Widow stayed quiet, and Lucas pulled the picture back. He glanced down at it one last time and placed it back into his wallet, and returned his wallet to the inner pocket of his jacket.

Cord said, "We'll do whatever it takes to get her back. We're Secret Service and ex-special ops. We aren't helpless. We can get her back."

Widow looked at Li.

He asked, "When was she taken? What time exactly?"

"We think she was abducted two nights ago at around nine o'clock. Maybe ten."

"How's it she's still alive? That's more than twenty-four hours ago."

Cord said, "The video message wasn't uploaded until last night. We heard nothing until this morning."

Widow said, "They wanted you to be afraid. They wanted you to be terrified. They wanted her parents to think the worst, as most parents do when their children go missing."

Lucas said, "Well, it worked. We're terrified."

Widow said, "How much time do we have left? Exactly."

"Air Force One lands at 6:30 p.m. After it lands, the president will disembark and face the press corps. That'll be our last chance. If Lane sees that the president is still alive when the cameras come on, then Raggie is dead."

"And you're certain he's serious?"

Cord said, "He's serious."

Li looked at both of them, her eyes wide and her mouth hung open.

"What about the president?"

Widow and Cord looked at each other.

Widow said, "That's what Lane wants. He wants Rowley to assassinate the president, in front of cameras for the world to see."

Li's expression was shock. She left her mouth hanging open. She didn't know what to say.

Cord said, "You understand you can't tell anyone, Li."

"But?"

"No one!" Cord barked.

She nodded.

Widow didn't respond, but he was thinking about her future. If Rowley went through with it, they could all end up in jail. He wished Cord hadn't told her, hadn't involved her.

He said, "I don't mean is he serious about killing her. Obviously, he can do that. I mean, how do you know that he'll return her unharmed if we do as he asks?"

Cord looked at Li.

He said, "You should leave."

"Why?"

Cord stepped back onto the patio, his shoes scuffing the concrete and making a low echo that bounced between the walls and the privacy fence and the neighbor's houses.

"Because you've heard too much already."

"What's that supposed to mean?"

Silence. She looked at her boss and then at Widow.

Widow said, "He's right. You should go home. Forget about this whole thing."

Li's face turned pale. She said, "What the hell? What do you mean? I'm not good enough to help?"

Cord said, "No. That's not it at all."

Widow said, "He means that you have your whole career ahead of you. Your whole life. After this thing is over, there will be hearings and investigations and trials. You'll be called in front of Congress and probably be on the news. He means that your career will be over."

Li thought for a moment and understood.

Widow said, "Whatever the hell happens, this thing will be over by tonight. I can call you after."

Li signaled for Widow to follow her off to the side.

She walked onto the grass. It was dry, and the dirt underneath was hard. She walked far enough away to be out of earshot from Cord and Lucas. She pulled Widow by the arm and then stopped in the middle of the yard.

She looked around for anyone listening.

She said, "I'm going to go home, but I don't think you should be involved, either. They don't want you to investigate this. It sounds like they only want you as bait, and bait gets eaten. Obviously, they know cops and have friends they trust in the bureau. Plus, there's Graine, who's a cop. They could call any number of people to search for this girl. They don't need you."

Widow said, "I don't think that they have much choice. If Graine were good enough, they'd have him out there investigating and not babysitting the mother. And if they could use any of their friends, they would have. You can't just call up anyone and say, 'Hey, I need you to investigate a missing girl. Oh, and by the way, she's the daughter of the Director of the United States Secret Service. Plus, the maniac who took her wants us to kill the president.'"

"I'm scared for you, Widow."

"Don't worry about me."

"They don't care about you. You need to be careful."

"I know. They want this little girl back alive. I get it. That's all they care about. But what am I supposed to do? Walk away?"

Li said, "This isn't your fight. Walk away."

"Not my style."

"You don't even know this girl."

Widow said, "I know her enough. She's fourteen years old. She's a fellow surfer, and she's been taken. She's out there somewhere, and she's scared that she's gonna die. And you know what? She's right. She's gonna die. Look at these guys. They're so desperate that they called up a hobo to help them."

Widow looked over Li's head at the edge of the privacy fence and then back into her eyes.

He said, "What I know is Lane's out there. He's pissed at me. And he's got Raggie. I'll do whatever it takes to bring her back alive."

Li reached up and kissed him. A long kiss.

She said, "You got a future."

Cord and Lucas stared at them.

Lucas said, "What is that?"

"Looks like Li is saying goodbye," said Cord.

"Do you think Widow will live through this?"

Cord paused a moment and then said, "There's no question Lane will kill Raggie if Rowley doesn't kill the president."

Lucas said, "Right. But I'm talking about this guy. Widow."

"Lane will kill him. No question."

31

WIDOW WALKED through the Rowley house one last time before following Cord, Li, and Lucas out.

They said goodbye to Graine, and to Karen Rowley, who looked like she was in the kind of shock that wasn't going anywhere soon. She kept her composure, but she said nothing. Even though she hadn't seen the video of Raggie, she'd still had the life scared out of her. Widow wondered if it was a good idea to keep the video from her. A parent's imagination could be much worse than reality.

Widow had no experience with kidnappings that involved ransoms, but he had some experience with abductions—Faye Matlind, a little Mexican boy, a girl named Jemma Hood, and the girls he found back in Black Rock, Mississippi, which seemed a lifetime ago to him now.

They stopped in the driveway, and Widow told Li to wait for him in the car. She did, and he turned to Cord and Lucas.

He asked, "What's the plan? You want me to turn myself over to Lane hoping maybe it'll buy some time? I get that. But what's really the plan here?"

Cord said, "We'll go with you, and Rowley will call Lane."

"He's not gonna trade her for me."

"No, he won't."

"What's the endgame here? You hope he'll extend the deadline if you hand me over?"

"That's exactly what we're hoping for."

"It's a stupid plan."

Cord asked, "You got a better one?"

"You guys are ex-Special Forces and now Secret Service. Tell me the truth."

"Obviously, we don't plan just to give you up. One dead man won't stop Raggie from being killed as soon as Rowley doesn't follow through and kill the president."

"I figured that. What's the real plan?"

"A rescue attempt."

"How?"

Cord said, "Simple plan. We put a tracking device on you. Then we send in the cavalry."

"That doesn't sound reassuring."

"I know. But it's all we got."

Widow said, "I guess that's our best option."

"We sit tight until Lane calls Rowley back, and then we get on the move."

32

LANE WAS IN VIRGINIA, not far from Widow and the Rowley residence. Of course, he was even closer to Raggie. She was in a room with her one wrist handcuffed to a steel pipe from the plumbing. She wasn't far from a sink, but it was too far for her to reach with her feet because she tried to kick at it—at the bottom. She doubted that leaking water would attract attention from any of the neighbors, but it was at least a small glimmer of hope. Better that she kept her mind occupied rather than worry about what the men who had kidnapped her were going to do to her.

She remembered seeing the man that she knew, but that was about all she remembered. She had been awake for a while but wasn't sure how long she had been there or how long she had been restrained. She had looked around the room several times, but it did no good. She wasn't in complete darkness. The room she was in had no natural light, and the lights were turned off, but somewhere there was a faint light from a digital source, like a clock. She was handcuffed to a pipe near an old farmer sink. There was a metal hose hanging over it like a restaurant dish room would have, but Raggie was sure she wasn't in a restaurant. She thought she was in an animal hospital because she heard lots of barking. And the barking was coming from the next room. It was an animal hospital or an animal shelter.

In the next room, on the other side of the barking dogs, Lane sat at an office desk and stared at his phone. He had just acted surprised to get a call he had been expecting.

Rowley called him from Air Force One, begging to see his daughter, begging for Lane to spare her, and begging for Lane to swap her for Widow.

Rowley had called with the proposition that they trade Widow for Raggie, but Lane quickly dismissed that. Then Rowley had begged him to reconsider, and he replied he wasn't interested. Lane countered with proof of life from Raggie and the promise to extend the original demand by an extra day. But he had no intention of extending it. He was on a deadline. The president would be dead on TV by the end of the day. And Raggie would be dead no matter what by the end of the day.

Lane texted Jekyll's burner phone: *Nice work. Widow's on his way to me. Our employer will wire you the rest of your money when POTUS is retired. I'll send you payment personally when Widow is in my hands.*

Lane set his phone down and turned in his chair to look at the monitor that had night-vision lenses. He watched a grainy and greenish live video feed of Raggie in the other room as she tried to kick at the pipes of a sink used to clean animals. She kicked and kicked, and the sink rattled. He wasn't sure what the hell she was trying to do—maybe trying to make the pipes burst and leak water everywhere. Or perhaps, since she was a surfer, water was a security blanket. Lane wasn't sure.

It didn't matter. The pipes were switched off. They had done that before locking her in there. Lane had learned a lot about abduction, and he knew it was good to give the captive something to do. The only time you needed to take away all hope was when you wanted to scare them. And she had already been scared enough when Grant popped her in the face before filming the video for her parents.

Grant had a great talent for that sort of thing. He hadn't hit her hard. Not enough to hurt her. It was intended more to scare her and leave a bruise.

Jekyll asked that they not hurt her too badly. No reason to hurt the girl any more than necessary. Of course, Lane didn't care what Jekyll wanted. Jekyll had some misguided notion she was important to him. Like his own family or something. Probably because he'd known her for her whole life, he harbored the false idea that he could still be a good guy. It was an illusion.

Lane turned away from Raggie's video feed and stood up. He was in good shape. And it wasn't his military background that had kept him in good shape. It was his time in prison. Ten years in an African prison was a long time. He had expected every day that the guards would come and take him to his death—or worse, to some sick and twisted fate like losing an appendage or being burned until he was unrecognizable. He'd heard stories of guys being set on fire and then put out and treated so they'd live on in misery.

Lane had seen Navy prisons, and he knew his accommodations were far from US standards, but by West Ganbola standards, they were the Ritz.

He stayed in that hellhole for nearly ten years, until one day, his employer showed up in his cell. He remembered the guy who'd walked into his cell. He had already known his employer—his savior. But now, the guy looked completely different from the last time he'd met him. This time, the guy had no right arm. It was completely gone from the shoulder, which was something he had in common with Raggie, an amputation. Except that this guy also had no ears. He could hear, but not very well. His external ears were completely missing. They had been severed from his head by a dull knife. It had to have hurt like hell. That was something Lane was sure of.

The man who had freed him was a man he knew only briefly, but he was now in a position of power within Sowe's government. In fact, some believed he was running it behind the scenes because Sowe was losing his grip on reality. As the old dictator grew closer to his golden years, he slipped in and out of senility. Sometimes it wasn't a big deal, but other times he had entire days where he couldn't grasp executive decisions. One such event that had taken place had saved Lane's employer's life.

After years of being tortured—starvation and sleep deprivation at first, and then later mutilation and so on—Lane's employer was surprised at being given a chance at a new life by Sowe. He was provided a document granting his release from prison if he renounced his old ways and joined Sowe's ranks. It was something he might've rejected years earlier, but after spending years experiencing the worst imaginable tortures by your enemy, change sounded good. And that was what happened to Lane's employer.

The perspective of the man with no ears and no right arm had changed immensely. The change was so drastic that he sided with Sowe on several issues. The main one being that Sowe wasn't his enemy. Sowe wasn't the one who had betrayed him. In fact, Sowe had always remained steadfast about who he was and what he represented. He was the dictator of West Ganbola, but he was also a strong leader who had protected the country and prevented invasion by its neighbors. Invasion was an actual threat. The small country's neighbors to the north were butchers. That was Lane's employer's opinion.

Sowe's elite torturers had spent years convincing Lane's employer that Sowe was the rightful leader of West Ganbola. Eventually, he believed it to the point where he was willing to die for Sowe. They had effectively brainwashed Lane's employer into believing in Sowe and hating the United States.

Although Lane didn't care about Sowe or his regime or his tiny country, he still had something in common with his employer, and through him, with Sowe. Lane hated the United States. He hated the American president. He hated Gibson Rowley and the other men who had left him for dead in West Africa.

And he hated Jack Widow.

33

THE MEN on Lane's payroll sat waiting in an apartment in DC, not far from the White House and the Capitol Building. It was the Lansburgh building, in the Penn Quarter of DC. It was located just south of Pennsylvania Avenue, midway between the White House and the United States Capitol. The cityscape views were amazing and came at a hefty price. Lane's penthouse apartment was two stories and double the regular price of rent.

The actual owner was a man named Marden Smith. He lived in Washington, the state, far from DC, and there was no chance that he would return soon. He had been paid rent six months in advance and had never met Lane in person, so there was no need to get rid of the guy. He knew nothing.

The mercs sat around, enjoying some light drinking and talking, like they were out in the desert around a forward operating base, preparing for a mission.

They weren't a real unit; they were a private one and not a military one. They had no loyalties to each other in the sense of brotherhood, like guys they had been in the field with. Their loyalty was exclusive to money, and they were getting plenty of it.

Lane was their leader because he had recruited them, but the guy who was paying them was top secret. There was no official chain of command other than Lane first. But if there had been a second in command, it would've been Grant.

Grant said, "Not too much of that bottle."

Silverti was the one who had been drinking the most. He was an ex-Marine, short and grayed around the temples and completely bald on top. He looked at Grant and started to make a rebellious gesture. But he saw the look in Grant's eyes and refrained. Better not to piss off one of the scariest guys he'd ever worked with. Silverti had known Lane for a year and respected him even though he wasn't too keen on their mission. But money was money, and he had plans for his future. He had plans to drink and live on a South American beach. Valentine had the same plans. They all did, probably.

Except for Grant. His plans were a mystery to Silverti and to the other guys. He probably planned on continuing with Lane to the next thing. He probably planned on never retiring. He was one of those guys who believed in dying a good death—like he couldn't wait to meet the man who would give him his final blow.

That wasn't Silverti's way. His way was to kill the guy who stood between him and getting paid.

Suddenly Grant's cell phone rang, and Silverti looked up just after the other guys did. They had all been bored, but that was part of the lives they all led once upon a time. Waiting was the biggest part of military life when you were out on a mission—especially for Special Forces. Whenever they were training or taking part in missions, they were waiting.

Grant answered his phone. It was Lane.

Lane said, "The deal is going down at sundown. We'll meet at the subdivision at five o'clock."

Grant said, "Okay. Same plan?"

"Yes. They all die. Except Widow. Take him alive."

"Okay."

"Come pick me up. We have to meet the boss at the airport."

"Do we have time?"

"Yeah. His plane arrives in an hour."

"Is it safe for him to be here?"

"He's safe here. No one's looking for him. It was more dangerous for me to come into the country than for him. The government probably thinks he's dead. Rowley certainly does. The look on his face when he sees us kill his daughter on video will be priceless."

Grant said, "How'll he see it? Won't they kill him after he kills the president?"

"Let's hope not. Let's hope they arrest him. That's what the politicians and the American people will want. They'll want to keep him alive so he can stand trial."

Grant said, "What about the Secret Service agents?"

Lane said, "Oh, they'll shoot him. Without a doubt. Let's hope he survives. Either way, his wife will see it. That'll be good enough for our client."

"Okay. Should I bring the guys?"

"Bring Silverti. Valentine can babysit the girl. Tell him to take the Range Rover and set up. Wait for us."

"Are you gonna tell him to keep his hands off her?"

"He's more scared of you than me. Not that I care, but our Secret Service friend does. For his peace of mind, do it. I don't want to anger our pal. We still need him."

Grant asked, "For what?"

"In case things go south, or in case Rowley gets cold feet. Our friend is keeping a close eye on him."

"Is Rowley really going to do it?"

Lane said, "He tells our friend he won't. He tells Widow he won't. But our friend says not to worry—he will when he thinks he has no other choice. He will. After we kill the rest of his crew and take Widow, then he'll do it."

Grant said, "Okay. I'm headed over."

The phone went dead in his ear, and he clicked it off. Then he slipped the phone back into his pocket and got up from the sofa. He gave Valentine his instructions and told Silverti to come with him.

They left the Lansburgh, one at a time. They each waited several minutes before exiting, not wanting anyone to spot them. Valentine went to the Range Rover, which was parked down the street. Grant and Silverti met on a street corner, walked into a parking garage, and got into a silver Mercedes GLE with legally tinted windows.

They drove off, and no one watched them.

34

AT DULLES INTERNATIONAL AIRPORT, plane engines roared as they powered and propelled huge passenger planes down runways and into flight. An equal number of aircraft landed on designated runways. The planes arrived from all over the world, from Zurich, Vienna, Moscow, Seoul, Tokyo, Bogotá, and even cities from the Middle East. Some flights had origins from African cities—Dakar and Johannesburg.

One flight on a Boeing 777-300ER, which was a long-range wide-body twin-engine jet, had originated in Dubai, but Passenger 88 had not. He had originated in Accra, Ghana, and had a layover in Dubai before traveling fourteen hours to the US.

He was a man of unimportant height and race, but he was remarkable in several other features. He was an African man who weighed a hundred fifty pounds and stood five foot ten inches. His right arm was missing, removed at the shoulder. If a doctor examined it up close, he would note that it hadn't been removed in the surgical sense of the phrase. He would describe it as *hacked off*. The instrument used would've been something dull, and the procedure would've been time-consuming. It had probably been done with a hatchet or a machete. But the only person who recalled the incident would be the man himself. And he wasn't going to relive the experience to relay the information to anyone.

Passenger 88 was a man of few words. He hadn't always been that way, but hard time in an unimaginable, dark prison would do that to any man. Some men found religion. Some men found redemption. But those types of men weren't in the same prison, not in the same reality that Passenger 88's prison life had been. Those types of men had the opportunity for such ideologies, but not Passenger 88. He hadn't been given this type of prison life. His was one of immense suffering and terror, and he was left with only two choices—die or join.

Now he was in the enemy's backyard. He was in America to ensure that the man who had betrayed him would now betray his own master.

Passenger 88 walked off the plane, down the corridors with wall-to-ceiling windows, and into the terminal. He walked past the Starbucks, the Burger King, and the duty-free store. He didn't go to the baggage claim because he had no baggage. He had checked a bag, but it wasn't filled with his belongings. It was filled instead with random clothing and toiletries he purchased just to pack them. He didn't want to draw attention from customs or the TSA or the security forces in Dubai by not checking bags on a one-way trip to the United States.

A single passenger with no bags on a long flight to the United States wasn't a person who planned to return to Africa and, even more disturbing, wasn't a person who planned anything that made any real sense. No one traveled from a far-off place like Africa to the United States without a return ticket and with no luggage. That would've raised red flags with the authorities. Immigration would've been notified. They would confront him to find out exactly what his plans were, and most of the time, they would deport this person back to his country of origin.

One time out of a million, they might deal with a person with alternative plans. They might deal with a man with dangerous plans. And one time out of ten million, they might deal with a dangerous man consumed by revenge. The chances of coming across a man like this were small, but the chances of a man like this planning to commit acts of terrorism were almost one hundred percent.

Passenger 88 was no different, but he wasn't stopped by the authorities, nor was he bothered by airport personnel. His passport was a perfect forgery, and he had a credible identity to go along with it. He was confident that his fake documents would work with no problems because he paid a fortune for them, and their creator was reputable. There was a complicated network of forgers, hackers, and corrupt bureaucrats who needed to supplement their incomes because governments didn't pay well enough. Why should their bosses and counterparts in other countries make so much more money?

When the immigration agent stamped his passport with the official seal of the United States, Passenger 88 didn't smile. He didn't show any sign of relief to have fooled them. Not until he walked through the end of security and past the terminal onto official US soil did he crack a smile. And when he walked right past baggage claim and beyond all the other passengers who had stopped to wait for their bags, his smile widened. He walked to the end of the baggage claim and had an overwhelming urge to look back. He pictured himself turning back and seeing his one lone decoy bag going around and around the carousel, no one noticing it and no one picking it up. He thought that when Rowley pulled a gun on the president on live TV and pulled the trigger, he would flashback to his lone piece of luggage going around and around, a forgotten symbol of how the US security forces had failed at their jobs.

He stopped and looked back, but there was no luggage on the carousel. It was what he should've expected. Never in the history of his flight experiences had he ever seen the baggage arrive before the passengers.

He turned and left the airport.

Outside, in the arrivals lane, he was greeted by a Mercedes with tinted windows. Inside, he met Lane and two of his guys. They didn't get out of the car to greet him. They just waited for him to open the back door and slide into the seat. He shut the door, and then the car drove off.

35

WIDOW RODE in the backseat of Cord's SUV. It was nice. Plenty of room for him compared to the cars he was used to hitching in. The interior of the SUV was silent. Even though he wasn't under arrest, he felt like he was because he sat in the back of a black government SUV. It felt like the backseat of a police car.

He wasn't under arrest, but he was awaiting an uncertain fate based on a stupid plan to get a young girl back from a madman. He wasn't in love with the whole scenario, but what choice did he have? It was ingrained in him to save those who needed saving. He couldn't help it.

They had been driving for forty minutes on the outskirts of DC. They stayed mostly on the interstates and highways surrounding Virginia. Cord didn't know where to go, so they just circled around, waiting for Rowley to call with news from Lane.

The day felt long. Mostly, they rode in silence. Widow was the first to speak in a long time.

He said, "Hey, guys, why don't we stop for coffee and food? I know the situation is tense, but we gotta eat. I know I do."

Lucas craned his head back and said, "Can't eat."

"You have to."

"We eat when Raggie is safe. Not before."

"You got a problem with me?"

Lucas said, "I don't know you. The only thing that matters to me is getting Raggie back."

"And we will."

"If you're so sure, then you can wait to eat."

Widow said, "Okay, try to look at it from my point of view. I'm probably going to my death for a girl I've never met. The least you guys can do is feed me a last meal."

Cord said nothing to that.

Lucas said, "You'll be fine. Do your part, and we'll get you both out."

Widow said, "Even death row inmates get a last meal."

Lucas turned all the way around in his seat and pointed his finger at Widow's chest.

He said, "Stop saying that! Stop implying it's your last meal! Your last meal means Raggie's last! Get it?"

Widow didn't react. He stayed quiet and looked straight ahead at Lucas. He wasn't angry. From what Widow could tell, Raggie was like a daughter to Lucas. All the guy wanted was the same as any parent would want. He wanted to get her back.

Cord said, "We can stop up here and go through the drive-thru at this McDonald's. But we can't leave the truck. Okay?"

Cord looked into the rearview mirror. His eyes met Widow's.

He said, "Get whatever you want. I'm buying. We'll sit in the parking lot while you eat. We need to wait for Rowley to call. We can't miss it."

Lucas turned back in his seat and faced forward. Cord turned into the McDonald's driveway and drove through the drive-through. He ordered two coffees. One for Widow and one for Lucas, even though Lucas never acknowledged it. Widow felt his appetite slip away, but he knew he had to eat.

Eat while you can and sleep while you can was a universal military motto.

Cord paid for everything, and they pulled around to an empty parking space near the exit. He left the engine on and handed Widow the coffee and a brown bag with a burger inside. They sat there in silence for fifteen minutes while Widow ate his sandwich and drank his coffee. After he finished, he crumbled the bag up into a ball and left it on the backseat. He kept the coffee in a cup holder.

Lucas spoke first. He said, "Something's wrong."

Cord said, "Relax. Nothing's changed."

"But why hasn't that bastard called Rowley yet?"

Widow said, "Therefore, it's not about the girl. It's about you. He wants to scare you. He wants you like you are—worried and desperate."

"Well, it's working."

Widow stayed quiet.

Suddenly Cord's phone rang, breaking the silence. He must've had the volume turned all the way up because it burst out like an alarm bell.

Cord picked it up and swiped the screen.

He said, "Yeah."

The voice on the other end said something that Widow couldn't hear.

Lucas watched Cord's face like a dog waiting for his master to give him an order.

Cord said, "Yeah. Okay." And then, "Got it. Text it to me."

He hung up the phone and looked in the rearview mirror.

He said, "Lane wants to meet with you. It looks like we got a plan."

Then Cord stopped talking and got out of the SUV. He walked to the rear of the truck and popped open the rear hatch. The door went up slowly on its hinges.

Cord leaned in and said, "Get out for a minute."

Widow took another swig from the coffee, returned it to the cup holder, and then unlatched his seatbelt and opened the door. He stepped out. Lucas did the same. They all met at the rear of the vehicle.

Cord reached into the rear cargo space and opened a small, rectangular black case. It must've been some sort of Secret Service kit because inside was an unloaded SIG Sauer P229. The magazine was fully loaded and in a separate groove that held it in place. Next to it was a miniature flashlight and a radio. Then there was a small compartment containing a bunch of random, everyday items. One of them was a small black-headed nail-looking device. It was less than a half-inch long.

Cord picked it up and showed it to Widow.

"This is a GPS tracking device. It works like a cell phone tracker. As long as the battery is good, I can see its location on my phone. To turn it on, twist the head like this."

He twisted the head and said, "Clockwise means it's on. Counter-clockwise is off. The battery life is short. It'll work for up to five hours, and then it'll be dead. To charge it, you need a special charger, which you won't have."

Widow asked, "So, if they take me, then you gotta find me within five hours, or I'm as good as dead?"

"We'll have you in two hours—or you're on your own."

Widow said, "Great. What's the range on this thing?"

Cord said, "Don't worry; it's good. We won't be too far away. After the exchange, we'll try to stay as close as we can while hidden. Hopefully, we can get to you in an hour."

Widow said, "Okay."

Cord activated the GPS and handed it to Widow.

"It works on an app on my phone. Slip it somewhere no one will find it."

Widow held it in his palm for a moment and stared at it. Then he knelt and overturned his shoe, trying to balance on one foot. He stuck the nail-shaped GPS device into the ridges on the bottom of his shoe. He pushed it in good and hard so it would stay.

Cord nodded.

Lucas said, "Good thinking. If anyone finds it, they'll think it's just something that got stuck in your shoe."

Widow nodded.

Cord said, "That was Rowley on the phone. Lane called him and agreed to give proof of life and give Rowley another day if we deliver you to him."

Widow said, "Sounds like a shit deal for me."

"It's the best we're going to get. Remember, we're right behind you. But ultimately, it is up to you."

Lucas asked, "You sure you want to do this?"

Widow nodded and asked, "How long do I have to wait?"

"Lane promises he'll give Rowley another twenty-four hours, but we won't wait that long. Forty-five minutes to two hours is all I'll wait before we come looking for you. I want to make sure you have time to locate her. If you haven't been brought to Raggie's location by two hours, we won't wait any longer. I don't care what Rowley says. I know you're going out on a limb here for us. We'll come and get you. You got my word."

Widow looked at Lucas.

He said, "Don't forget about me."

Lucas smiled. It was slight, but it was there. Widow bet that under different circumstances, Lucas was probably a warm guy. Maybe he even laughed a lot. Many of the cops Widow had known growing up had a great sense of humor. Most of them knew that there was a time to be serious and a time to laugh—and both were equal in the eyes of a policeman. Their jobs were so stressful that having a good sense of humor was imperative for mental stability. And in Widow's experience, the sicker the sense of humor, the better the cop.

"Where are we going?"

Cord said, "First, we'll meet with Graine. Then we go to and meet with Lane in a suburb about fifteen minutes from here."

Lucas asked, "Where's Graine going to meet us?"

"He left a half-hour ago. Rowley called him straight away. He should be here soon."

* * *

SEVEN MINUTES LATER, Graine pulled into the parking lot and up to them and stopped. He drove a green F150 pickup. Chrome rims. It looked brand new.

Cord said, "Here he is,"

He walked over to the driver's window.

Graine rolled the window down, and the two of them spoke for about ten seconds. Widow was out of earshot and couldn't hear them, but he saw Graine pull a Heckler & Koch MP5 up from his lap. He handed it to Cord, who took it in his hand, not even looking around to see if anyone was watching him. Widow guessed that being a Secret Service agent made him not care about what bystanders saw or thought.

Cord reached into the window with his free hand and grabbed a second MP5. He nodded at Graine, who nodded back and rolled up his window.

Cord returned to the back of the SUV and handed one of the MP5s to Lucas. Both men checked their weapons. They pulled out the magazines, saw the rounds, and then reinserted them. They readied their weapons and were now locked and loaded.

Widow felt naked. He wasn't used to leaving his life in the hands of others.

Cord looked at his watch and then at Widow and asked, "Ready?"

Widow said, "As I'll ever be. Let's shoot the moon."

Cord looked puzzled. "What?"

"It's from Hearts."

"What?" Cord asked again.

"It's a card game. It's an expression. Like throwing a Hail Mary."

Cord nodded.

Widow stood up and looked back at Graine, who smiled at him. Then he returned to the backseat of the SUV.

Cord and Lucas got in, and they drove off. Cord programmed an address in the suburbs into his dashboard NAV system, and they followed the instructions.

36

WIDOW THOUGHT OF LI. For a split second, he thought about telling Cord to pull the SUV over and jumping out. He imagined telling them to take a dive off a cliff. He imagined returning to Li's apartment and to all the glorious pleasures that came with being there. He focused on her bed and the accommodations that came along with it.

Li was quite a woman. And for a moment, as Widow had done from time to time, he pictured settling down with a woman like her. There were certainly a lot of perks. But then the overwhelming fear of stagnation set in.

Widow recalled a line from one of his favorite books; actually, it was a novella. It was Stephen King's *Rita Hayworth and the Shawshank Redemption*.

The line was: "Some birds aren't meant to be caged."

It was a great line. A great novella. A great movie too.

Widow looked forward out of Cord's windshield and saw they were coming up to a subdivision on a huge piece of land—acres of land.

Windsor Estates was spelled out in huge block letters on a brick sign out front.

Widow glanced back and saw Graine still following close in his truck.

They drove through the open gates and passed an abandoned guard post. Widow wondered why no one was there. The first couple of houses they passed were huge and looked expensive. They were much newer than the houses in Rowley's neighborhood and probably twice the price even though they were much farther outside the District.

They drove the length of the main street and gazed at the houses. They were all large and had different designs. Some were brown. Some red. All were brick with long driveways.

Widow noticed something else. The driveways were empty. As they drove on and turned a corner and then took a curve to the right around a small but thick forest of trees, he realized why. He realized why Lane had picked this subdivision as a meeting place. It was because it was so new and expensive that the only street that was developed was the entrance. The rest of the place was a maze of unfinished mansions and large houses. Some were closer to completion than others, but none were habitable. Not yet.

It was a new construction development.

Probably no one even lived in the first set of houses they passed. There were front yards with unmanned bulldozers and small cranes. There were piles of lumber and stacks of covered brick. One house was half-built and had a half-constructed chimney protruding out of it, but no roof. Another had a hole dug for an in-ground swimming pool but no driveway. None of the houses toward the end of this street had glass installed in the window slots.

And there wasn't a construction worker or a person in sight.

Widow looked forward and said nothing. He looked down at the navigation screen and saw that they had another turn to make, and then they would be at the location.

They made the last turn and came to a short street with several unoccupied houses that were still under construction. The street was littered with vacant trucks and the same kinds of vehicles they'd seen in the previous yards. It looked like they ran out of money while constructing the houses. Probably couldn't sell any of the ones they'd already built, and that's why construction had stopped. Maybe the finance company had pulled the plug because of the lack of sales. Or maybe the city had shut them down because of violations and fines that needed to be paid. Whatever the reason, it was impossible to imagine that they weren't in danger in this location. There were countless hiding places. Rooftops. Abandoned vehicles. It was a Secret Service nightmare. Even without the military-style training from his mother, Widow could still tell it was bad because of the looks on Cord's and Lucas's faces. They appeared less than confident.

They reached the end of the NAV system's directions, and Cord pulled over to the side of the road. He put the SUV in park and left the engine running.

He turned to Widow.

"From here, we go on foot. It's the house up ahead," Cord said and pointed it out.

They all stepped out of the SUV and shut their doors, leaving the engine running. They waited for Graine to pull up behind the SUV and park. He got out, and they all started up the long drive.

Widow stayed to the right. Lucas was center. Cord on the left of him. And Graine stayed to the rear.

Widow scanned the house. Before he scanned past the front door, the garage door automatically started opening at the top of the drive. Widow and the others turned immediately to it.

He saw a dim light inside, probably from a bulb hanging from the ceiling. The light spilled out from under the lip of the door as it retracted upward. Like a giant mouth opening wide to consume him, the garage door stopped when it was all the way open.

He saw a dark figure standing there in the center of an empty garage. The figure's voice spoke. It was a voice from the past.

"It's good to see you again, Mr. Widow."

Widow said nothing.

The figure stepped forward into the light. It was John Lane. He stepped out of the garage and out of the darkness and onto the driveway.

He walked forward, slow, and stopped.

"Or is it Commander Widow, now?" he asked.

Widow called up the driveway.

"It's just Widow."

"You out of the Navy, Widow?"

"I've been out. Long-time."

"Did you retire?"

"No."

Lane nodded.

He asked, "What *was* your last rank?"

"Commander."

"O-5?"

Widow nodded and said, "Senior Officer."

Lane smirked and showed both hands out in front of him. He slow-clapped.

"Nicely done, Commander. Impressive. Why don't you and your friends come forward?"

Lane had changed little from the last time Widow saw him in that bungalow in Africa, fifteen years ago. He was still a well-built guy. He looked younger than Cord and Lucas and Rowley, but he was close in age, somewhere in his fifties. He had thick gray hair and a beard to match. He wore a black windbreaker with a black shirt underneath and green camo pants.

He stopped clapping and moved his hands out and up and farther apart so that the agents could see he wasn't carrying a weapon. He was empty-handed.

Lucas didn't wait any longer. He stepped forward and pointed the MP5 over the door and lined Lane up in his sights.

He shouted, "WHERE IS SHE?!"

Cord stepped out with him and backed him up even though this wasn't a part of the original plan. He didn't want to leave Lucas out there alone, nor did he want to show any disunity between them in front of Lane. Standard military and Secret Service SOP when confronted with the enemy.

Widow stayed where he was. They were all at the end of the driveway. Widow prepared his knees to make a leap in case he had to hit the deck if they started shooting.

Lane said, "Guys. This wasn't a part of the deal."

Lucas shouted, "WHERE?"

Cord called out just loud enough for Lucas to hear him.

He said, "What're you doing?"

Lucas ignored him and repeated his request. "WHERE?"

Lane raised his hands higher.

"Would you shoot an unarmed man? A man who's not carrying a single weapon?"

Lucas raised his gun higher, stock in tight to his shoulder, and cheek tucked down. He stepped forward. The SUV's engine idled behind them. He walked up further, keeping his sights on Lane, covering him. One false move, and he intended to squeeze the trigger.

Lucas said, "I'm not going to ask again. I'm going to shoot you if you don't tell us. Right here. Right now. No more games."

Stupid move, Widow thought.

Widow looked around, scanning the house. The lights were out in every window. Depending on how many guys Lane had brought with him, every single window could've had an armed bad guy positioned in it. There could've been a dozen guns aimed at him for all they knew.

The only move Widow had left was one he hadn't learned in his years as a SEAL or as an NCIS agent. It was from elementary school. It was the fire safety rules. When on fire, always *Stop! Drop! And Roll!*

When the first bullet was fired, he figured he'd stop, drop, and roll to the right. Then he could fast-crawl to a tree that was big enough to hide behind.

Cord side-looked at Lucas.

"What're you doing?"

This time, he said it loudly enough for Lane to hear.

Lucas said, "NO MORE BULLSHIT! WHERE IS SHE?!"

Cord didn't question his friend anymore. This was the play they'd made, and he was committed.

Lane said, "I don't have a weapon, but that doesn't mean I'm completely unarmed. You know that there're other guys here with guns. They'll shoot you dead as soon as you fire one shot."

Lucas said, "I don't need more than one. You're not going to walk out of here, alive or not. One way or the other, this'll end here."

Graine flanked and moved behind Lucas. He also had his MP5 up to his chin and focused on Lane, eyes squinting through the thick glasses.

He said, "Lucas! What da hell are you doing? You're going to get her killed!"

Lucas said, "I'm doing my duty! I swore allegiance to the president. Either they will release Raggie now, or they never planned to. We can't let them push Rowley into doing this."

Lane stayed quiet and stared into Widow's eyes, and then he looked him up and down, fixated on him.

Graine said, "He isn't really going to go through with it. Rowley knows they'll kill her."

Cord said, "No. He will."

Graine looked over at Cord's profile for a brief second and then back down his sights at Lane.

He asked, "What do you mean?"

"Gibson'll do it. If he thinks it'll save Raggie, he'll do it. He may say he won't, but trust me. He will put a bullet in the president's head if he thinks it'll save his daughter's life."

Lucas said, "ENOUGH! WHERE THE HELL IS SHE?!"

Lane said, "Shoot me. I won't tell. And you won't get out of here alive."

Lucas stepped forward, farther from Cord and Graine. There was no going back now. If there were guys stationed in the house, they had Lucas dead to rights.

Widow looked up at the house's windows again. He scanned the second level, where the roof was missing. He squinted his eyes and searched for any sign of a sniper or any movement.

There was nothing. Either these guys were really, really good, or there was no one in the house.

He refused to believe that Lane would come out like this, unarmed without his guys. It made little sense.

Widow focused his vision on one hole in the upper wall. It was the perfect position for a sniper—up higher than the street, good cover. A sniper could snap out of cover and take a shot and then snap right back in.

He glanced back at the agents. Cord was moving forward now, as well. He followed close to Lucas's position, but he stepped farther out to the left. He kept his position wide from Lucas. This seemed logical to Widow and was most likely a Secret Service tactic.

The only one who seemed out of place was Graine. He trailed behind Lucas like a shadow, staying ten feet back from him. Widow closed his eyes and imagined the different ways this could play out. He calculated two ways, then three, then four—and, suddenly, he realized something. It was like being struck by lightning.

In no tactical way did Graine's positioning make any sense.

Widow thought back to Li, and to Cord and to Rowley.

What were the odds that Widow would get arrested and booked and found so easily in that same twenty-four-hour period of Raggie's abduction? He might've been arrested at the same time.

Calderón had caused him to get arrested. Opportunity had forced him into this position. His history with Lane and Rowley had caused Cord to seek him out.

One thing led to another: cause and effect.

But that's a lot of coincidences. Widow knew Rowley. He knew Lane. He had worked with them before. He knew he would be on Lane's target list if Rowley was. If Lane had killed all the other guys from his unit. But what were the odds that he would be found so easily? He was willing to buy some of it as coincidence, sure, but all of it?

Widow looked back at Cord and asked a question.

"How did you know to find me?"

Cord said, "What?"

"How did you know to find me? How did you even know about me? Was it just from Rowley?"

"What're you talking about?"

Widow turned back and stared at them, his hands down by his sides.

"How did you find me?"

Lucas said, "This isn't the time!"

Widow asked, "Who found me?"

Cord said, "Graine."

Widow asked, "He's the one who found me?"

"Yeah. He's the cop."

Widow turned and looked at Graine.

"How long have you been looking for me?"

Graine said, "What? Two days. Lane revealed himself. And a simple sweep found you."

"Explain that to me?"

Graine paused a long beat.

He said, "I stumbled upon you. It was luck, really."

Lucas asked, "What the hell does this have to do with anything?"

Widow stared at Graine coldly.

Graine said, "Gibson told me about you. That's all."

Widow shook his head.

"No. I don't think so. No way. I live off the grid. Raggie was kidnapped two days ago. Rowley just found out about Lane. You're telling me she was kidnapped just as I was arrested and showed up in the system? I don't buy it. I can believe that it's a coincidence that I show up in the system as you're searching for me. Or I can believe that she was taken. But all at the same time? No. I don't buy that for a second."

Graine said nothing. He quivered from behind the stock of his MP5.

Widow asked, "How long you been looking for me?"

Graine said nothing.

Cord said, "What're you implying?"

Cord lowered his weapon just enough for Widow to see his whole face.

Widow said, "I've known two types of people my whole life more than any others—sailors and cops. I grew up with cops. I've worked with cops. I was an undercover cop in the NCIS. I worked a lot of cases. Sixteen years. And I never met a cop who was that lucky."

Graine stayed quiet and looked through his thick glasses at Widow.

Cord said, "And?"

Widow said, "Either you're the luckiest cop that ever lived, or you're a regular Sherlock Holmes. But I don't think it's either. Because if you were so good or so lucky, then why're you on the sidelines, babysitting the mother? Why not be out there looking for Raggie like the top cop you seem to be?"

Graine stayed quiet.

Widow said, "You found me. You told Cord about me. I bet you came up with this harebrained scheme?"

Cord looked back over his shoulder at Graine. Lucas remained trained on Lane.

Widow said, "These guys definitely didn't have any faith in you. If they did, then why not let you off the leash? Why not go out there and find Raggie yourself? Why are all of Rowley's close friends in the Service, on his team, and not you?"

Graine stayed quiet.

Widow said, "I'll tell you why. I think you aren't a good cop. I think you weren't good enough for Rowley to put you on his Secret Service detail. And those glasses...I know little about prescription glasses, but I've never seen glasses that thick on a person before unless he was virtually blind. Yet you were just driving, which isn't a big deal, because plenty of people with strong prescriptions drive. But right now, you're looking down your MP5 the right way. You're aimed at Lane, who's a good thirty yards away from us. And you made it as a detective in some department in Missouri—I'm told. I don't doubt that there're cops with bad vision, especially in some small town out in Missouri, but they don't make detective easy. To be a detective, you must be able to detect.

"And I doubt your bad eyesight came on overnight. No way. They test you before letting you have a gun. And the Navy would've tested you before that. Your vision might be bad, but I don't think it's that bad. And I don't think you were so unlucky for your whole career and then, suddenly, lucky enough to stumble upon all those clues. Not by yourself."

Cord said, "Graine, what the hell is this? Did you know Widow ahead of time?"

Widow said, "And one more thing. How did Raggie get taken in the first place?"

Lucas shifted his footing. His face twitched, and his eyes closed tightly. An expression that Widow had never seen before came over his face. It must've been utter betrayal or intense disappointment or both. Widow wasn't sure. Lucas swiveled and spun one hundred eighty degrees—fast.

He trained his MP5 on Graine.

He asked, "You? You took her?"

Cord asked, "How could you? You're like a brother to us!"

Graine said, "Guys! I don't know what he's talking about! Come on!"

Widow said, "A fourteen-year-old girl who surfs and was attacked by a shark, survives, and goes on is a tough girl. She wouldn't be easy to kidnap. No way would she have been tricked into getting into a stranger's car. No way!

"Plus, I don't think her mother would let her go out to meet her friends alone. Not living the life they live. A Secret Service agent's wife? A mother whose daughter almost lost her life in a shark attack? No. I think she thought you would shadow her. That you would watch over her like you always had. Isn't that right? Did you tell Karen that you would stay close?"

Graine stayed quiet.

Widow said, "This time, when Raggie didn't come back. What'd you tell Karen?"

Graine remained quiet. His brow sweated.

Widow asked, "Did you tell her you were sorry? Did you blame it on your bad eyes? These people trusted you with their lives, with their daughter, but you aren't obligated to protect them, are you? Because you're not Secret Service. You aren't good enough to be an agent. You're not like Cord. Not like Lucas. Not as good as them. Is that right?"

Graine said nothing.

Widow asked, "Is that why you betrayed them?"

Graine kept his gun pointed straight ahead. He didn't shift the target from Lane. He let go of the underside of the barrel with his left hand and lifted his hand slowly back to his face. Not too fast—he didn't want Cord or Lucas to squeeze their triggers. He touched the frame of his glasses and blinked a few times as if straining to stare through the thick lenses. Then he jerked them off and tossed the glasses into the grass. They landed three yards from Widow.

Widow stared at Graine, who suddenly looked like a different man, like he transformed right before their very eyes.

Widow thought, *Stop! Drop! And Roll!*

Graine said, "You guys always got all the good shit. Better jobs! Better pay! Better lives! Gibson always favored you two over me! His wife loved y'all over me! That kid loved y'all over me!"

Lucas spoke in a low voice.

"Doug?"

Graine said, "I was always the odd man out!"

Cord asked, "Why?"

"Listen to me! I'm telling you!"

Lucas said, "But you're one of us!"

"Do you know how much I make a year?"

Cord asked, "This is about money?"

"Lane is paying me a lot of money."

Cord said, "Doug, he's not going to give her back?"

"I was! I'm not a monster! Raggie will be fine! But not that bastard president!"

Cord asked, "What did he do to you?"

"He's out there campaigning and giving speeches while guys like us are dying and doing the heavy lifting. Isn't that a good enough reason? Does that satisfy you?"

Cord said nothing.

Graine said, "But really, for me, it's the money—or maybe the chance to do something. I don't care about politics. Just money. I'm old, and an old man deserves at least a taste of the good life."

Lucas couldn't wait any longer. He moved into a shooting stance and raised his MP5 to aim at Graine. He squeezed the trigger.

But nothing happened. No bullets fired. No muzzle flash. Nothing.

It wasn't like in the movies where a guy squeezed a trigger, and there was an audible click. There was no click.

Graine smiled.

The MP5s that Graine had handed them had been fully loaded. That wasn't the issue. If you wanted to trick someone into thinking their gun was loaded and operable, you didn't take the bullets out. As anyone with gun experience knows, a gun without bullets is easily detectable. An unloaded gun is lighter than a fully loaded one.

Graine said, "Sorry, old friend. I removed your firing pin."

Cord tried his MP5. He fired at Graine, but the same thing happened, which was that nothing happened. It didn't fire. He lowered his MP5 and tossed it to the ground. It clattered on the driveway.

Graine pointed his gun at both men, waving it back and forth between the two.

Widow had no idea what feelings or thoughts were going through Lucas's head, but he imagined they weren't good. And he felt stupid for not seeing this earlier.

Lucas said, "Let Raggie go. She's not a part of this."

Graine said, "That's not up to me."

He set the selector on the MP5 to semi-auto and pulled the trigger in two quick successions.

POP! POP!

Two bullets fired from the gun—the first hit Lucas in the neck.

Widow watched as a red mist burst from the back of Lucas's neck. Blood and tissue and veins followed it.

The second bullet would've been a dead-on headshot, but because Lucas's head whipped back as the first one hit, it ended up hitting the right side of his face. Another misty red explosion burst into the air.

Widow didn't *Stop! Drop! And Roll!*

37

INSTEAD OF *STOP! Drop! And Roll!*, Widow bent his knees and glanced quickly at Cord.

Cord was a good agent with excellent training. He was prepared to die in the line of duty. That was a reality hammered into all Secret Service agents long before they were allowed within a hundred yards of the president. Maybe Graine had been rejected because of his unwillingness to do just that. Widow remembered how much Li had wanted to become an agent. He remembered how important it was to her. Missing the test had been the end of her world—no question about it.

Cord had been one of Rowley's best friends and most trusted agent. Taking a bullet for Rowley wasn't a question. For Cord, it was like breathing. He would do it automatically.

And taking a bullet for Rowley's daughter wasn't a question either. But would Cord take a bullet for Widow? That was a question Widow didn't want to be answered. But he got the answer.

Graine shot Lucas again, who was now lying on the ground fifteen feet from Widow. His body twitched, and he gagged. Blood pooled under his frame like a spilled pot of tomato soup. After the three shots at Lucas, Graine swiveled and aimed in Cord's direction. Graine had fooled both of his friends and had faked his intentions and his abilities.

Cord didn't use his mind to make his split-second decision—he did it instinctively. His reaction had a mind of its own. It was probably a maneuver he had tucked away in the large deck of maneuvers he'd trained his body to do in all likely scenarios that he might encounter protecting the president. He went for the SIG Sauer holstered on his hip. But rather than drawing it quickly and firing at Graine, he turned toward Widow and threw the gun at him.

Graine had left the MP5 in semi-auto function, so he had to pull the trigger every time to fire a bullet. He pulled three times in rapid succession.

POP! POP! POP!

The spent brass flew out of the ejection port and bounced off the ground. The bullets flew in Cord's direction.

Widow made a dive toward the SIG Sauer as it overshot and flew past him toward the tree.

The first bullet caught Cord in the shoulder. The second one missed him. And the third nailed him in the chest. His vest caught it, but it still hurt like hell. He grabbed his chest as soon as he hit the ground, forgetting at first about the one that had penetrated his upper shoulder until the pain hit him.

Widow rolled, grabbed the SIG Sauer, and scrambled to the tree.

Graine fired after him but missed on purpose. He didn't want to damage him. He hadn't been paid yet for his capture.

Lane shouted, "Don't shoot him!"

Graine said, "I know! I know!"

Widow knew Lane hadn't brought his guys, or at least they weren't in the house. The whole thing had been set up to make it look like they were going to be ambushed from the front when the actual plan had been for Graine to ambush them from behind. If there had been guys in the house, they would've come out blasting by this point. Of course, this didn't mean that Lane's backup wasn't somewhere nearby. If so, they certainly heard the gunshots. If Widow was going to get away, he'd better not wait any longer.

He hugged close to the back of the large tree. He didn't look back, but wondered if Cord had survived Graine's bullets.

Graine said, "Widow! Come out!"

Widow stayed quiet and released the magazine from the SIG Sauer, checked it. It was fully loaded—thirteen rounds in the magazine and one in the chamber. Fourteen rounds from a handgun versus an MP5, plus Graine's sidearm. He didn't know what the second weapon was, but he was sure it was something reliable. Probably a Glock. And Lane probably had a gun somewhere within reaching distance. And then there were Lane's guys, who were probably on their way and carrying who knows what kind of guns.

The odds were not good, and they would only get worse.

Graine said, "Come out, Widow! There's nowhere to go!"

Lane said, "Wait!"

Widow couldn't see what they were doing, but he knew.

Graine said, "Come out! You got ten seconds." And then he counted out loud. "Three...Four...Five..."

Widow peeked out over his right shoulder. A quick glance at the drive up to the house and then back. He saw Lane holding a gun about forty yards away, moving parallel to Widow's position and trying to get a look at him from the north. Graine was exactly where Widow feared he would be. He stood over Cord; his MP5 pointed down at him.

"Seven...Eight...Nine..."

On ten, Graine did nothing. He paused and waited till what would've been eleven, and then on twelve, he pulled the trigger. Just once. One quick gunshot. He didn't even look down at Cord. He kept his eyes on Widow's position.

The bullet plugged another area on Cord's bulletproof vest, and Cord screamed in agony. He didn't speak. He just wailed in pain.

Graine said, "Okay! Five seconds this time!"

Widow closed his eyes. Thought about what he would have to do to get to Cord.

Lean out over his right side. Take aim. Fire two shots. Hit Graine.

Two rounds to the center mass were what he wanted because that was the most likely target he could hit with only one second of aiming. Then he'd pull back to the tree, wait one second longer for Lane to fire. Maybe a second and a half, depending on how good Lane was with a gun. And Widow was sure he was plenty good. If Rowley's description of Lane was any indicator of his ability, then the best-case scenario was that Lane had been an average special ops shooter ten years ago. If he was out of practice, it meant that now he would most likely be slightly better than poor because shooting is a perishable skill. However, even with deteriorated skills, he'd still be able to hit a target as big as Widow at that range.

The worst-case scenario was that Lane had picked up right where he left off after prison and had spent the last year practicing. Maybe he'd improved.

Graine counted again. "Five...Four..."

And suddenly, Widow's odds got significantly worse because a Range Rover came barreling around the corner and down the street, its high beams bright and pointed straight at Widow. He reached up with his hand to block out the light. He was sure that the occupants in the truck weren't on his side. Lowering his gun, he stayed tucked behind the tree.

The Range Rover hopped the curb and skidded in the grass like a dramatic scene from a bad movie. Three guys jumped out—mercenaries from the looks of them. Two had M9 Berettas, and the other one had an MP5. No suppressors.

The one driving popped out fast. He hit the dirt and scrambled around to the hood. He extended his arms across the top of the truck and pointed his M9 at Widow.

"Drop it!" he shouted in a thick British accent. He didn't repeat himself. He was confident. Widow figured he must be the wrangler of the bunch, the guy behind the guy. He was probably the second lieutenant.

Looking over his left shoulder, Widow saw Lane had made a half-circle around the tree and was now pointing his gun at Widow's head from twenty-five feet. No chance he was going to miss his shot, no matter how little he might've practiced his shooting skills. Even in the darkness, there was still plenty of city light on the horizon that it wasn't completely black. And the bright lights from the Range Rover had Widow lit up like a spotlight on a stage. There was no way out, and he knew it.

He tossed the SIG Sauer to the ground and stayed standing.

Grant, the one with the British accent, screamed, "Get down!"

Widow stayed quiet and didn't move. He kept his hands by his sides.

Lane said, "Do as he says!"

Widow stayed standing.

Grant repeated his orders. "Get down!"

Widow said, "I'm not getting down. You have me. No need to treat me like a dog."

Lane looked at Grant and shrugged. He said, "Put the cuffs on him."

The other two mercenaries moved closer. They stumbled slightly, but it wasn't completely blundering, more like they just woke up. Or perhaps they were a little drunk.

Widow held his hands down and said, "You can put cuffs on me, but you'll find that won't keep me submissive. If you want me to cooperate with no trouble, let Agent Cord live."

Lane closed in and lowered his weapon, but stayed too far away for Widow to reach him. Smart.

Lane said, "Trouble? Do you think you can cause trouble for us? We aren't just guys with guns. We're former Special Forces guys with guns. You're not going to cause trouble for any of us."

Widow said, "You have no idea the kinda trouble I can cause you."

Lane flashed an angry scowl.

"It's a shame that you will die so slow. You know, I'm not as angry with you as with the others. At least you tried to save Chang. Do you remember?"

"I remember."

"At any rate, you will die a slow death, Commander Jack Widow."

Widow said, "Tough talk from a coward holding a gun."

"Oh, you think you can take me? You want me to put down the gun and fight you? Some kind of deal where you and your friend walk free if I lose?"

"You would lose."

"There'll be plenty of time for chitchat later. Right now, I've got to deal with another dead president."

"Let Agent Cord live, and I won't cause you any trouble."

The two mercs neared Widow. One had the handcuffs in his left hand while his right hand was held up like he was trying to tame a lion. The second guy stood five feet behind him, a gun aimed at Widow's center mass.

Lane said, "We're going to kill him now. And you will die much later."

The first guy reached out to grab Widow's wrists, which were extended outward, limp, and submissive. He stepped up and grabbed Widow's left wrist with his right hand.

Widow took the chance and jerked his arm straight down, delivering a perfectly timed head-butt straight to the guy's forehead. He had been blessed with a head like concrete, which made for a pretty good weapon—and one that couldn't be taken away from him. However, his head wasn't designed to stun. It was a finishing weapon, usually delivering a fatal blow. But he didn't want to kill the guy—he needed him alive. He pulled back on the head-butt so that it had just enough force to stun him, yet still enough power to shatter the bones in the guy's nose. Blood spewed from the center of his face in a gush like a red waterfall.

Widow pulled back and spun the guy around. He clamped his left hand down over the guy's hand, and the guy dropped the handcuffs. Widow grabbed the guy's other hand and pulled both hands across the guy's chest and over his shoulder, then pulled the guy in tight and squeezed the bones in his wrists.

The guy's nose was broken from the impact of Widow's head. He was eager to grab his nose and pinch it, a normal reaction to a nose-bleed, but not realistic here because he couldn't release his hands from Widow's grasp.

Widow was thankful the guy wasn't drunker. Unconscious people and drunk ones were two of the worst types of people to use as hostages. You can't hold up an unconscious person and cover your body with them like a human shield. Deadweight was heavy and could often be immovable. A drunk person was just as bad. Their body movements were unpredictable, and their behavior erratic.

Widow pulled hard on the guy's wrists. He screamed in agony.

Widow looked over his shoulder at the others. Lane was still behind him, but Widow was counting on him not to shoot. Lane wanted him alive and unharmed, because his plan was to do all the harming later.

The wrangler merc stepped forward and away from the others. Widow's eyes were dead in the sights of his M9. In his British accent, he said, "Let him go, son!"

"Don't shoot!" Lane said, "Widow, let him go. I can shoot you right now in the back, and then we'll have to haul you around everywhere. You won't like it. It'll be more uncomfortable for you in the long run."

"You won't shoot. I weigh two twenty-five. I'm heavy. It'll take all day to drag me around. Let Cord live, and I'll let him go. I'll come with you of my own free will. No hassle."

Graine said, "I'll kill Cord if you don't let him go!"

Lane said, "Shut up!"

He turned to Widow.

"Okay. Okay. We'll let him live. We'll take him with us. You've got my word."

"You'll let him and the girl live?"

"Now, you know I can't promise you that."

Widow knew he'd refuse, but he wanted to try. In his experience, it was better for the bad guy to assume that you knew you were completely hopeless. He wanted Lane to think he was holding all the cards.

Widow said, "Then promise me they'll live longer than me. Promise you'll keep them alive and consider letting them go. After you get what you want, what difference will it make to let them go? People are going to know who you are anyway. No way will you get out of the country without people knowing your identity."

"You're right. Fine. You've got my word. I'll let them live if you give up."

Widow acted like he was considering it, and then he squeezed the guy's wrists one more time—hard. The guy screamed, and Widow let go of him. He dropped to the ground and cupped his nose with his both hands.

Grant said, "Cuff him!"

The guy with the MP5 walked over to Widow with his gun extended, which was a big mistake. It gave Widow a second opportunity to escape. The guy must've been a little drunk as well—or perhaps he'd been absent on the day his Special Forces buddies were taught how to secure a prisoner. Widow could've taken the weapon from him. He could've shot him in the chest and knelt fast, switching the firing selector to full auto. Then he could've opened fire on the British guy and snapped to the left and repeated the action on Graine. But Lane was still behind Widow. Depending on how fast he reacted, which probably would've been plenty fast, Widow would've been shot in the back and died before he got to the guy on the ground. And even in the best of circumstances, Graine would've killed Cord for sure.

Widow let the handcuffs lock down on one wrist and then the other.

The guy grabbed the chain that linked the cuffs and jerked Widow forward.

Lane said, "Grant, pick up Silverti!"

The British guy said nothing, but holstered his Beretta behind the small of his back and walked over to Silverti. He reached down, grabbed the guy by the arm, and jerked him up to his feet. Grant said, "Walk."

They walked back to the Range Rover, and Grant shut Silverti into the backseat. Widow saw Silverti reach up to the console. He pulled out a white rag and held it to his nose. Then he leaned back against the seat.

Lane came up behind Widow and holstered his gun.

He said, "I'm going to enjoy killing you more than the president."

Widow said, "Don't forget your promise."

Lane nodded, but it wasn't reassuring to Widow.

The guy who had put him in cuffs, whose name Widow hadn't picked up on, hauled him down to the Range Rover and lifted the rear gate. He shoved Widow in.

Widow sat upright, back against the backbench. He had to cross his legs Indian style to fit. The guy slammed the hatch down, and it snapped shut. He watched as Lane went over and talked to Graine. This was the moment that scared Widow because he had gambled that Lane was a man of his word. It turned out to be a safe bet because Lane pointed at Cord, and Grant placed handcuffs on him as well. They removed his bulletproof vest first and tossed it into Graine's vehicle. Then they turned Cord over onto his stomach and handcuffed him with his hands behind him, which they should've done to Widow.

Next, they rolled Lucas's body over, and Grant and the other guy lifted him by the arms and legs. They carried him back to the open garage of the house from which Lane had emerged. They disappeared inside and came out a few moments later without the body. They had left Lucas behind, abandoned like a dead piece of meat. Lane shook hands with Graine, who got back into his truck after collecting the MP5s with the missing firing pins and tossing them into the back.

Widow watched as Graine drove past him. They didn't make eye contact.

Lane and Grant returned to the Range Rover, dragging Cord along with them. They put him in the back with Widow. He lay in pain across Widow's lap. Then they went to the front of the truck and got in, Grant in the driver's seat and Lane in the front passenger side. The other guy got in next to Silverti.

Lane turned and looked back at Widow. He said, "We'll get to know each other soon enough, but for now, just relax."

38

WIDOW HAD MADE A MISTAKE, and so had Cord. They had assumed that after Widow traded himself over to extend Raggie's life, Lane would take him back to where they had stashed her. He didn't.

The other mistake was the GPS tracker on his shoe. That was useless now. But he left it.

Instead of driving to Raggie's location, they took the Range Rover down the street and turned a corner. The unfinished, abandoned subdivision project was much larger than Widow had guessed. They drove for at least ten minutes before they rounded another empty block with high trees and undeveloped land, coming to a stop at a house that looked finished as far as the exterior went. They pulled into the driveway, and Grant killed the engine on the Range Rover.

Widow looked at Cord. The agent's eyes were open, but he looked like he was in a great deal of pain.

Widow asked, "Does this hurt?" He poked gently at Cord's ribs, first the upper and then the lower.

Cord squirmed in agony both times.

Widow said, "Looks like they're broken. How's the shoulder feel?"

"Hurts like hell."

"We need to dress it before you bleed out. I need to flip you and check to see if the bullet came out."

Cord nodded and said, "We're stopped. Better do it now."

Widow nodded and grabbed Cord's arm. He hauled him up and flipped him over for a second, then gently rolled him back.

"It went through, but we gotta wrap these wounds."

The rear hatch swung up, and the guy whose name Widow didn't know said, "Time to go in."

He grabbed Cord by the arm and pulled him up and out. He said, "On your feet."

Cord struggled, but made it to his feet.

Widow said, "He needs his wounds cleaned and bandaged."

Grant said, "No way! He can suffer!"

Lane said, "That's not necessary. If Widow wants to clean and bandage him up, let him. There's a first aid kit in the truck. Get it for him."

Grant turned and walked to the rear of the truck. He leaned inside and came out with a white box with a red cross on the lid.

Lane said, "Take 'em to the room and let 'em figure it out."

Grant nodded toward Silverti and said, "What about his nose?"

"Take out the tape and some bandage. Leave the rest. They'll need it more."

Grant opened the kit and took out a couple of large bandages and the medical tape. The rest he shoved into Widow's cuffed hands.

Widow took it and walked behind the guy and Cord. They entered the house. He glanced over his shoulder and saw that Lane wasn't stupid. He followed right behind with his gun drawn.

The inside of the house was nothing but some unfinished cabinetry, unfinished walls, and concrete floors. The stairs were plain wood and had no railing. The guy with no name started to take them up the stairs, but Cord groaned at the bottom.

Lane said, "Not up there. Take them to the master."

The guy shrugged and led them down a hall with unpainted walls. In the master, there was no furniture except for a couple of folding chairs. The wall near the bathroom was lined with exposed beams.

Widow heard a motor humming. The noise was coming from an external generator.

At the far end of the wall, there appeared to be a command center set up. Two MacBooks were open and running programs. He could see that one was a CCTV feed. Widow focused and saw Raggie. She was alive in another location in the dark. She probably didn't know she was on camera. The picture was grainy, and the screen was dark green, so the camera must be set to night vision. Blackness shadowed the outskirts of the screen. There was no sound.

The other guy said, "Have a seat," and pointed to a long wall with no windows.

Widow looked around the room. Checked out the bathroom. And then he said, "Where's the girl?"

The guy said, "Forget about her. Sit down."

Lane walked into the room and said, "Did you think we were going to take you to her? That would've been dumb on our part. We can't have you knowing where she is. Like I said, I underestimated you once, but I'm not doing it a second time. Not that you'll escape, but in case you get a lucky break, I don't plan on having you anywhere near her."

Damn! Widow thought.

Lane said, "Sit down."

"I need the cuffs off both of us, so I can help him."

Lane nodded and said to the guy, "Toss him the key. Don't hand it to him. Stay out of his reach."

Smart guy, Widow thought.

The guy threw the keys to Widow. He kept the MP5 pointed downward, but his trigger finger was on the gun and ready. Widow had startled the guy with his actions at the other house. Now, the guy wouldn't let Widow get the advantage. He was going to make it harder, but Widow wasn't worried.

Cord couldn't stand any longer. He dropped to his knees and turned his hands out toward Widow. Widow put down the first aid kit and picked up the keys from where they'd landed. He unlocked Cord and then himself, which was awkward and took him a moment. Cord had leaned back against the wall. He grabbed his shoulder.

Cord said, "Widow, I'm feeling woozy. Not sure how much longer I'll be conscious."

Widow said, "Hang on."

He dropped the handcuffs and the key to the ground and opened the first aid kit. Inside, he found gauze, some dressings, and a roll of bandage. There was a sewing needle and some black string, probably for stitching. There was also a bottle of rubbing alcohol.

Widow grabbed the bottle and said, "Take off your shirt."

Cord struggled to lean forward and unbuttoned several buttons.

The process was too slow, so Widow said, "Move your hands."

He grabbed both sides of Cord's shirt and pulled them in opposite directions, ripping the buttons right off. He released the fabric, and Cord pulled his arms out of the sleeves. Underneath it, he wore a white cotton T-shirt that was now soaked in blood. He pulled it over his head and kept it balled up in his hand.

Widow picked up the bottle of alcohol and said, "This'll hurt."

Cord nodded.

Widow poured a quarter of the bottle over the entry wound from the gunshot.

Cord screamed in agony.

Widow turned him around and did the same to the exit wound. He examined both wounds and then pushed his hand against the back wound, pressing hard to stop the bleeding. He kept his hand there.

He said, "We need to stitch up the exit wound. It's pretty big. I think the front will be okay with tight wrapping."

Cord said, "Do it!"

"Lean forward and try not to move."

That was when Widow noticed for the first time that Lane was smiling. He seemed to enjoy seeing his old teammate in agonizing pain.

Widow knew little about sewing, but he got the gist of it. He didn't concern himself with trying to make a straight line. Under the circumstances, he thought faster was probably better. He grabbed Cord's shoulder tight with his hand, applying a tremendous amount of pressure to it to keep Cord from squirming around too much. Luckily, the needle was already threaded with string. That saved a lot of time because Widow was not good at things as tedious as putting the tiny end of a string into the barely larger hole at the end of a needle.

He had to make more than a few stitches into Cord's wound to pull it shut. The entire process took five minutes, during which Cord struggled not to scream.

By the end, Lane's smile had grown even wider.

39

Widow finished sewing up Cord's wound and then wrapped a dressing tightly around his shoulder so that the bleeding at the entrance wound would clot. Then he wrapped the rest of the dressing snugly around Cord's chest, under his arms, and around his back to pull his ribs together. He wasn't medically trained and had no idea if it would work, but his idea was to use the dressing as a splint. He thought it might keep Cord's ribs from moving around too much.

A short time later, Widow was sitting on the floor and leaning against the wall with his hands cuffed behind him and around the exposed wood framing. Cord lay on his back, his arms extended above his head, and cuffed around a different stud. The nameless guy had been left to watch over them. Alone. That was fine by Widow. He had been hoping for that. Even though he and Cord were both restrained, it gave him better odds.

The guy was busy on the computer. He watched Raggie half the time and amused himself on the computer the other half. He started laughing out loud. It looked to Widow like he was watching *YouTube* videos. Widow had heard of that site and how people went there to watch pets doing funny things or kids trying stupid and life-threatening stunts.

Widow whispered to Cord, "How're you feeling?"

"Not my best day."

Widow nodded.

Cord said, "They killed Lucas."

"I know. And they almost killed you."

"I was in the Marines. Did you know that?"

"I didn't."

"So was Lucas. We served together. I've known him for twenty years. I think his dad fought in Korea. He was a good soldier. A patriot."

Widow said, "I came from a military family, myself. I could tell he was a good guy. He really cared about Raggie."

"Is she alive?"

"Over there. On the laptop. You can see her. It looks like a live feed. She's being held somewhere else."

"Does she look okay? I mean, is she healthy?"

"She looks scared. I can't see her very well. We're too far away, and they've got her in the dark."

"How can you see her?"

"Night vision cameras. She probably doesn't even know they're watching her."

Cord said, "She knows. She's a smart one. The only reason they even got to her was Graine. That bastard! I'm going to put a bullet in him!"

Widow said, "Relax. First things first. We gotta get out of here."

"How the hell are we going to do that?"

Widow shrugged. "I got no idea."

40

RAGGIE DIDN'T LIKE any of the men that she had seen so far. But then again, they were her abductors, so there was no reason to like any of them. But she particularly didn't like the one who had been sent to watch her now—not one bit.

He had wandering eyes. He had looked at her twice now. He walked in, past the barking dogs, and opened her door, and turned on the light. He said he just wanted to check on her, but she knew he wanted to let her know he was there and that they were alone.

The first time she saw him was when they filmed that stupid video that she didn't want to be a part of. And the second time had been an hour ago when he showed up to replace their leader—the quiet one.

This guy was called Valentine. She'd heard his name. She tried to remember all their names so she could tell her dad later. She knew he would rescue her. There wasn't a doubt in her mind that the Secret Service wouldn't let her die. But then again, Graine had been one of her dad's friends. He wasn't Secret Service, but he had been a cop and was once with her dad when he was in the Navy. She had known him ever since she was a little girl. But she didn't know him as well as she knew Lucas.

Lucas had been like a second father to her. Sometimes he felt more like her real father than the one that she had because he was always around whenever he wasn't working. He came to all her birthdays and every major event in her life. She remembered one year he took her to Australia to watch a huge surfing competition on Bells Beach. It was one of the most favorite weeks she had in her whole life.

Lucas would find her—that she knew for sure.

But she didn't want to wait. One thing her dad had taught her was never to leave your life in the hands of others. Always try to ensure your own safety. Pack your own parachute and that sort of thing.

What if Lucas wasn't coming? What if no one was coming?

She had to take matters into her own hands, but then she thought about how she only had one hand. She smiled a bit for the first time since she was taken.

Raggie had to escape or die. It was better to die trying than to die the way they wanted her to. But how the hell was she supposed to get out?

She was sure that they were watching her with a camera that could see in the dark. What the hell was that called? The neighbor kid back in South Africa would know. He was always playing video games. Dark vision? Whatever. She needed to get their attention. She was frustrated because so many things had to fall into place for her to escape. She needed one of them to get close to her. Then she needed that person to remove her one handcuff. But how was she going to do that? She didn't know yet.

After that, she needed to use her one hand to grab a weapon. Her first choice would be a Glock. That was a gun her dad had taught her to use—she was comfortable with it because it was lightweight and easy to fire. She wasn't big on guns, but he had insisted on her being competent with them. He wanted her to know how to handle one safely.

Here, though, the weapon she had chosen was one she found lying around. She knew she was in a veterinary clinic—the barking dogs and the giant farmer sink made that pretty obvious. Even though it was dark, she had found the sink's pipes using touch and sounds. She had slipped off her shoe and felt around with her toes. While doing that, she discovered a big bottle, like a gallon jug. It was mostly empty. She could hear the liquid in it swish around every time she tapped it with her foot.

Since she figured her captors were watching her, she kicked at the pipes while pulling the bottle back to her. That way, they wouldn't realize what she was doing. She moved the liquid bottle over to her, and she studied it. Without lifting it in her feet and possibly giving away her potential plans to her captors, the closest she could get it to her face was to rest the bottle next to her right hip. By twisting her back and peering over, she could look at the label.

After being locked up in the dark for hours, her eyes had adjusted somewhat to the lack of light. She couldn't see too far away, but she could see well up close. The label was bright white, which was a good thing, but the small print was impossible to see. She could, however, clearly see the large letters showing what was in the bottle. It wasn't what she had been hoping for—but much better. She thought a veterinary clinic was probably required to lock up all hazardous materials and narcotics. But the chemicals that people left out were cleaning products.

Raggie had hoped that the chemical inside of the jug was bleach. But it wasn't bleach—it was ammonia. That was the word she could see clearly on the bottle.

Ammonia caused severe chemical burns. Raggie had seen on *YouTube* some effects of ammonia when it contacted skin. There were stories all over the internet of people who had ammonia thrown in their faces. As she recalled, most of these stories were gruesome. She remembered one where a guy in Iran had thrown it in a woman's face and then raped her. Later, the guy was caught. Iran had a crazy law that whenever someone committed a vile crime against someone else, the victim had the right to call for an equal punishment against the aggressor. The woman had lost her eye because of the chemical, so she had called for the prisoner's eye to be taken out and for him to be raped by other inmates regularly. The judge in the case agreed to the severe punishment, and to this day, the rapist was still getting his.

Raggie remembered this story. How could she forget? But she wasn't a savage. She was a good person. But, it was kill or be killed. She didn't care if one of her captors lost his eyes. All she needed was for one of them to come close to her. She hadn't heard a peep from anyone in almost twenty-four hours. So Valentine seemed to be her best chance.

* * *

VALENTINE WATCHED from the next room. He smiled. Raggie was just the right age.

He was still drinking. He'd stolen several of those small liquor bottles from a motel in Memphis three days earlier. His vice hadn't always been such a problem, but he was running out of luck. He'd pissed off a lot of his employers because of his excessive drinking.

One such employer that he'd pissed off was a mobster in Memphis. Some rich moron who liked to hire ex-military for different things he considered being special assignments. Most of it was spying on the guy's competitors or protecting him during meetings with other mob families from Atlanta. It was boring, low-level stuff, even though he liked to think it was important. He liked to think it was like the jobs he had in his heyday. But nothing he had done in Tennessee or anywhere else in the US compared to the dangerous operations he performed ten years ago in Iraq or Afghanistan.

But even in the small-time jobs, Valentine was messing up. His drinking had gotten worse. And that's why when a job came along that got him out of Memphis, his employer had given him rave recommendations. Of course, he was taking a risk doing this because the kind of guys who were looking for a couple of extra men for an operation on American soil weren't the kind of guys you lied to. Not that Valentine's old employer was wise to this. He probably didn't know exactly who he was lying to. He had no idea how insignificant he was compared to some of the hardened warlords Valentine had met in the past.

Besides, Valentine wasn't planning on messing up the mission.

At that very moment, he wasn't that drunk—not like he had been before. But the girl was looking good on camera. They were going to kill her, anyway. What difference did it make if he had a little fun with her? As long as he didn't leave any visible marks, they would never even know.

She wouldn't be a problem. She was restrained, and she only had one hand. But he figured he had to remove the handcuffs because he liked it when a girl used her hand.

He wasn't worried. She was a hundred pounds soaking wet. No way was she going to overpower him. Besides, she had been locked up for twenty-four hours. She looked like she hadn't slept, and her kicking and screaming had slowed down a lot. She wouldn't be a problem.

But just in case, he decided it would be best to make it quick—in and out. No trouble. And he would have to leave his gun behind. He would be preoccupied and probably have his pants off for a good ten minutes. Couldn't take the chance of her getting his gun.

He took a swig from the little Jack Daniels bottle, emptying it, and stood up from the desk with the monitors that provided a constant stream of video. He looked away at the door that led into the next room. The dogs had quieted down. They were all taking their afternoon naps, he guessed. Opening the door would wake them up, and they would start barking again. But that was a small price to pay for a good time.

He withdrew his Beretta M9 from the holster. It was the gun Grant had given him. They had all received a gun. He had one full magazine with no backups. They hadn't planned on using weapons. Not really. The gun was more of a precautionary measure. The mission was a difficult one. Its goal was to get some guy—someone Valentine didn't know and didn't care about—to assassinate his friend and boss, the United States president, on national TV.

Their role was manipulation. Apparently, this Lane guy had succeeded in a practice op just like this one in Africa. Valentine was impressed by these guys so far. They'd pulled off the African thing. He saw it on the news. But this wasn't Africa. This was the United States of America.

He had his doubts about the whole scheme. Valentine wasn't a fool. He knew that out of all the guys they had; he was the weakest link. But, hey, his job was babysitting. That required little sobriety. Suddenly, he questioned the act he was about to take part in. Then he pushed his doubts aside, just shrugged them away like a piece of lint on your shoulder.

You only live once, he told himself.

He ejected the magazine from the Beretta and put it into his pocket. He left the gun on the desk next to the keyboard.

It was impossible to shoot a man with his own weapon when you had no bullets. In case the girl got free and got his gun—both impossible—then at least she would be screwed when she tried to shoot him.

* * *

THE DOOR OPENED, and a pool of light flowed into the dark room.

Raggie saw for the first time the details of the space in which she was being held captive. It was a small room, much smaller than she'd thought. She'd imagined it was this huge space with a table for examining dogs, a scale, some empty cages of different sizes, and the farmer sink for bathing the animals. But the room wasn't like that at all. It was more like a big closet. It reminded her of one of those decompression chambers she'd seen in documentaries about space shuttles. The astronauts left the shuttle and went out into space, and then they returned with their spacesuits on. Next, they entered one room and let it seal, and then they went back into the shuttle and removed their breathing gear.

On one wall were the chemicals and drugs used for the animals. They were locked up in a large cage with wheels on the bottom. The next wall had equipment and machines she had never seen before. There was even a large tank of some sort. And then there was a large, empty counter for examining animals or administering narcotics or performing surgery.

In the corner, above the counter, was a camera pointed down directly at her.

She tucked the bottle of ammonia behind her. She had slipped the top off with her toes. It had taken her forty-five minutes. She pulled her knees up to her chin and made it look like she had run out of energy. Then she swiveled in such a way so that the jug was hidden from where she thought the camera was. She rotated her toes back and forth like a wrench. The top had slowly come loose, and then finally, it was off.

She was ready for the guy. She just needed him to unlock her handcuffs.

But then the guy did something she hadn't expected, and her plan was severely compromised. He flipped on the light in her room, and she was overcome with blindness.

She felt a terror consume her like that day she had been pulled under the surface of the Indian Ocean by a ragged-tooth shark.

Valentine said, "Be a good girl, and this'll all be over quick."

41

WIDOW AND CORD tried to figure out how they would get free and escape without getting shot. The answer to the question presented itself like the luckiest thing that could've ever happened to them. The only thing that would've been better was if the guy tasked with watching over them while Lane and Grant were gone suddenly had a severe heart attack right in front of them and dropped the keys to their handcuffs at Widow's feet.

That wasn't what happened. Instead, the guy suddenly sat upright in his chair and stared at the monitors like he was watching a football game, and his team was about to lose, but they caught an interception in the last seconds of the game. The player ran full steam toward the end zone, but he was tackled at the last second. There was no cheering from the guy. He screamed at the monitor, a loud sound that Widow guessed was negative.

The guy stood, knocking the chair over.

He repeated, "No! No! No!"

He sifted through his pockets, frantically searching for something. Widow assumed he was looking for his cell phone. The guy searched each of his pockets a second and third time. No phone.

Whatever the guy had seen on the screen had freaked him out so badly that he started pacing the room. And then he did the most bizarre thing—he asked Widow for help.

He said, "Have you seen my phone?"

Widow stayed quiet.

The guy said, "Look! If you know where it is, you better tell me! Your little girlfriend's life might depend on it!"

Widow craned his head and looked over at the monitor to see what had the guy so frantic. It wasn't football.

Widow saw Raggie wasn't alone. Her eyes were tightly shut because someone had flipped on the light. The night vision was now impaired, and the screen had gone from a grainy green color to a bright white color, but Widow could still see Raggie.

A man stood over her. He stood over Raggie in a way that made his intentions obvious.

Widow quickly closed his eyes and retraced the guy's steps over the last fifty-five minutes they had been alone. Within three seconds, he knew where the phone was.

The guy had stepped outside the house twice and smelled like smoke, so Widow assumed he left to smoke a cigarette. It made little sense for him to leave the unfinished house, but the guy had. The only other place he had gone was to the bathroom.

Widow craned his head and looked past the guy and down the short hallway to the master bath. The door was open, and Widow saw a roll of toilet paper they must've brought with them on the back of the toilet—and on top of that was a cell phone. A smartphone. If it was a burner, it was a pricier one. Maybe the guy had sprung for his own so that he could use the internet.

Cord looked confused and said nothing. He hadn't looked at the monitor yet.

Widow said, "You got me! It's in my pocket. I took it off you earlier. You dropped it, and I guess you didn't even feel it fall. Maybe you were too drunk."

The guy said, "I'm not drunk."

Widow said, "Whatever. I don't care. It's in my pocket."

The guy said, "How'd you get it in your pocket?"

"I did it when you uncuffed us earlier. I thought if I could get free—maybe ask you for a bathroom break—I'd call for help. I was waiting for an hour. Right now, it's close."

The guy came forward and got close to Widow.

He knelt and asked, "Which pocket?"

Widow stayed quiet.

The guy said, "Now!"

Widow spoke with a little intimidation in his voice like he was scared. "Okay. Okay. It's the front left pocket."

He had said left pocket on purpose because he watched the guy earlier. When he had the MP5 in his hand, his right hand was on the handle. His right index finger was in the trigger housing. The guy was right-handed, and right-handed people always reach into a stranger's left pocket with their right hands, which was what Widow had wanted.

The guy reluctantly reached into Widow's left pocket. He should've patted him down first to see if there was a phone there, but it wouldn't have made much difference.

The guy's hand went into Widow's pocket, and Widow squeezed his thigh muscles as hard as he could. The guy's hand was caught instantly in a tight grip, wedged between a rock and a hard place. The guy pulled back, but the more he pulled, the tighter the grip became, like Chinese finger cuffs.

A great invention, Widow thought.

Suddenly, Widow landed a vicious head-butt. He had cocked his head back the whole time the guy was moving forward and down toward him. At the perfect moment, Widow's head thrashed forward. The front of Widow's forehead connected with the guy's face, and for the second time that night, he broke a nose. But this time, he did more damage—much, much more.

He hadn't held back. The impact made a loud crack, and the guy's nose ruptured and fragmented. The bridge was completely cracked open in several places, and his face was covered in blood. The force of the blow had sent him flying over Widow's legs, his hand still locked in Widow's front pocket. He hung there, limp and motionless.

Widow wasn't sure if he was dead or not. He hoped not, because they might need to get information out of him.

Cord said, "Damn! I think you killed him."

Widow said, "Maybe. Maybe not. Doesn't matter."

"How're we going to get free? Not with the keys. We can't reach his pockets with our hands like this."

Widow said, "I guess with some regular squats."

"What?"

Widow stayed quiet and drew up his knees. He squirmed around and got his feet under his butt. Sitting on the backs of his legs, he pushed up and out, away from the wood. Widow hadn't done squats in years, but he remembered the basic principle. The wood behind him was relatively new, but Widow was strong. He had strong leg muscles and a strong back.

He pushed—hard. His feet and shins strained. He heaved upward and jerked forward like a working ox pulling a fully loaded cart out of a ditch. As he strained, his face turned a crimson color as if he'd burst a vein.

He opened his eyes and stared at the monitor across the room. He saw the man still standing over Raggie. He saw her eyes were sealed shut from the brightness of the light, but she knew what was happening. He could see the terror on her face. She squirmed as far away from the man as possible. The handcuff tugged at her one wrist.

The man was taking off his belt, and Widow knew that next he would remove his pants. Widow pulled even harder.

Widow pulled and strained and groaned like a bodybuilder in his toughest competition. The force he exerted was tremendous. Finally, he heard a low crackling sound. The force of his pull and the weight of his body weren't enough to break the board, but luckily for Widow, the nails were cheap, and the work was sloppy. In a mass-produced subdivision, often minimal work was done, and minimal quality was the result. This subdivision was no different. In fact, it was worse because the investors had obviously mismanaged and miscalculated everything from the production of the properties to the costs of labor to the units that they would sell during the early stages of development. Therefore, they ran out of money early on. And because of that, Widow had the advantage.

The wood splintered and cracked at the place where the nails had been driven into the plank at the top of the board. Upon hearing this sound and feeling the slight give of the board, Widow's effort was strengthened by his willpower. He pulled even harder—harder than he thought he could.

A second later, the board tore free from the planks at the top. It sent Widow flying forward onto his face, but he wasn't injured. He didn't waste a second thanking his luck. Instead, he shimmied forward on his belly and freed himself from the wood.

Cord's energy was returning after seeing this feat. He shouted, "Yes!"

His sentiment echoed in the room, which was good because it told Widow that no one else was there. Otherwise, they'd come running to find out what the commotion was. But there was no one. No mercenaries locked and loaded. No bad guys. No Lane.

They'd left Widow and Cord alone with the guy whose name he still didn't know.

Widow dropped onto his back and pulled his wrists up underneath his legs. He kicked his shoes off to get his hands easily around his feet and in front of him. He spun around and felt through the guy's pockets for the keys and found them in the guy's front left pocket. He undid his handcuffs and then Cord's.

Cord said, "What about Raggie?" He got himself up on his feet and wobbled over to the monitor. He could see what was happening before he got there, but like a good Secret Service agent, he stayed calm. He didn't panic.

Widow said, "Don't worry about that. Get the gun. Cover the door."

Cord didn't question him.

Cord grabbed the MP5 and checked the magazine. It hadn't been fired. Full magazine. He wobbled over to the door and knelt. He propped himself against the frame and took aim down the hallway. No one was getting past him.

Widow scrambled into the bathroom and grabbed the cell phone. He prayed there was no passcode like many people had. There wasn't. He hit the home button, and the screen lit up.

Widow pressed the phone icon. He swiped over to the recent calls screen and scanned through them. There were several calls on the phone, all to the same group of numbers and the same area codes. It must be the same group of cell phones. Probably all purchased at the same time in a package deal.

He pressed the first one and put the phone up to his ear. He listened and heard a ring. The phone rang once. Twice. Three times. Then a British voice answered and spoke one word.

"Problem?"

Grant, Widow thought.

He clicked the phone and hung up on the guy.

He dialed the second number listed. The phone rang.

Lane's voice answered.

"Is everything okay?"

Widow hung up again and dialed the third number.

Cord said, "What're you doing? Calling the cops? They can't help us!"

Widow said, "Relax."

The phone rang and rang a few times.

Widow turned and walked to the monitors. He looked at the screen. He saw Valentine had unlocked Raggie from her cuffs. Her wrist was in his hand as he tried to lead her somewhere. The phone interrupted him, and he stood up with his pants down around his ankles. He dropped Raggie's wrist, and she scooted in tight underneath a sink.

Valentine pulled his pants back up and buttoned them. He left the belt and zipper undone. He reached into his pocket and scrambled to retrieve his cell phone. He got it out and put it up to his ear. He said, "What? I'm in the middle of something!"

Widow said, "If you let the girl go right now, I won't beat you to death."

Valentine froze in place. He looked left and looked right out of instinct or habit or just plain stupidity. Widow wasn't sure.

Widow said, "That's right, asshole! I can see you!"

Valentine turned around and looked up at the camera. He said, "Widow?"

"You got it! And I'm coming for you!"

Valentine said, "Where's Mitchell?"

Widow looked back and down at the other guy. Mitchell, he presumed, but Mitchell didn't move.

Widow said, "He doesn't look so good. Might be alive still."

"Lane'll kill you."

"If I were you, I wouldn't concern myself with what Lane may or may not do."

Silence.

Widow said, "Don't you want to keep your pathetic life? Don't you want to keep breathing? Because if you don't walk out of there right now and disappear, I will find you and end your breathing. Believe me. That's a fact."

Valentine started to say something, but he didn't. He looked dumbfounded—a deer in the headlights.

Widow watched and smiled. He didn't know Raggie, but he had formed a mental picture of her in his head as a tough girl. She was a girl raised in a family of military and Secret Service agents. She and Widow had a similar upbringing. But one thing separated them— Raggie might've been even tougher than Widow because she'd survived a vicious shark attack. She lost her hand yet rebounded back to the ocean and to surfing despite it.

When she moved back to the sink and pulled back out with a jug in her hand, Widow smiled. She was smart. She hadn't known about Widow, and she hadn't sat back and waited for the agents to come and save her. Instead, she had designed her own plan for escape.

Widow said, " Last chance before you get hurt."

Valentine lifted his hand to the camera to flip it off.

That was when Raggie exploded to her feet and said something that was not quite audible to Widow but looked like, *"Hey, asshole!"*

Valentine spun around and caught a face full of ammonia. She didn't splash it on his face; she heaved it, jug and all, like a grenade or a Molotov cocktail. The liquid sprayed into his eyes, and Valentine dropped the cell phone. It fell to the ground and shattered into tiny plastic parts.

Widow lost the signal and couldn't hear anything anymore, but he could watch.

Raggie had flung the liquid into Valentine's eyes, and now he was clutching at them helplessly. She pushed him as hard as she could. He spun and grabbed at thin air. He fell back into the sink, nailing his head on the counter.

It wasn't a fatal blow, or even enough to knock him out because he was still squirming around. He reached up one hand, trying to get a grip on something, and the other hand clutched at his eyes. Widow thought he saw thin wisps of steam coming off his face, but he wasn't sure if it was real or just a trick of the light. Did a chemical burn emit steam after skin contact? He wasn't sure.

Raggie looked up at the camera like she wanted to talk to it. She heard Valentine's side of the conversation and must've known the caller was watching Valentine from the camera. She must've also known that he wasn't one of them. He was a good guy.

What Widow hoped she figured out was that they might not have been the only people watching the feed. Widow figured Lane or Grant might've been watching from another location.

He tried to redial the phone to warn her to get the hell out of there, but there was no answer. The phone rang and rang. She wasn't responding. Therefore, there must be no ringing on her end.

Raggie waved at the camera and then scrambled out of the frame and out of the room.

Valentine remained, still, trying to stand. He looked like he was in a lot of pain. He was probably screaming at the top of his lungs.

Widow could only hope.

42

RAGGIE WALKED past the barking dogs and carefully opened the outer door to make sure Valentine had been alone. She saw no one. She turned back to the room with the caged dogs. They were barking stridently. Then she ran back to the other door. She didn't want Valentine making it out of there, so she inspected the door, looking for a lock. There was none.

She looked around hastily, but then heard some scuffling from the next room. Valentine was moving around. It sounded like he was on his feet. She reacted and reached over and grabbed a rack full of caged pharmaceuticals. She pulled and jerked with all her might. The cage wobbled. She leaped up and put all her weight into the downward force. The cage came crashing down. She dodged it and rolled out of the way as the large metal apparatus crashed down in front of the door.

Valentine had found the doorknob and had opened the door, but its motion was instantly halted by the obstruction of the cage.

He screamed profanities at Raggie.

"You little bitch! Get back here! I'll kill you! I'll kill you! Let me out!"

Raggie had stepped back into the noise of the barking dogs and couldn't hear anything Valentine was screaming. She checked the door to make sure he wouldn't escape. It looked like he was secure, and his phone was broken. There was no need to worry about him making any calls. Unless he had a backup phone, which some people did. Her dad, for instance, carried two different cell phones. One was for some guy he called *POTUS*, and the other was for everyone else.

Raggie looked around the room one last time and decided that she shouldn't be the only free bird that night. She smiled. It was good to have a sense of humor. Without hers, she would've gone nuts a long time ago. She unlocked the cages of all the animals in the room. There were five cats, one of them with several kittens. They followed their mother out of the cage and ran out the open door. Then nineteen dogs ran out after the cats and waited in the front room, barking. One of the dogs was a weird breed she hadn't seen before. It had puffy fur like a poodle; only it was huge. It came up to her and stared. It didn't bark like the others.

She looked at a medical tag attached to its collar. It read, "Name: Max. Breed: Shepadoodle. Age: 8."

She said, "Max, let's get out of here."

The dog looked at her as if he understood completely.

Raggie wondered what the hell was a Shepadoodle? Whatever it was, this was a great dog. It seemed to have an automatic instinct to protect her. It escorted her past the office, where she stopped and stared at the laptop screens. She couldn't see Valentine. He was out of the shot because he was banging on the door.

Then she saw another screen that was programmed to *CNN*. News anchors were waiting at Dulles International Airport. It was a press event. She couldn't hear anything because the sound was turned all the way down, but she read the text on the screen. It basically said that the president was going to land soon and give an important speech about the state of Africa.

Raggie thought of her father. She needed to let him know she was okay, but she couldn't call him. First off, there was no phone anywhere in sight, and second, he was on Air Force One and couldn't receive calls. At least that's what she thought.

The last thing that she remembered was riding in a van with Graine and then waking up here. Maybe they had been attacked? Maybe he was dead? Either way, she didn't know who to trust—except she knew she could trust Agent Lucas. She needed to get home and tell him what happened. Tell him that Graine was probably dead, and these guys had kidnapped her.

Off to the side of the laptop, she saw a black object. It was a gun. It looked like a Beretta M9. She wasn't an expert on guns, but she had seen plenty of Berettas. She lifted it. It was light—too light. And then she realized that, of course, the magazine was missing. She looked around the desk. No magazine. She looked back at the monitor, showing the room she had been in. Valentine must have it on him.

She left the gun and turned and left the office. She went to the front of the veterinary clinic and walked to the entrance. The animals were all lined up, waiting to go out. Luckily, the keys were already in the door and not in Valentine's pocket. That would've been a difficult situation.

She unlocked the door and pushed it open. Somewhere behind the desk, a buzzer sounded, showing that someone had opened the door. It was probably to alert the staff, but this time, no one was entering, and everyone was escaping.

She waited for the dogs to run out first, and then the cats mixed in. The last to leave the building was the litter of kittens. And then she and Max.

43

WIDOW STOOD over the guy called Mitchell and checked his pulse. He was barely alive. He pulled him over to another exposed wooden stud and handcuffed him to it the same way he had been handcuffed.

Cord said, "He's not going anywhere."

Widow said, "He'll be lucky to live through the night."

"We can't call the paramedics. Not yet. They'll bring the cops, and they'll have tons of questions. They aren't dumb. They'll put two and two together. Plus, this guy probably has a rap sheet that runs into the classified arena. And a sheet like that will alert the FBI. And then they'll notify the Secret Service once they've identified a man who may or may not be a terrorist within a hundred-mile radius of the White House. That's SOP."

Widow said, "He'll probably die."

Cord shrugged and asked, "You care?"

"I'm not a priest. If I were, I'd read him his last rites."

They picked up the MP5 and checked the guy's pockets, finding a spare magazine and a Beretta M9.

Widow said, "Why didn't he pull the gun on me before he checked my pocket?"

"Guess stupidity is why he does this type of work."

"I guess."

Widow took the MP5 and gripped it beneath the front magazine and barrel. He gave the Beretta to Cord, who tucked it into his holster where his SIG Sauer used to be.

Cord said, "I wonder where they put my SIG?"

"Grant took it with him."

Cord nodded.

Widow walked with Cord, his arm around his back, and his hand locked around the back of Cord's belt for support. They walked out of the house and to the street.

Cord said, "What now?"

"It doesn't look like they're around. They might be headed to Raggie, or they might be headed to another location, but certainly, they'll be near a TV. It'll be 6:30 soon."

Cord asked, "What time is it?"

Widow said, "6:05."

"How do you know that?"

"It's just a thing I do."

"We should call the cops. Raggie is free."

Widow said, "We should call Rowley."

Cord nodded.

"Do you know the number?" Widow asked.

Cord nodded and said, "He's on Air Force One, but he'll answer."

Widow walked Cord to the neighbor's driveway and then behind a half-finished, enclosed patio near the front door. He set him down on the concrete. Cord sat upright.

Widow handed him Mitchell's cell phone and said, "Make the call. Tell him not to worry."

Cord nodded and asked, "What about you? Where're you going?"

"I'm going to get us a ride."

Cord said, "Our SUV is probably still there."

"I know. I'm going to go look. Do you know how to hot-wire the thing?"

"Not necessary. We always keep a hidden key. You never know when you need to roll. And you can't be ready to roll when you've lost your car keys."

"Where is it?"

"Under the rear passenger tire well."

Widow nodded and said, "Be right back. Call Rowley. Then call the cops. Get them over to the house. Tell them to take Graine into custody and put out an APB for Lane."

Cord nodded and started dialing the phone.

Widow took off running toward the SUV.

44

MOMENTS AFTER RAGGIE ran from the veterinary clinic, Grant pulled up with the Range Rover and stared at the open front door. He pulled his Beretta M9 out of its holster and jumped out of the SUV, leaving the engine running. He surveyed the parking lot but saw no one around, only a couple of cats.

He entered the clinic and scanned the corners with his gun out, ready to fire. No one. He entered the office and looked at the monitor and saw an empty room, but he knew the room wasn't empty because he could hear Valentine pounding on the door with his fists. He was screaming and yelling. It sounded like he was in tremendous pain.

Grant entered the second room. No dogs. He knew all he needed to know—the girl was gone, and Valentine was locked up in the next room.

He walked to the other door and holstered his weapon. He reached down and lifted the steel-mesh cabinet that the girl must've thrown down to block the door. He shoved it aside and then stepped back. He pulled the M9 out again and said, "Step back."

Valentine recognized his voice.

Grant opened the door and found Valentine with his eyes swollen shut, and his face freshly scarred and disfigured.

Valentine said, "Thank God! Grant, she tricked me. I need a doctor."

Grant said, "Where is she?"

"I don't know. She ran off, I guess." He was clutching at his face and yet not touching it with his hands because every time he did, it burned even worse.

Grant said, "How long?"

"I don't know. I really need a doctor!"

"How long since she got out?"

Valentine waved his hands through the air like a blind man trying to find his way. Grant slapped them aside and repeated his question once more.

Valentine said, "I think maybe ten minutes ago. Maybe not even."

Grant said, "Are you sure?"

"Yes. Get me to a doctor!"

Grant shot him twice in the chest, watched him stumble backward, and left him to die.

In the parking lot, Grant pulled out his phone and dialed Lane. When Lane picked up, he said, "The asset is out."

Lane remained calm and said, "Call Mitchell. Check on the other two."

"Think they planned this?"

"No. Probably good luck on their part—and bad on ours. But I'd guess they're probably free as well."

Grant said, "Why do you think that?"

Lane said, "Because Mitchell is watching her on the other laptop and he didn't call us. My guess is that Widow got out at the same time. He's turning out to be a pain in the ass."

"Should I look for her?"

"Forget it. She'll hide from you."

"What about the police?" asked Grant.

"Don't worry. I'll handle that. Just call Mitchell."

Grant said, "And what if you're right? Should we abort?"

"No. The target will be retired in less than thirty minutes," Lane said.

Grant hung up the phone and got back into the Range Rover. He pulled out of the parking lot slowly, checking for any sign of Raggie. But there was nothing.

* * *

THE MAN with one arm and no ears sat in the center of the backseat of the Mercedes even though the front passenger seat was free. He liked to sit in the back like royalty, a side effect of his indoctrination into Sowe's regime—once a tortured enemy, now a loyal assassin.

He leaned forward and spoke into Lane's right ear, but not in a whisper or a hushed voice. It was his regular, thick West Ganbolan accent. He said, "Is this going to be a problem?"

Lane didn't turn to him. He simply said, "No problem. We're still on schedule. We planned for contingencies. Don't worry."

The man with one arm and no ears sat back and remained calm, unusual for a terrorist in his position because anyone who was part of an international conspiracy to assassinate the American president on American soil and in front of the entire world would naturally have been nervous when a critical part of the plan went to hell. But he wasn't a normal terrorist. He had hand-selected Lane, and he trusted him.

The man said, "What's the next step?"

Lane said, "We picked these guys because they were expendable. We didn't care about their competency because we were going to kill them. However, we didn't expect Widow to be so resourceful, but that's why we've got Graine."

The man said, "And what is Jekyll, or Detective Graine, going to do about it?"

Lane said, "I'm calling him now."

He pressed his phone to his ear, waiting for an answer.

The phone rang.

* * *

JEKYLL AND GRAINE were the same man, and right then, he sat on the sofa, listening to Karen Rowley babble on and on about her daughter and how much she missed her. He listened to her claims of being a good mother and how she would be so much better when Raggie returned. This seemed to go on and on.

He had one eye on the TV in the living room and the other on Karen Rowley so that she thought he was the nice guy they all thought he was. The act must continue a little longer. They knew little about him. Sure, he'd formed a bond with Rowley, Cord, Lucas, and Karen. But he'd also formed a bond with Lane. The bonds of brotherhood seemed to be important to Rowley. He was always gabbing on about the family and kinship and the Navy.

When Graine tried out for the Secret Service and was declined, even though Rowley had promised him he would make it, he resented them—all of them. He knew them from his days in the Marine Corps. Instead of joining them in the Secret Service, he became a cop back in his hometown and stopped talking to the rest of them—until one day.

Lane had reached out to him from prison.

That was years after there was a slight change in the regime back in West Ganbola. Sowe was still in charge, but he had kept his public appearances to a minimum. A rumor was going around that he'd befriended one of his enemies—some guy he tortured for years—and, in a kind of demented brainwashing, the enemy had become his friend. Eventually, the enemy became his most trusted ally—not in the sense of friendship, but more because Sowe had taken and hidden his enemy's family.

But the enemy was promised they would be taken care of and was even granted visits where he had to fly on a plane with no windows, under guard, and then blindfolded on the ride to their location. All he knew was that they were in Africa and probably still in the country. The man with one arm and no ears could fly to them for two months a year. There, he tried to forget the evils he did for Sowe. He had betrayed his friends and his countrymen. He had betrayed everyone but his family.

When Lane had reached out to him via his old Marine Corps email, Graine had been astounded that Lane could use the internet. As the months passed, the two became friends. Lane had told him about how nicely he had been treated after the first year. He was still a prisoner, but eventually, he was entrusted with certain responsibilities involving security and intelligence. He told Graine about how the other prisoner who had no ears had become his friend. When this prisoner was released into a high-level government position, he joined forces with him. After all, it was his own country that had abandoned him.

Graine and Lane kept in contact for years. Graine thought of telling the others, but after such a long time keeping it a secret, it had become more of a dark secret. A secret they wouldn't understand. He and Lane were friends now like he used to be friends with the others.

Graine used to feel that same bond with Rowley and the others, but it had faded. Their bonds had fallen apart pretty much around the time they had all gotten into the Secret Service, and he didn't.

He had always been good to Rowley. He caused no problems. He never dreamed that one day he would agree to this plot to assassinate the president or betray his old team or kidnap an innocent girl. But the moment things changed for him was the day he came home and found that his wife had packed up her things and left with their three young boys. Graine was devastated. He blamed himself at first. The only person who even listened to him anymore was Lane. He couldn't tell the others.

Once he got to a place where he was nothing but angry, he thought he should find his wife. The woman had taken years of his life and his children. He wanted to find her. He wanted to get even. He thought maybe hadn't been good enough to get into the Secret Service, but he was good enough to locate a single woman with three young boys. He searched and searched. But he found nothing.

He thought maybe he wasn't very good as a cop, either. That's when he reached out to one of the other members of Rowley and Lane's old unit. It was a guy who was there that day — one of the names on Lane's hit list, a guy named Haverly.

And what did he find? He found Haverly had also been a Secret Service Agent. He did some digging and found that Rowley had gotten him on as well.

Haverly agreed to meet him at the mention of Rowley's name.

Graine had rented a decent car with decent gas mileage because his old truck wouldn't make the drive from Missouri to Pennsylvania, where Haverly lived.

Finally, he had arrived at Haverly's house. Haverly lived alone, which probably helped to end his life. The two of them sat around, swapping military stories, the one grunt to another sort of thing.

They drank and drank. They ate barbecue. And they drank some more. Everything was friendly. But the jealousy of this other friend of Rowley exceeding him in life got under Graine's skin.

He had never been the kind of person to take immediate action. He never was intuitive, and his past employers would never have described him as an outgoing employee, but he was good at some things—like keeping secrets. He was used to taking his time.

He returned home to Missouri, and he waited. Then a few days later, he visited an unstable nurse he knew whom he'd saved from an abusive boyfriend. From time to time, he listened to her babble on and on about her depressing life. One day, she went further than usual. She had planned her own suicide.

Graine tried to console her, as usual, but for the first time, he didn't talk her out of it. No more "you've got too much to live for" or "you're worth more than that" or "what about your family?" No more of that. Not for Graine.

This time, he was asking, "How would you do it? How would you take your own life?"

She explained she had access to a lot of narcotics and that she'd choose the least painful and fastest way to go. He asked her about the most painful. She replied that there were many options. He asked her about the options where no one would know how she died. He wanted to know what drugs would simulate a natural death.

She told him there were a bunch of those, but the problem was that they were all traceable. There was no such thing as a drug that simulated natural causes but was untraceable. Everything was metabolized and could be found in the blood. Then she stopped and explained that there were a few drugs that could kill someone but would mirror normal metabolites found in the blood after death. An overdose of potassium chloride, for example, would kill someone, but it would mimic a cardiac arrest.

When he asked again about the pain factor, she grew a little hesitant. She asked why he wanted to know and said she didn't want to feel any pain. He told her he asked out of curiosity. She explained to him that a drug called succinylcholine was probably the best answer in a case where someone wanted to inflict a great amount of pain, yet make a murder look like a heart attack. Essentially, she said, succinylcholine would have to be administered by injection. It would first sedate a person's muscles and organs and cause paralysis. Everything would stop working except for the mind—the person would still be conscious and see, feel, and hear everything going on around him.

He remembered her saying, "This would be a cruel way to murder someone."

He had asked her if she could get some of this drug. She asked why, and he explained it was for a case. He needed it but couldn't ask officially because of the case. He told her it was a small-town thing, and he didn't want to start up the rumor mill. It would look bad for him if it turned out he was wrong.

The nurse helped him to get some succinylcholine. He had gotten the needle on his own. He called Haverly from an untraceable line and said he needed to see him. Of course, this was after he had rented a car from Joplin Regional Airport, which was a four-hour drive from where he was. He rented it with a false ID and then drove back to Pennsylvania.

He called Haverly and told him he was already in town and needed to see him immediately. There was a Rowley problem he wanted to talk about.

Graine went to his house, confided in him about his correspondence with Lane, and told him he knew what they did to Lane, to Chang.

Haverly was taken aback by this. He didn't know what to say. In a moment of terrible judgment, he allowed Graine to stay the night.

Haverly was sleeping and never felt the needle go into his arm. Graine could've let him sleep, but he woke him up to watch him die. He shook Haverly, but said nothing. He just watched as Haverly's eyes opened wide when he realized he couldn't move. His organs were stopping one by one, like a demented game of dominoes. His lungs stopped working, but that's not what killed him. His heart stopped, and in less than a minute, he was dead.

* * *

BACK IN THE ROWLEY HOUSE, Graine's phone rang. He prayed it was Lane calling to tell him he no longer needed Karen Rowley, and Graine could put a bullet in her head and be off. But he didn't say that.

Graine answered the phone.

"Hello?"

Lane said, "The girl has gotten away. We need to move to the backup plan."

Graine said, "I see, sir. That's an old case."

He looked at Karen Rowley and said, "I've got to take this. It's Karter, my boss. He's calling about a case I worked on ten years ago. I'm sorry."

Karen Rowley nodded and said nothing, staring off into space the way she did every time Graine left her alone.

He stood up from the couch and walked out of earshot of Karen Rowley. He kept walking until he was well down the hallway, past the kitchen. He said, "Where the hell is she?"

Lane said, "We don't know. Not far from the veterinary clinic. But it doesn't matter."

"And why is that?"

"Calm down. If she goes to the police, you can handle it."

Graine said, "How am I supposed to do that? I'm not a magician!"

"Figure it out! It won't matter soon, anyway. Call Rowley. Tell him he must do it as soon as they land. Nothing can interfere."

Lane hung up the phone.

45

GRAINE HADN'T BEEN in the Secret Service, but he'd been around long enough to have some friends in the FBI and on various police forces throughout the country. He had made plenty of friends back when he was in the Marines, and one guy came to mind.

He hadn't talked to him in a couple of years, but Special Agent Mark Leger was a longtime FBI agent and close to retirement, so close that he had a retirement party starting at the end of the workday. This was his last week.

Graine searched through the phone contacts on his regular cell phone, found the number, and dialed it. The phone rang, and a husky smoker's voice answered.

"Doug?"

"Mark. How are you, old friend?"

"I'm okay. How's it going? I didn't expect to hear from you."

Graine said, "I know. I'm sorry for not calling sooner. And I'm especially sorry for not calling you after Liz died."

Silence on the other end.

Graine said, "I'm a terrible friend."

Leger said, "No, not at all. This is a nice surprise. What's up?"

"Listen, Mark; this isn't a social call. I need a favor. It's a matter of national security but not in a tell-your-boss way. It's more of an embarrassment."

"I'm listening."

"You remember Gibson Rowley?"

"I never met him, but yeah, the Director of the Secret Service isn't a secret in my circles."

"Well, it involves his daughter."

Leger said, "You probably need a different agent. I don't handle national security. I don't have the clearance for anything like that."

Graine said, "Just listen. She ran away from home. She's not in any danger. Just a rebellious teenager. It's a private matter, and Rowley prefers to keep it that way."

"What do you want me to do?"

"The word from one of her little friends is that she ran off with this college kid. In a band. You know the type?"

Leger said, "Sure. I got daughters. Hell, I got a granddaughter now."

Graine pretended to care, saying, "Seriously, we'll have to catch up soon. But let me tell you about this. It's time-sensitive."

"Sure. Go ahead."

"I need you to put the word out that she's got some story made up about what really happened to her. But the truth is we already know she was with this guy and they got into a fight, and she ran off. The Secret Service has already talked to him."

"Whoa. The father—the Director of the Secret Service—hauled him in because he ran off with his daughter? That's a scene I'd pay to see. Bet the kid was scared shitless."

Graine said, "You've no idea. But listen. She's still out there. We think she'll go to the cops and tell some bullshit story to explain why she ran away to begin with."

"What kinda story?"

"You know, teenager stuff."

"What, like she was kidnapped or something?"

"Yeah, like that."

"I get it. You want the cops to act like it's serious?"

Graine said, "Yeah. Exactly. Just have them bring her home. We'll handle it here."

Leger said, "DC is a big place. I can't control every cop in the district."

"No problem. I know exactly what precinct she'll be near."

"Well, for an old friend, I can see what I can do."

Graine smiled and gave him the information.

A minute later, he congratulated Agent Leger on his retirement and texted Lane. Then he walked outside the house and pulled out his pack of cigarettes. He lit one and took a couple of drags from it. He held it between his lips, pulled out his cell phone, and dialed Rowley.

The phone rang, and Rowley picked up. The quality of the connection was far from good, but it was audible enough.

Rowley said, "You got word about Widow? Did Lane take the deal?"

Graine said, "They took Widow, but there's something else."

Rowley swallowed hard and said, "Doesn't sound good."

"It's not. I'm sorry."

"What is it?"

"We never really talked about this out loud, but we all thought it. We asked ourselves what if this was an inside job?"

Rowley said, "What happened?"

"It's Cord. He fooled us."

"What? What did he do?"

"He's the inside man. He's been working with Lane and the other terrorists this whole time."

Silence fell over the phone line. Rowley said nothing.

Graine said, "It was Cord. He pushed Widow into a death sentence, I'm afraid."

Rowley made an audible gasp on the other end of the line. He was stunned.

"And Lucas is dead. Cord killed him at the meeting, and then he handed Widow over like he was nothing." Graine said. "I know. I was there. I saw the whole thing. I barely got away with my life."

Rowley said, "No! No! It can't be."

"I'm sorry, Gib. I'm so very sorry, but if you don't put a bullet in the president as soon as you land, they'll kill Raggie."

Rowley didn't respond with words. He threw the phone against the wall of the cabin. The glass screen cracked and the plastic fragmented with the impact.

The president looked up, along with everyone else.

Rowley got up and headed to the bathroom. He spoke to no one.

All Graine heard through the speaker of his phone was the repeated alert sound from the cell phone company saying that the connection had been lost, and then the line went dead. The screen on his phone said, "Call dropped."

He pocketed the phone and smiled.

46

WIDOW MADE it back with Cord's SUV. He helped the agent into the passenger seat and buckled him in.

Widow said, "They moved Lucas. I'm not sure where."

"Bastards! We gotta get back at them!"

"First, let's make sure that Raggie is home safe. Did you call Rowley?"

"I tried, but the line's busy," Cord said.

"Try again."

"I will. Let's get going."

Widow nodded and got in the driver's seat. He put the SUV in drive and hit the gas. They sped off through the subdivision and out onto the main road. They drove through a small strip with stores, gas stations, and some light traffic. They found the interstate and pulled onto it.

Cord said, "I'll call the house. We've got to warn Mrs. Rowley."

Widow said, "No! Graine is there. Call the cops. Ask for an APB. We'd better have them pick up Raggie first."

Cord nodded and dialed.

He got the local cops. He gave them his Secret Service badge number and told them it was an emergency. Cops were trained to keep their mouths shut when they heard that. Secret Service calls were treated as national security orders.

The officer took a minute to check out Cord's name and badge number. After that, he confirmed Cord's identity and connected him to his watch commander, who took his instructions. Cord told him to put out the APB for Raggie. He told him she was important and should be brought straight to a police station. She was to wait and not leave with anyone until he got there.

When Cord got off the phone, he said, "Okay, done. At least we don't have to worry about her."

Widow said, "You forgot to give them this number."

"Shit! I don't know what it is. We'll call them back later and check. We know she'll be safe and out of Lane's hands. I've got to get through to Rowley now. The president is scheduled to land in twenty minutes."

Widow said, "Call him again."

Cord dialed Rowley's cell again and waited. No one answered. He put the phone down and stared out the windshield at the freeway. He said, "Hit that switch on the other side of the steering wheel." He pointed at a black switch.

Widow hit it, and the SUV's emergency lights flashed on. Bright blue rays flashed across the blacktop.

"Hit the gas. We need to get to Rowley's house!"

Widow said, "Call someone else in the Secret Service. Tell them about Rowley."

"He won't hurt the president. Don't worry."

"Cord! Don't be an idiot! He still thinks his daughter's life is in danger! You've got to warn your guys! Tell them to take him into custody!"

Cord stayed quiet and stared ahead.

Widow said, "Cord!"

"I can't. What if he knows about her already? He won't do it! He'd never do it!"

Widow stayed quiet.

Cord looked torn and desperate. He looked as much like a man stuck between a rock and a hard place as any man Widow had ever seen before in his life.

Widow said, "I know he's your friend, but you gotta do the right thing."

"Even if I had someone to call, how do we know we can trust him?"

"There's no one else."

"How can you be sure?"

Widow said, "You can't have that many corrupt agents. That's a damn impossibility. I bet that one hundred percent of your guys are on the straight and narrow. And zero percent are corrupt."

Cord said, "But how can you be sure?"

"Trust me. Graine isn't an agent. He's a lowly detective somewhere in the middle of Missouri—not a state known for its honest police departments. Police corruption is a part of life there. And that's a failure of the executive branch as much as it is for the local counties who hire these guys. But if I know anything about politicians, you can bet your ass they'll take care of themselves first. And you don't get better politicians than presidents."

He paused.

He said, "The Secret Service is clean. Besides, I know a little something about how hard it is even to pass the entrance exam."

Cord nodded, then said, "I can't call anyone. There's no one to call. Not on Air Force One. Only one person has a working cell phone because of security—the Director of the United States Secret Service."

Widow said, "What about the president? Surely, he has a cell phone?"

"I don't have that number. I don't rank high enough for that privilege."

"What about the pilot? Tell him to turn the plane around. Rowley can't shoot the president if they don't land."

Cord said, "The pilot? Do you know who the pilot of Air Force One is?"

Widow shook his head and checked his side mirrors. He moved into the left lane and around an ambulance that was driving slowly on the right side.

Cars turned their blinkers on and moved to the shoulder. Some faster than others. Some of them drove slowly, trying to give the appearance of driving safely. From his experience, Widow knew that about ninety percent of drivers did this when they saw a police vehicle flashing its lights behind them because they didn't want to get in trouble. This was something that pissed off a lot of officers on duty. They were trying to get to a crime scene as fast as possible, and the rules of the road were eating away at their time.

Widow said, "No."

"Calling the pilot is out of the question. First, I'd have to call the Pentagon and have them radio him. In theory, this should be an easy thing to do. But the guy who pilots Air Force One is an Air Force general, and when the commander-in-chief is on board, the Air Force sees it as their job to guard him. Our powers are diminished in their presence."

"Cut the bureaucratic bullshit! You're the Secret Service!"

"I know that. I'm not saying we shouldn't try it. I'm just saying that it won't happen in ten minutes. They'll have landed before I'm done fighting with my Pentagon colleague about passing on the message. National security is often rivaled by bureaucratic hamstringing."

"What the hell do we do?"

Cord said, "Trust Rowley. I've known him for a very long time. He'll do the right thing—the patriotic thing—before he succumbs to his own desires. He'll sacrifice his own life and Raggie's, too, before he'll hurt the president."

Widow said, "Do you really believe that?"

"I do."

Widow looked down at the cell phone's clock and said, "Five minutes till we find out."

47

RAGGIE STUMBLED around barefoot in the dark. She made it a couple of miles away from the clinic, and Max had followed her the whole way. Walking around in unfamiliar neighborhoods in the more questionable areas of Washington DC wasn't her idea of an ideal situation, but it was light years better than being back in captivity.

She had passed a few guys earlier, and they looked even more questionable than the neighborhood. One of them had called out to her. "Hey, girl. Where ya goin'?" On the surface, it sort of sounded like a question from a concerned citizen, but its meaning was more like "Hey, girl. Why don't you come over here and follow me into a dark alley for a couple of minutes?"

He wasn't the type of person who was going to help Raggie, so she pressed on. The only reason the guys didn't follow her was because of Max. He barked at them in a tone meant to warn. It said, "Stay away!"

Raggie thought that when this was all over, she would definitely keep him.

She walked on, feeling more dehydrated than she ever had before—even more than the first day she was in the hospital after the shark attack. That was different, though. She hadn't been deprived of water back then. It was the drugs that had made her feel dehydrated. This time, she'd had no water for twenty-four hours.

Raggie walked on and turned onto another street. She didn't know where she was, but she figured if she headed toward the brightest lights, eventually she'd come to a more civilized part of the city.

After another five minutes of walking, she ended up at a gas station. It had bars on the windows and was more than rundown. But it was promising because there was a police car was parked in front of it. She walked into the gas station and saw a cop paying for coffee. He was a middle-aged black guy with ears so big they looked like mushrooms sprouting out of his head. He looked at her with concern and asked, "Miss, are you all right?"

She walked up to him, with Max trailing behind. The door swung shut behind them.

The store clerk said, "Hey! No dogs, girlie!"

The cop repeated himself.

Raggie saw the grave concern on his face and realized she must look like someone who had just awakened after sleeping in a dumpster.

Raggie said, "Help me."

The cop left his coffee and said, "What's wrong? Is someone after you?"

She said, "I was kidnapped."

He grabbed her shoulders and stared at where her hand used to be. He said, "Are you injured?"

She shook her head and said, "My arm was already like that, but the guys are still out there. They're friends of my dad."

The officer said, "Come with me."

He took her by her one hand and led her out into the parking lot. He opened the back door to the patrol car and sat her down. Max jumped in after her, and the officer didn't question it. He closed the door and sat in the front seat. He spoke into the radio and got headquarters on the line. The night watch commander explained to him in radio codes and cop talk that Raggie didn't comprehend that the FBI had already informed them about this girl.

A moment later, the police officer received information on who she was and a message on his console computer requesting that she be taken back to her house and back to her parents. It informed him that this was a special favor for the FBI, and that was more than enough information for Officer Daftshaw. At forty-three, he was a lifelong cop. Twenty-one years on the force qualified him as a professional. If he had been in the military, he could've retired already. That was a thought that plagued him to this day. He often wished he had gone into the military instead.

Back in the nineties, he had the choice, but he didn't want to get injured and thought soldiers had a much higher probability of being shot by the enemy. Of course, the joke was on him because his second year on the streets, he was shot in the leg by a woman. Sometimes he still felt pain in his right thigh, especially when it was going to rain.

After Officer Daftshaw read his message, he looked out of his window at the sky. Not a cloud in sight, but his leg was aching something awful. He thought for a moment and changed his mind. Something nagged at him. Something he couldn't put his finger on. He decided it would be prudent to call Raggie's parents just in case. The father was Secret Service; he would want a phone call immediately. Their home number was listed.

Daftshaw turned back to the Raggie and said, "I'm going to take care of you, okay? Don't worry—everything's been sorted out."

Raggie nodded.

Daftshaw said, "I'm going to step out and make a phone call. I'll be two seconds."

Raggie said, "I need to call my dad."

"Okay. Let me talk to him first, okay?"

He didn't wait for her to respond. He got out of the car and stepped in front of the hood. He pulled out his cell phone and called the number from memory.

Daftshaw waited, listening to the phone ring. A voice answered and said, "Rowley's house."

"This is Officer Daftshaw with DCPD. I'm calling to speak to Mr. Rowley."

Graine said, "This is he."

"Mr. Rowley, I have Nicole. She's safe and sound."

Graine paused a beat and then said, "That's great news, Officer. Where are you?"

"I'm at a gas station outside the city."

"Fantastic! Thank you so much! I've been worried! Please bring her home!"

Daftshaw said, "We got your message from the FBI. I apologize for this unpleasantness, but I must ask, why the FBI?"

"What do you mean?"

"Procedure calls for her to be brought to the station. She doesn't have any physical injuries except for a small bruise under her eye. But it's enough to cause alarm. Sir, if there's been a crime here, it shouldn't be overlooked even if the FBI asks us to."

"Officer, I'm Gibson Rowley."

Daftshaw said nothing.

"If my name means nothing to you, Google me. I'm the Director of the United States Secret Service. Nicole ran away with her boyfriend. She's a minor, and this whole embarrassing scene could cause considerable problems for me and possibly for the president. Certainly, the media will make a heyday of it. I'm sure you've seen the claims in the news of late about the Secret Service scandals. Agents drinking and getting hookers, and so on. Please, Officer, just bring our daughter home. We don't want any problems."

Daftshaw thought for a moment and said, "Okay, sir. I understand. We'll be there soon."

"Okay. I'll inform the gate. Just come straight here and don't stop."

Daftshaw said, "Sounds good." He hung up the phone and returned to the car.

Raggie said, "Can I call my dad now?"

"You'll see him soon. I've been told he's worried about you. They know the whole story. Everything's going to be fine. Just relax."

Raggie sat back on the seat. Her eyes felt droopy and tired, and almost with no warning, she was asleep.

Max laid his head in her lap.

48

AIR FORCE ONE flew into Dulles International Airport on a privately designated runway. The press corps was gathered and allowed to wait near the president's hangar for a special briefing.

The president had just left a summit in Africa's western region to help soothe tensions in the area. The recent assassination of a president-elect by his oldest son on international television had sparked a domino effect of unrest and political aggression. The struggles between democratic and socialist countries in the region weren't evenly matched. Most of the countries weren't real democracies, and what happened in West Ganbola was perceived as an act to destabilize the region.

Rowley leaned against the sink in the bathroom and stared at his face in the mirror. Not that he didn't recognize himself, but he didn't recognize the man who was contemplating killing the president. He closed his eyes and thought about Raggie.

Even though Rowley hadn't been in the Navy in years, he still wore his dog tags every day beneath his suit, tie, and a bulletproof vest. He also wore his United States pin on his jacket. He looked down at it, and the stars and stripes stared back at him.

Rowley looked away from it and closed his eyes again one last time. He saw his little girl as she lay in that South African hospital bed after the shark attack. He felt guilty now for not being there sooner. He felt guilty that he had to leave while she was in surgery because the president was moving. He felt guilty that he'd never even told anyone she had been in surgery until after the president had left the country and was safe.

What was he going to do? He had been a patriot first and a father second for his whole career and for Raggie's whole life. Now he had to decide which duty was more important. He had to decide which was more important—his president or his daughter.

Rowley opened his eyes and looked at the flag pin one last time. Then he unpinned it, threw it in the toilet, and flushed it.

He took out his department-issued SIG Sauer. He pulled back the slide and checked the round, clicked the safety to fire, and holstered it. The agents assigned to guard the president closely didn't have safety buttons on their holsters. They needed to have quick, fluid access to their weapons. Their safety was in their training.

He was locked and cocked, ready to do what he needed to do.

Ready to fulfill his duty.

He splashed water on his face, wiped it clear, and stepped back out into the plane.

49

"WE'LL NEED BACKUP," Widow said.

Cord said, "I don't know who else to call."

"You need to make more friends."

"I mean I don't trust anyone else."

Widow said, "I know someone we can call. Dial this number." And he repeated the digits straight from memory.

Cord dialed them without question until he got to the last one. He recognized the number. Before he hit the call button, he looked over at Widow. They were nearing the exit closest to Rowley's house.

Cord said, "I don't know about this."

"Call it. We need her help. Trust me. She can do more than you think."

Cord was silent.

Widow said, "Trust your people."

Cord hit the call button and waited for the phone to ring. It rang and rang. He had almost given up when a female voice answered and said, "Hello? I'm in the shower."

Cord said, "This is Cord and Widow. We need your help. Rowley's house. ASAP!"

He hung up the phone.

50

LANE and the man with no ears drove through the gates of the subdivision first, and Grant followed in the Range Rover.

Lane led Grant down a couple of streets and through several turns. They looked around at all the old Victorian houses. Some had flagstone steps leading up to gates with more security that was hidden to the layman, but they noticed it right off. Some houses, the larger ones, had Secret Service agents standing watch at their front entrances. The agents stood in plain sight, meant to be deterrents as much as guards. Grant noticed security cameras hidden in trees in some yards. He smiled at the absurdity of it.

Americans are so predictable, he thought.

Lane parked the car in the driveway of the Rowley house, and Grant parked behind him. They got out and walked to the door. Grant rang the bell.

A moment later, Karen Rowley opened the front door and welcomed the men into her home. She said, "I'm so grateful you helped us. Doug told me you all worked with him in the Marines. My husband trusts you. Please come in and make yourselves at home."

Lane said, "Thank you so much for your hospitality, ma'am. We just want to help bring your daughter home safely. Where's Doug?"

"He's in the family room. He said it was important to watch the news at 6:30."

"It's imperative, ma'am. Please come join us. We'll discuss your daughter soon."

Karen Rowley nodded, a little confused. But she had been so out of it since Raggie's disappearance that it all seemed normal to her. She led them through the foyer, down the long twisting hallway, and into the family room.

Grant stayed close to Lane and didn't speak. He didn't want to let his British accent slip. The last guest to enter the room was the African man with no ears.

Karen Rowley stared at him, flummoxed. She always told Raggie's cousins that it wasn't polite to stare at her daughter's stump, and yet she found herself unable to stop staring at this man. She raised her hand over her mouth to cover her shock at his appearance.

The man said, "Mrs. Rowley. I knew your husband. Back in Africa. I'm here as a friend to offer my help as well."

She said, "I'm...I'm sorry. I don't mean to stare. Who are you?"

He said, "My name's Michael Chang. I knew your husband long ago in the bush."

She said, "You were in the Navy?"

"You could say that. I was in an army, just not the American one. I was in a rebellion, and your husband was on my side."

"A rebellion? I know nothing about that. Did my husband help you?"

The man with no ears and no right arm smiled and said, "Your husband helped me to find out who I really am. He helped me."

51

Officer Daftshaw pulled up to the driveway of the old Victorian house, parking his car on the street because there was no more room in the driveway. He turned back to Raggie and saw that she was still asleep. She reminded him of one of his kids on a long car ride. Of course, the ex-wife had gotten custody of them, but she allowed him visitations—ironic since he was the one who paid child support and paid for most of their school clothes, supplies, and part of the rent. But he didn't complain. He'd been the one who was never home. He was happy just to see them on the weekends.

Daftshaw turned off the ignition and went around to the back door. He opened it and reached in and shook her. Raggie opened her eyes slowly, feeling like maybe the whole ordeal had been a bad dream, but that lasted only a second until she saw Daftshaw.

She said, "We're home."

He said, "You're home. Come on, let's go."

She smiled and leaped out of the car with Max in tow.

Daftshaw followed her up through an open gate and a bricked-in privacy fence. The house looked more like a small fortress than a home that people lived in.

They went to a side entrance instead of the front door. Daftshaw could tell it was the way Raggie had always entered her own house. And why not? It was her home.

His instincts had told him to ring the doorbell, which was also procedure, but he didn't. He should have, because as soon as he followed her in, he felt something was off.

They walked in through the kitchen. Raggie ran through a large dining room and straight into the next room with Max following. She grabbed onto her mother and hugged her like she hadn't seen her in years.

The thing that was very wrong was that there were four other men in the room, and three of them had guns drawn as soon as he showed his face in the dining room.

Max barked. One of the men, a guy with a British accent, said, "Shut that dog up!"

Raggie grabbed Max by the snout and fought him to keep it shut.

Daftshaw didn't even reach for his gun. He was a slow draw and knew it. Plus, he might've stood a chance against one guy with a gun, but not three.

Lane said, "Welcome, Officer. Please come in."

Daftshaw entered the living room. His heart pounded. Some old part of his brain, the part that cared only about survival, knew he was going to die.

Lane pointed his gun at the officer and said, "Take off your belt slowly and toss it and your weapon over to us."

Daftshaw did as he was told and then put his hands up.

Lane said, "Have a seat."

Daftshaw sat on the couch.

Karen Rowley and Raggie held each other tightly.

Karen Rowley said, "Please don't hurt us, Doug. Please. Don't let them."

Graine said, "Shut up! I've listened to you and your mouth for hours! Just keep it shut!" He waved his gun around and then pointed it in their direction, swinging it back and forth between them like a pendulum.

Lane holstered his gun and said, "Take it easy. We need them."

Graine backed off and holstered his gun, but kept the safety off.

Grant kept his gun out and trained on the cop.

Chang said, "It's time. Keep them all silent."

Lane nodded.

Grant moved in close and picked up the cop's gun and belt. He removed the gun, a Glock 19 loaded with nine-millimeter parabellums. He ejected the magazine and jerked the slide back in a quick, fluid motion. The bullet in the chamber ejected, and bounced and rolled on the carpet.

Grant picked up the magazine and bullet laid them on the coffee table. He stuffed the empty gun into his waistband, then walked in closer to the cop and sat out of grabbing distance. He kept his gun pointed at him.

Chang sat on the coffee table, pointed the remote at the TV, and switched to *CNN*. He turned the volume up and remained glued to the events flashing across the screen. They cut to Air Force One. It had just landed and was taxiing up to a crowd of onlookers.

Blue siren lights flashed in the background from Secret Service vehicles and swept across a sea of faces. The camera was trained on the side of the plane as it pulled to a stop. It was the cleanest plane Raggie had ever seen.

The fuselage was painted white. There was a blue stripe across the side of the plane that curved down from the all blue top face of the nose. Above the wing, in a big blue font were the words *THE UNITED STATES OF AMERICA*. Slightly underneath the strip, near the front of the wing, was the presidential seal. The tail had the American flag painted on it.

The camera was behind the second row of people and panned out to a wide shot, which showed the plane taxiing to a stop. A large metal staircase attached to a white truck pulled up to the plane. The camera turned and focused on the tail end. A staircase dropped out of the plane, and people with suitcases exited. They seemed to be mostly Secret Service agents in suits and ties.

A group of agents walked out and then stopped to form a security perimeter around the front wheel of the plane—two on each side of the wheel and two by the nose. Two more agents stood on either side of the plane, near the engines, just underneath each of the wings.

The camera zoomed in on the front exit door. The hatch opened, and a Secret Service agent stepped into view. He pushed the hatch, and it swung open until it banged against the fuselage. It took a few minutes for the top of the metal staircase to inch in for a perfect fit around the door. The agent stepped out and checked it. He looked at the railings and the platform to make sure it was secure. The Secret Service handled more than just human threats. They safeguarded the president against all enemies—even gravity and poor craftsmanship.

Raggie had never seen the president exit Air Force One before. She didn't know how much of an ordeal it was—or how boring it was. The camera focused on the open hatch at the top of the stairs. Other than the noise from the aircraft's engines, absolutely nothing else was happening.

Chang seemed to be frustrated by this because his one hand squeezed the remote control in a kind of quiet tantrum. He squeezed it so tightly that Raggie could hear the plastic, making cracking sounds from the pressure.

The news anchorman seemed to sense the boredom of the CNN viewers because he talked over the still images. He droned on and on about some kind of summit and about how the president returning was such a big deal because he'd never visited Africa so far in his presidency. The entire affair seemed to take forever, but it was only about fifteen minutes.

President Asher was a tall man in his late forties. He was one of the youngest presidents in American history, but not the youngest. He finally emerged from the hatch and walked out onto the landing of the stairs. He waved to the spectators. He was the only person to emerge.

Chang said, "Why's he alone? Where's Rowley?"

Raggie and her mother stared at Chang.

Raggie wasn't aware of who these guys were or what exactly was going on, but she had a sense that it was something involving her father and the president. And she knew it was something bad. Her mother seemed to have absolutely no idea because she asked, "What does this have to do with Gibson? Doug? Talk to me!"

Graine said, "Shut up!"

Karen Rowley looked down and away. Raggie reached out her hand to hold her mother's.

Lane said, "Relax. He exits alone. He's the only one who uses the staircase at the front. Everyone else comes out the back."

The president quick-stepped down the stairs on long, wiry legs. He made it to the bottom and had to walk through his security before he was greeted by a group of men in suits, all guys that Raggie didn't recognize. They stood far from the press corps, shaking hands and talking for another five minutes before Raggie's dad emerged in the background.

Chang stood up as soon as he saw Rowley. He stepped closer to the TV and stayed glued, waiting for something bad to happen.

52

WIDOW AND CORD parked down the street from the Rowley house and waited for their backup to arrive.

Cord said, "We can't wait long."

Widow said, "We won't have to. Look, there she is."

They watched a black Ford Taurus pull up with the lights off. The driver killed the engine and stepped out of the vehicle. Li met Widow at the front of the car and said, "You boys need my help?"

Widow looked her up and down and then again in reverse order. She'd dressed quickly and sped all the way over. He knew that because she was there in only twenty minutes. She probably used the siren lights embedded in the grille. But how she looked so good in that short amount of time, he had no idea.

She wore black slacks, a black long-sleeved top, and a black hat with the bill turned to the front. None of that backward crap. She looked deadly and sexy as hell all at the same time. Widow smiled.

He said, "We couldn't be more grateful."

Cord said, "Did you bring a gun?"

Li reached back to the pancake holster behind her and pulled out a Ruger SP101 double-action revolver, stainless steel with a black pistol grip.

Widow said, "A three fifty-seven? That's quite a piece. You know how to shoot it?"

Li said, "I can shoot you with it."

"Why didn't you wear a vest?"

"I don't have one. I work support, remember?"

Widow stayed quiet.

Cord said, "You two can flirt later. Let's hurry. My shoulder isn't getting any better."

Widow said, "You stay in the truck."

"No way! I'm going in with you!"

"Forget it! You've been shot. You won't be any help. Besides, someone needs to stay on the street. Once we start shooting, this block will be crawling with agents and cops. You'll need to make sure that none of the bad guys get away."

Cord protested, but the pain in his shoulder and ribs hurt like hell.

He said, "Just get in there and save that family!"

Widow said, "Get on the phone and start calling people."

Li said, "Why don't we just get all these other agents to storm the house with us? They're already here and armed."

Cord said, "These guys aren't worried about getting away alive. They're willing to die, and they'll kill Raggie and Karen. The agents on this block are sworn to protect these other families. They'll secure their own first. We don't have time to explain things to them. It may already be too late."

Widow said, "It's not."

"How do you know that?"

"If the president had been shot, this street would already be up in arms. No one's outside. Everything's quiet. Nothing's happened yet."

Cord said, "And it won't. Rowley won't do it."

Li said, "How do you know?"

"I know. But that won't save his family. Get in there."

Li followed, and they jogged up the street, weapons concealed.

Widow said, "After this is over, I'm taking you out to a nice dinner."

Li said, "After this is over, you'd better."

53

THE PRESIDENT SHOOK hands with Kerry Fife, his chief of staff, like he hadn't seen him in decades, even though they had just spoken on Skype fifteen minutes earlier. The handshake was for the cameras.

The president's advisor to the western region of North Africa was with them as well as the vice president. A fourth man who walked up late to the group was the West Ganbolan diplomat to the United States. He came to greet the president and thank him for his visit as their people mourned the loss of the president-elect.

His boss was President Sowe, who was the runner-up in the election and the previous president. By West Ganbolan law, when a president died in office, his minister of defense became president. But when a president-elect died before he was sworn in, then his strongest opponent in the election took office. Here, it was the last president.

President Asher wasn't a fan of Sowe, and everyone knew it. In fact, Asher downright hated Sowe. Sowe was a vicious and brutal dictator. He was behind the assassination of Biyena, and everyone knew it. But the region needed a leader, and the US couldn't publicly interfere with the sovereignty of another country unless it was planning to go to war. No one wanted a war in Africa. No one was interested in a little country that had no strategic value and no resources. Nothing would be gained in winning a war there except a victory for democracy.

Asher had been advised just to play nice and go along with the old regime. It was better than a civil war that would suck the neighboring countries into its vacuum. Asher shook the man's hand.

The commentator on *CNN* went on and on about the drop in approval ratings that Asher was taking for supporting Sowe, but Asher's advisors had warned him that sending troops there would be even worse. Americans didn't care about western Africa.

* * *

AT THE TAIL end of Air Force One, Rowley stared at the crowd of reporters and onlookers. His assistant director, a tall man named Renth, was standing five feet from him, asking about the flight. Rowley didn't pay him any attention or respond.

Renth asked, "Everything okay?"

Rowley said, "I need to speak to him."

"He's on camera right now..."

Rowley didn't wait for him to finish—he just walked away. He walked under the wing of the plane for what seemed like an eternity as the cameras flashed and recorded video. He looked to the left at the crowd. No one was watching him. They were focused on the president. Reporters stood with microphones in hand, staring into large cameras at an audience of millions—faces they never saw and people they never met.

The sky was three-quarters dark blue and one-quarter bright red and orange from the last moments of the remaining sunlight. Clear skies with no cloud cover stretched into the pending darkness. The top of the airport peeked out in the distance behind the cameras and the reporters.

Rowley had been born fifty-six years ago in June. He was born left-handed and was one of ten percent of Americans who were left-handed. The Secret Service employed 3,211 special agents, which meant that he was part of a group of 321 agents who fired their guns with their left hands.

He walked toward President Asher, his right hand clasping and pinching the place on his lapel where his flag pin had been only twenty-one minutes before. He raised his left hand and rested it near his gun, outside the bottom of his jacket. He kept his mind clear. He thought about nothing but Raggie.

Everything around him grew blurry—except for Asher. He looked at Asher with shark eyes.

Rowley walked under the wing, past the two agents near the staircase. Then he passed under the nose. He sidestepped from behind an agent who stood directly under the cockpit of the plane. The agent stared at him from behind and said nothing. Another agent stared at him, and Rowley could hear one call out to the other. They were the world's best-trained armed guards, and their protective instincts were kicking in on high. He knew it, but he didn't stop his approach to the president.

He cleared a third agent and a fourth and a fifth. He walked up behind Asher and then peered over his left shoulder for a split second. In that second, he saw the first lady's face and then the president's youngest daughter standing next to her.

He thought of Raggie.

He turned his head back and opened the flap of his jacket to expose his gun and holster.

He stopped five feet from President Asher.

Chief of Staff Fife looked at him strangely.

Asher was speaking to the diplomat from West Ganbola, still shaking his hand. The guy's face was blank, and he seemed to not care less about his handshake with the president.

Rowley cleared his throat and pulled his gun out of the holster.

In a split second, the agents standing around the president both reacted and stood down—their first instinct was "gun!" and then their next thought was Rowley. They didn't know what to do. There had been no training in the classes or in any manual on how to react to their boss pulling a gun on the president of the United States.

Rowley said, "I'm sorry, sir."

Asher turned and looked at Rowley. He said, "Gib, what's going on?"

Rowley paused a beat and looked at the faces of the other men, his gun in his hand but down by his side. He clicked the safety back to safe and reversed the gun in his hand, pointed it out butt first. He pulled his Secret Service badge and ID out of his inside jacket pocket. He held them both out to Asher.

He said, "I resign my position as Director of your Secret Service. I ask that you accept my resignation immediately. I ask that you have the agents take me into custody. I'm a risk to your security."

Asher looked at Rowley and then over his shoulder at the other agents. Everyone looked more confused than he was.

He said, "Gib, this isn't the place."

Rowley said, "This has to happen now, sir." He looked back at the agents and nodded at them.

One of them approached and removed his hand from his gun. None of them drew their weapons, but the two agents closest to him kept their hands on their weapons. The agents farther back near the plane stared in confusion. They prepared for something to happen, but they didn't know what was going on.

The press corps was out of earshot, and the plane noise was too loud for them to pick up anything even with their advanced microphone technology. But everyone knew something was happening. The news commentators looked around, speechless. Some stared at each other, while others just watched and said nothing.

A Secret Service agent stepped up to him. He didn't put handcuffs on Rowley, but he took his SIG Sauer and badge. He pocketed the badge and stuffed the gun into the waistband of his trousers; then he placed his free hand on Rowley's wrists in a kind of securing gesture.

The agent looked at the president.

Asher nodded, and the other agents came in close. They gripped Rowley under his arms and walked him off to the west, away from the press and the plane.

Asher looked at the other men and shook his head. He didn't know what had just happened or what to say.

* * *

CHANG THREW the remote violently at the TV. It shattered into three pieces. The batteries flew out and rolled across the floor.

Raggie and her mother held each other tightly. They weren't sure about what had been supposed to happen, but they both knew it hadn't happened the way Chang had wanted it to.

They sensed that the next thing to happen wouldn't be good.

Chang stood with his back to the rest of the room. He said nothing for a long moment.

Lane stepped forward and said, "Now what?"

Chang turned and said, "Do it!"

Lane turned to Grant and said, "Do it quickly. I want to be out of here in five minutes."

Grant smiled, stood up from the sofa, and nodded.

Lane reached behind his pants and pulled his Beretta M9 from its holster. He reached into his right inside jacket pocket and pulled out a long, black object.

The first person to recognize it was Daftshaw.

He leaped to his feet and said, "No! No! Come on! We know nothing! Let the kid go! She's just a kid!"

Lane smiled and secured the suppressor to the end of his gun.

Grant said, "Shut up, mate!"

He shoved the cop down hard against the coffee table. Daftshaw fell backward and landed on the coffee table. He was a little overweight by department standards, and his heavy weight shattered the glass top and got him stuck in the table frame. He struggled to get back to his feet.

Raggie and Karen Rowley screamed as Lane pointed the Beretta at them.

Grant then brandished a suppressor for his own gun and fastened it.

Daftshaw repeated his protests over and over. He struggled and fought to free himself from the table.

This was Grant's favorite part of the job. He moved the M9 in a slow movement to point it at the cop.

Daftshaw stared at the hole at the end of the suppressor, and then he squeezed his eyes shut.

Grant pulled the trigger in rapid succession. Once. Twice. Three times. The bullets burst out of the muzzle in soft sequence, each time making a sound like a loud purr. The gun fired three shots—one in the center forehead and two in the chest—tight proximity.

Raggie and her mother screamed.

Max broke free and ran from Raggie. He galloped away and up the stairs.

Raggie called out, "Max!"

54

WIDOW AND LI crept up the front to the side gate. The outside motion lights shot on like watchtower spotlights searching for escaping prisoners. Li's heart nearly leaped out of her chest, and she froze. Widow felt stupid for a split second for not noticing them before.

Widow whispered, "Come on. Just the motion sensor."

They moved into the side yard and walked on the grass until they reached the patio.

Li stayed low and was barely visible to anyone who might be looking. Widow was a different story, but he could get low enough. They maneuvered through a clutter of patio furniture—four table chairs, two lounge chairs, a table, two side tables—and a nice barbecue grill.

They moved close to the house and pressed their backs against the wall. Widow wasn't familiar with hand signals, but he wouldn't have been surprised if Li knew them. She'd studied hard for the Secret Service test, and her whole life had been focused on that. She didn't have a military background, but Widow was certain she'd probably studied everything she could get her hands on for that test. She was the type to go the extra mile, to turn the corner and keep going. She wasn't the type for questioning herself or ever looking back.

He whispered, "Stay here. Wait thirty seconds. After I'm out of sight, breach this door. Right through the glass."

He gestured to a set of double French doors. He said, "Make it loud, and then take cover."

"Where are you going?"

Widow said, "Back door. Remember—thirty seconds after I'm out of sight."

Then he stopped and turned back. He said, "Don't shoot the glass. Save the ammo for the bad guys."

She said, "What do I use?"

Widow reached down and grabbed a garden gnome. He said, "Throw this as hard as you can."

Li said, "Okay."

Widow turned and crept around the side of the house. He started counting in his head. He turned another corner on the side of the house. He looked through the windows as he passed. The lights were off until he got to the backyard. He stopped and froze, with his back hugged tightly to the corner. He peeked slowly around it and saw the lights from the back of the house shining out across the grass. Long rectangles of light stretched out into the darkness.

He looked up at the sides of the house and traced the brick to the roof. He saw the motion sensor lights at the top, staring down into the yard. The moment he set foot in the back, everyone in the house would know he was there.

He waited and counted. Twenty-seven. Twenty-eight.

Li went early.

Crash!

Widow heard the window shatter and then something in the kitchen —like knives or silverware—crashing to the ground. The sound echoed through the house and outside around the sides to where Widow was. It ricocheted off the bricked-in privacy fence like a bullet.

Widow leaped up from the corner and scrambled forward. He stopped dead five feet from another set of double French doors at the back of the house. He spun forty-five degrees and dropped to one knee. In half a second, he lifted the MP5 and took aim into the house through the windows.

His eyes quickly scanned the scene through the glass doors—Left! Right! Back left again!

Two men stood in the room, and two females crouched down tight together—Raggie and Karen Rowley. One of the men had no right arm, and something was wrong with his ears. No, his ears were missing. He was unarmed. No problem. The other man—Grant—had the same Beretta M9 from before, but this time, it had a long suppressor on the end. Both men faced the direction of the kitchen.

Where were Lane and Graine? Widow wondered, and then he thought, *the kitchen.*

In old westerns, the good guy would've duked it out with the bad guy—or, in this case, the bad guy's main henchman.

Not Widow's style.

The girls were clear enough for a kill shot.

A bullet fires fast. Out of a Heckler and Koch MP5, it travels out of the barrel at a speed of thirteen hundred feet per second, but a second isn't the shortest measurement of time.

Widow liked numbers, always had, and he knew a lot about them. He wasn't good with physics—he only knew the basics that everyone knew. Not that he didn't find physics interesting. One thing he knew about physics was a thing called *Planck time*, which was the measurement of *Planck units*. It had something to do with measuring the speed at which light travels in a vacuum. The thing that was important about it—right then at that moment—was that light speed could be measured in the smallest known measurement of a second, known as an attosecond.

An attosecond equals ten to the negative eighteenth power of one second. The way Widow had always thought of it was that an attosecond was to a second what a regular old second was to thirty-two billion years. Very short and fast!

Widow couldn't move at the speed of light, but it sure as hell felt like he was. He switched the fire selector to three-round burst and squeezed the trigger in a period of time that felt to him like an attosecond.

Three bullets exploded from the gun, and a cloud of fire and smoke burst from the muzzle. The bullets shattered the glass and rocketed across ninety-nine feet of space. They ripped three nine-millimeter holes into Grant's back and head. A fine red spray puffed out from the other side of him along with parts of his lungs and facial muscles and teeth, staining the Rowley's white carpet and splattering a white wall.

Raggie and her mother screamed, and the African guy with no ears spun around to stare at Widow. Aside from Shepard back in Red Rain Indian Reservation, Widow couldn't remember the last time he had seen someone so scarred up.

Chang said, "Who're you?"

"Shut up!" Widow said, and burst through the shattered glass like a one-man SWAT team. He said, "On the ground! Now!"

Chang wasn't the kind of guy to be intimidated—not after the things that he had seen and done—but one look at Widow's face and he dropped like a sack of potatoes.

Widow heard a dog bark and saw a big dog covered in curly white hair, a mix of God knew what. It ran down the stairs and barked at the guy on the ground. The dog didn't even look at Widow. It seemed to be interested only in restraining the guy on the ground.

Widow flicked the gun up and pointed it toward the opposite hallway that led through a dining room and into the kitchen.

Raggie said, "There's two more!"

"I know," said Widow. "Grab your mom, and get the hell outta here! Go through the backyard!"

Raggie stood bravely and led her mother by the hand out through the shattered glass of the French doors. Max stayed behind for another second, watching the guy on the floor and growling loudly. Then he darted out the door and chased after them.

Widow stayed until he was sure they were out and away from harm. Then he looked at Chang and said, "If you move, I'll kill you in a way you've never seen. Whatever did that shit to your face will seem like heaven compared to what I'll do!"

The guy with no ears looked up at him, and Widow knew he wouldn't move. The guy had a fear in his eyes that Widow had seen before. It was the kind of look you couldn't fake. Widow thought about shooting the guy just to be safe, but he had already wasted enough time. Besides, with those shots fired, the neighboring Secret Service agents would be by soon enough. They would find him and take care of him.

He walked back to Grant's body. He knelt and picked up the silenced M9 that Grant had dropped. He tucked it under his armpit and held it there as he looked over the body. Seeing another gun tucked into Grant's waistband, he pulled it out and checked it, one-handed. It had no bullets. It looked to Widow like Grant had taken it off the dead cop in the coffee table and ejected the rounds.

He looked back at the guy with no ears.

He asked, "You responsible for this?"

The guy looked up slowly and shook his head.

Widow asked, "Are you the guy in charge?"

The guy said nothing.

Widow dropped the empty gun and pointed the silenced one at the man with no ears. "Name?"

The African guy said, "Chang."

Widow nodded.

He said, "We thought you died."

Chang said, "Sowe spared me. Taught me things."

"He do that to you?"

Chang nodded with his hands behind his head.

"You the guy behind all of this?" he asked again.

Chang said nothing.

Widow looked at the dead cop and said, "You responsible for that?"

Chang said, "Consequences. Casualty of war."

Cause and effect. One thing led to another.

Widow was taught never to use a gun in the field that he'd never test-fired before. So he test-fired the silenced M9. He aimed it at Chang and squeezed the trigger four times—three bullets for the dead cop and an extra for himself. He ejected the magazine and fired the chambered round into Chang also, making it five bullets—and one very dead African.

The gun worked just fine, but he didn't need it. He tossed the silenced M9 and turned toward the hall that led to the kitchen.

He glanced up the back stairs and thought, *two left*.

He hoped he'd find them both in the kitchen, but he knew there was a second staircase at the front of the house. He figured if one of them was missing from the kitchen, he was most likely upstairs.

He headed quickly down the hall in a crouch. He stopped at an open doorway and peeked in, his head behind the MP5, stock jammed hard into his shoulder. His eyes hit the far corner and then darted to the others. Nothing there. Just empty furniture and darkness. He scrambled the rest of the way to a corner near the kitchen, just inside the dining room.

He heard gunshots—two very loud ones that sounded like cannons firing and three muffled ones. The two shots were from a .357 Magnum. No question. The other three were from a gun with a silencer attached. Unmistakable. He wasn't sure what type of gun it was, but he figured it was Lane's M9. Then there were three more shots that sounded like they came from a SIG Sauer—Graine's gun.

Widow tucked in tight and took a quick glance around the kitchen doorframe. He saw Li crouched behind an island. He didn't see Lane or Graine.

Li looked at him and gestured to an open doorway at the far corner. That's where they were—on the other side—probably hugging the wall.

Graine was an old man, a has-been cop, and a traitor who had misled his friends for years. He may have been a special ops soldier at one time, but that didn't change the fact that he was a has-been.

Lane was a different story. He was from the same unit as Graine, but he was younger and had personal motivation. He also had a skill set that had probably only gotten better with time. More than likely, he ran bullshit missions back in Africa for whoever that guy in the living room was. There was something about him that Widow knew all too well. He was a guy who thought he was still in his prime and he was probably right.

What would Lane do here? he thought.

Simple—Lane knew Li wasn't alone. They'd heard Widow fire a three-round burst, and they had probably heard his voice. Lane would instruct Graine, the weaker of the two, to stay behind and take care of Li while Lane headed to the second floor up the front staircase and then down the back stairs to flank Widow from behind.

Widow wished he knew some of those special ops hand signals that Li probably did. But he didn't, so he did the best he could. He held his hand up and gave her the universal signal to stay put. And then he pointed up at the ceiling. She nodded. He wasn't worried about her. She could handle herself.

Widow leaped to his feet and ran in a crouch back the way he'd come, being careful to check every corner before turning it. He made his way back to the family room and stopped. The guy with no ears still lay face down on the floor, dead as a doornail. Widow slumped back into the darkness of a far corner. He got down on one knee, pressed his back to the corner, and pointed the MP5 at the back staircase.

He waited. Seconds crept by slowly—and nothing. He waited longer. Still nothing. He barely blinked, moving his eyes from side to side and up and down, not keeping them trained on one location for too long. Eyes blurred when you stared at one thing for too long.

No one came.

He heard another two gunshots from the kitchen. He waited. The seconds ticked by. He counted them. The first shots from the SIG Sauer were one minute and ten seconds apart. And then the shots of the second set were spaced one minute and eleven seconds apart. The third set came, and there was one minute and nine seconds between. The spacing was intentional—an ambush.

He smiled and waited.

Finally, he heard a fourth set of two rounds fired at one minute and ten seconds from the last. Then he saw a foot creep down from the top of the staircase. He silently slid his back up the wall and steadied the MP5 in a rock-solid stance. He breathed in and breathed out.

He saw the guy's other foot come down on the second step from the top. He waited patiently as Lane's legs came fully into view, then his chest and then his face. Lane crept down the stairs with his silenced Beretta M9 pointed out, ready to fire.

Widow stood still in the corner's darkness, waiting for Lane to either see him or reach the bottom. Lane never saw him. When his foot hit the floor after the last step, Widow moved out of the corner—slowly. He stared down the iron sights of the MP5. Lane's center mass filled the middle of his reticle.

Widow whispered from the darkness. He said, "Lane."

Lane twisted fast and pointed his M9, but he wasn't fast enough.

A burst of bullets exploded from Widow's MP5. The three bullets ripped through the flesh and bone in Lane's chest, and he flew backward onto the stairs in an explosion of red. He slumped down, and blood spurted from the wounds in his chest. His silenced M9 fell to the carpet. It was useless.

Widow stepped out of the darkness and over Grant's corpse. He moved toward the staircase, his gun trained on Lane. He stopped with his right foot on top of the fallen M9.

He stared into Lane's eyes—up close and personal—for the first and last time.

Lane tried to speak, choking on the blood gurgling in his throat.

Widow said, "Guess what? I just killed you."

And in seconds, the life drained from Lane.

Widow looked over at the dead guy with no ears, and then back at Lane. Only one left. He stared at Lane, wondering how much he weighed. Holding the MP5 in his left hand, he reached down and grabbed Lane's belt with his right. He deadlifted him straight up. He wasn't a big guy, just average size. Still, carrying dead weight like a suitcase wasn't easy. But the adrenaline and the combat instincts in Widow's bones magnified his strength. He lifted Lane's corpse up and hauled him up the stairs. Lane's arms and legs hit the edges of the steps limply as Widow climbed. Once at the top, he dropped the body on the second floor and dragged Lane through the hallway and around corners until he reached the front staircase. He didn't go down them. He stopped at the top.

He called out, "Graine!"

55

GRAINE WAITED and fired his gun every seventy seconds, as instructed. He wasn't trying to hit anything. Whoever came down the stairs would see a flash of a small man with a gun and not much else.

Graine wasn't as young as he used to be, and his usual role was a more behind-the-scenes contribution. He didn't like all this exposure. This was Lane's show, not his. Why should he keep sticking his neck out? Rowley may not have gone through with killing Asher, but the damage was done. It looked like he was going to tell everything and deal with the shame for the rest of his life. He would go to prison. Even if his family lived, they would never speak to him again. He clearly chose his country over his daughter's life. Graine didn't quite get all that patriot shit. Well, he understood it to a point, but sacrificing his own for this country? That was cold even by his standards.

No matter the outcome, Rowley was finished.

Graine's money was in an account in the Cook Islands, so why should he stick around? He'd fire one more shot, and then he'd be out of there. He should just take off now while Lane was occupied, and none of the agents from the neighborhood had arrived yet. He knew they would come any second. Probably the cops, too.

He went. He didn't even fire the next rounds like he was supposed to do. Seventy seconds had already passed. It had now been more than ninety. He turned and headed out the front door when he heard a voice call from the top of the front staircase.

It was Widow. Widow had called down. He said his name.

Graine froze, trained his SIG Sauer at the stairs.

He said nothing. He waited. It seemed like an eternity, but at the first sign of Widow walking into view, he would unload the rest of his magazine into the guy.

Widow said, "Graine, I'm coming down. Don't shoot. We can talk."

Graine readied himself, his finger tight on the trigger.

* * *

Li heard Widow call down from the front stairs. She lifted her head and looked over the counter. She took a chance and darted toward the opposite wall. She hugged it close and crouched down low, moving slowly across it. She stopped three feet from the doorway. Graine was somewhere on the other side. She thought about shooting through the wall—surely a .357 Magnum would rip through it—but she didn't know his exact location. Four bullets left. Maybe she'd hit him, and maybe she wouldn't.

She waited.

* * *

Widow pulled Lane's corpse up onto its feet and tossed him down the stairs like a rag doll. Lane's body plummeted down the stairs like a heavy bag. He bounced and bumped against the railing. Blood and loose entrails splattered out across the stairs.

Graine reacted, firing his SIG Sauer. The bullets did their job, tearing through and shredding his target. The problem wasn't that his aim was bad. The problem, he realized too late, was that he hadn't shot Widow. He'd shot Lane.

Lane's corpse lay sprawled at the base of the stairs. It was a grisly heap of meat. It looked like someone had used him for target practice.

Then, like a phantom, Widow was suddenly at the top of the stairs, crouched down on one knee. He wasn't dead.

He barked, "DROP IT!"

"Okay. Okay," Graine said.

He dropped his gun and slowly raised his hands.

Widow said, "Li?"

Li stepped out into the doorway with her gun drawn, like a trained agent.

She said, "You got him!"

"We got him!"

Li smiled and pointed her gun at Graine.

Widow asked, "You got handcuffs?"

Li said, "You know it!" She didn't move her eyes from Graine. She said, "Turn around slowly and touch the wall! Spread your legs!"

Great cop voice, Widow thought.

Li shoved him against the wall and frisked him from top to bottom. She used one hand, keeping the gun shoved deep into his back, and then she holstered her gun.

She said, "You're under arrest for treason and for conspiracy in the attempted homicide of President John Asher. Plus a hundred other things, I'm sure."

She cuffed him. The sound of the metal locking was loud in the stillness. She jerked on his cuffs like they were the reins on a workhorse.

Graine said nothing.

She took him toward the front door, but Widow stepped in the way.

He looked at Graine and said, "Remember my face! I hope you think about it every day while you rot away in prison."

Graine started to speak, but Widow catapulted off his feet, whipping himself forward. It was his third head-butt today, but by far the most enjoyable one. It wasn't intended to crush Graine's face—something he could've easily done—but to break his nose and his front teeth.

The results were perfect. Graine flew off his feet and hit the door. A cracking sound echoed through the foyer, and blood spurted out of Graine's broken nose. He spat out four whole teeth and fragments of others. The man writhed on the ground.

Li said, "Why did you do that? That's police brutality."

Widow said, "I'm not a cop, and no one is going to think you did it. No offense."

She said nothing.

They could hear distant sirens closing in.

He said, "Sorry. I couldn't help myself."

"Wait for me out there. There'll be a lot of questions."

Widow said, "You take them. I'm going to slip out the back."

She said, "What? Why?"

"Questions and red tape aren't my thing."

"What the hell do I tell them?"

Widow walked away. He stopped and turned. He tossed the MP5 at her, and she caught it.

He said, "Tell 'em you did it. Cord won't refute it. Believe me, he and Rowley will want to keep as much of this a secret as they can. They'll probably never even mention me, and no one would believe them, anyway.

"Oh. One last thing."

She looked at him blankly.

"Tell Cord, there's a guy down in Miami. The cops are holding him. Have Cord take care of him for me. He's a good man. Just made a dumb mistake."

"What's his name?"

"Jorge Calderón."

He turned again and walked down the hall. Stepping through the shattered French doors, he walked into the backyard and disappeared in the darkness by the back fence.

56

Li took Graine out to the cops and the Secret Service agents. Cord was taken immediately to a hospital.

Questions were asked and answered. More questions followed after that, and they too were answered. Soon people tired of asking questions.

Li spent the entire night in a debriefing room at FBI headquarters. She sat in a cold room with a hot cup of black coffee, which made her think of Widow. She wondered where he was and if she would ever see him again. She sat, staring off into space. No one had been in to see her for forty-five minutes. She was questioned so much that she felt like she was the main suspect. And she had said as much to the last agent who questioned her.

He insisted she was not under any suspicion. She was regarded as a hero.

Finally, she was told she could go home for the night but needed to return first thing in the morning. She nodded and left the room. She walked down a long maze of hallways, past cubicles with agents transfixed by their computer screens. She passed security downstairs, and they buzzed her out of the building.

On the street, she was stopped by a tall Secret Service agent named Renth.

He said, "Agent Li?"

Li nodded.

"Come with me, please."

Li yawned and covered her mouth. She looked closely at the man's face. She recognized him. He was the assistant director of the Secret Service. She nodded and followed him around a corner to a black sedan.

He said, "Get in, please. Someone would like to see you."

She headed toward the front passenger side, and Renth told her to go to the back. She got in and leaned back in the seat.

Renth didn't close the door behind her. Instead, he handed her an iPad. The screen was on. He said, "Take this."

She took it, and he shut the door, leaving her alone in the car. Then she heard a familiar voice. She looked at the screen of the iPad and saw President Asher staring back at her from a FaceTime connection.

She said, "Mr. President?"

Asher said, "Hello, Miss Li."

"Hi," she said, not knowing what to say.

Asher said, "Agent Li, I wanted to thank you personally for your brave service tonight."

Li said, "Thank you, sir."

"I'm sorry I can't meet with you in person, but this is the only way, I'm afraid."

She said nothing.

Asher said, "I hear from Special Agent Cord that you were an essential part of foiling this terrible plot."

She said, "Thank you."

"Anyway, I just wanted to thank you personally."

Again, she said, "Thank you."

Asher hung up.

Li didn't know what to think. Never in a million years did she think the president would speak her name.

Renth opened the door and took the iPad from her. He leaned down and said, "Want a ride?"

"Sure."

He closed the door and got into the driver's seat. He started the engine and looked back at her in the rearview mirror. "Where to, Special Agent Li?"

She said, "I'm not a special agent."

He said, "You sure are. Executive orders. Sorry, there's no getting out of it."

He reached over into the next seat and then tossed something back into her lap.

She looked down and saw a Secret Service badge that had no name engraved on it. It read: "Temporary Agent."

Li stared at the badge with a feeling of accomplishment. She didn't know what to say. For her whole adult life, she had the goal of making it as a special agent, and in one day, it had been both taken away from her and then given back—and given back by executive order. If she'd had more sleep and was more herself, she would have cried with joy.

But right now, all she wanted to do was get home and see Widow and go to bed. He said he would call her later, but she hoped what he really meant was that he would wait for her. Where else was he going to go?

Renth said, "Where you wanna go?"

Li said, "Home. I'm exhausted."

Renth turned and faced the street. He started the car and asked, "What's your address?"

"Not far. Ten minutes maybe. Head east."

Renth followed her instructions. They drove on through several lights and intersections and then through a small section of down-town. At this early hour, traffic was moderate—not as bad as it would be in a half-hour, but not as light as it had been an hour earlier.

Once they reached her apartment, Li thanked Renth again and got out of the car. She walked up her stone pathway and then to the elevator. The whole trip home, she had one thing on her mind.

A major flaw Special Agent Li had was that even though she was extremely organized, she was also a little forgetful when it came to everyday things. One of the things she had forgotten more than once in the past had been the keys to her apartment.

She started hiding an extra key across the hall underneath the carpet in a place where it was torn up a little—something okay for most normal people but probably not the best idea for a United States Secret Service agent. The slight tear in the carpet helped her remember where she hid her key.

The thing she thought on her ride up in the elevator was that she hoped Widow had found her key and was now waiting in her apartment. She hoped he was waiting for her in her bed, already asleep. Perhaps she could slip in without waking him. Perhaps she could snuggle up behind him. Perhaps she could tuck in close and sleep the day away.

When she got off the elevator, instead of checking to see if the spare key had been used, she went straight to the apartment door. A smile of anticipation lit up her face. She unlocked the door, wondering if Widow was there, waiting.

* * *

Special Agent Cord woke up in a hospital bed the next afternoon. His chest still hurt like hell, but the staff of George Washington Hospital was taking very good care of him. His nurse was an attractive young woman, and that didn't bother him one bit.

He looked around his room and saw flowers and empty chairs. He smiled and breathed out, hurting from his broken ribs. His chest had been tightly bandaged, and he could see that the bandages Widow had wrapped him with after stitching his bullet wound had been changed.

He glanced at the TV. It was turned off, something he was glad to see because he was sure every channel would be filled with news reports about what had happened, and that was the last thing he wanted to think about.

He laid his head back down and stared up at the ceiling, enjoying the silence. He thought about his dead friends and thought about Jack Widow.

He wondered where Widow was now. He had underestimated him just as he had underestimated Kelly Li. He'd also underestimated Douglas Graine, and because of that, one of his friends was dead, and probably another. His oldest friend and boss would most likely lose his job and his future retirement—and that was the best-case scenario.

Cord tried to turn his mind off and not think about it. He tried to concentrate on the silver lining—Raggie was alive.

* * *

RAGGIE AND MAX slept the entire next afternoon, snuggled up under piles of blankets in a bed at her aunt's house in Virginia. Her mother looked in at her and smiled. She was glad her sister had finally gone to work, because even though it was only the afternoon, she was exhausted, too. She had stayed up all night thinking—and she had a lot to think about.

She needed to think about her future with a man who had chosen duty to his country over duty to his family. Even though she could understand why, she wasn't sure if this life was right for her any longer. She needed to think about a lot of things, and only time would give her the answers.

But for now, Raggie was safe, and it was obvious they had a new family member in Max the Shepadoodle.

She had tried to call her husband, but they weren't allowing him phone calls right now. He was currently being detained with no formal charges. They were holding him as a person of interest until they decided whether to charge him. Either way, she figured she was going to need the time apart.

Rowley was a fiercely loyal man—incredibly so—and it was likely he would tell them most of the truth. But she didn't think he would tell them about Cord and Lucas's involvement. He would tell them they were acting on his orders. Cord would be fine. He would retire with a full pension. He would be promoted, for sure.

None of this mattered to Karen Rowley now, however. All she wanted was to spend time with her daughter. She walked into the extra bedroom and made eye contact with Max as he lifted his head and looked at her. She lifted the covers and scooted in next to Raggie, who didn't acknowledge that her mother was getting in next to her but was aware of it.

Even though Raggie was exhausted from her ordeal, it would be awhile before she could sleep deeply like most people did, in that vulnerable way made possible by complete trust in the outside world. Her fears would keep her always partially alert for a long time. But she knew she would eventually move past it. Eventually, she would sleep like a normal person. Just as she had gotten over a shark attack and learned to embrace it as a strength, telling her friends, "Hey, I survived a shark attack. What've you done?"

But for now, she would sleep with one eye open.

* * *

WIDOW WAS DEAD TIRED. He figured Li would be awhile. He also figured that she wouldn't mind if he let himself into her apartment. So, he found a spare key hidden underneath a torn carpet out in the hall. He used it and let himself into her place. He showered and waited for a while. But she hadn't come home yet.

Eventually, his laundry finished, and he took it out of the dryer, folded everything nice and neat and set it on the counter in Li's bathroom.

He slipped into her bed and closed his eyes. He wanted to wait for her to come home. He fell asleep.

PATRIOT LIES: A PREVIEW

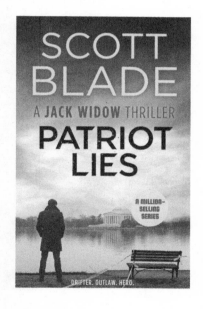

Out Now!

PATRIOT LIES: A BLURB

A dark lie. A darker truth.

They killed a homeless veteran.

They tried to cover it up.

Jack Widow won't let that stand.

Widow passes through DC. Hanging out, reading the morning paper, he learns about a homeless vet found burned alive on a park bench. The Vet has no known family. No one's expected to attend his wake. Widow must go.

He meets a lawyer who claims there's a sizable inheritance at the service: a stock portfolio worth fifty million dollars.

What's a homeless vet doing with that amount of secret money?

Widow follows a trail of murder and treason that leads him to a terrifying conspiracy.

Readers are saying about Scott Blade and the Jack Widow series...

★★★★★ Scott Blade and Lee Child are cut from the same cloth! Do yourself a favor and check this series out!

CHAPTER 1

THE OLD MAN on the park bench was outside, freezing on a cold October night.

It was typical for him. October. August. January. July. None of it mattered.

Every night, he slept somewhere that didn't belong to him. He slept wherever he was. Sometimes he was in the same place as the night before. And sometimes he wasn't.

The locations changed, but two things remained the same. The exact time of year meant nothing to him, all but one day, his daughter's birthday. He always remembered the date and the year she was born, but he never knew if he was on that exact date or not. He didn't know because he couldn't keep up with what day of the week *he* was in.

He knew the current month was October. He recognized October by the cold setting and the leaves changing colors.

The second thing that never changed was that he was drunk. He drank himself to sleep every night. He was a man trying to forget.

An empty bottle of Old Crow Whiskey lay out sideways on the brick sidewalk below him. The last drops streamed back and forth, slowly, across the inside of the bottle, like a carpenter's level.

The old man had drunk most of the bottle, but not alone. He'd shared it with other homeless men. One of them he knew by face. One he knew by name. And three of them he had never seen before in his life and would never see again.

The three he didn't know were friendly enough. They drank with him that very night. They helped him to the park bench and left him there. It was one of his nightspots, a good spot, too, because it was nestled in a tree-covered nook in the park that was often well-hidden and overlooked. A pedestrian passing by on the street would miss it unless he was looking for it.

The night trees weren't the same as the day trees. Technically, they were the same trees, but not to him. The night trees whistled in the wind. They swayed heavily, making creaking and rocking sounds like growing pains, all in the night's stillness.

Cars barely passed along the four streets that surrounded Lincoln Park.

Everything was quiet in a way that made him think of the open desert nights in Iraq.

The bench was all metal, painted deep red. It was hard and cold and not long enough to support a tall man. Luckily, the old man wasn't tall. He stood five-foot-nine and a half, when he wasn't hunching over. That half-inch used to be very important to him, when he cared what people thought. Those days were long gone. And it showed.

He let his beard grow wild to where even his friends from twenty years ago wouldn't recognize him. He'd let his pores clog. He hadn't showered in days. He couldn't remember the last time a razorblade had touched his face. He couldn't remember the last time he had brushed his teeth or combed his hair or laid hands on a bar of soap.

Not to mention, he couldn't remember the last time a woman had touched him. No woman would touch him now. He knew that for sure. Now, all he got were dirty looks and people avoiding him.

Lincoln Park wasn't his first choice for spending a cold October night. He usually rotated between the back of a 7-Eleven on Benning Street or the Kingsman Field Dog Park on Tennessee Avenue or one of the ten churches in less than ten square blocks or the back alley of a yoga studio over on Tenth Street, past the Maryland Avenue overpass.

But not tonight.

Tonight, he slept in Lincoln Park. Not planned. He had gotten drunker than usual. It was just the way things worked out. He'd ended up there by a series of events that seemed random, like every other day of his life. Nothing had been planned. There was no predestined reason for him to be drinking with the other homeless guys. Nothing seemed out of the ordinary.

Early that night, he'd met a guy, got a ride, and found a bottle of booze, which he shared with other homeless guys. He got drunk, too drunk, and now here he was, sleeping on a park bench. It was all a typical night, except this time he spent it with drinking buddies and a full bottle.

His drinking buddies numbered five guys. There was the one he knew by name, the one he knew by face, and the three he didn't. When you're homeless, you take all the drinking buddies you can get —random or not.

The five of them gathered around a trashcan fire to stay warm. Autumn nights in DC could be relentlessly cold. Not like winter nights, but still he risked catching a cold; at worst, he could freeze to death.

The five homeless guys stood around and bullshitted about bullshit and not much else.

Within forty minutes, he was buzzed. Within two hours, he was piss-drunk. Thirty minutes after that, he was fast asleep on the park bench. His homeless drinking buddies were gone. The trashcan fire burned out.

He was alone.

The old man slept for nearly an hour before the black Cadillac Escalade pulled up to the curb on East Capitol Street from North Carolina Avenue. Both one-way streets were marked with clear one-way markers.

The Escalade's engine ran and purred under the hood. There were four guys in the truck. The driver left the engine on and hopped out with the rest, shutting the doors behind them.

They wore all black. Black jackets. Black pants. Black boots. They matched, like a secret private security force.

The first guy led the way into Lincoln Park and over to the homeless guy on the bench. He walked as if he knew the way in advance, like he had been there before, like he had rehearsed it at this exact location.

He approached the old man's position as if he knew exactly where the old man was perched, like there was a tracking beacon on him.

The second guy followed the first guy. The third and fourth guys followed halfway over to the old man, and then they branched off, walking toward different entrances to the park. Three of the guys formed a perimeter, as if they were guarding against anyone coming in or going out.

The first guy led the way to the bench and pointed out the sleeping homeless guy to the second guy. Then, the second guy turned and faced away as if he were standing guard. He stuffed his hands into his coat pockets to look like just a guy standing around.

All four men carried firearms in concealed hip holsters under their clothes. All four holsters' safety buckles were unsnapped. All four firearms were chambered with a nine-millimeter bullet. All four weapons were well-oiled and well-maintained. All four weapons had been fired before. All four men had killed before.

The first guy walked over to the sleeping homeless man on the bench. He carried a brand-new bottle of Clyde Brothers' Whiskey. The price tag was two hundred bucks, far more than a cheap bottle of Old Crow.

The first guy couldn't use the Old Crow, not that there was any left to use. He needed a flammable whiskey. Old Crow wouldn't do the job. Not the right way, even if it was a full bottle.

It's a myth that any old bottle of alcohol will make a good accelerant. It's true that alcohol is highly flammable. The right bottle of alcohol makes for the perfect Molotov cocktail. But most cheap alcohol is cheap for a reason. There's not much pure alcohol left in a cheap bottle of whiskey. Not enough to do the job that the first guy needed it to do.

To get the most bang for your buck, you need a cask strength whiskey. Bottom-shelf whiskey is watered down, which reduces its strength and its cost.

Cask strength isn't the highest proof nor the strongest alcohol content in a whiskey, but it burns well enough. Cask strength whiskey will catch on fire and burn just right.

The first guy stood directly over the homeless man, watching him sleep, listening to him snore. The homeless guy snored with his mouth wide open.

The first guy looked up. He looked left, looked right. Making sure no one was watching.

He saw no one, just his guys.

The wind gusted around him. It brushed through Lincoln Park. It whistled through the crevices and ridges over the Emancipation Statue, a life-size memorial that portrayed President Lincoln, standing over the last enslaved man to be captured under the *Fugitive Slave Act of Missouri*.

All around, the first guy heard nothing over the wind noise, except the usual weeknight sounds of Washington, DC.

Horns honked far off in the distance. Sirens wailed, but far away. Mechanical motor sounds rumbled along the city streets. Tires rolled over pavements. Worn brake pads hissed. A dog barked to the south. But no one was around. No witnesses.

The first guy tore the seal off the top of the Clyde Brothers' bottle and pulled out the cork. He tossed them both to the ground. He held the bottle out at full arm's reach and tipped it upside down, spilling the contents all over the snoring homeless man.

The alcohol gushed out, drenching the homeless guy and the bench beneath him in whiskey.

The homeless man was so drunk that he didn't wake up to the liquid dousing him all over. Not at first.

It wasn't until the first guy doused the bottom fourth of the bottle all over the homeless guy's face that he woke and reacted.

He half-leaped up and waved his hands over his face as if he were being waterboarded.

The homeless guy's eyes popped open in time to see the first guy standing over him, emptying the bottle of whiskey all the way until there was nothing left but glass and the label.

"What? What the hell're you doin'?" the homeless guy asked.

The first guy finished pouring the bottle over him. Then he tossed it over his shoulder. It landed off the track into some bushes. The bottle didn't break.

The homeless guy stayed lying on the bench. Frantically, he wiped the whiskey out of his eyes and spat some out of his mouth.

He squinted, staring up into the starry night above. Things were blurry, as if he were looking through a glass of water.

He saw the first guy standing over him. The first guy's features were all covered in shadows and blurred.

"What the hell's going on?" the homeless guy asked.

The first guy reached his free hand into his coat and came out with something palm-sized. He balanced it in his hand and pressed on it with his index finger. Then he swiped left. It was a smartphone.

"What're ya doing?"

The first guy said, "Hold up a second, Commander."

The homeless guy's eyes widened, as if he saw someone he thought he knew, but he couldn't see the guy's face, and he didn't recognize the voice. But the first guy had called him *Commander*, like people did back when he was a commander in the Navy.

"Who are you?" the homeless guy asked.

The first guy ignored him and said, "It's time."

"Time for what?"

The light from the smartphone's screen lit up the guy's face. The homeless guy's eyesight improved, and he focused. He looked over the first guy's face. He saw a clean-shaven chin and deep blue eyes, and not much else to speak of. The first guy's face was average and unremarkable. It was strangely forgettable. In a police lineup, he would blend right in. No one would identify him in a crowd. Besides his eyes and a pair of broad shoulders, everything else about the guy was average, like he was built for spycraft—an average-looking guy with no memorable traits made him someone who could pass through crowds with no problem. Witnesses would never remember enough details to describe him. There was nothing to remember. He was a vague man walking.

The guy was in his late forties. He had broad shoulders, with a lean lower half like a marathon runner, and short black hair, sprinkled with gray.

"Do I know you?" the homeless guy asked. He legitimately wasn't sure. Part of him glimpsed some vague recognition from a deep past that he tried to forget.

The first guy didn't answer. He clicked a button on the phone's screen, and the phone rang—once. Someone answered it on the other end of the line. The first guy put it on speaker.

He said, "Found him, sir."

The first guy reversed the phone and faced it to the homeless guy.

The phone's bright screen lit up the homeless guy's face. Blue back light bounced off the homeless guy's unkempt beard.

The first guy stared at him.

"You look like shit, Commander."

The homeless guy reached up for the phone as if he was going to take it, but the first guy jerked it back.

"Don't touch!" the first guy shouted.

The homeless guy stayed laid out where he was, like he was. He didn't budge. He didn't move. He just stared up at the screen. The first guy moved it in closer to the homeless guy's face.

The homeless guy stared at the screen until he realized that someone on screen stared back at him.

The face was familiar. He knew the eyes. They were dark brown, not black, but they were just as soulless as the last time he'd seen them—twenty years ago. Unlike the first guy, these were not eyes he would forget. He saw them nearly every day in his dreams—his nightmares. They were eyes from a dead past that he wished would stay buried. He thought about that face often. He tried not to. He tried to forget it. He wanted to forget, wanted never to see it again, but here it was, staring back at him.

The first guy stared at the homeless guy from behind the phone's back light and asked a question.

"This him?"

The voice on the screen replied.

"Turn his head to profile. Let me get a good look at him."

The first guy barked an order at the homeless guy.

"Turn your head!"

The homeless guy did nothing.

The first guy reached a gloved hand out and grabbed the homeless guy's beard on the left side and jerked his head to face the right —hard.

The homeless guy struggled, but it was useless.

The first guy barked, "Stop!"

The homeless guy stopped fighting back and gave in.

The voice on the screen ordered, "Show me his eyes."

The first guy jerked the homeless guy's head back to center, released his beard, and reached up to his eye sockets. He got a grip on one of the homeless guy's eyelids and pulled it open wide as far as it would go. In any other human being, the whites of the eyes would've been what showed up, but not here. The homeless man's whites were too bloodshot to be called *white*.

All that was visible were pupils, irises, and blood-red veins throughout his eyes.

The voice on the phone said, "He's piss drunk."

The first guy said, "Yes. Part of the plan. It's how we got him alone."

The homeless guy said, "What? What's going on?"

The voice on the phone said, "Hello, Henry."

The homeless man said, "Who?"

"Henry Eggers. I know it's you."

"No one. No one calls me that anymore. Henry Eggers is dead now."

Eggers looked at the face on the phone. He lifted his head off the park bench's metal armrest and squinted his eyes, trying to focus on the face on the phone's screen.

Both the face on the screen and the first guy waited a long moment until they knew for a fact that Eggers recognized the face on the screen.

They knew because terror swept over Eggers' face.

The face on the phone asked, "You remember me, Henry?"

Eggers said nothing.

The face on the phone said, "Yeah. You remember me. I found you. Can you believe it? It wasn't easy. Finding you was hard. And I've got the resources to find anyone. Anyone, Henry."

Eggers swallowed and said, "I didn't know you were looking for me."

"I've been looking for you for a little bit of time now. Months, in fact."

"How are you?"

The face on the phone's screen ignored the question.

"Henry, you look like shit."

Eggers said nothing.

The first guy said, "He smells like shit too."

The face on the phone asked, "What's happened to you, Henry?"

"I'm between jobs right now."

"Funny."

Eggers paused a beat. For a reason nothing other than he was completely blank on what to say next. Finally, he spoke.

"To what do I owe the pleasure?"

The face on the phone stared at him, hard. Then he spoke.

"I've got to ask you a question."

"Okay."

"Answer honestly, now. This'll all go a lot easier for you. No lies. Understand?"

"Okay."

The face on the phone asked, "What did you do with your money?"

Eggers stayed quiet, but his eyes opened wide. They darted from side to side as if he was tortured by old, unforgotten memories.

A solid minute went by. The face on the phone knew it because he had been watching the time on his phone.

"Henry!"

"What?"

"Where's the money?"

Eggers paused. He tried to grip the bench and pull himself up, but the first guy plunged four solid fingertips into Eggers' chest, shoving him back down on his butt.

"Stay!" the first guy barked.

"Answer the question!" the face on the phone demanded.

Eggers cleared his throat and said, "I don't know."

The face said, "Henry, where's the money?"

Eggers said nothing.

The face said, "Last chance."

The first guy reached into his pocket and pulled out a Zippo lighter. It looked both expensive and familiar to Eggers. It looked familiar because it was. One time, long ago, the lighter had belonged to him.

It was a gift from a commanding officer he had back in his Navy days.

An engraving on the polished silver casing read his full name and rank and nothing else.

Eggers said, "I'm not Henry anymore. You don't need to worry about me. I'm one of the forgotten people now. Like a ghost. I'm nobody."

The face repeated, "Where's the money?"

Eggers said, "I don't got it."

The face on the phone called out for the first guy by name.

The first guy pulled the phone away from Eggers and stared at the face on the screen.

The face said, "He's useless. Do it."

The first guy smiled. Eggers saw it in the light from the phone.

Eggers was drunk and ancient, but once upon a time, he had been somebody. Those old instincts might still be there somewhere, down deep. He hoped they were. He hadn't thrown a punch in more than twenty years. The last time he was in close quarters combat, he'd been more than a decade younger and ten pounds heavier, but it was all muscle. Now, he was a shriveled shell of that guy. He was a husk of someone who used to be a highly-trained sailor. He hoped the muscle memory was still there.

Eggers reached down and mustered the strength and the nerve to go for it. He exploded to action and slapped the back of the phone in the first guy's hand and slammed it into his face.

The first guy, not stunned, but surprised, stepped back a foot, unfazed. The effort wasn't the most powerful thing ever, but it had served its purpose.

Eggers didn't need to engage in a one-on-one boxing match with a guy twenty-five years younger than him and built like a brick house. He only needed to surprise him, buy himself a few seconds to get up and run.

Eggers rolled off the bench and stumbled to his feet. Everything was hazy. The darkness and the city lights beyond seemed to blur together like a watercolor painting with the colors running from being left out in the rain.

Eggers might've been drunk-beyond-drunk, but he had experience in this. He knew how to maneuver in the dark, in a state of intoxication. Eggers had been drinking away his regrets for long years. He knew how to live in that world.

He scrambled away from the first guy and took off running.

The first guy reacted. He dropped the Zippo and reached down and jerked a SIG Sauer P226 out of a concealed hip holster.

He pointed the gun at Eggers' back as he ran away.

The face was still on the phone.

He barked, "Don't shoot him!"

The first guy stared through the iron sights. Both of his eyes were wide open. He had Eggers lined up. He could've squeezed the trigger. But he didn't.

"No bullets!" the face on the phone ordered.

The first guy lowered the gun and said, "Roger."

The first guy called out to the other three guys.

"He's heading on foot to Thirteenth Street!"

Eggers ran as hard and as fast as he could, which was to say not quick at all.

He saw Thirteenth Street's lights just ahead of him. He saw a taxi pass on the street.

"Help!" he tried to call out. But his voice sounded hoarse from not having used it in a long time.

He tried again.

"Help!"

Another car drove by.

He kept running. The exit from the park was right there. The street was so close. He almost made it, but he didn't.

Instead, he felt instant pain in the back of his head. He heard a loud, echoing shatter so close it was like it was inside his skull. The next thing he knew, he was on the ground.

He was dazed, more dazed than he ever felt drunk.

Eggers rolled his head to the side and put a hand down on the brick walkway. He pushed himself up and turned to see what hit him in the back of the head. It had been a full bottle of Clyde Brothers' Whiskey, but now it was an empty bottle. It was a broken, empty bottle, shattered all over the brick from hitting him.

The first guy had thrown it at him.

Eggers looked up, while the first guy approached him from the park bench. A gun was in his hand and pointed right at Eggers' face.

Eggers tried to push himself up and stand on his own feet, but then he saw three other men. They came from three different directions around him. They were all dressed in black, looking like they were up to no good, which they were.

No one came up from behind him, from the street, but that made no difference now. He would never make it to the street, and he knew it.

Two of the other guys reached under his armpits and scooped him up to his feet. They kept their grips locked on him. They pulled both of his arms out to his sides as if they were going to put him up on a cross.

He got a look at one of the other guys. He was a massive, bald guy. He had fists like concrete blocks.

The bald guy stood nearby with a gun in his hand. Not a SIG Sauer P226, like the first guy's, but a Glock 34. The thing Eggers deduced about them at that instant, which he should've recognized before, was from their guns.

Special Forces operators are usually trained in as many weapons as possible. The different divisions of the US military service all have their own unique standard-issue weapons. The Army used to have the M1911, back in the day. Then they upgraded to the M9 Beretta for a long, long time. But recently—he couldn't remember the year exactly—the Army had switched to the SIG Sauer P320 after it won a "Modular Handgun Systems" competition.

The thing that Eggers recognized about the weapons these guys carried was that if there was a shortlist for preferred weapons by Special Forces operators, they would both make the cut.

His brain coupled the choice of weapons with the way they were dressed and the way they placed themselves in a perimeter, along with the face on the phone. And he knew—they had been Special Forces in their pasts.

The first guy lowered his weapon but kept it in hand at his side.

He approached Eggers and raised the phone's screen to face him again.

Eggers looked at the face that stared back at him.

"Henry, I'm sorry it's come to this. Take care of him."

The face said nothing else and hung up. The screen went black.

The first guy slipped the phone back into his pocket.

He said, "Hold him tight."

Eggers felt two of the other men wrench out his arms, holding him locked in place.

The first guy twisted back at the waist and rotated fast and forward. He whipped Eggers across the face with his pistol.

The gun *cracked* across Eggers' lower jaw. Teeth splintered. He spat out two. Blood trickled out of his mouth.

He wanted to beg and plead, but he didn't. The old sailor that he used to be was still there, down deep in his core. Sailors don't beg or plead. They stand tall.

He pushed his feet down into the brick and tried to stand up tall.

He spat out blood toward the bald guy.

"Tough now, are you?" the bald guy asked.

Eggers stayed quiet.

The first guy hit him again with the pistol and then a third time—both across the face. The third one was flat on Eggers' forehead. He felt nothing after that. The blow was hard and dazed what was left of him to daze.

The first guy said, "Drag him back to the bench."

The others lifted Eggers off his feet and took him back to the bench. They forced him to lie flat like he had been when he was asleep.

One of the other guys took out a zip tie and forced Eggers' wrists between the bars on the armrest of the bench. He ziptied his wrists around it.

The men all backed away.

The first guy reached into his jacket pocket and pulled out a pack of cigarettes. He took one out and returned the pack to his pocket. He knelt and scooped up the dropped lighter. He flicked open the top. He stuck a cigarette into his mouth, struck a flame, and lit it. He returned the Zippo to his pocket and puffed away on the cigarette.

He smoked it until it was half–gone. Then he stared down at Eggers and asked a question.

"Want a cigarette?"

"I don't smoke."

The first guy nodded and puffed one last time. Then, he said one final thing to Eggers.

"Hooyah, brother."

The first guy took a long step back. He looked into Eggers' eyes, a taunting, sinister look that would haunt Eggers for the rest of his life.

Eggers struggled against the zip tie and the park bench's metal, but it did not free him.

The first guy took the smoked cigarette out of his mouth and tossed it onto Eggers and the bench. The whiskey that covered his body lit up instantly.

The cask strength whiskey did as advertised. It burned and burned.

The other three men gathered around the first, and they all stood around and watched Eggers burn to death.

After he was dead, the first guy took the cigarette pack out again and spilled a bunch of the cigarettes out on the ground, and he dug a store-bought cheap lighter out of his pocket and struck it twice, so it seemed used, and he dropped it over the cigarettes. He did all of this so the cops would find them. He kept the Zippo. Couldn't leave that behind. It was easier to trace back to his boss.

The cops wouldn't look close enough and wonder how Eggers lit his own cigarette. They'd figure he'd used a match, or they might find the cheap lighter.

One of the others cut the zip tie around Eggers' wrist, avoiding the flames as best he could, but the fire was hot. He couldn't get a grip on the zip tie's remains. It fell somewhere into the flames.

The first guy said, "Forget it. It wouldn't make a difference."

The four men left Eggers' body to burn out on its own. They walked back to their SUV and hopped in. They drove off, following the street signs to their next destination as if nothing was out of the ordinary.

A WORD FROM SCOTT

Thank you for reading **Foreign & Domestic**. You got this far—I'm hope you enjoyed this installment of Widow.

The story continues...

To find out more sign up for the Jack Widow Book Club and get notified of upcoming new releases. See next page.

Next is **Patriot Lies**, out now!

THE SCOTT BLADE BOOK CLUB

Building a relationship with my readers is the very best thing about writing. I occasionally send newsletters with details on new releases, special offers, and other bits of news relating to the Jack Widow series.

If you are new to the series, you can join the Scott Blade Book Club and get the starter kit and other exclusives: free stories, special offers, access to bonus content, and info on the latest releases, and coming soon Jack Widow novels.

Sign up at <u>ScottBlade.com.</u>

THE NOMADVELIST
NOMAD + NOVELIST = NOMADVELIST

Scott Blade is a Nomadvelist, a drifter and author of the breakout Jack Widow series. Scott travels the world, hitchhiking, drinking coffee, and writing.

Jack Widow has sold over a million copies.

Visit @: ScottBlade.com

Contact @: scott@scottblade.com

Follow @:

Facebook.com/ScottBladeAuthor

Bookbub.com/profile/scott-blade

Amazon.com/Scott-Blade/e/B00AU7ZRS8

Made in United States
Orlando, FL
17 February 2024

43799380R00211